LOVERS FOR TODAY

SIXTEENTH BOOK IN THE BRIGANDSHAW CHRONICLES

PETER RIMMER

ABOUT PETER RIMMER

~

Peter Rimmer was born in London, England, and grew up in the south of the city where he went to school. After the Second World War, aged eighteen, he joined the Royal Air Force, reaching the rank of Pilot Officer before he was nineteen. At the end of his National Service, he sailed for Africa to grow tobacco in what was then Rhodesia, now Zimbabwe.

The years went by and Peter found himself in Johannesburg where he established an insurance brokering company. Over 2% of the companies listed on the Johannesburg Stock Exchange were clients of Rimmer Associates. He opened branches in the United States of America, Australia and Hong Kong and travelled extensively between them.

Having lived a reclusive life on his beloved smallholding in Knysna, South Africa, for over 25 years, Peter passed away in July 2018. He has left an enormous legacy of unpublished work for his family to release over the coming years, and not only they but also his readers from around the world will sorely miss him. Peter Rimmer was 81 years old.

To read more about Peter's life, please visit his website: https://www.peterrimmer.com/novelist/author/

OTHER BOOKS BY PETER RIMMER

～

～

The Big River

The Asian Sagas in order:

1. Bend with the Wind

2. Each to His Own

The Pioneers in order:

1. Morgandale

2. Carregan's Catch

Novella

Second Beach

PART 1

MAY 1997 – ESCAPE TO THE WILD

1

"*L*and in sight, Mr Holiday... Can I come in?"

"It's your boat."

"But you chartered it. Good morning. We'll be coming into Table Bay in about two hours if the wind stays. Lucky there isn't a south-easter blowing. We can eat breakfast before going into the yacht basin. Come on up when you're ready. How are you feeling today, Jane? No morning sickness? My wife says having babies is never easy. We'll be passing Robben Island where the great Nelson Mandela was incarcerated for eighteen years of his twenty-seven-year sentence. And now he's president of South Africa with a Nobel prize for peace. Can you imagine giving up so much of your life for a cause? The things we humans do to each other. Colonialism. We Americans had to fight the British. Oh, sorry. You have a British passport. The flag's flying at the masthead as we come into South African waters. Good old stars and stripes. Two months on the high seas. Tomorrow, my wife and I sail back to America. We've enjoyed having you both on board. Now you'll be on your own. When the coast guard sees the foreign flag, they'll probably come alongside. Have your passports ready. There's one last favour. I want to buy a copy of one of your books in Cape Town and have you sign it for me. Did you enjoy the trip?"

"You saved my life, Stanley. The booze is right out of my system. Blown out with the wind. By the time you leave tomorrow, I'll have hired a camper and we'll be off up the road. Just have to remember to drive on the left. I'm back in Africa. It feels good. See you up on the deck, skipper. Africa. My beautiful Africa. I'm home."

"Sorry to have barged in."

"It's my pleasure. What day is it?"

"Thursday the fifteenth of May, according to the local radio. Eight-fifteen local time. Now, look at that. My wife's brought you both a cup of coffee. Have a good trip up the coast. Don't forget to buy yourselves a map. It's been a pleasure doing business with you, Randall. What would we do without the internet? And the sun's shining."

"The sun always shines in Camelot. A good sleep and a cup of coffee. What more could a man want? We've arrived, Jane. We've reached our destiny. I think she's still asleep."

"How long are you going to stay?"

"Who knows? In this life, you're never sure what's going to happen next. Wake up, Jane. A cup of coffee. Can't keep nodding off or it goes cold."

"What's going on?"

"We've arrived. We're here. Africa. Welcome to Africa, Janey."

"I'm just so comfortable I don't want to move. Never felt happier in my life. Good morning, Yvonne and Stanley. Another lovely day? Thank you both so much for looking after us so well. One, long, beautiful voyage neither of us will ever forget. The perfect memory."

"Don't bother to buy a book, Stanley. When I get back to New York, I'll post you a signed copy. Are our finances in order? Have you got everything you want? This coffee is quite delicious. Tell you what, Jane. You stay in the cabin and I'll go up on deck and let my nostalgia for Africa flow out of me all on my own. You enjoy your coffee and go back to sleep. Pregnant ladies need to rest. In Cape Town, we'll find a doctor to give you a check-up. He'll be able to tell us if it's a boy or a girl."

"I don't like doctors looking inside me. Let nature take its course. We'll know in four months' time if all goes well. And it will. I feel fine. The baby feels fine. We're going into the wilds. To Lawrence and Tonga territory. I want you to show me everything. Finish your coffee and off you go, my love. What a lovely voyage. Never before sailed the seas. You are such a nice couple. And it all started through the sailing magazine."

When Randall climbed up on deck he went to the railing and held it with both hands, the yacht leaning with the wind as the bow cut through the ocean waves. The land was closer than he had expected, the flat table of the mountain looking out over the bay, the faraway sounds of the city competing with the slap of the waves on the hull. All Randall could do was smile and let his mind drift up the African continent to the home where he was born, the farm high above the distant Zambezi escarpment his father had called World's View. Was it his imagination or could he smell the rich smell of Africa in his nostrils as Stanley, now at the tiller, guided them into the bay? Once again, the world was his oyster. He was home. Back where he belonged. Just the two of them, all the horrors of people left behind: no publicist; no agent; no media. Just himself, Jane and the stories of Lawrence Templeton-Smythe and Tonga he made up in his mind.

When they came into the small yacht basin using the auxiliary motor, no one had come anywhere near them. Hand in hand, each of them holding a large travel bag, they thanked Yvonne and Stanley for the last time and went ashore, walking straight into the small yacht club where Randall used the phone to hire a camper. Two hours later, they went through customs before picking up the Dormobile that had been delivered to the yacht club. When all the papers were signed, the deposit given with two months' rental for the vehicle, they were on their way out of Cape Town.

"That was easy, Janey."

"You can say that again."

"Everyone's relaxed in Africa. They take you at your word. People don't worry. We've an unlimited credit card and a pile of South African rand."

"When do we stock up with food?"

"When we pass through Malmesbury. We're on the N7 heading north. Relax, my American lover. In Africa, we take everything easy. By the time we reach the Skeleton Coast, the temperature will be warmer. I've not been before, but I remember Dad telling me that Harry Brigandshaw... I have told you about Harry Brigandshaw? Anyway, apparently Harry found an enormous diamond in a whirlpool in the ocean off the coast. Don't know why he was there. Years later, that diamond saved his children, financially. I've always wanted to go. So here we are making our way to the Skeleton Coast, finding ourselves nice little campsites along the way. At night we will pull out the double bed behind us and live like hoboes. We're as we are. We don't have to worry about our appearances. No one cares. We can just relax and enjoy ourselves. No one knows who we are. Here I'm just Randall Crookshank, a thirty-nine-year-old born in Rhodesia. No one will tie me to Randall Holiday, the famous author. Any more than they will know you wrote the film script for the blockbuster movie of Tracey Chapelle's book. They may have seen *Lust* on the screen. They may have read my books. But they won't connect us, and as sure as hell we are not telling them. We're free, bound by neither fame nor fortune... Just look at this place and tell me it isn't beautiful. We'll drive for maybe six or seven hours and look for our first campsite. Are you excited, Jane?"

"Never more in my life. I could live here forever. We could find a little spot and write our books together."

"There are two sides to today's Africa. The beauty of the place and the politics. Never be fooled by appearances. By what the politicians say. As much as I love Africa, I can't live here again. We have our first child on the way. We have to think of our children."

"Are we going to have more than one? We're not even married."

"We agreed to stay as we are. Stay as lovers. My last two marriages ended in divorce. We're going to be different and live with each other and our children because we want to. When your first book comes out in three months' time and makes you a fortune, we will pair some of our money and buy ourselves a nice little country house with a few acres in England, far from the madding crowd of New York and far from African politics. There, in peace, we'll watch our children grow up and be happy. Lots of dogs and cats. Big log fires in winter. Mozart playing under the timbers of a beautiful old house. There'll be no wolves howling in my head. And definitely no alcohol."

"How are you managing to drive on the left-hand side of the road? It's so weird."

"I learned to drive on this side. Give me your hand. We're free, Janey. We've got away from the bastards."

"What bastards?"

"People. All those people sucking up to us and telling us how clever we are. All bullshit. The only thing I want from a reader is to know they enjoyed reading my book as much as I enjoyed writing it. None of all that celebrity crap. Until we have to fly back for the launch of your book, we have peace. You and me in paradise. We're on the road, love. And we're happy. All that matters in life. Being happy."

"Didn't you like being Randall Holiday?"

"For a time. And then it caught up with me. Too much fame and too much money can kill a person. If you hadn't got yourself pregnant it would have killed me. I would have done an Ernest Hemingway and shot myself to get away from the howling wolves in my head."

"Wasn't it the alcohol?"

"Fame drives you to drink."

"I thought it was Meredith walking out on you."

"She married me for my money. Let's not talk about it. We have our new lives together. With a life of peace and quiet in the English countryside, we won't have to put up with people. Holiday was my writing pseudonym. A name I'm going to keep as far away as possible... Just look at that beautiful mountain... They called it the Cape of Good Hope. Hope, Jane. Let's hope. You, me and our children. In peace. In quiet. Just ourselves."

Was he trying to rationalise with himself? Randall wasn't sure. Was he really going to stay sober for the rest of his life? Was there ever the chance of living with a mate without the fights and arguments? Was it all false hope? She was pregnant, that much was certain. They were on the road, moving forward into the next stage of their lives.

Half an hour out of Cape Town it began to rain, the banging of the windscreen wipers breaking their silence. In the small town of Malmesbury, they stocked up with food and made their way back to the N7, the road going on and on. By the end of the day, when they drove off the road and followed the sign to the campsite, the rain had long stopped. They parked under a tree next to an open fireplace with a small wooden table and two benches on either side to sit on. A man came across from the small house at the entrance to the campsite.

"How long are you staying?"

"Just tonight."

"Eighteen rand for the site. You have to buy your firewood."

"The firewood?"

"Another five rand."

"There we go. Keep the change."

"Where are you heading?"

"Namibia. The Skeleton Coast."

"You a local?"

"Not quite. A bit further north. I was born in Rhodesia. We live in America."

"Lucky you. This country is headed for the same rocks as Zimbabwe. You watch. In seventeen years' time, they'll be doing the same things to us whites as Mugabe is doing now. And this reconciliation by Mandela is to give them time to take over the economy. He wants us to drop our guard."

"Everything will turn out fine."

"For a few. Not for us Afrikaners. The blacks hate us. And for very good reason. You can't lock a man up for twenty-seven years and expect him to love you. It's only three years into the new government. Once they get proper control of the reins, they'll take it all back from us. Three-quarters of the whites have now left Zimbabwe. You're one of them. Lucky you. My family have been in Africa over three hundred years. There's nowhere for me to go. I can't get a foreign passport. In twenty years they'll have tossed us Dutchmen on the rubbish heap. Thanks for the tip. America. You lucky bastard. Do you have a job in America?"

"Not really."

"What do you do?"

"I'm an itinerant storyteller. I tell people stories round the campfire."

"Do they pay you?"

"Not today. We're on holiday. When the sun goes down, come and join us. It's my first night in Africa for many years... Do the owls call?"

"Sometimes. Mainly the crickets from the river."

"Everything is going to turn out just fine."

"That's what they all say... Itinerant storyteller. That's a new one. What does itinerant mean? My English isn't that good."

"A man who travels from place to place. Like a preacher. It started long before the written word. Before books."

"What kind of stories do you tell? I'm Koos van der Merwe, by the way."

"Call me Randall. Old stories. Tonight, I'll tell you the story of the first white hunter to roam the old lands that became the country we called Rhodesia. He was an English aristocrat who hunted elephant for their ivory. The third son of a lord with a good education but no prospects of an inheritance. Lawrence came to Africa to make his fortune and then go home again."

"Can I bring my wife?"

"You can bring the whole family."

"There's just the two of us. Now the government's changed we don't want children as we can't see a future for them."

"How old are you, Koos?"

"Twenty-eight. My uncle owns the campsite. We run it for him. It's a job. Can't complain. But if these people take back the land as Mugabe is now doing in Zimbabwe seventeen years after independence, we'll end up with nothing. No land. No house. No job. My uncle says once you lose political power in Africa, it's only a question of time before you lose everything. Anyway, it could be worse. We could be shooting each other. Half of the new post-colonial Africa is in turmoil. Civil wars. Revolution. Everyone trying to get their hands on the assets; the minerals; the land; control of the big companies by what Mugabe calls indigenisation. There are two new English words the blacks are using that I understand: indigenisation and expropriation. What would be the point now in building up a business in South Africa when in a few years' time the government here will tell you to do what Mugabe is telling the whites who own companies in Zimbabwe: give fifty-one per cent of your company to the indigenous people for nothing and you can carry on doing all the work but you won't have control of your business. The people don't benefit. The poor sods without jobs. Just a few of the elite who use their wealth to keep Mugabe in power. And they have the cheek to call it a democracy... What time does the storytelling start? My wife and I get bored just watching the local television. We hate listening to the news."

"Come over when you see my campfire burning."

They watched in silence as the man walked back to his house, both of them staring at his back.

"The poor man is paranoid, Randall."

"So would you be if you were an Afrikaner under a black government. They're frightened of retribution and they have nowhere to go... Right. Let's set up camp. That pile of wood next to the fireplace must be ours. I'll pop up the top in the camper and we can make the bed. Just look at this. Pull out the table, pop up the roof, turn the two seats on either side of the table into a double bed and *voilà*. We have a nice little bedroom for two. This camper is perfect. I'll cook the T-bone steak over the fire. Can you make the salad? Once the fire has burned awhile, I'll stick the spuds in the coals wrapped in tinfoil."

"That poor man."

"Life is never easy. You just have to make the best of it."

"We're the only people in the campsite."

"Wrong time of the year, I suppose... Now you see why three-quarters of the whites in Zimbabwe have left the country. As much as I would love to live in Africa, it just isn't possible for a white man. The two races are far too divided. Hatred is a terrible thing. In the end, it explodes. We'll come back on holiday but not to live... There we are. They really have provided us with everything: sheets, blankets and a duvet. Not surprising the high price of the rental. Those people were organised. Know how to run a business. And that's Mugabe's problem. Why his economy has sunk into the shit with eighty per cent youth unemployment. Can't run anything without management. That man Koos has made me realise how lucky my family are to be out of it. Life's a constant roller coaster... There we are. That didn't take long. The fire's started and the sun's gone down. Gets dark quickly in Africa. The river must be on the other side of those trees from where the crickets are singing."

"You think he'll come back to listen to your stories?"

"Who knows?... I'm hungry. Let's get the food started. First a cup of tea. Look at that. They even provided us with a kettle we can boil over the fire. And behind that pile of wood, there's a water tap. I'm tired from driving all day."

"What a pity."

"What are you talking about, Jane?"

"Africa. As the sun disappears it's even more beautiful. Just look at that sunset. You're right. Our child must be born in America and have American citizenship."

"He could also be born in England and be part of the European Union... There he goes. Did you hear that? It's an owl. Just wait. There she goes. His mate has answered him. Owls call to each other."

"It's getting cold."

"Why I needed to buy all that wood. You'll toast nicely in front of the fire. And we can eat at that wooden table placed perfectly next to the fire."

"I wouldn't mind a glass of wine."

"Neither would I. But we've agreed, Jane. No more drinking. We were a couple of drunks. Back in your day, you said you never stopped drinking. How you ended up working in a laundry on a pittance of a salary. We've got to stop. Control ourselves. Or we'll destroy ourselves and our children."

"Maybe he'll bring some booze for the itinerant storyteller."

"I hope not. Thank goodness there was no booze on that yacht. Give me a hug, Janey. We're so lucky you are pregnant. Now we have to be responsible."

"What a strange world it is. Is it luck when things turn your way? If I hadn't lived in that run-down apartment next to Tracey Chapelle before she found a publisher for her book she called *Lust*, I would never have got a job with your literary agent and written the film script for *Lust*. In my days of alcohol addiction, I threw away my degree in English with all the drinking and partying. Threw away the best years of my life. Or so I thought. Not long thirty-nine, the same age as you, and pregnant by the most wonderful man I could ever have imagined. And here I am in Africa, the horrors of my past forgotten. Having said all that, I'd enjoy a nice glass of wine with my love."

"My trouble is once I start, I can't stop."

"Mine too... That fire is burning nicely. The warmth is so nice. It's all quiet and peaceful. Oh, love, I'm so happy."

When they went to the table the light from the fire ran high up into the tree above the bench where they sat and ate the steak and Jane's lettuce salad, the spuds in the fire to come later.

"I don't think he's coming."

"Oh yes, he is. Here they come... Hello, Koos. Come join us round the fire."

"We waited for you to finish your supper. This is Petra, my wife."

"Hello. I'm Jane. And this is Randall. You must be cold. Come and sit round our big fire. We're so enjoying the peace and the singing of the crickets."

"Are you really going to tell us a story, Randall? We so love a little company."

"Sit you both down. It all began in the year 1886 when Lawrence Templeton-Smythe was taken by Andre de Klerk to the kraal of Chief Mogumbo of the Shona, a Bantu tribe who had migrated down from the north centuries before, displacing the indigenous people, pushing them south and taking their land. In exchange for guns and ammunition, Chief Mogumbo gave Lawrence permission to hunt elephant for their ivory. Tonga, a young man of the tribe, went with Lawrence as his servant and to show him the land that had been settled by his ancestors. Andre, with the commission in his pocket from the arms deal delivery, rode on his way back to South Africa leaving Lawrence and Tonga with two horses, six oxen and the big wooden wagon they were to fill with the tusks from the slaughtered elephant. When this part of the story begins the last wagonload was almost full of ivory and the now friends who had taught each other their different languages, English for Tonga, Shona for Lawrence, were about to part company forever. Tonga would go back to the kraal of Chief Mogumbo. Lawrence would go back to England with

the ivory he had built up over three years and stored in Beira, a port on
the coast of Mozambique, with enough money from the sale of the ivory
to purchase an estate bigger than that of his father, who had inherited
the Templeton family estate passed down by his feudal ancestors who
had been given the land and their title of Baron Templeton of Peaslake in
the eleventh century in exchange for their services to the king of
England..."

When Randall finished telling his story the fire had gone down, his
audience captivated. He got up from the bench and piled wood on the
fire, the flames breaking out again sending light up into the tree. Sadly,
Randall knew it was the final end of his story he had been talking and
writing for over a year.

"Now what do I do? I hate finishing a book. It leaves a great void."

"You'll think up another one."

"I hope so, Jane."

"So you write books as well as telling stories around a campfire?"

"I'm afraid I do."

"Have we read any of your books?"

"I don't know, Petra."

"What's your name?"

"Does it matter?"

"Are you famous? Koos, go and get us a box of wine. You do drink,
Randall?"

"We shouldn't. We're both alcoholics. And Jane's pregnant."

"You're not going to tell me who you are?"

"I'd prefer not to. We ran away on a yacht. You should have children
of your own. Don't worry about the politics. Life goes on down the
centuries much the same. Feudal barons. White tobacco farmers given
six thousand acres of crown land. Dictators dispensing other people's
property to those who keep them in power, trying to pretend they are
running a modern democracy. And is democracy a solution when the
stock markets crash with the currency and your money becomes
worthless and you don't have a job? No one through history has ever
found the perfect way to run a country... Has he really gone to get some
wine? Oh, well. There. Now the fire's burning properly."

"Koos constantly worries about what they are going to do with us
Afrikaners now they control the army and the police."

"When there's nothing you can do about it there's no point in
worrying. You just do your best. Go on living day to day. None of us are

ever in control of our lives. We just think we are... Well now, look at that, Jane. A box of nice South African wine. Five litres. And it looks as though it hasn't even been opened. Glasses. We need glasses. Oh, well done, Koos. That other little box is full of wine glasses. Let's get started. Jane, my pregnant Jane, is allowed one glass of wine."

"You've got to be kidding."

"Maybe two, love."

"That's better. When we've had two or three, we stop counting."

"There we go, Koos."

"What's this for, Randall?"

"The wine. Thirty rand for the wine. Can't drink your money, now can we? Wine, women and song. Who's going to sing? Africa. My beautiful Africa. I'm back... Anyone want a spud? Baked potatoes in the fire. Open them up and toss in a pat of butter... Thank you, Koos. Cheers, everybody. Now it's your turn. Tell us the stories of your life."

"Only if you tell us who you are."

"After your stories and the wine. Maybe. I don't so much as want to think of anything other than the present. A campfire burning beautifully. A box of red wine. And two new friends. Cheers, everybody. Here's to happiness."

"Our lives are pretty uninteresting. We met at primary school. You could say we grew up together and then we married. We haven't travelled. Been nowhere, really. We do the best we can with this job. When you live in a rent-free house with a vegetable garden and chickens you don't need a whole lot of money to live comfortably. We read a lot. Our house, that also serves as an office, has a small library for the campers if they want to read. The books are free, provided they return them. Petra reads all the time. We have one employee who looks after the camp. He and his family have their own little house. We share the eggs and the vegetables. A perfect life if it wasn't for the politics. Now I don't know what to do. We feel so unsettled. All the talk of land expropriation and nationalism gives me the shivers. They can do what they like and there is nothing we can do about it."

"Can they, Koos?... This wine is quite delicious... You've probably heard of the fourth estate, what they call the media and its power over governments. Politicians are scared of the press. Well, there's a fifth estate with even more power over how politicians run their countries. It's called the markets. The stock markets and the currency that can plunge a country into chaos at the drop of a hat. Upset the financial markets and they'll destroy you. Ask Robert Mugabe. They have to print new banknotes with extra noughts on them every six months, as the old notes become worthless. No one wants to invest in Zimbabwe. Maybe the Chinese for political reasons but only so far. When Mugabe tries to swipe fifty-one per cent of their investments they'll turn on him. The Chinese want the minerals but they'll only go so far. So don't worry yourself sick about the new South Africa. Like everyone else in this global economy, they'll have to behave themselves or the people they are correctly trying to bring out of poverty will be worse off than before. It's all very well for politicians to talk and make promises, but if they can't fulfil those promises, they'll lose the backing of the people. There'll be riots in the streets. They'll be kicked out of power and pay for their sins. Never forget the fifth estate. It's the economy that drives a country, not the politicians. And the economy is controlled by the financial markets which maintain or destroy the value of a paper currency and increase or decrease the wealth of the country through the stock and property markets. Rising stock prices lead to increased jobs as people invest in the future. You can shout your mouth off with promises as a politician in pursuit of people voting for you. But in the end, it's all about the financial stability of the country. Africa, in particular, is desperate for direct foreign investment if it is to drag its people out of poverty. The new black government isn't going to destroy its tourism. Relax, Koos and Petra. Have a family. There's always a future through children. How the world goes on. From generation to generation to the last syllable of recorded time when all our yesterdays have lighted fools the way to dusty death. And that last bit is Shakespeare... How's that spud?"

"What's a spud?"

"The potato you're eating, Petra. Sadly, I'm enjoying your wine. It's called the slippery slope once we start. But who cares tonight? We're among friends. Forget the rest of the world. We're enjoying ourselves. Let me stop talking about politics. I hate politics and most politicians."

"You think it's all talk?"

"I hope so, Koos. All fingers and no action. How's the wine going down, Jane?"

"Just perfectly... Just listen to those crickets."

"Are you two married, Jane? I don't see a ring on your finger."

"We want to stay lovers, Petra. No, we're not. And probably never will be. But we're going to have a family and live happily ever after. I can't wait for my baby. They say a few glasses of red wine are good for both of us. Cheers, everybody. To happy days. There's nothing more exciting in a girl's life than being pregnant... What's that over there, Koos? It's some kind of animal. It's staring at us in front of those bushes behind the water tap. Big ears like rabbits only twice the size. Almost the size of a small pony."

"It's a bushbuck. The fire attracts them. If one of us gets up it will run... Give me your glass. It's empty. They call box wine plonk but it has the same effect as expensive bottled wine. The same percentage of alcohol. So you think my family could stay in Africa for generations, Randall? Running the family camping site for the tourists. Once a year I go to the travel convention in Durban to talk to the travel agents and drum up business. Tourist operators come from Australia, America, and Europe. My uncle says a successful business or product is all about marketing. You got to sell yourself. Half our bookings come from travel agents I met in Durban. Nothing better than personal contact. The rest of the business comes from passers-by like you and Jane who see that big sign on the main road... He's still staring at us. Big horns and big ears. Hasn't moved. Wonder what he thinks of us? What we are doing here. Oh, look at that. He's sitting down. Still staring at us, sitting in the long grass. I love the bush. And everything in it. No better place to live. And you meet all kinds of people. Are you a famous author hiding from the crowd? I'm quite content doing what I am. I just hope that Mandela, and whoever succeeds him, leaves us alone. I don't want much from life. Peace and quiet and my lovely Petronella. I like to call her Petra. Sounds nicer than Petro. You can keep all those big cities. Why not, Petra? Let's stop worrying and start a family. Anyway, unlike our friends here we don't have an alternative... The fifth estate. I like it. Makes me less panicky. Glad I brought you the wine. Give me your glass, Randall. Funny name. The only Randall I ever heard of is Randall Holiday, the author of *Masters of Vanity*. I loved that book. So did Petra. The story of people chasing money to satisfy their egos. Your surname wouldn't be Holiday by any chance?"

"My surname is Crookshank. I can show you my passport."

"There we go. Filled to the top. And now we have a lovely bushbuck to keep us company. Just look at him. Hasn't taken his eyes off us. What a lovely fire. Books. I love reading books. One of the joys of my life. Takes me away from the real world and all its horrors. If you don't marry, Jane's baby will have her surname."

"And the world goes on."

"That it does, Randall. Whatever we humans get up to. Unless we blow it to pieces. Then we won't have to worry what's coming next."

"Live for the moment, Koos. Tomorrow never comes, is what they say. Tomorrow is always tomorrow."

Smiling inwardly at the luck of writing under a pseudonym, Randall sipped his wine, content, happy and beginning to feel ever so slightly tiddly. Letting the others talk while he enjoyed his wine, he leaned comfortably on the table as he stared at the animal, not twenty yards from where they were all sitting on the wooden benches on either side of the table, the light from the fire reflecting in the eyes of the animal with the large rabbit ears. Knowing his mind and his stomach would pay for drinking the wine, Randall no longer cared. The inevitable slide down the slippery slope of alcohol had begun for both of them. Was it good for a pregnant woman to drink red wine? He wasn't sure. And there was no point in worrying. They had both agreed to let nature take its course. Worry and fear were most likely more dangerous for a baby in a girl's womb than an evening of red wine. Rationalising as was his habit when he drank, Randall enjoyed the evening, the crickets singing, the wild animal just visible in the light of the fire, the three layers of stars above twinkling in the black of the night sky, a tiny sliver of a moon as he waited patiently for the call of an owl. Every time a glass was almost empty, Koos put it under the small tap that protruded from the bottom of the box and filled it up. They were all getting drunk but no one seemed to care. All they had to do was walk to their beds, no worry about driving cars or bumping into people. Petra and Jane were discussing having babies and how much fun it was going to be to bring up their children, Randall's mind wandering off on its own. Would he let Manfred publish the story of Lawrence and Tonga once he had written down and not just spoken the final chapter? He wasn't sure if the story would resonate in the modern world of cities teeming with people striving for whatever they could get to show off to their friends. He was never sure when he finished a book if it was any good. And would he go back to writing about Shakespeare's friend, the man who had helped write the bard's great plays, a man from Randall's imagination who may well have been real? Or would he find a new story to write about and give his life purpose? He was never sure what would come when he sat at his desk with the blank white page in front of him and the ballpoint pen in his right hand. Only when the bushbuck jumped up and ran away did he come out of his reverie. A car was coming into the campsite, its headlights washing over them as it swung to a stop next to the entrance. The car's horn hooted.

"Better go, Petra. Business calls. We'll leave you the wine, Randall. Seeing you paid for it."

"Do me a favour and take the box with you. That way we'll stop drinking."

"Are you sure?"

"Take it, Koos, or we'll drink the lot and start my nightmare all over again. I never again want to hear the wolves howling in my head. Thanks for the company. My word, that man is impatient. Hooting horns is so rude. We'll be off early tomorrow morning. Have a good life, both of you. Have a family. And try not to worry. There he goes. My owl. He's hooting. There she goes... You think owls love each other like humans? To me, that sounds like a lover's call."

"I enjoyed your story."

"I'm glad. The only purpose for telling a story is to amuse the listener. Entertainment. May you both be happy together for the rest of your lives."

Watching his two new friends run off to attend to their business, the wine box in Koos's right hand, he hoped the night of drinking would not bring back the alcohol craving he had left behind on Stanley's yacht. Jane was staring at him, no longer smiling.

"Why did you let him take the wine? We've paid for it."

"To hopefully stop me calling at the next bottle store we pass on our road north and buy a case of whisky."

"I was enjoying myself."

"So was I. That was the trouble. There's a bit left in Petra's glass. He left the glasses behind. Oh, Janey, we want to be happy with our lives without drinking ourselves stupid. Finish your wine and Petra's and then we'll go to bed and spend our first night cuddled up in our camper. Do you think we helped them? Just hope what I said about their future was right. Trouble is, you only find out when it happens, the good, the bad and the downright terrible."

"I'd love to live in Africa."

"So would I, Janey. But we ain't going to do it. Too many bad memories of Rhodesia. We had a six-year bush war before Smith gave in and handed the country to Mugabe. It was never going to end. The farms were constantly under attack. Maybe South Africa has learned from our mistakes by handing over the government in a democratic vote and avoiding war. Maybe they'll see that without the skills of the white man to run the economy they'll all end up down the toilet. They say we learn by our own and other people's mistakes. For people like Koos and Petra I really hope so. Good, he's parked on the other side of the camp. The headlights are out. Quiet returns. What a shame."

"What's a shame, Randall?"

"That I let him go off with our wine. Come, Janey. To bed, to sleep, perchance to dream. We have another long drive tomorrow. Tomorrow, we're going to share the driving."

"I can't drive on the wrong side of the road."

"Of course, you can't. We'll slip out with the dawn, never to return. Two more days of driving and then we'll park off on the Skeleton Coast and fish for our supper. Hear the sound of the waves on the shore. The call of the seagulls. Swim in the sea. Get ourselves a suntan. Finish your wine. You're right. It's a bugger. That wine box was still half full. Or half empty. Whichever you prefer. How's our baby? Do four-month-old babies go to sleep in their mother's womb?"

"You're nuts."

"I know I am."

"A whole case of whisky?"

"Try not to even think of it. With luck, we just stopped short and won't have hangovers. I'm going to douse the fire in case the wind comes up."

"You don't have a fishing rod."

"But I will have when I buy one."

"She'll make a lovely mother."

"So will you, my Jane."

2

———————

*a*fter climbing through the back door of the Dormobile camper they went to their bed, the night dark and totally silent, the crickets no longer singing. Moments later rain pattered on the pop-up roof above them, the sound gentle and pleasing. Randall folded his body around Jane from the back, feeling her pregnant stomach. The next thing Randall became conscious of was the crow of a cockerel. The light was coming up. Quietly, Randall detached himself from his lover and pulled on his trousers before getting out of bed. It was time to hit the road.

Half an hour later, dressed, happy, having drunk their morning cup of tea – Randall had made more from the water he had boiled over the morning fire – they drove out of the campsite. As they drove through the gate an excited Koos ran out of his house waving a book over his head. Randall waved back and drove on without stopping.

"What was that all about? Why didn't you stop? He was calling your name."

"He had a copy of *Masters of Vanity* with my photograph. It was the first book they published. After that, I told them not to put my photograph on the back cover... Have you got a hangover?"

"No, thank goodness."

"Did you dream? I always dream lovely dreams when I'm happy."

"I dreamed of a house full of lots of laughing children. There's nothing more beautiful than the sound of happy children... Are we buying a case of whisky?"

"No, we are not. One more stop at a campsite and then we'll drive off the main road and we'll be on the Skeleton Coast. Two more long days of driving. They always say there is no pleasure without pain. Are you sure you can't drive on the wrong side of the road?"

"I suppose I can try."

"That's my girl. If we end up living in England, you'll be driving on the left-hand side of the road anyway. I hope he saw my windows were up and thought I couldn't hear him calling my name. I hate being rude. Being too high and mighty. Keeping quiet about my books isn't as easy as I thought it would be. I just can't stand people gushing all over me just because they read one of my books. It's the books that matter. Not the author. It'll be your turn next. Why publishers want to put the author's face on the back of the book, I have absolutely no idea. We all had fun together last night. That's what matters. Not a person's fame. We all look the same under a bus. In three hours we'll stop by the side of the road and use the little gas cooker they hired us to make a cup of tea. We'll have ourselves a bit of breakfast. Not a car on the road. Just perfect. Welcome to beautiful Africa, the home of my dreams."

"Why can't we live here? You never know, the new South Africa might just work."

"Once bitten, twice shy. It's for them to find out. Luckily we have all our papers in order to cross into Namibia. One of the great secrets of life is being organised. Being prepared. Thinking ahead. It's been plain sailing, literally, since we left New York. And it all seems so far away. A distant land of distant people. Now, it's just the two of us. Or two and a half of us. We have everything we want right here as we drive on and on up the long road... I wonder what they are all up to?"

"Who, Randall?"

"All those billions of individuals who inhabit this planet. All those little lives we try to think are so important. Is my life any more important than anyone else's? I don't think so. And in the end, we all turn to dust, lost, forgotten, our lives totally irrelevant except for that link in the chain, the next link breeding in your stomach, a boy or a girl with a short life of seventy or eighty years if they are lucky, full of pain and problems and striving for money to survive. Poor kid. I'm melancholy today, Jane. It's that wine. When I've been drinking, I find it difficult to think positively... I love this camper as it doesn't have a radio. For the weeks we spend on the road, the beach and in the game reserves, we won't have to listen to the news. There's nothing you can do about other people's problems. Let them fight their wars. Have all their arguments. Why must I be involved? You know that old cliche: no news is good news. That's what I want."

"Wouldn't you like some music?"

"Maybe Mozart. A little Haydn."

"And a book to read?"

"I don't want to read or write. I'm going to let my mind float."

"We were going to sit and write on either side of the table. All we have to do is pull back the seats, fit in the two poles and put back the top of the table. Nothing will disturb us. We both write with a pen."

"Let's see. You never know when that urge to write will hit you. When you want to open your mouth and blurt it all out, cleaning the system... Did you ever imagine being in Africa when you were working in that laundry?"

"Not in my wildest dreams. But I had a job. That's what mattered. I could just pay the rent. That petty pace from day to day you so like to quote from Shakespeare. Do you really think someone else wrote his plays?"

"They are so diverse it's difficult to imagine one man with so much knowledge and experience. A great storyteller matched with a great philosopher. Hard to imagine it all coming from a single mind. He must have had some help. How much we'll never know. In those days without the media, a writer could keep his privacy. All the public wanted was to go to the Globe Theatre and watch his plays. How it should be. He could hear the nightly applause without all the rest of the nonsense. He wrote, produced and acted in his plays to have fun. Can you imagine him and his friend thinking up *A Midsummer Night's Dream*? They must have giggled themselves stupid. They were having fun. Making fun for everyone... Do you know what I am talking about?"

"Not really. Pull over. There's no traffic on the road. I'm going to see if I can drive. You're right. It's so far away. Another life. Another existence. Out you get. I'll slide across... Everything feels much the same. Get in. Here we go, love. We're off again. I'm okay. We can share the driving. What are we going to call our baby if it's a boy?"

"Kimber."

"Kimber's a girl's name."

"It's also the name of an old schoolboy friend."

"And if it's a girl?"

"We'll call her Kimber. Kimber-girl. Kimber-boy. Just Kimber."

"You're nuts."

"How are you finding the driving?"

"Like a duck to water. Just weird moving the gear stick with my left hand."

"What are you going to write for a new book? A sequel to *Love in the Spring of Life*?"

"I'll have to dream up a new one. How do you do it, Randall?"

"All you have to do is start at the beginning and let the story tell itself."

"What story?"

"That's the problem. You have to have a story."

"I could go back to my drunken heyday."

"There we go."

"Then we'll need a case of whisky to bring back all those memories."

"You're trying too hard, Jane."

"Worth a try. Now let me think. A story. I want a story."

"You see it wasn't so difficult."

"What wasn't?"

"Driving on the left-hand side of the road."

"I would like to be a playwright."

"You are one. You wrote the film script to *Lust*."

"I wonder how she is. We both owe a lot to Tracey. The three musketeers. All of us writing books and sharing an apartment. And she's so happy now she has a baby. Shakespeare's life lived in the theatre must have been so much fun. Please finish your book so I can read it... Now, where was I? A story. I want a story."

Smiling to himself, Randall looked out of the window at the passing trees and grassland, putting his mind in neutral, letting the world float by. When Jane stopped the car at a picnic spot on the side of the road, Randall had fallen asleep.

"Why are we stopping?"

"Teatime. And then it's your turn to drive."

"How long have I been sleeping?"

"A couple of hours. There's a little table and bench over there. Three cars passed us, all driving too fast. I always like to keep within the limit... I think I've got a story. *Love in the Autumn of Life*. Those years after bringing up your children. Your wife is dead and you live all alone. Then luck comes along and you meet someone in a similar predicament and fall in love. A different love – mellow, sweet and gentle, not spurred on and controlled by sex. The love of company, of finding a true companion. Someone to share your life."

"You're talking of your father. Jim and his new friend, Sophie?"

"Exactly. They're so happy. They'd met when they were both virgins, loved, maybe, and then lost touch. When my father stayed in England to get his degree at the London School of Economics. Then all those years later they met in Harry B's, barely recognising each other when I introduced them. Then it clicked and they journeyed back in their memories to those ten days on the boat across the pond to England and their two weeks of sightseeing together in London. It's just as romantic as me and Harvey, the story of my first book that's launching in August. Love in the spring, and love in the autumn. I won't tell Dad it's about them. But if it publishes, they'll recognise themselves. I'll bring in her squabbling children who only think about themselves, and a husband who shot himself and the son who says they're better off without him. Poor Sophie. Hell on earth... Have I got a story?"

"Oh, you've got a story, no doubt of it."

"I want to start writing when we camp by the sea up there in Namibia. I can feel it coming. My mind is racing. Should I take notes?"

"Never take notes, Jane. Let the story build and rest in the back of your mind, so when you sit down to write it will flow out of you like a gentle stream running around the rocks, fresh, new and real, not patched up from a pile of notes you wrote months ago... The little gas cooker is lit. The kettle's on. You want an apple? Or shall I make a sandwich? We're getting there, Janey. In more ways than one... Doesn't she have a lot of money recently left to her by her deceased father?"

"What's that got to do with it?"

"Love, what we like to think of as simply a passion for another person, is more likely a mutually beneficial relationship. With all that money in Sophie's kitty your father can retire and live in comfort."

"He will have a pension."

"Pensions are rarely enough."

"So you think Dad has joined up with Sophie because of her money, not because of their unrequited love?"

"It's possible. Money talks. She's lonely. Says her children, all three of them, are only interested in themselves. She won't care not leaving them her father's money. Why not spend it with her Jim and take him on a cruise around the world in the comfort of a first-class cabin? Love in the autumn has to be mutually beneficial or it doesn't work. Mostly in life, we love what people can give us, which to start with in a relationship is sex. Later there is more to it than just sex. You and I are going to have a mutually beneficial baby together. We can write together. We were friends, real friends before we became lovers. We were both lonely and then your pregnancy joined us together and gave us both what we wanted. For us, money isn't part of the game of life as we both have more money than we know what to do with. Or you will have when your book sells in the millions."

"You think Dad's after her money? That's horrible."

"I hope not. Just think of it for your new book. A good story has a twist in the tail. A twist that brings reality back from the hope and desire of our imaginations... How's the tea?"

"But they love each other. Why they are so content and happy."

"But what are they thinking, Janey? What's the truth inside of both of their heads? We all like to waffle, mostly to convince ourselves that what we are doing is love, the romantic kind of love. But love has many meanings."

"We drank too much of that wine last night."

"Did I? The truth often hurts. Let's hope the love between your father and Sophie is that perfect love that can come in the autumn of life, not something brought by materialism, by spending money. Yes, things can happen. Like me getting you pregnant and opening up a whole new, better world for both of us. I'm not really talking about you and me, or Jim and Sophie. I'm talking about the book you are going to write to give it depth and a real story that resonates with your readers. Life is never perfect. Except in romantic fiction. Give your book a story that will last. Give it something of value."

"Let's hit the road."

"Why not? Just let me drink my tea. My turn to drive. Next stop Keetmanshoop and a campsite in the Kokerboom Forest."

"Can we buy that case of whisky?"

"You think we should? Let's just see. Have I upset you?"

"Just a little. Dad would never be influenced by her money."

"Are you sure? There's nothing better than a life of comfort. Especially in our autumn years. Why did Sophie's husband shoot himself?"

"I don't know. And it was her second husband."

"Now we're getting somewhere. You've got a book, Janey... What a beautiful day. The sun is shining. The birds are singing. And there's not another car on the road."

Back behind the wheel, Randall smiled. The day, the road, his whole life was in front of him as he listened to Jane expanding her story. She was a romantic like so many women. Always living in hope. Never really understanding how complex and horrible life could be, the way they had all lived in the colonial days in Rhodesia, in a paradise for fools, no one wanting to look ahead and see where it would end – in war, death for some, the loss of their land and everything they had worked for. Splashing money around on fancy trips for Sophie. Would their new lives together have worked so well in a couple of rented rooms, with nothing much to do but sit and look at each other? All the running around gave them something to do, the luck of Sophie's inheritance.

"When you've written for the day, make sure you make notes of what happened so that further down the story you won't contradict yourself. It'll take a year or so to write your book but only hours to read it. You got to maintain the correctness of the story. Can't change the name of that cruise ship or the reader will see it's wrong... Go on. I'm interrupting."

By the time the light began to fade they were driving into Keetmanshoop, both of them tired from the driving.

"Do we or don't we, Jane?"

"What?"

"Buy the whisky. There won't be any ice in the campsite. We can drink it with a little cold water. We're not in a hurry. If the Kokerboom Forest is what I hope it is, a lovely hideaway among the trees, we can park up for a couple of days. Make friends like we did with Koos and Petra. Shouldn't be too difficult to attract friends with a whole case of whisky."

"You want to face your reality? That we're a pair of drunks?"

"Something like that. And you don't have to giggle. Here we are at a red robot and look at that..."

"A robot? Are you kidding?"

"Sorry, that's a traffic light to you. Here in Africa we call them robots. Become a habit of mine. Right there ten yards on our left is a bottle store with one empty parking spot just in front of it. Now that can't be a coincidence. The lights are green. What whisky shall I buy? How about a nice case of VAT 69? Good Scotch whisky. Should keep us happy for a couple of days. We'll just have to drink very slowly to look after our baby. And there we are nicely parked. A coin in the metre and into the shop.

They can give us the directions to a campsite in the forest. The locals will know. We've got enough food for three days. All we need is the whisky. Now, you really are smiling, Janey... What a shame."

"What's a shame?"

"All those wonderful years in Africa gone for my family forever. I wonder what World's View now looks like? All those tobacco-curing barns. That big grading shed. And our beautiful house. We even had cricket nets to practise our batting and bowling. All gone. Never to be seen again. All my father and Bergit have is the memory. My lovely stepmother. Anyway, at least they're comfortably off living in London. You see, my father was looking forward. Using his brains. Spent some of the profit from the good years when the weather was right to buy a share in a block of flats in Chelsea with an artist. She's famous now. Livy Johnston. She married and divorced Frank Brigandshaw, the son of Harry Brigandshaw who was the reason my father came to Africa. Actually Frank wasn't Harry's son. It's a long story. In those days you could get your money out of the country. One of the prime spots in London, right on the Thames. Nothing better than living close to a river. My father wasn't a fool, thank goodness. Paradise he knew, but he faced reality."

"You're off again."

"Probably. It's whisky-buying day. Let's go."

"Why are you being so nostalgic?"

"I'm back in Africa, Janey. Back in my Africa, where I was born. Where I grew up. Before I found out what the world was all about. Now just look at that. The VAT 69 is on special. Give me a case of that nice whisky and tell me how I get to the best campsite in the Kokerboom Forest."

"Cash or credit?"

"Cash. Is there discount for a case?"

"No. Not when it's on a special. My best friend's father owns the Kokerboom campsite. There's only one. Went to school with his son. I'll write down the directions. Give Eugene my regards. Eugene Steenkamp. He works for his father, kind of a family business like this place. My dad owns the bottle store."

"Can we get any ice for the whisky at the campsite?"

"Just ask Eugene. He'll look after you. There's your change. Now let me get the case and take it to your car. Lucky you found a parking lot. Saw you both get out of the camper. Where are you from?"

"America, New York. I wanted to show my lady, Africa... Thanks, Eugene. All I've got to do is follow the directions. What a lucky day. A parking spot right outside. My favourite whisky on special. And Eugene's going to give me a bucket of ice to drink with your whisky. What do you think of that, Janey? Don't get no better nowhere. Don't worry. I'll carry the case of whisky... What's your name?"

"Fred Whitemore. Strange name for today's Africa. My ancestors came from England."

"What do you think of the new South Africa?"

"Going just fine. Now, with Nelson Mandela as president, everyone has a future... Have a nice day. Don't drink it all at once."

"We'll try not to."

"My friend Eugene likes whisky."

"Does he now? How old is Eugene?"

"Nineteen. We're the new generation."

"And he drinks whisky at nineteen?"

"Why not? The Steenkamps all drink. You'll see. I like that camper."

"So do we. Where can I buy some whisky glasses?"

"Right here. How many you want?"

"Make it half a dozen. Can't drink whisky on ice out of a teacup, Janey. Oh, my goodness. Are we going to have fun... Keep the change, Fred."

"You've given me a hundred rand!"

"It's also your lucky day."

"Are all Americans rich?"

"It's all in the exchange rate. A dollar goes twice as far in Africa. Janey, can you carry the glasses? How long will it take to get to the campsite?"

"Half an hour. Americans. Wish we had more American tourists. You don't have much of an American accent."

"It's a long story."

3

*B*ack in the Dormobile, the whisky and glasses in the back, Jane gave him a quizzical look.

"Now what's the matter, Jane?"

"You don't even have a trace of an American accent."

"He was just asking a question in a roundabout way. You drive, I'll read out the directions. I have the accent of an old British colonial. Nothing I can do. How I was taught. Does it matter so long as we all speak English? Strange, that one. The Empire has gone. But the language lives on. Every educated person on the planet wants to learn English. It's the universal language everyone understands or wants to understand. At least something is left from that little island set in the silver sea. Drive on, my Janey. The journey of life continues. We still have half our lives to live with a bit of luck. What happens then, God only knows. Met a man once who said he'd had previous lives. He could remember them. He was some kind of preacher who made people remember their previous lives. If there are previous lives there must be more in the future. Or so the story goes. Made a living out of it. Some kind of therapy. The things we people do to make a living. But if it helped his gullible clients to better enjoy their present lives. Who cares?... Right at the robot. How's last night's wine? I can still feel the effects. Why is there always a price to pay when you have fun? There you go. According to Fred, we just follow this road for half an hour, and we'll see the campsite on the left-hand side of the road. At least with our whisky, we can douse the remains of our hangovers. And start all over again. There's a big sign on the side of the road. 'Holiday Camp'. Fred's note says we can't miss it... Are you hungry?"

"But I don't have a hangover, and yes I am starving."

"Stop laughing. Mine has been creeping up on me all day. First, I'll get a fire going while you lay out the food. Then we'll open the first bottle of whisky."

"What about the ice?"

"Depends on Eugene."

"Do you think we had previous lives, Randall?"

"I have absolutely no idea. I have enough trouble handling this one. We made a deal to always live in the present... Just look at those lovely trees. Not fir or gum. They're indigenous to this part of Africa. Nothing like them in Rhodesia... How's it going?"

"The driving's fine."

"I meant your story. Can you feel it building?"

"Comes and goes... Sheep. Look at all those sheep... What are we having for supper?"

"Lamb cutlets."

"Those poor sheep."

"Life, Jane. How it goes."

"Do you think the sheep have more than one life?"

"Now you're being ridiculous."

"Am I? If what that man said about his multiple lives is true, why shouldn't the sheep live again? The only difference between us and the sheep is that no one eats us. Hopefully."

"You got to live. Got to eat. Life in all its glory."

"Did he tell you what he did in his previous lives?"

"Not the psychic."

"Where did you meet him?"

"At a writer's convention in New York. He'd written his story down in a book. Said he used his book as a calling card. Charged a hundred dollars for a one-hour session. People were lining up once they read the book, according to his publicist. I met a woman at the convention who had received ten sessions of therapy after reading his book. She was ecstatic. After the fifth session, it all came back to her. She'd been in the French Resistance during World War Two, twenty years before she was reincarnated as the lady I met at the book convention."

"How old was she?"

"At the convention? Thirty-something. Didn't have any kids. She was on her own."

"Could she speak French?"

"I should have asked her. If she couldn't speak a word of French, how did she remember being in the French Resistance? Would have knocked it all on the head. Just as well I kept my mouth shut. She was hoping to find more of her previous lives. She had been suffering from depression when she read the book. He'd changed her life. What's a thousand dollars if it stops you feeling miserable?"

"How did the psychic feel inside of himself?"

"They don't care when they're making money. Let's talk about raindrops on roses and bright copper kettles and all my other favourite things."

"You are nuts."

"It was a song. Made people feel better about themselves. The trick in life is to make other people feel happy, even if you charge them a thousand dollars. Or I'll just shut up and let you think of *Love in the Autumn of Life*, your next bestseller."

When Randall saw the big sign on the side of the road twenty-five minutes later, having timed the journey on his watch, the sun was setting, sending the last fingers of sunlight into the heavens. They stopped at the gate next to a house. A young man came out carrying a board holding a sheaf of papers.

"Are you Eugene?"

"How did you know?"

"Fred Whitmore sends his regards."

"Just sign in. Good old Fred. How long are you staying?"

"We don't know. We'll pay for tonight and see what happens tomorrow. You got any ice you can give us? We brought a case of whisky."

"I'll bring it to you when you've made camp. Welcome to the Kokerboom Forest, Mr Crookshank."

"Call me Randall. Look at that, Jane. The place is full of happy campers. I can even hear the music. There you go, Eugene. Keep the change. Just don't forget the ice. Bring the whole family if they'd like a drink. Tonight is party night. Money. What would happen in a world without money? That one over there, Janey, under those trees. Lamb cutlets coming up. There's a nice pile of wood next to the fireplace."

"You didn't pay for it."

"He didn't ask me. Did you see? His eyes positively shone when I mentioned the whisky. And the world goes on. And here we are on the other side of the world. Let's you and me get organised. Tonight is whisky night. The birds are singing. The frogs are singing. Just listen to those crickets. I'm beginning to forget what my apartment in Manhattan even looks like."

Forty-five minutes later when the fire was going and the food ready on the table, other than the meat, Eugene brought them a large bucket of ice.

"What did Fred have to say for himself?"

"That he thought the new South Africa has a future for everyone... You want a drink?"

"Why not?"

"Sit you down. Everything is ready. We'll cook the chops when we've had a couple of drinks. Nothing better than a glass full of ice doused with whisky... There you go. Are your parents going to join us? You've made our evening with the ice. One favour deserves another. So, tell me what you think of the new South Africa, and what's it like living in Namibia that was once South West Africa?"

By the time the mother and father joined them around the wooden table, Eugene was on his third whisky. Whether he was just trying to convince himself about his future under black rule, Randall wasn't sure. They had cooked and eaten their supper.

"Don't get up. How many drinks has he had? We do the rounds every night. Everything in order? You can leave the ice bucket on the table. Is he boring you, our son? Enjoy your evening."

"When you've finished the rounds, come and join us."

"Are you sure?"

"We have a whole case of whisky."

"Now you're talking."

"Randall and Jane."

"Corinna and Dirk. What's he been telling you?"

"What a wonderful future the people of South Africa have, as does Namibia."

"I wish. This place will go the same way as Zimbabwe. Once they've taken over running the country by booting whites out of their jobs, they'll turn the whole economy over to themselves by what they are calling black economic empowerment."

"Don't be silly, Dad. We're all going to work together and turn Africa into the new powerhouse. The prospects are mind-boggling."

"You hope. Enjoy your whisky. See you later, Randall. Don't believe a word he says."

"Why are you always so negative, Dad? Think positive. Then it will happen. My generation is going to pull the black people of this country out of poverty once and for all. We're going to create a market that will give the economy an annual growth rate of ten per cent for years to come. Like the Chinese. Their economy has doubled in the last ten years. And they're under communist rule. The Chinese are going to help us. You see. They want our minerals and we want their capital and expertise."

"Don't know where he gets it from, my son."

"I read. Ask questions. Pick brains of the overseas holidaymakers. Like Jane here from America. We all got to work together in Africa if we are going to succeed."

"And if it doesn't work?"

"At least we will have tried. You got to share, Dad. You can't be greedy. Don't you agree with me, Randall?"

"Oh, I'd like to. You have just no idea how much I would like to."

"Disparity of wealth. That's our problem. The gap between the rich and the poor is greater than any other country on earth. Either we bring them up the wealth ladder or their poverty will destroy all of us."

When the mother and father walked off on their nightly rounds, Randall sat sipping his whisky as the young man talked on about the future. At nineteen, the boy had brains. Determined not to tell him 'hope springs eternal' and start an argument, Randall's mind wandered off. He remembered those early days in Rhodesia where everyone in the farming block they had called Centenary (due to its first white farmers settling on the land a hundred years after the birth of Cecil John Rhodes) thought they had the same glorious future that Eugene Steenkamp was exhorting. When the parents came back, they drank one whisky before carting their half-drunk son back to their house, pained expressions on the faces of both parents.

"Peace and tranquillity returns, Jane. You know what? It's time for bed. We've got to control our drinking now you are having a baby. I'll pull out the bed. Should have done it before I started drinking."

"If he's right, why don't we buy a place in this beautiful country and write our books in peace?"

"We've been down that road. And we ain't going to do it, my love. A house in the English countryside is our alternative. Despite the foul weather. We have the money to buy the right place. Oh, don't get Eugene wrong. Some of the blacks will do very nicely thank you. The political elite. The rest will scream and shout and get nowhere. The political elite in Zimbabwe are already stashing their ill-gotten gains in offshore bank accounts to hide their money from the next generation of predators. But we'll have to see. I wish young Eugene the best of luck. All he can hope for is luck and keeping himself out of the firing line. The secret for the whites in the future South Africa is to not show off their wealth. Never look rich in a poor man's country or it will drive him crazy and make him seething jealous. Disparity of wealth. The new catchphrase. He had that one right."

"Are you really going to bed?"

"Let me sort out the back of the Dormobile and then we'll see... The music has stopped. They've all gone to sleep. All I want now is the call of the night owls. Mostly in life, you have to make the best of what you have. Tourism. Probably the right business to be in if you are a Eugene Steenkamp in the new southern Africa. Tourists from Europe and America like the familiar. People like themselves. We'll just have to see. Whatever you do or wherever you go, you can never be certain you have made the right decision. Will the well-thinking blacks in this country use the whites to create that new African powerhouse? Possibly. Will a sharply increasing population create the market for a growing economy? Zimbabwe's population has multiplied five times since I was born. And all the new technology, like computers and cell phones, can open the whole world to a young man. The kraal will no longer be isolated in a lifestyle that hasn't changed for all those centuries. And just maybe, they'll be able to visit New York on some new-fangled device without moving from under a tree. And who knows what a phone will look like in twenty years' time? And with billions around the world wanting that product, the price will plummet. A smart black government might just give the school children that phone or computer for nothing. Technology, Jane. Could revolutionise Africa as it has done China, India and the rest of the Far East... I'm waffling. It's the whisky. Let me go and make the bed."

"Then why put up with the English climate when we could live in the sunshine?"

"You're at it again."

"You're biased because of what's happening to all your old farming friends in Zimbabwe."

"By the end of this century in three years' time, they'll have kicked every white farmer out of the Centenary. They're not using them to mentor the new emerging black farmers. They want them out. Right out. Right out of the country. The roof's popped. They hate us, Jane. And for good reason. When you've been pushed around in South Africa for three hundred years by a bunch of Dutchmen, you're not going to want to make friends with them. Did servants ever love their masters? I don't think so. They feared losing their jobs and sucked up to them to get life's basics: a roof over their heads and food. The rest was plain humiliating. And no one ever liked being humiliated. Underneath the false smiles lurked a deep resentment. Now, for the blacks, it's time for revenge. One double bed ready."

"Can I have another whisky?"

"Just one."

"Give me a kiss. We're having fun. I've put more wood on the fire."

"I can see... That ice bucket of Eugene's did the trick. The ice hasn't melted."

"I'd love to live in Africa. There's so much space. You're not on top of people all the time. Even in a holiday camp, there's lots of space between the campers. Thank you for bringing me to Africa, Randall. I'm so enjoying myself."

"That's the whisky."

"Whisky always helps."

"Until the morning after. You want a cold spud? There you go. Just a touch of salt. And the night comes down."

"What are we going to do tomorrow?"

"Tomorrow, we'll walk the forest. Take a picnic lunch. Go exploring. Eugene said the sun will shine tomorrow. We'll find a river and lie under the trees and listen to the beautiful sounds of nature. With luck, we'll see wild animals... This whisky is quite delicious."

"I told you so."

"How's our baby?"

"Fine. Just fine... It's so wonderful to feel happy."

4

By the time they went to bed the first bottle of whisky had been finished with the help of Eugene and his parents. Having drunk slowly and eaten a good supper, each drinking down a pint of cold water before they climbed into the double bed, they hoped for a good night's sleep untroubled by alcohol. Eight and a half hours later, the morning sun streaming through the window woke them from their slumber. Neither of them had woken during the night. When Randall leaned up on his elbow and peered out of the window, he could see the camp was half empty.

"You stay where you are and I'll make the tea. It's the man's job to make the morning tea. Believe it or not, I don't have a hangover... But there's still one problem."

"What's that, Randall?"

"We still have eleven full bottles of whisky staring at us. Oh, well. Today's a day to relax. No driving... Did you dream?"

"Just before waking I was breast-feeding my baby, the baby all cuddled up in the crook of my arm... I love yawning and stretching in the mornings. It's all so peaceful. Please kiss me good morning... I was under a tree, next to a river, me and my baby alone. It was such a lovely feeling as the baby suckled. We were in Africa. I could hear the same birds and crickets you so love. It was all perfect. Thank you, my love. A soft, beautiful kiss on the mouth. I'm so glad you shaved off your beard. You'd better put your trousers on. When are we going into the forest?"

"When we've drunk our tea and eaten our breakfast."

"I'm still nicely sleepy. I'd better be careful. Don't want to let my tea go cold, do I? Wake me if I nod off. You were so lucky being born and brought up on an African farm. After the forest, I'm going to put back the table and start to write my book. I want to go down that rabbit hole into the world of my book. Do you go down a rabbit hole when you write, Randall?"

"Every time. Why writers like to be hermits so they can live in their books down that same rabbit hole that comes with writing or reading in the quiet of one's mind. A world alone inside a book."

"Isn't it weird for you to imagine all those readers around the world at this very moment visiting your rabbit hole and disappearing into your books? You're in their minds and they are in yours. I can't wait to go down my rabbit hole. It's my world where I can stay for as long as I write... You could sit on the other side of the table and go visit Shakespeare and his friend. How does that sound?"

"Let's just see what happens... Tea coming up. You can go back to sleep. 'Oh, what a beautiful mornin''."

"You can't sing."

"Never could. I'm always out of tune."

"The birds are singing. You must never upset the birds. Why is it some people sing out of tune? It's like not being able to speak properly. Except for those with a lisp, everyone I know speaks fine. But lots of people can't sing in tune."

"I've never heard you sing."

"And you never will. Wake me with a cup of tea. It's so lovely just talking and finding out about each other. We're writing books to each other. There's nothing more perfect than being with a lover and wanting to share. And you're wrong about one thing. Whatever happened in their pasts, many Africans will want to make friends with the whites. It's human nature to want to chat with each other and make friends. And when they all find out how similar they are in their minds, the colour of their skins and what they look like won't matter. Maybe you people have a guilty conscience, using all that cheap black labour to grow your tobacco."

"You have a point."

"I always have a point."

When Randall came back with the first cup of morning tea Jane was fast asleep, the back door of the camper still wide open.

"Wake up, sleepy head... Now, what's the matter?"

"You startled me. I was having a bad dream. I'd lost our baby. Look at me. I'm sweating with fear. Shaking. The worst nightmare of my life. You think last night's whisky can have hurt my baby, Randall? Please come and hug me. It was so horrible."

"If drink was a problem when having a child, Phillip and I would never have been born. My mother was permanently half drunk. It killed her in the end. She drove off into the bush pissed out of her mind and ran out of petrol. When she tried to walk to find some help she was attacked by a pride of hungry lions. Maybe her drinking has given me an inherent liking for a couple of drinks. But it didn't kill me inside her womb. My poor mother. Phillip can't even remember her and he's two years older than me."

"Must be awful to lose your mother so young."

"It was. Neither of us will ever get over it. Her death is my problem, not the alcohol in her body. Without our stepmother, Bergit, I don't know what would have become of us. We would never have pulled our lives back together. Don't sweat, Jane. Enjoy your tea."

"I want a hug... Do you know I never used to drink much tea before I met you?"

"Yes, I know. Everything's going to be fine. Don't worry. Worry can do more harm than a few glasses of wine. Now, does that feel better, Janey? A morning hug and a morning cup of tea. Don't nod off again and let it get cold. I'm making breakfast. Get up when you are ready... Your mother died when you were seventeen. You were lucky compared to me and Phillip. Stop worrying about the baby. Relax. The last thing you need is stress. Why we came on our journey, to get away from all the noise and nonsense of people. A slow, gentle journey that will end when we go back to New York for the launch of your book in August. Then in September, you'll have a beautiful, healthy baby in the best clinic in America."

"The tea's hot."

"As it should be."

"Now what are you doing?"

"I'm dancing the light fandango. Another of my favourite songs. I can dance the light fandango on my own but I can't sing. Good, you've stopped looking worried... Half last night's campers have upped and gone on their way. All those journeys we love to take."

Worried about Jane and not sure if alcohol wasn't a problem, Randall went back to the fire and with a long toasting fork made the toast before scrambling the eggs. By the time he put the breakfast on the wooden table, Jane was dressed. They ate together in a comfortable silence before wandering out of the campsite into the forest. A narrow path took them through the trees and wound its way down to a stream.

"What's in your backpack, Randall?"

"A tin box stuffed with tomato sandwiches and a flask of tea."

"Don't get us lost. This place is wild."

"Trust me."

"What's that sound coming from the top of the trees over behind the river?"

"Vervet monkeys. Look carefully and watch for movement and you'll see them. They're not very big but very cute... Now just look at this for a perfect spot. I'll lay towels on the ground under the tree and make a blanket we can lie on while we listen to the sound of tinkling water. Look at all those tiny birds up in the trees flitting from branch to branch among the leaves. They must be picking something. Well, this is it. Perfect peace and harmony of birds and wild animals. I'm going to lie on the towel with my back against the tree and read my book."

"Did you bring my book?"

"Naturally. Writers need to read. Now there we are. No talking. Let's live for an hour or two with nature and enjoy our books. What would the world do without books?"

"Do you think my nightmare was brought on by drinking too much whisky?"

"I hope not. Stop worrying. We've found paradise on earth, Janey. This is it. What every man and woman on earth craves in their wildest dreams."

At the end of a perfect day, when they walked up the winding path through the forest and back to their campsite, the ice bucket was still on the wooden table, the fire no longer smouldering, the sun going down behind the trees. Randall relit the fire and idly took the top off the ice bucket.

"Well, I'll be buggered. It's full of ice. Good old Eugene. You want a drink?"

"The glasses have been washed and dried."

"What makes me think we're going to have company? How quickly the temperature drops when the sun goes down. I'd better go and pay them for another night. It's your turn to make the food. We've got a couple of nice big steaks and plenty of lettuce. Spuds, steak and a salad. Wasn't lying next to that stream just a perfect way to spend a day?"

When Randall returned from paying the bill, the salad had been made and everything was ready on the table. The campsite was filling up with travellers, bringing noise and the distant chatter of people.

"When are they coming?"

"I didn't see Eugene. Maybe filling the ice bucket was a thank-you for last night's drinking."

"Or he's found another tourist to drink with. Someone his own age. Teenagers like to drink with their own. Pour us a drink. Everything's ready."

"How are you feeling, Jane? Did the day under the trees chase away your nightmare? Good. Here you go. We're back on the booze."

"And tomorrow?"

"We'll carry on up the road. The further north we go, the warmer the climate."

"I wonder what Tracey is up to? I so enjoyed living together in her apartment. She was so good to me. Saved my life."

"Looking after her baby. Writing her book. Drinking. Probably found herself a man for the night."

"And she's still not sure who fathered her baby?"

"That was the idea. Multiple partners. So she wouldn't have a man to tell her what to do."

"Wouldn't it be strange if our baby is related to her baby? They'd be half-brothers or sisters."

"Let's not go down that path. What Tracey does is her business. She didn't want us to have a blood test so that's final."

"Make us all one big family. The world is so strange."

"It was a one-night stand. I was drunk and even fell asleep on the job."

"A child needs both parents. You won't run away will you, Randall? I love sitting around the fire. My whisky tastes so good. And the bed's made up. All we do is enjoy our food and drinks around this lovely fire and climb into bed when we're ready."

"Maybe we should stay another day? There's no hurry."

"The three musketeers may be thousands of miles apart but we're still close to each other. She'll be thinking of us on our long journey, the same way we are talking about Tracey... I can't wait to have my first baby. You must so miss James Oliver and Douglas. Poor kids living without their father. Why do so many of us ruin our lives?"

"Amanda wanted to live with her rich lesbian lover. Meredith preferred a younger man: she only married me for my money. I was the fool not to see what she wanted. I thought she wanted me. I was horribly wrong. Do you think my two kids miss me?"

"Of course they do. Let's just see. With that nice big house in England, there'll be plenty of room for visitors."

"They don't want me to see their children."

"Time will tell. In this strange and complicated world, you never know what's going to happen. A year ago I would never have dreamed I'd be in Africa and pregnant with my first child. We're all going to be one big family. A few years and who can tell what we'll all be doing?"

"You want me to put the steak on?"

"Let's have a couple of drinks. Why did you call him James Oliver? Two names instead of one?"

"After my two best friends. Didn't I tell you? I wonder what happened to James Tomlin and Oliver Manningford? We lose touch with people. Sad. Very sad. All about living in too many countries, I suppose: Rhodesia, England and America. People drift apart with time. We all lived in the same boarding house. Must be twenty long years since we all first met. Young, innocent and trusting of people. In our youth, we only look on the bright side of life. The longer we live the more sceptical we become. It's something in our brain that changes when we reach our mid-twenties. People say the longer you live, the more you comprehend as you go through life's realities. Young love, the heart of your book, believes everything in the future is going to be perfect. We don't question our own motives and see the consequences, let alone the motives of our future partners. There was another old saying: 'Fools rush in where angels fear to tread.' Young men rush off to war with excitement to fight for their country. They don't see the horrors and misery of war when they sign up. They don't even think they are about to kill other people, let alone that those people are much the same as themselves. I would love to have stayed nineteen in Mrs Salter's boarding house with James and Oliver and the rest of our friends forever and ever. Never growing old. Never realising the true realities of life. And do you know, I don't even know what's happening in the lives of my half-sister or brother,

Myra and Craig. I should. They're family... Now, what's wrong with this? A nice whisky with lots of Eugene's ice."

"Did you ask them to join us?"

"It's up to them. Let them decide. They may drift by when they do their night check of the camp. Strange to think our baby is going to go through that same life. We'll enjoy watching him if it's a boy or her if it's a girl. See all those wonderful years again. Lots of people say the best days of their lives were their school days... How's the Scotch going down? The fire's burned down enough to put the spuds in the coals all nicely covered in tinfoil... There he goes. A night owl... And again.... And again... There's something wrong. He's called three times and she hasn't replied."

"I'm so happy, Randall. I thought once I reached my thirties without a life partner or children, I'd just drift into my old age with nothing. That I'd be empty. A life alone in an empty world with little or nothing to live for."

When Randall put the steaks on the grill over the coals, they had drunk a third of the bottle of whisky, each of them reminiscent about their pasts, content with each other. High above, the stars were out in the heavens, the night growing cold as they leaned close to the fire. After eating their supper they sat in harmonious silence holding each other's hand as they sipped down the first half of their bottle of whisky, the camp settling down with the night. Three times the owl hooted for his lover without success. Were they going to be all right together for the rest of their lives? Randall hoped so. For both of them, it was their last chance for happiness, a happiness money could never buy. Was he going to take out the unfinished manuscript of *Shakespeare's Ghost*, the new title he had found for his book about the Bard's playwriting companion, and try and write tomorrow, himself and Jane at the same writing table but far, far away down their own rabbit holes? Peace on earth and tranquillity with not a nasty thought in their minds, the characters so alive they could see them as clear as crystal in a place they wanted to be.

"You found the ice. The camp's quiet. Everyone's settled down."

"Where's your wife?"

"Just me tonight, Randall. Can I have a drink? Corinna and I have had an argument. She thinks Eugene should go off and find himself a proper job. Make himself a career, instead of bumming off his parents. Can I put some more wood on the fire?"

"It's your wood. Thanks for the second bucket of ice. Sit you down."

"Eugene's quite happy helping me run the holiday camp. He's going to build himself a cottage and be independent."

"What about girls?"

"Thanks, Randall. I really needed a drink tonight. You're right, Jane. He's never had a girlfriend. He sees the occasional pretty girl his own age but the next day they've gone. Maybe Corinna's right. I hate arguments. She's always right. I just don't know what Eugene can do. He finished school in the middle of his class. Never talked of university. With the new government in place, they did away with National Service so he didn't have to go in the army. Corinna says he drinks too much but what else is there to do? He'd do the same in town. He'd end up working for some supermarket, working for someone else for the rest of his life and ending up with nothing but a small pension. Here, we own the place: our home and our business."

"Go and tell her to join us."

"She won't talk to me. It's best she sleeps on it and we'll have it out again in the morning. Wives and kids. Never easy. Do you mind if I stay for a few drinks? You can stay another night and enjoy the forest and we won't charge you. Why is life always so complicated? She doesn't even want to talk to Eugene. She'll be sitting there seething on her own. Why do wives always think it's better on the other side of the fence? She's never satisfied. That one went down well. Straight down the hatch."

"Want another?"

"Thought you'd never ask. Thanks. I needed company. My poor wife. Stuck in the middle of an African forest isn't everyone's cup of tea."

"She seemed happy enough yesterday. Let me go and talk to her. Girl to girl. We've plenty of whisky. And we too like a little company every now and again."

"Will you, Jane? Thank you."

"After a few drinks and lots of chatter your argument will be forgotten. You want a baked potato? We had steak tonight. It's so nice sitting around the fire with a drink."

And the game of life went on, making Randall smile, the game never changing. They both watched Jane walk across to the house, shining her torch, her jacket pulled tightly over her shoulders against the cold.

"She's nice, your Jane."

"She is, isn't she? How's that for a tot of whisky, Dirk? Nothing better than drowning our sorrows."

"Where does it all end?"

"You tell me."

For a long while, neither of them spoke as they waited. The camp had gone quiet, only the sound of crickets mingling with the night, a moon looking down on them from the heavens. Randall felt for the man, remembering his own arguments with Amanda and then Meredith, the constant nagging. Had he ever seen a truly happy marriage? He wasn't sure. Leaning across the table, he poured whisky from the bottle into Dirk's glass, the firelight flickering in the man's unhappy eyes. Once their child was born, would they too start nagging each other? What Eugene did was his own business.

"Here they come, Dirk. I can see the torchlight."

"Is it both of them?"

"I'm not sure."

When Jane sat down at the table, she picked up her glass and drank.

"She doesn't want to come, Dirk. Should have minded my own business. Your wife snapped at me. Eugene's locked himself in his bedroom."

"You want some more, Janey?"

"Keep pouring."

"I'd better go."

"What for? Let's get drunk and forget the damn world."

"We won't write tomorrow."

"Who cares? There you go, Jane. You did your best. You tried. Cheers. Let's just enjoy ourselves. Don't worry about it. Worry is the curse of life. Instead of worrying about the present tell me the story of your life, Dirk. Jane and I love other people's stories. It helps us with our work."

"What do you do, Randall?"

"We write books. Both of us. Jane's first book launches in August in New York."

"Randall Crookshank. Never heard of a writer by that name. What's your book called, Jane?"

"*Love in the Spring of Life.*"

"We were so happy when we were young, Corinna and I. We were twenty-two when we married. A whirlwind romance."

"Good. Now you're smiling. Tell us more. The night is still young."

What seemed to Randall like an hour later, the story was interrupted by a female voice from out of the dark, the moon down behind the trees.

"It was a perfect time of my life, too."

"How long have you been standing in the dark? You must be freezing cold. Come and sit by the fire. Randall, give my poor wife a drink. I've done a deal with Randall, Corinna, for the whisky. We're not charging him for tomorrow. I'll go and get Eugene."

"I'm here, Dad."

"Now you've both spooked me. Randall tells me they are writers. You've always said you wanted to write. Tell my son how to start."

"It's quite simple. You start at the beginning. Page one and let the story flow."

By the time the family left to go back to their house, the second bottle of whisky was half empty, all five of them as tight as ticks, the argument between Dirk and Corinna long forgotten. As Randall fell asleep in the back of the Dormobile, he was smiling, Manhattan, New York, America, a million miles away. His last thought was wondering if Eugene Steenkamp would ever write himself a book, giving the boy a life's purpose in the middle of his African forest. Next to him, Jane groaned in her sleep. Outside the owl called, answered by its mate as Randall slid gently into his dreams.

PART 2

MAY TO SEPTEMBER 1997 – BACK TO REALITY

1

Jane woke to the dawn chorus of birds with a dry mouth, a headache and a guilty conscience: drinking was not good for her baby. Pulling the bedclothes aside, she eased herself off the bed, trying not to wake Randall. Wearing a sweater, the bottom of her tracksuit and her walking shoes, she opened the back door of the Dormobile and stepped into the morning, where a cold wind was playing through the trees. With her hands tucked into the ends of her sleeves, she stood listening to the birds. Very quietly, Jane closed the door of the camper. Smiling, despite her hangover from the previous night's drinking, she walked off alone into the trees as quickly as possible, the exercise beginning to make her warm. There was no sound from the other campers nor the silent house standing at the gate. In her mind, she was thinking of her new book, a book she wanted to start despite her headache. As she walked, her characters began to talk to her as the window to her new story opened up. Her hangover, thankfully, began to subside as she walked on through the forest. In her head, Jane was nineteen years old, among her old friends in a world where everyone smiled and people believed what they were told. Love, that pure love of trusting youth, was back in her life, all the worry of whether Randall would stay with her once the baby was born gone from her mind. Would they ever marry, she doubted. They had both been through too much. They called each other their love but were they in love? If he wanted to drink, what else could she do but join the party? A woman of her age trying to hold on to a man never found it easy, especially a man with fortune and fame. The chances were that when they returned to Manhattan they would go through the launch of her book and the birth of her baby and end up going their separate ways.

"Forget about the present, you silly woman. Whatever happens, happens. At least you are going to have a baby. You'll always have someone to love."

When Jane got back to the campsite, Randall was still asleep in the back of the Dormobile, and Jane was itching to start writing her book.

"Up you get, my love. I want to pull open the bed and put in the table. My new book is shouting at me to start. Do you mind? The walk has got rid of my hangover. How do you feel? You want to write? You want some tea? Who did you meet in your dreams? Her name is Margaret. Margaret Neville. She wants to go to drama school and be in the theatre."

"What on earth are you talking about? I was fast asleep."

"My book. I have a new book. Talking last night to Eugene about starting a book has brought it all back into my mind. I'm nineteen again. Inside Margaret's head. It's all so wonderful. All I need is a place to write. Please help me, Randall. That's better. You're smiling. What are you smiling about?"

"There's nothing more beautiful in life than writing a book."

"Are you going to write with me?"

"Of course I am. What else can I do if you want to write? You put on the kettle and I'll turn the back of our camper into the perfect writing room. But first, give me a kiss. That's better. Now everyone's happy."

"You know the strangest part? Margaret is English. She lives in that beautiful country of England where we want to live, make our home and live happily ever after."

"Always the romantic."

"A girl has to dream."

By the time the kettle boiled, Randall had pulled open the double bed making it into two seats on either side of the table he had fastened back to the floor.

"Forget my tea. I'm going to try and walk off my hangover. Enjoy your writing. Look at that, the sun's coming up over the trees."

Turning off the small gas cooker, she took her pen and packet of white paper from her suitcase and slid in to sit at the table. With six sheets of paper placed on top of each other on the table, she picked up her pen and began to write the story, her mind in another world. By the time she finished writing her second page, she looked up to find Randall, head down, writing on his side of the table. Looking down, she went back into Margaret's mind. When the story stopped talking, Jane returned to the present, sliding herself out from the table. To her surprise, the camp was alive with people, some coming, some going, their noise now heard, no longer blocked by the rabbit hole where she had been all morning. Happy with her writing, she walked away to stand under the trees. When she looked back at the Dormobile she could still see Randall bent over the table oblivious to the world around him. Avoiding contact with people, Jane walked on out into the forest where she sat down on the grass under a tree, next to a bush, the warm sun through the leaves on her cheeks. Maybe, just maybe, she told herself, they had started a life together bound by the writing of their books.

"Margaret Neville, we're all going to be happy. You're going to find the perfect lover and both of us are going to have our babies. By the time I've finished writing your story, I'll be living in your England, the new hope of my dreams far from the noise and turmoil of cities, in your beautiful English countryside... Are you hungry, my baby? Let's go and make us some lunch. We'll be as quiet as two mice until your father has finished his writing. Oh, little one, it's all going to be perfect. And when you are grown up and nineteen years old you can read all about Margaret Neville. Not only will you understand Margaret's mind, you'll understand your mother's and the book will help you avoid some of life's pitfalls. Life's to be enjoyed, my sweetheart, not to be worried about. Your mother must stop worrying. From this little thing in my belly, you're going to grow into the most beautiful woman. Your father and I are going to be so proud of you."

Still smiling at the happiness in her thoughts, Jane looked around at the trees, a slight breeze moving the leaves, the birds singing to each other. When she returned to the campsite, carefully avoiding any contact with people, Randall was nowhere to be seen. Taking the coolbox with the food from the back of the camper, Jane walked to the wooden table where they had sat under the stars the previous evening, next to where Randall had made up the fire ready to cook later. Singing softly to herself out of tune as was her habit, she made the sandwiches and the tea. When everything was ready, Randall walked back through the trees.

"How was your writing today? I've made us some lunch and the kettle's boiled. I'm hungry. Come and sit with me. It's nice and warm in the sun."

"Shakespeare's visiting his friend at his friend's country estate. He's been in the library of the big house all day researching the history of kings and queens. In the evening, they sit together in the grand dining room, the two of them alone waited on hand and foot by the servants while they discuss Will Shakespeare's research. It's been a lovely day for me. When I came out of my book, you were gone. Thanks. Cheese and tomato. My first cup of tea of the day. Where'd you go?"

"Away into the forest. I didn't want people to interrupt my thoughts. Do your characters stay with you after you've finished writing? Why are Shakespeare and his friend dining alone? Where are his friend's family?"

"They stay with me all the time, mostly in my subconscious as the day's writing subsides from my conscious mind. He's alone, poor man. All that great big mansion and there's just himself and the servants. When his friend Will Shakespeare isn't visiting to discuss their plays, he dines alone. Must be terrible always being alone. In those days, servants kept their place, standing at the long dining room table serving the food but never talking. His wife is dead. His daughters are married. His sons are far away on their travels. So there he is, poor man. Rich and all alone. He was lucky early in his life when he was young to have gone backstage after watching one of Shakespeare's plays at the Globe Theatre. He's now not that old. Married early. A little older than Will. They had struck up a friendship that time backstage when he showed Will his first play. Writing plays is his only escape from boredom. Never be alone, my love. It's a terrible way to live. Will's friend had never had to work a day in his life as the heir to his father's estate, everything done for him from the day he was born. Writing was his only outlet, but as an aristocrat, there was no way to get his plays staged as it would not have been considered proper for such a man to open himself up to the world and its people and leave himself open to ridicule for exposing himself. Which is where Will came in and how the two became friends. Can you imagine? That great dining hall with log fires burning at both ends of the room, the best food and finest French wine?"

"You're writing your book out loud again. I love it."

"What are we going to do after lunch? We can go for a walk down to the river and lie under the trees. Tell me more about your own book, Jane. It's a bit like Will and his friend. We won't open the bar until six o'clock. What do you think the chances are of another bucket of ice?"

"Pretty good. We can all talk about books. Writing opposite each other at the table was the most wonderful experience of my life. We're so lucky to be able to write. How's the tea? You want some fruit? I can always go and ask Eugene for a bucket of ice when we come back from our walk. So who wrote Shakespeare's plays? Was it Will Shakespeare or his friend?"

"Nobody knows in my book as they aren't telling. Shakespeare staged and managed many plays at the Globe Theatre, not all of them his. Maybe Shakespeare used his friend's plays as part of his research. Or maybe he put his name to his friend's plays to safeguard his friend's privacy. I never say in the book who wrote what when it is put on the stage."

"But they must know."

"All I say is they read and discuss each other's work. When a new play comes out, the programme says it's written by Will Shakespeare, those plays familiar to all of us. They both get what they want: Shakespeare his research, his friend the company and, just maybe, the satisfaction of seeing his plays performed on the stage. Oh, in my book we see the friend sitting alone in his box at the Globe Theatre watching the play with that deep look of gratitude and satisfaction on his face. But he never claims the plays are his. For Shakespeare's friend, writing the play is more important than fame."

"So you're going to the end of your book without saying who wrote what?"

"I suppose that's a way of putting it. It's the play that lives forever. Not the writer. What's in a name, Jane? Nothing. That which we call a rose by any other name would smell as sweet. We have the plays of Will Shakespeare and always will, if you'll forgive the pun."

"Are you pulling my leg?"

"I hope not. Will Shakespeare and his anonymous friend are pulling your leg: 'Have another glass of this delicious French wine. How was the lobster? Wasn't the cook's soup so nice? Let's go stand by the fire. When's the next opening night? I'll stay at the club as usual. To friends, Will. Let's drink to friends.'"

"You're muddling me up."

"That's life made to look like fiction. Or the other way around. Take your pick. Here we go. Another walk in the garden of Eden with my lover."

"People want to know who wrote the plays."

"Do they really? Why? Would *A Midsummer Night's Dream* be any different if it was written by Charley Porcupine? Or Freddie the Terrible? People don't know who wrote my books. Holiday or Crookshank. Who cares? When they put down our books after having enjoyed their read, you and I are the last people that matter. Anyway, his friend is rich. He doesn't need any more money. He's having fun. When life is fun, that's all that matters. When there's no fun and you're sitting at the top of that long dining room table all alone, that matters. They're having fun."

"Most people want acclaim. They want money."

"Then they are fools if there isn't any fun. Who wants all that celebrity crap? Do you? Our fun is writing our books at the same table and coming back from our long walk to a nice fire, a good meal and a bottle of whisky. That's all Will and his friend ever want in my book. Give me your hand. Let's dance the light fandango. I'm happy. We're happy. And we are having fun. That's all that matters, Jane."

"You got to have money."

"Enough, Jane. Just enough."

"You've never had to work in a laundry for a pittance."

"Then I was lucky."

"Why do we have to buy an estate in England? We can go to Rabbit Farm, far away in the Isle of Man."

"Our child will want company. School and school friends. The Isle of Man is too remote. It was fine for me when I was alone writing my books, telling the story over drinks to my only neighbour who now farms my land. I'm not going to sell the place. It's my backup if everything goes wrong. But nothing is going wrong now you and I are having our child. We're going to forget the turmoil of our pasts as we move into the peace of our forties. Tranquillity. Peace of mind. Somewhere just far enough away but a place to bring up happy children... Now, tell me more about your book."

"Let's just walk and think about our stories. Work out the plot. See where our stories are going so tomorrow we'll know what to write."

Not quite sure what was in Randall's mind, Jane walked on silently, the mention of Randall needing backup making circles in her mind. Trying not to worry, all she could do was hope. Life, she told herself, was one long journey that would only end when she died an old lady. He was right. The trick in life was to have fun and live in the moment. And there she was again, Margaret Neville, back in her mind. As they walked on through the trees, Jane was back in her new book, planning the plot, all her worries forgotten.

By the time they reached the stream and sat with their backs to a tree, Jane had drifted back to her past, to the time of her mother's first fit. They were all in the kitchen helping to make breakfast. It was a Sunday morning, the fear to Jane as real as she sat under the tree as it had been when she was thirteen years old. For no apparent reason, her mother fell to the floor and went into convulsions as the family stared. A week later, Jane's mother was diagnosed with brain cancer. For six months after the first operation, everything appeared normal, neither Jane nor her eleven-year-old sister having any idea of the seriousness of their mother's illness. The brain tumour kept growing despite the surgery as their lives disintegrated. Looking back as she sat in companionable silence with Randall, Jane blamed her mother's long illness on the problems that came later in her life: the breakup with Harvey; the years of drinking and sleeping with different men, most of whom she could barely remember; all those jobs that came and went in the libraries and the bookshops, fired more times than she could remember for not pitching up to work. Many times when she woke up too late to go to work, she had no idea where she was or who was sleeping next to her. Jane blamed everything and everyone for her own stupidity until the day she had to take the job in the laundry, her father refusing to help her, Conny now married and living in Denver. All those years in the eighties were a blur, drowned by alcohol. Despite the warm sun through the trees, it made Jane shudder. Apart from being pregnant, was what she was doing any different? Would the past stay in the past?

She got up from the towel she was sitting on and walked down to the water where she stood quietly alone. She bent down and picked up a stone, throwing it into the water. At least her father now had Sophie, and Jane had a book that with luck was going to make her rich and independent. Money was the most important thing in a thirty-nine-year-old girl's life, despite what Randall said about fame and fortune, easy for him to say when he had both. What was life all about? Jane wasn't sure. But if *Love in the Spring of Life* sold a few million copies she would have one answer: money. Smiling at the thought of the upcoming launch, Jane sat and hunched down over her knees. Her mother had been thirty-eight years old when she died, two years short of her forties. So short a life with little purpose other than her two children. Thinking back again to those years she had shared a bedroom with Conny, she hoped her sister

was happy, that her sister's husband was happy, their two kids were
happy. But did anyone ever know what other people were feeling? Jane
was never sure. All she was sure about was having her baby, launching
her book and hoping her affair with Randall would last as long as
possible, the thoughts making her smile. She was going to be a mother, a
good mother, and bring up her child. Think positive, Janey. And never
rely on other people.

Looking back up the bank of the stream, she inwardly smiled at
Randall and the luck that had come into her life when he had made
her pregnant. How she had never fallen pregnant in her years of
debauchery was nothing short of a miracle, as, like Tracey, she would
have no idea who was the father of the child. On the edge of the
stream on a small, smooth rock with her head on her knees, Jane
smiled at her memories. What a life! The worst of the debauchery was
the Thursday Night Club, as they liked to call it, an evening of drink,
music and good food that ended in the reason for all those young
single girls and men gathering: fornication. Drunk, they picked on
whoever they fancied, everyone being promiscuous together, changing
partners, getting sexual highs from watching the others at it. Some of
the girls, never the men, thank goodness, played with each other for
the men to see, sending the men's hormones skyrocketing. Every
Thursday night there were new girls who had heard of the debauchery
on the grapevine and had phoned the ringleader of the club, Marlon
Webber, for an invitation. Thinking back sent Jane into silent giggles.
They were young, having fun, using their youth and good looks to the
maximum. Did they do anyone any harm? The girls, if they had their
heads screwed on properly, were on the pill. So far as Jane
remembered, none of them had become pregnant. And what else was
life for, other than having fun? Randall was right: if it wasn't fun, forget
it. Some of the men, she could still recall their faces, but few of their
names. They were Joe and Pat, Ricky and Mack, Henry and Ron, and
who cared? None of the girls' names came back to her. The Thursday
Night Club. What a world! But what the hell? No one was hurt.
Everyone had fun. And their lives went on, most of them into
marriages and children where their pasts stayed in the past never to be
mentioned to wives, husbands and children as they all ploughed on
through a normal life of work, family and the daily routine. At least
they had done something with their youth instead of thinking young
love, like her own love for Harvey, would last forever - as she had

written in her book. That would fool the lot of them, make Jane her fortune and give her independence.

As her mind revolved around her memories, Margaret Neville re-entered her thinking, making Jane wonder if the girl who aspired to a life in the theatre might not enjoy a few nights in a Thursday Night Club with some of her fellow actors. Jane smiled at the thought of her readers enjoying Margaret's debauchery, pushing the sales of Jane's second book through the proverbial ceiling. You've got it, Janey, share that fun with the world and let them see how naughty a nice girl can be in pursuit of life's meaning, of looking for a meaning to life and giving it, even for short moments. What was wrong with debauchery? She'd put it in her book. First, she'd let Margaret get into the Juilliard School in New York... Good old Marlon Webber. Wonder what happened to him? It all made Jane smile. Anyway, there was one person who was never going to hear about her frolics in the Thursday Night Club and that was the child in her womb. Unless, of course, she read her mother's book and asked where the story had come from. Or would it be a him who asked that question? Life really was full of pitfalls. Picking up another stone, Jane threw it out into the water.

"The river flows on."

Lying back with her feet almost touching the water, Jane drifted off into a sleep where she dreamed she was in drama school being taught how to act.

"WHAT'S GOING ON?"

"Who are you?"

"Randall. What's the matter? You look scared out of your wits."

"Do you ever wake, not sure what is real or your dream? I wasn't here. Gives me the shivers. The fear of not quite knowing whether it is life or death. The in-between of now and the hereafter."

"I have no idea what you are talking about. We'd better go back. I need a drink."

"You always need a drink."

"Why were you so frightened?"

"Not knowing which life I was in... What time is it?"

"The sun will go down in an hour. Come on. A bucket of ice and a bottle of whisky. What are we eating tonight?"

"You tell me."

"So you like Africa? Were you dreaming?"

"I'm still not sure."

"Smile, Janey. The world hasn't come to an end. How's your new story building in your head?"

"It's coming. In more ways than one."

"That's better. You're giggling. Give me your hand. There we are. My beautiful pregnant lady. It's so nice to let the days drift by. The birds are singing. Listen to that lovely call of a dove. You look worried. Don't worry. There's nothing to worry about. We don't have to plan anything. Well, maybe our books. Let the rest take care of itself. We're lucky, you and I. Just think of all those millions of people having to get up every morning and travel to work. Some work twelve hours a day. What kind of a life is that? Count your blessings, Janey. Writing is fun, not work, and when you get it right it brings a return of millions. Can you imagine being a family doctor for sixty hours of the week, listening to everyone's moans and groans? Drive me nuts... Now, what are you doing?"

"Throwing stones in the water."

"Hold your lover's hand and we'll walk through the trees in perfect peace and tranquillity. We don't have to put up with people. Not like all those other poor sods."

Still feeling the strangeness from her dream, Jane did what she was told, shuddering inwardly for herself and her unborn child. As they walked hand in hand her troubled mood receded, caused, no doubt, by the previous night's drinking, the after-effects of alcohol Jane knew so well from her drunken past. All those mood swings. All those guilty feelings. And did they really love each other or was it mutual convenience: someone to drink with as they waited for their baby? Jane wasn't sure, despite the comfort of Randall's hand.

By the time they sat down around the fire with a full bucket of ice, two glasses and the whisky, Jane decided not to care. The meat was ready to be cooked over the fire and Randall seemed happy. They were on their own, which was pleasant. No sign of Eugene and his family. No need to make polite conversation.

By the third glass, Jane was enjoying her whisky. Should she tell him about the Thursday Night Club, Jane asked herself. Better not. He could read it in her book and decide for himself whether she was writing fact or fiction. The camp was quiet, the other campers equally enjoying their solitude. Sipping at her whisky, she half listened to Randall's story, as, like everyone else Jane had known in her life, he talked on and on about himself. On the fourth drink, it was Jane's turn to return the compliment. Once again, she was back in those early days when life was full of roses. Through the cool of the evening and the warmth of the fire, they prattled on to each other, both of them enjoying their evening and the comfort of companionship, Jane no longer digging in her mind for the truth. What the hell, she told herself. Did anything really matter? They had eaten well, were getting nicely drunk and having fun. The panic from waking and seeing what for a moment she had thought was a stranger standing over her was gone. She would sleep well and write again in the morning. There was peace on earth and happiness to all men. What else could she want, she tried to tell herself for the umpteenth time. The secret in life was telling each other what they wanted to hear. Boosting each other's egos. Making each other feel better, the whisky only part of the trivia. Life to Jane, as the whisky took control, was one long load of bullshit as they strove to get what they wanted, and alcohol was the false friend that made life seem worth the living. With Randall prattling on, her fear of being alone, the fear she had had so desperately before she fell pregnant, had gone for the moment, washed clean by the whisky and Randall's charm.

Jane smiled as she listened to the itinerant storyteller. He was never boring, her luck at having a man who knew how to tell a tale. In the past, after that terrible morning with her mother having convulsions on the kitchen floor when the laughter had stopped, she had taken to reading books to escape from reality. Books became her only comfort as she watched her mother get worse and worse. Her poor father. Looking back, she could see he had known right at the start of her mother's illness that it was only a matter of time before she would die. And then it came to Jane: at least something had come out of their misery. In her hours of escape, she had fallen in love with literature, making her study for her degree in English. And now through the sheer luck of life, her father had found his Sophie, the first, tentative love in her father's life, making him happy and bringing back the laughter that had once been so much part of her family life. Interrupting her thoughts to laugh at the end of Randall's story about his brother Phillip, she put out her glass for a refill.

"I'm going to write tomorrow, so this is my last one."

"You enjoyed my story?"

"I always enjoy your stories, my love."

"Then one for the road. Tomorrow, when we've finished writing, we'll carry on with our journey. We're going north. To the Skeleton Coast. From the forest to the sea... Are you happy, Janey?"

"I think so. I hope so. I'm sure so... Give me a kiss."

"First your last whisky of a beautiful evening... How's that for a kiss?"

"Perfect... It's all so quiet."

"Then we'll soon to bed and make love. You want to make love, Janey?"

"I always want to make love."

Not sure if she was lying, Jane drank her whisky as slowly as possible, both of them quiet as they watched the flames from the fire die down. The bed was made up, everything ready, the night owls calling deep in the forest, the sound of crickets and croaking frogs playing nature's symphony, a sound as beautiful as any music.

"Let's go, my love."

"I'm coming."

"I hope so... Do you ever fake an orgasm, Jane?"

"Why would I ever want to fake an orgasm? We're going to need each other and that duvet tonight. It's cold. Thanks to our writing we've controlled our drinking. Clean heads tomorrow. Up nice and early. A good write and off up the road."

"Did you climax nicely, Jane?"

"Twice."

"That's my girl. Sleep tight. Don't let the bedbugs bite."

"Do we have bedbugs?"

"Of course not."

Smiling with Randall's arms around her, Jane waited to slip into her sleep. And she hadn't been lying to Randall. Not only did he know how to tell a good story, he knew how to bring a girl to her climax, an unselfish lover, unusual in Jane's experience. Together, in harmony, Jane drifted into sleep, into a dream inside a dream. Twice Jane woke in the dark of the night, her thoughts and dreams all mingling into one. As her conscious mind took control, Jane wondered what she was doing in the middle of some African forest far from her roots with a man who wasn't even an American. Feeling her stomach with both hands while lying on her back made her understand the reason.

2

*J*ane's journey went on and on, the days of writing, driving, looking at the scenery all blending into one. The days became weeks, time for both of them of no importance. By the time they drove off the main road and reached the Skeleton Coast, they had both written three chapters of their books. Parked on the edge of the beach they were alone, far from people, sleeping in the camper, writing opposite each other at the table in the camper, running across the sand and bathing in the sea, both of them naked as the waves rolled into the shore, seagulls calling, the birdsong mingling with their laughter. Randall had bought his fishing rod on the way up the long road, casting his line over the breaking waves into the deep of the ocean, catching their supper, the fish grilled on the fire he made next to the Dormobile. By the end of June her stomach had grown into a mound she held with both hands. Time was running out. America called as the launch of her book drew closer. When Randall turned the camper around and headed south back to Cape Town, it was the middle of July. The journey home had begun.

AT THE END of the month when they returned the camper and took a taxi to Cape Town airport, Jane's mind was out of the story of Margaret Neville as the fear of the launch not being successful took control.

"You know what, Randall? I've got a funny feeling there's two of them. Two babies, not one. I'm going to have a check-up when we get back to New York. How about twins? That'll be something. It's been a perfect journey and our writing kept control of our drinking. We're about to go back into the world, my love. All that noise and people. Everyone after something. The thought of facing the media when my book's launched makes me sick to the stomach."

"Do you want to go back?"

"Some of me. Part of me. I'm frightened out of my wits that the launch is going to be a failure. That my book won't sell. That the critics will rip it apart."

"Your film script for *Lust* was a howling success. By now the publishers will have sent copies to all the newspapers across America."

"That's what frightens me. Are the reviews going to be good? Is my book really any good, Randall?"

"I've read it twice. So has Manfred. The publishers had many readers before they accepted. And they know how to build up the hype. You gave them a good book. Now it's up to the marketing. They'll have copies stacked up in the windows of thousands of bookshops across the country. *Love in the Spring of Life*. The title alone will grab the public's attention. Stop worrying."

"Is Tracey really picking us up at the airport?"

"With Phillip and Martha. So they say. Of course they will. It's journey's end. We're going home. And when your book has joined the list of bestsellers, you're going to have our baby. Why do you think there might be two?"

"When I feel the movement in my belly, it comes from two directions."

"First stop Johannesburg to change aeroplanes and then it's good old New York City."

"It's been a wonderful trip. Utter peace."

"Now it's back to the crowd, Janey."

"Are we really going to live in England?"

"Let's see. One step at a time. First your book. Then our baby."

"Do you think we'll ever get married?"

"Do you want to be married?"

"All girls want to be married. Third time lucky, Randall. There it goes again. It's like one side moving against the other."

"They've started fighting with each other already. Little buggers. The doctor will know what's going on with all those scans... And that was my beautiful Africa. Gone with the wind."

"We'll always have the memories. Would you have liked to have written *Gone with the Wind*?"

"You bet I would."

"So would I. One of the greats. Are you going to give *Shakespeare's Ghost* to Manfred to publish?"

"Maybe. It's still not finished. Thank you, driver. Keep the change. Let's get a trolley to put the luggage on. We can book it through to New York. All we'll have to do is change planes at Johannesburg. One journey ends and another begins. And the world goes on despite us. How it is, Janey. Come on. Give me your hand. You know what? I'm quite excited. My lover is going to publish her first novel and give pleasure to millions of people. That's what it's about, Jane. Not the money. There is nothing more satisfying in life than giving other people enjoyment. Makes the whole rat race of life seem worthwhile. And the story of a good book never ends. Your characters will live on and on. All they will know is your name as the author of the book. They'll be reading it long after we are dead. But the characters will stay alive forever. Think of Shakespeare's plays four hundred years on. Every educated child in the world knows *Hamlet* and all the other characters in Shakespeare's plays. If the world lasts another thousand years, they'll still be performing his plays. There's nothing more anyone could have done with a life."

"I'm not Shakespeare. Don't be ridiculous."

"But you've written a good story."

"It may make people feel better with their lives as they hope their own love will last. But it never does. You know that better than anyone. Can I have a seat near the window? I want to look down for what may be the last time at your beautiful Africa. What a journey. Crossing the ocean on a yacht. All those campsites in the plains and the forests. Warm sun as we drove further north to those glorious beaches we had all to ourselves. A world apart. No wonder you always hanker for those years of your childhood on World's View. You were so lucky to have had such an upbringing on an African farm."

"But it didn't last."

"Nothing lasts."

"There we go. Luggage on the conveyor belt. Just hope we find our suitcases in New York."

"Why did you give the camper owner your fishing rod?"

"Can't fish in New York. I told him to lend it to his campers."

"He'll charge them."

"You're probably right. Money. Why does it always come down to money?"

"Money is the breath of life."

"Is it?"

"You'd soon find out if you ran out of it. No money, no home, no food, no nothing. Why this lovely world revolves around money."

"You're thinking of all those millions of sales. You'll have to give a speech at the launch."

"Never spoken in public in my life before."

"There's always a first time. There you are, Janey. A seat by the window. Now what I want is a nice cup of tea."

"I'm going to wear a big, flowing dress to hide my growing belly. I'll be real pretty."

"You're sure there are two of them?"

"One of each. A boy and a girl."

"Now you are talking nonsense."

"One of each, my love. Come to think of it, there are twins in my family. My mother's sister had them... Let's sit in silence and thank our lucky stars for such a wonderful journey. Peace. Utter peace in your African paradise, a place I will remember for all the years of the rest of my life. Thank you, Randall. It's the first time I've been truly at peace with myself since they diagnosed my mother with brain cancer."

JANE'S PEACE was destroyed the moment they stepped through with their luggage at John F. Kennedy Airport, both of them tired from the endless journey, changing planes three times on the way. Tracey had an amused smile on her face. Next to Tracey stood Phillip and Martha, both looking bewildered. As Randall pushed their luggage trolley towards his brother, Manfred Leon, their literary agent, moved forward surrounded by what Jane feared was the media.

"Was it based on a true story? Who's the real man in your book? What was his name? Are you pregnant? Is Randall Holiday the father? Are you married?"

Jane looked from Tracey to Manfred, not sure what to say. Manfred took her hand and led her out of the airport to a limousine.

"Smile at them. The interviews are going to be at the launch. How are you, Randall? Quite a party... Okay, chaps. Jane Slater will give each of you interviews at Friday's launch. Don't take their photographs. They both look exhausted after their long journey. We've already printed two hundred thousand copies. The book is flying off the shelves all through America. We have four studios bidding for the film rights to *Love in the Spring of Life*. Jane herself will be writing the film script after her success in writing Tracey's script for *Lust*. Thanks for coming. All we told you was the time of Miss Slater's arrival. Wonderful to see you all... Get in, Jane. All of you. Organised a limo for your homecoming. There's plenty of room for us all and for the luggage. Let's get out of here, driver. Thanks for waiting... Are you really pregnant, Jane? My word. What a world. Two of my best authors having children. Or is it three of you? Are you the father, Randall? None of my business. Where do you want to go?"

"Right back where we came from."

"Seriously, Randall."

"Home. If we can call it home. How's the Big Apple, brother? Thanks for meeting us. That was quite a reception. Now you know what it feels like, Jane. Fame. You're famous, Janey. Two hundred thousand at the first print! Tracey, where's your baby? How is she?"

"With the nanny. She's fine. So, here we are again. The three musketeers. We had your apartment dusted and cleaned. So, tell us about your journey?"

"How was Africa, Randall? Am I interrupting you, Tracey? Did you get up to Zimbabwe? Dad's curious. You must give him a ring the moment you get back to your apartment. I don't know how you three do it. All that media attention would drive me nuts. Tomorrow's headline: 'Famous author pregnant'. Two of the newspapers have worked out that your male character is based on your affair with Harvey. Both of them have interviewed him. He loved the attention. Your book has made your old lover famous. What's the matter, Jane?"

"I feel sick."

"Do you need a doctor?"

"I need more than a doctor. Never mind. Lovely you were all there to welcome us home. What's on the agenda, Manfred?"

"A little dinner with Phillip and Martha. It's the best launch of my career as a literary agent. And it's only just started. They love your book, Jane. The whole world is going to love your book. Everyone is excited. Your publisher. Your publicist. Not to say me. There's nothing better in life than winning. Congratulations, Jane. You made it. Now all three of you have made it."

Not sure if she was deliriously happy or frightened out of her wits, Jane sat quietly in the corner of the limousine listening to everyone's chatter as she looked through the window at all the bustle of passing cars and people. Was it all going to be worth it? Jane wasn't sure. Was the turmoil going to be good for her baby any more than all the whisky she had drunk on her journey, a journey to get away from all the noise and people now screaming back in her life? With Martha talking about her Carmen and Tracey talking about her Allegra, Jane drifted into her dreams, the dreams where life was simple and no one wanted anything. A place in the forests and plains of Africa, where crickets sang and frogs croaked surrounded by peace and tranquillity, where the air was clean and the sky blue.

BACK ON THE thirty-first floor in Randall's Manhattan apartment, Jane walked across the lounge, up the three steps and past the dining room table to look out of the big plate-glass window, not sure what had happened to her life. Staring through the window and seeing nothing, she slowly shook her head.

"They all want a piece of you, Jane. You'll just have to get used to it. Stories about celebrities, however banal, sell newspapers. And in the end, if it suits them they'll rip you apart. Success is not all plain sailing. Good for Tracey. The place is nice and clean. Do you want to go to Phillip's dinner party? We've half an hour. I can phone and say you must rest for the sake of our baby. So many of us crave attention, most of us fools. When the baby is born at the end of September, I'll put this place on the market and we'll make another run for it. Staying here they'll chew us up piece by piece."

"We'd better go to Phillip and Martha. All that way to the airport to meet us. I don't want to be selfish. The babies feel fine again. I am still sure there's two of them. Look how huge I am! But we won't stay long. For the next five days until the launch, I'm going to rest. Not go out. Just stay here... Just look at it all. Why do people want to live on top of each other? High-rise after high-rise. Bricks and mortar. Concrete. Building after building with people crammed into them like rats... So Harvey likes to be famous, poor sod. He'll probably write his memoirs. Or get someone to write them for him. What's it all about, Randall?"

"You tell me."

"Are you sure we can't go back and live our lives in peace in Africa? What am I really going to do with all the money?"

"Not Africa, Jane. It's far too volatile. I know that now. We'd get nicely settled in and then there would be a revolution. The continent is far too unstable. No, we've made our money. For me, it's the English countryside and back to the home of our ancestors. Back to where both of our families came from. We'll find our peace again. Are you going to have a shower before we go? Even the bed's made up. We'll have a nice dinner and make our excuses... Now you know why the wolves howled in my head. The predators. The news media. We've got to hide, Jane, or they'll destroy the pair of us. Just a little countryside estate with a little house and tell no one who we are. We'll be an ordinary couple with an ordinary life. We'll tell them we are married. You can say you're Mrs Crookshank. Change your name and the name of the baby by deed poll. Of course, we'll write our books. We love writing books. Gives us something to do. We'll send them to Manfred without telling him where we live. All they'll get from us are the books. No more book launches. No more book fairs. No more interviews with the media. It's not worth it. Stop staring out of the window and come and sit down. I'd better phone Dad in England. It'll bring back his memories of Africa. We'll come through, Jane. Just got to be careful. Good, you're smiling. Mind the steps. There we are. Sit, Jane. Sit you down. That's my girl. That really was a circus. Just the launch now. All you have to get through. We owe that much to Manfred."

"Give me a kiss."

"My pleasure."

"Are we going to grow old together, Randall?"

"I hope so. Trouble is in life you never know. No one ever knows what's coming next. Except a nice hot shower. If we're going to be late, I'll phone my brother. They'll have the wine out by now. They won't mind if we are late. And when we've had a nice supper and a couple of glasses of Phillip's wine, we'll come down from the forty-ninth floor and sleep nicely here through the night and most of tomorrow morning. Remember, I soundproofed the bedroom. In bed, we can't hear the noise. You see we're lucky, Jane. We have the money so we can keep away from the whole damn lot of them."

"Did Tracey look happy?"

"Who knows? People only tell you what they want you to hear. She looked good enough. Talked a lot about Allegra. And she doesn't have to put up with me or any other man."

"I don't mind putting up with you, Randall."

"How sweet of you, Janey. Now off you go for that shower."

Instead of getting up, Jane sat worrying while she listened to Randall's phone call to his father in London, the long story over the line making her sad to be back. And now Harvey was back in her life, dragged out of the past by hungry newspaper reporters looking for stories, the happy ending of her book clashing with Harvey's rendering of their nasty breakup that turned her into a philandering drunk.

"When do you want to go and see the doctor? Dad and Bergit are fine. Send you their love. The weather in England in July is perfect. So nice for them to have the Thames so close. I always love rivers. Especially the Zambezi. They say if you drink the water of the Zambezi, you will always go back to Africa."

"Did you drink the river water? I'm going to forget seeing a doctor. Let it all be a surprise. Let nature tell us what is coming into our lives... What's a deed poll?"

"A document like a marriage or birth certificate. The new-fangled mobile phones make life so much easier. So quick to get through to Dad."

"What am I going to say to the press when they ask me why I made up the happy ending to my book?"

"Avoid the question. Tell them all about those happy times before he went off and married a girl from a rich family. Take their minds in a different direction. With luck, they'll forget what they asked you. People lose track when you interrupt their train of thought."

"And if they persist?"

"How long are you going to be in the shower?"

"Do you think drinking can hurt my babies?"

"You really are sure you're going to have twins... There are so many stories of what's good or bad. I don't think our ancestors worried. Certainly not my mother. Why, do you want a drink?"

"I was just worrying."

"Stop worrying. There is nothing worse than worrying."

"I'm not looking forward to the launch."

"Neither am I. Too many newspaper reporters. Good old Manfred. He sure knows how to hype a book."

"He'll want to know where we live."

"And who, may I ask, told the press about Harvey? It was either Manfred or your publicist. Did you tell Manfred about Harvey?"

"I might have done."

"There you go. We'll give him a postal address."

"Who?"

"Manfred."

"What about a phone number?"

"We'll tell him we don't have a phone."

"He'll know it's a lie."

"We all tell little lies when it suits us. Ask him if he told them about Harvey? You'll see. Better still, we'll tell him we need complete seclusion to write our books and that we'll come out of hiding when we've finished writing."

"But we don't want to come out of hiding."

"Then we won't send him the new books. They'll stay in the drawer in manuscript form for our children to make money from when we are dead. It'll be part of their inheritance... Are you in the shower yet?"

"My belly is so big. All I want to do is have my shower and climb into bed."

"We won't stay long."

"And when we've had a couple of drinks?"

"Life's all about waiting to see. To see how it goes. The food will be good. They both do the cooking. Bergit taught both of us how to cook a really good meal. Good food is good for the baby."

"Babies."

"We'll see."

"I wonder what Harvey's wife will think of the book."

"They both got what they wanted. She got Harvey. He got a directorship in his father-in-law's company."

"And what will the father think?"

"Who cares? Harvey's given him grandchildren. Don't tell me the father-in-law didn't have an affair or two before he got married. No one is different to anyone else... I'm going to pour us a whisky."

"Come and join me in the shower."

"Now you're talking."

"Do you really love me, Randall?"

"What's love? We're lovers. We're happy. That's what counts. No one in my experience has the slightest idea of the meaning of love. It's just a word to make someone feel comfortable. Usually, when we want something."

"I don't want anything."

"You want a drink. And a baby. And peace and quiet in a nice little place in the English countryside."

"And you, my love. A whisky after?"

"Yes, afterwards."

"You'd better phone Phillip. We're going to be late. How did your brother meet Martha?"

"On a holiday to Zimbabwe. Phillip ran a safari camp in the Zambezi valley, you remember. It's amazing how meeting another person changes a life so drastically. Phillip still hankers for the bush. So does Dad. He went quiet on the phone when I talked about Africa. I could almost hear his mind drifting back into his past. There we are. Our whisky waiting with lots of ice. Just how we like our whisky. Cheers. To happy days."

"Take your pants off and step in."

"We need a bigger shower. My word, that belly of yours is real big... Why do they say 'real big' in America? It's 'really big'."

"You haven't phoned Phillip."

"It doesn't matter. I left the phone in the lounge. Amazing to think that in eight weeks' time he'll pop his head out."

"Stop trying to look at my fanny."

"You learned that word from me. We all pop out of the womb. How life begins."

"Does Phillip like living the life of an investor in information technology in America?"

"Hopefully. It's the game of life. You grow up on a tobacco farm in a place called Rhodesia. Run a safari business in a place called Chewore, literally in the middle of nowhere. Meet a girl by chance and end up on the forty-ninth floor of a New York skyscraper with a nice little daughter called Carmen, named after our mother. His whole world changed when he heard her say 'Hello, my name's Martha.' This shower is so nice."

"It is."

"We'll have big log fires in England in winter. Fires in every room. A nice cosy writing room with a fireplace. We'll be as happy as pigs in shit."

"Are we going to write together? I loved it in the Dormobile."

"Dogs. We'll have lots of dogs. And cats. One big writing table with room for both of us to sit on either side."

"We'll have to work out what to do with the kids when we're writing. How many acres are we going to have?"

"We'll have to see. Pass me the soap. getmethatbook.com is going to make Phillip a fortune. Can't have it both ways if you want financial security. Ask any wife. He's locked himself in. You know, he once tried to write his memoirs of his days in Chewore. Said he couldn't write. We're lucky, Jane. Our stories run. Tracey is lucky. We three can live in our books and escape the turmoil of life. I suppose we'd better get out. Duty calls. Eight more weeks and we'll have a family. And the world goes round."

"Life goes on, my love."

"How it works. It's all so simple. The game of life."

"Do you like the game of life, Randall?"

"I do at the moment. Could it really be twins?"

"We'll just have to see."

"You're pinching my words."

"Everyone pinches something when they get the opportunity."

"I'm going to pinch your bum."

"You wouldn't dare. Come on. Let's get dried. They'll be waiting for us. Why didn't you put on the music?"

"I forgot. I was too busy talking to Dad. We'll ask Phillip to play Mozart. Or Mahler. We both love Mahler's Second Symphony. All that lovely choral singing of girls' voices. Come on, Jane. It's time to go to a party."

UPSTAIRS, when Jane walked into Phillip and Martha's apartment, the whisky after the shower had done its trick. Even the exchange of looks between old lovers didn't make her jealous: if Allegra was Randall's daughter it was none of her business, something from their past. At least she was certain of the father of her own child which was more than could be said for Tracey. Walking up the same three steps to the dining room table, Jane sat herself down between Manfred and Martha as Phillip put plates of food in front of the guests.

"You must be exhausted after your long journey, Jane. In the last months of my pregnancy with little Carmen, all I wanted to do was sleep. Just eat your supper and don't think you are being rude if you want to go straight down to bed. A good meal and a good, long sleep is what you need. Are you excited about the baby?"

"Never more excited in my life, Martha... What is it?"

"Risotto. Phillip did the cooking, didn't you, darling? Welcome home, Randall and Jane. Everyone lift their glasses. Jane's not staying long, so eat up and enjoy yourselves before the star of the evening leaves us. To Jane Slater and *Love in the Spring of Life*. Phillip's getmethatbook.com has been working on your book for the last ten days according to Perry Mance, the CEO of the company. We're all so excited for you. Can you imagine, if Phillip hadn't met Perry in Harry B's, getmethatbook.com would never have started. Even the best ideas don't work without venture capital. The luck of life, Jane. And what would you three authors have done without Manfred? Cheers, Manfred. To all your hard work... How's the food, Jane?"

"It's lovely. You were all so kind to meet us at the airport. What would we do without friends? The wine is lovely. So is that classical music."

"You must be so glad to be home. Home, sweet home. So tell us, Randall, all about your trip. Phillip can't wait to hear about his Africa. And if I hadn't gone on that trip to Zimbabwe we wouldn't be here with all of you. To a million sales of your book, Jane. Phillip and I are so envious. But as hard as we've tried, neither of us can write a story. I just don't know how you do it. You have no idea how lucky you are. And I'm not just talking about money. Writing a good book must be so satisfying. Lucky you, Jane. To success and happiness, everyone. It makes the world go around... Phillip, your risotto is delicious. A husband that can cook. Now that's real luck. Home-cooked food. Nothing better. What a lovely evening we're all having. Friends and family. And good luck with your baby, Jane and Randall... Now, look at this. Here comes Ivy and my little Carmen. Ivy, as you know, is studying for her degree in ecology. Works perfectly, doesn't it, Ivy? Carmen sleeps in Ivy's room where Ivy has her desk. Looking after a child gives a carer lots of free time to work at her books."

"Say goodnight to Mommy and Daddy, Carmen."

"Goodnight, Mommy. Goodnight, Daddy."

"Off you go, my lovely little girl. She's so cute. And inquisitive. She's always asking questions. You're welcome to join us, Ivy."

"My best time to study is after I put Carmen down to sleep. No interruptions."

"Suit yourself. A glass of wine, maybe?"

"Can't think and drink, Martha. Goodnight, everyone. Enjoy your party. Come along, Carmen. It's time for your bed."

"Sweet dreams, Carmen. Off you go with Ivy."

"I love Ivy."

"Of course you do. Now kiss Daddy goodnight... Are you going to employ a nanny, Jane?"

"We're going to live alone in the English countryside away from all the noise."

"Are you now, Jane? Lucky you. Phillip, pass me the wine... There you go, Manfred. A nice full glass of the best French red wine. All that lovely money, Phillip. What would we all do without lots and lots of lovely lolly? There are thousands upon thousands of books listed on the getmethatbook.com website. Including yours, Jane. Every time a book is ordered, Perry and Phillip make money. And when they buy your book, Jane, as they will, so will you. Everybody wins. The reader finds what they want to read in this ever-growing online library, and everyone is happy. It's like the old days when the librarian told you what to read. Librarians dedicated to literature."

"Out of so many books, how will they search for my book?"

"There's what is called a search engine where the reader types in what they're looking for. When the book they are looking for is listed on the screen, the book can be ordered, and it is then shipped to the reader. Modern technology is mind-boggling... How's the food, everyone?"

"Just perfect."

"Now that's what I call a chorus... Wasn't it lucky for Phillip and Randall having a rich grandfather leaving them all his money? We all need startup money. Nothing better than a famous Hollywood actor for a grandfather. To Ben Crossley. May his soul rest in peace."

"How old is Carmen, Martha?"

"Two and a half, three in January... You did know that Ivy is from South Africa?"

When Jane finished the risotto and a bowl of fruit, even the wine could not keep her at the dinner party. With Randall happy to follow, they went down in the lift to the thirty-first floor. Without a word, they climbed into their double bed, not a sound penetrating the soundproofing. Randall leaned up and slightly kissed her mouth as the day and her dreams mingled into sleep: the sun was shining on Ivy as she ran down to the beach, a warm African sun that made them all smile. Carmen was laughing as Phillip ran with his daughter into the warm blue sea.

3

*W*hen Jane woke in the morning, she thought she was in the Dormobile parked under the trees. It took her a while before she came fully awake to the reality of being in America.

"Oh, shit."

"What's the matter, Jane?"

"We're home."

"Go back to sleep."

"Give me a cuddle. I had a dream about Ivy and Carmen. We were all on the beach in Namibia. At least we can't hear all the noise. A real, quiet room in the middle of New York. Please hug me. We have the whole day to ourselves. We don't have to put up with other people... Did you see Tracey was flirting with Manfred?"

"They too were lovers, Jane. How Tracey found herself an agent. How she got *Lust* published. I think she seduced him on purpose."

"Girls and boys go out to play... Did you sleep well? There's nothing better in life than a good night's sleep... Are women that obvious?"

"Some of them. Depends how naïve you are not to see what's going on."

"Do you think I intentionally got myself pregnant?"

"You weren't on the pill. Or you forgot to take it. It doesn't matter, Jane. We both want the baby and here we are. Others have them adopted or aborted. Most men run away when they find they've made a girl pregnant: they don't want the financial responsibility."

"So Tracey screwed Manfred to get him to read her book."

"More likely to promote it to a publisher. Rumour has it, she then slept with the publisher. The one thing a pretty girl has to sell is her body. All she has to sell sometimes. It's her way of getting what she wants. 'If you want to have sex again, darling, you'll have to marry me.' Happens when we are young. Now, we're two old codgers trying to find a purpose in life. You've told me more than once the baby is more important to you than a marriage."

"I'd still love to be married to you, Randall."

"But what comes first? What's the motivating force? We're getting close to the middle age when it isn't just looks that draw people. In our case, neither is trying to force the other to do anything. We'll stay with each other because we want to be with each other, not because of some valueless marriage certificate. Our child will bind us. We will be the child's parents. Amanda and Meredith were after my money. Anyway, don't let's go down that path again. Life is a lot simpler than people make it out to be. We use what we have to serve our ends. To get what we want from life. Mostly it's about getting money. From Manfred, the agent, to Godfrey Merchant, the publisher for Tracey. And now she has enough money to have her baby without having to put up with a husband. Good for Tracey. Why her books read so well. She knows what she's talking about. Knows what people really want under all that self-righteousness of trying to convince ourselves we're not all a selfish bunch of bastards. We all like to fool ourselves and other people. They love your book because the story ends the way we want our own lives to end. In peace and joy with the love of our life. And then steps in Harvey from the past. Makes you want to laugh if it wasn't so sad. He talked to the press because he wanted something. He wanted attention. We all want attention, Jane. From the very beginning. Little Carmen wanted attention as does every child on the planet."

"Will Harvey hurt the sales of my book?"

"Possibly. Could work both ways. There's nothing better than publicity. Manfred knows what he's doing. All publicity is good publicity for a book. People will get curious and want to read about it. It's all about getting attention. Vincent van Gogh cut off his ear to get attention just before he sold one of his paintings right at the end of his troubled life. Now his paintings cost millions if you can find one for sale. No, Harvey's part of the hype. Leave it all to your publisher, your agent and your publicist. I'm sure they know what they are doing. They're in business to make money. You want some tea? I'm hungry. I'm going to make us some toast. We're going to be all right, Jane. You and me. We both have been through the mill and understand life. Do you want some marmalade on your toast?"

"You think they'll invite Harvey to the launch?"

"Who knows? Probably. Why not? And when you see what he turned out to be, you'll thank your lucky stars."

"But he might still be gorgeous."

"Hope springs eternal. I love your naughty smile. What does his wife think about him now he's shouted his mouth off?"

"Do you think my publishers paid him?"

"That, Jane, even for me would be taking it too far. But what goes on behind our backs is another world."

"What are you going to do today?"

"We're going to spend the day in bed."

"And tomorrow?"

"The same. Right up until the time we have to come out of this little foxhole and join the world of a famous writer."

"I'm not famous."

"But you will be when you've sold a few million copies and they've made a movie of your lovely book."

"You don't like being famous?"

"I hate it. It's not worth it. All that fame can kill a person. Drive them mad. Too many famous people have killed themselves to get away from it all."

"Please don't kill yourself, Randall."

"I'll try not to. In our nice little estate in England, the wolves won't howl in my head. We'll be able to live in peace and do what we like best."

"You mean drinking?"

"I mean writing our books. Our one true satisfaction in life where we can analyse the depths and truths of life and come up with some of the answers to allow ourselves, and hopefully our readers, to live in peace in this godforsaken world, where war, thuggery and downright meanness are as common as dirt."

"Make the toast, Randall. You worry me."

"I worry myself. Why the wolves screamed at me night and day."

"It was probably too much alcohol. Anyway, that's all in the past tense."

"We always blame the booze. Tea and toast coming up."

"You're not looking forward to the launch."

"There's a price to pay for everything. The success of the launch is for you, not for me. One night for the trumpets to play. It will put you on a high. The great feeling of floating halfway up to heaven. Far better than drink or drugs, so they say. Acclaim, Jane. That pounding feeling that comes from a room full of people telling us we are wonderful: the shouts and screams they throw at celebrities. The high of highs, my Janey. You'll be so excited your heart will want to burst. You see, now you're smiling. How's our baby this morning?"

"Our babies are fine... Do you like dreaming at night?"

"The only place to go. That place of our dreams where the world is not real. The other world. And when we wake, the dreams are gone and we're back in the shit. What you meant just now when you exclaimed 'Oh shit.' Let the day begin. Africa is lost in our dreams."

Alone, lying on her back, the door closed, everything silent, Jane thought back to her days working in the laundry, washing other people's dirty linen, not sure if she was any better off now than she was then. Were the two of them just living a story? Jane wasn't sure. Did Randall always mean what he said? Jane wasn't sure. And even if there were two of them in her womb, would they give her that feeling of permanence, of belonging, of having a real life of substance, not the day-to-day drudgery of daily living? Looking back on her life, Jane tried to remember those moments of bliss when all around her was happiness. There were brief moments that flashed into her mind but none of it had ever lasted: moments with Conny in their shared bedroom when they were children; playing sport in a team at school and winning a match; that first sublime moment with Harvey when she thought she had fallen in love forever.

When Randall opened the bedroom door and came in with the tray, her only solace was having the babies she would love for the rest of her life. The panic at the thought of the launch had temporarily gone.

"Now what's the matter?"

"Life, Randall. What was it all about? The toast tastes good. I was trying to make myself happy by thinking of those lovely sunny days walking up that lovely empty beach collecting shells. There were no skeletons on the Skeleton Coast. Just the sea and the sand and the sound of the waves coming into the shore. The Dormobile in the distance within the scrub. You and me."

"Why weren't you smiling?"

"Those thoughts had drowned in other thoughts I'd rather not talk about. Feel my babies. They're kicking. Did you feel that?"

"I did. Oh, my goodness."

"It's so strange to be so quiet in this room surrounded by walls, knowing all around us are people. People below us. People above us. Your brother and Tracey in the same building. Everyone thinking their thoughts as they struggle through their daily routine. Anyway. Enough of that. It's tea and toast. Get back into bed, my love. Are you happy, Randall?"

"I try to be. I want to write but my writing mind has gone blank."

"Let's both of us try and be happy. The tea's hot!"

"We can read our books. That's what we'll do. We'll escape into that other writer's world and get away from ourselves and our negative thoughts. Or we can go into the living room and listen to music. In New York, you can't even go for a walk. Not a real walk. Down there, you have to fight your way past people and avoid bumping into them on the street... It's all so far away."

"What is?"

"Africa, Janey. There we are. And now both of us are tucked up in bed. What on earth are we doing here?"

"A book launch. My book launch. And having my babies."

"Then we'll make another run for it."

"That's my boy. I love running away with you, Randall. Why do we always want to run away? Sad, isn't it?"

"Life's sad, my Jane. As much as we try and tell ourselves everything is wine and roses."

"Please don't mention alcohol."

"Better not."

"Everyone, listen up. The moment has come. The moment you have all been waiting for. Give a big hand of applause for the author of *Love in the Spring of Life,* the book of the month. Jane Slater, everyone. Congratulations, Jane."

"Thank you, Godfrey. Thank you, everyone. In particular, I want to thank my publisher Godfrey Merchant standing here next to me for publishing my book or none of this would have happened. Thanks to Tracey Chapelle who helped me out of a quagmire into your wonderful world. Tracey, thank you so much for asking me to write the film script for your *Lust* that motivated me to write my book. To all the members of the press gathered here tonight in the Warwick Hotel for giving my book such wonderful write-ups. I'll be available to you all evening. Enjoy the drinks. Enjoy the food. Enjoy yourselves. My heart and thanks go out to all of you. Let the band play. Let the music begin. Let the party swing."

Stepping down from the small, improvised podium, Jane stretched out her hand to the passing drinks tray as the applause continued. Randall was right. She was feeling as high as a kite without the help of alcohol.

"Well done, Jane. That was quite some applause. How does it feel to be famous? You don't recognise me, do you? Why are you looking so shocked? It's Harvey. It's me. They invited me. You used our story to make yourself rich. To get famous. Why shouldn't I get on our bandwagon?"

"Where's your wife?"

"Probably at home. Who cares?"

"Do you still work for her father? You look a wreck. Your clothes are dirty."

"Not at the moment. Been out of a job for six months. When they told me about your book, I hoped it was a chance for me to get some money. I'm stone broke, Jane. Do you have any idea what it's like to be stone broke? Nowhere to stay. Nothing."

"Didn't they pay you for your press interview?"

"I wish. Can you lend me some money?"

"Don't be ridiculous. Go home to your wife."

"She kicked me out when I fell out with her father."

"Why did he fire you? I presume he fired you."

"Caught me with my hand in the till."

"You were stealing!"

"A man has to build his own nest egg. Everything from my salary went to support the family. She still gets money from her father. Why didn't you recognise me? Have I changed that much?"

"You're as fat as a pig. Even your voice has changed. Will you excuse me? That man over there from the *Times* wants to interview me. Make the best of the party."

"Aren't we going to see each other again? I loved your book. You must still love me or you would have ended the book far differently."

"What on earth happened to you, Harvey? I'll ask Godfrey Merchant to give you some money. Find yourself a job."

"I tried. When they check my credentials with my father-in-law, he tells them I'm a thief. What am I going to do?"

"Have another drink. Now excuse me. A book launch is business. I feel sorry for you, Harvey. Never thought I'd ever hear myself say that... And your children?"

"They too want nothing to do with me. They don't want to cross swords with their grandfather."

"Of course. He's rich. And buys them things."

"Please, Jane. You never married. You must still love me. It's all in your book."

"I'm seven months pregnant under this voluminous skirt."

"Do you know who the father is? You're not wearing a wedding ring."

"He's standing right over there smiling at me."

"That's Randall Holiday the famous novelist."

"And the father of my twins."

"Do you live together?"

"Of course. Now, if you don't mind..."

"Will Godfrey Merchant really give me money?"

"I said so, didn't I? When did I ever lie to you, Harvey? You were the one who lied."

"I'm sorry."

"Too late to be sorry."

"But you've made all that money out of me. Out of a story."

"Now wasn't that just lucky."

"I'll write my own story and tell the world the true ending to *Love in the Spring of Life*."

"Be my guest. You were the one who destroyed our love in your pursuit of money... Francis. You wanted to interview me. Fire away."

"Can I tell the public what I just overheard?"

"Go away, Harvey. The truth is the truth. And we think it's twins."

"You're not sure?"

"Randall and I both like surprises. Don't we, Randall? Now, where were we, Francis? You can ask me every question in the book. You'll just have to be quick. There are an army of journalists here tonight who want to talk to me."

"Book of the month, Jane."

"Isn't that wonderful, Francis?... Pick what you want from the lady's tray of drinks. It's all work for you tonight, young lady... Please, Harvey. Push off."

"No one cares about me anymore."

"You've only yourself to blame. Go away. I have work to do."

"You're a bitch."

"Probably... Did you hear that, Francis? Let's you and I go stand in the corner."

Wanting to cry, Jane took the arm of the journalist, gave Randall a look of pain and turned her back on Harvey, the one and only love of her life. Like so many other nights in her life, the night went on from drink to drink. When the interviews were finished, she left with Randall through a side door.

"That was fun, Jane."

"You must be kidding. Anyway, it's over."

"Harvey upset you, didn't he? Write it down in a book. Get it out of your system. How I've got through my life... We drank too much."

"Who cares? Half the room was drunk in the end. My poor babies. Will they be all right? I'm so bad, Randall. I'm a bad, bad person."

"Are we going straight to bed?"

"I couldn't sleep a wink after all that nonsense. It's all churning in my head."

"You want another drink?"

"Of course I want another drink. And that was meant to be the night of my life. What's wrong with me, Randall?"

"Home sweet home."

"There's nothing sweet about it tonight."

"Tracey having fun chatting up the men."

"At least that was something. What a world."

"I'll put on some nice music. A little Mozart. It'll calm your nerves. The music of Mozart always cheers us up. His music sounds so happy. Sit down on the sofa and try and relax. I'm going to look after you, Janey. And no. Please don't cry. It's over. Once the baby is born, we're going to run and get the hell out of the way. Far, far from people."

"All they want is money."

"You can say that again. Money is what life is all about. We couldn't run if we didn't have money."

"Poor Harvey."

"You can say that about half the people on the planet."

"Should I tell Godfrey to give him a slice of my royalty?"

"If it makes you feel better."

"He was such a wonderful person."

"We're all wonderful when we want something."

"Are we that bad?"

"I try to hope not... Mozart and a glass of wine. Relax. Think of your baby. The world will still go round. Been the same since we evolved from the apes. Or wherever we came from."

"When will it end?"

"Who knows. Cheers, my love. A couple more months and your life will change forever for the better. A baby. Cats and dogs. Peace in the countryside. To peace, Jane. Let's drink to peace. To perfect peace. No howling wolves. No one worrying us. Just you and me and our children."

"Are we going to be happy? I just so much want to be happy."

"We're going to make ourselves happy. That's the secret. We're the lucky ones in this crazy, materialistic world. We've made our money. A man like Harvey in his forties isn't going to be lucky trying to start again. Unless he hid the money he stole from his company. Put it in some offshore bank account."

"You think he's putting on a front? Why would he do that?"

"If his father-in-law laid a charge against him with the police, he'd go to jail. Seeing him out in the street begging for his bread might seem punishment enough. Satisfy the old man's hatred. Who knows, Jane? Who cares? It's his problem. That old cliché: 'you make your bed and then you have to lie in it.' There's no real point in feeling sorry for the man. Enjoy your drink. Think of the good parts of tonight. I've never heard a room full of people applaud quite like that before. They must have truly loved your book. And that's what counts. Think of all those millions of readers who are going to love living in your book. Not wanting to put it down. Remembering your story for months afterwards. You loved Harvey and you've written it down for the rest of the world to see. For them to see how beautiful love can be. Let that give you joy, the same joy you are going to give to so many people. That's better. Now you are smiling. Yes, and you have made a piss-pot full of money out of the story of you and Harvey. So give him some from the piss-pot. In two months, we'll have vanished. None of the people tonight will ever know where we have gone. Give him a monthly stipend to get rid of the thought of your Harvey, that early Harvey of your memory, living in poverty. Godfrey can arrange a monthly payment into his bank account if Harvey still has a bank account. There'll be a way. Don't remember him as he was tonight. Think of him as he was when you were both nineteen, when the world was perfect."

"Will you really look after me?"

"Of course I will. As you are going to look after your baby."

"Babies, Randall."

"Of course. There are two of the little buggers. Let me feel them. Not a murmur. Fast asleep, Janey. Are you feeling better?"

"I don't know what I'd do without you."

"I've heard that one before."

"You're laughing, Randall."

"I'm happy for you. We just launched your book. Book of the month. Selling like hot cakes. Everyone clapping. A night to remember. Let's have another glass of wine."

"Poor Harvey."

"Stop thinking about him or you'll drive yourself nuts."

"Are we really going to escape?"

"We write books, Jane. We can always escape... There. How does that look? One nice full glass of wine. Cheers, my love. To happiness. To an older, gentler life without worry. You and I are going to grow old together in peace and harmony, bringing up our babies. Why don't we write children's books? I'll go on being an itinerant storyteller. Talking story to the kids and then writing it down for all those other little brats who don't have itinerant storyteller parents. We can write the kids' books together. Find someone in the English countryside who can draw the pictures. Books for little children all have pictures. We're going to create an artists' colony in the woods. Painters, creative writers, all kinds of music writers. We'll find a new Mozart. A new van Gogh. Only this time our van Gogh will be happy and won't end up with one of his paintings being used in the chicken shed. After he died, they found one of the most valuable paintings in the world being used as a board to keep in the hens at the side of the coop. Can you imagine what an artist felt when they did that with one of his paintings? A nice secluded unknown art colony totally free of celebrity. We'll have music evenings with lots of wine. Private exhibitions of our friends' paintings. Book nights when the writers read their work out loud... How's the wine going down? You want a sandwich? A world, Jane that isn't full of shit."

"What else happens in an art colony?"

"Long walks in the woods. Playing with cats and dogs. Riding horses. Singing in the rain. You always got to sing in the rain in England."

"Have you ever sung in the rain?"

"Not yet. There's always a first time."

"You're crackers, Randall."

"And street parties. Don't forget the street parties in the summer. And the children will all love each other. No fighting. No envy. No bullying. We'll have our own school with very special teachers, all of them artists."

"And what happens when the children grow up?"

"They marry each other and have babies. Themselves become artists. They won't even know the meaning of materialism. Oh, now listen to that. It's Mahler's Second Symphony."

"Won't our colony be invaded by outside people?"

"We'll keep them out by hook or by crook."

"And how do you do that?"

"I have absolutely no idea, Janey."

"I did love the applause."

"Why not?"

"Does that kind of world of yours really exist? Where everyone is nice to each other."

"We'll have to find out. Dream, my Jane. You got to dream the world and its people are not all evil."

"I'll make the sandwich."

"That's my girl. And here comes the choral part of Mahler's symphony. You see, there is real beauty. Just listen to it... You can talk to me from the kitchen."

"Are we really going to write kids' books?"

"No."

Spreading the butter on pieces of sliced bread, Jane fell silent. Everyone talked on about their paradise but none ever found where they wanted to go. So often in relationships, something else came along changing people's direction. Another young woman for Randall. Stealing money for Harvey. Refusing a blood test for Tracey so no one would know the father of her child. A crazy, ongoing world where only fools thought they had found their paradise. Would Africa be like living in a fool's paradise for both of them? Was an apartment in Manhattan any worse or better than a house among the woods in England? In Jane's experience, you solved one problem in life and along came another which you only found out about when it happened. Putting Bovril, slices of cheese and raw onion in between the bread, Jane cut the sandwich into pieces and made another one thinking one each would be enough. From the sitting room, the symphony played on, making Jane's mind wander. At least in her life she had done something of value by writing her book that all those people at the launch said they so loved. Or was the applause for her book created by her publicist with all the hype, people so easily manipulated?

"There's no point in making yourself miserable."

"What did you say? Where's my sandwich?"

And slowly, quietly Jane's great day came to an end.

4

---

*S*ix weeks and three days later, at one of the most expensive clinics in New York City, Jane gave birth to Kimber and Raphael, the excruciating birth-pains finally coming to an end. Her waters had broken seventeen hours earlier on the thirty-first floor, sending both of them into a panic. When both babies were positioned and feeding as she lay on the hospital bed propped up by two big pillows, it was the most exquisite moment of Jane's life. Miraculously, nothing had gone wrong. With the young nurse watching her, feeling tired, relieved and happy, Jane closed her eyes and quietly fell asleep. When she woke from her perfect dreams, the babies had gone, and Randall was smiling down at her.

"You see, having your first babies at the ripe old age of thirty-nine wasn't so bad after all. The doctor says mother and children are in perfect health."

"How long did I sleep? Have you men any idea how painful it is to give birth?"

"You poor darling. An hour or more."

"When can I go home?"

"We will need to check with the doctor, but probably in a couple of days."

"Have you held them?"

"Just one at a time. I was scared of dropping them. And in a few weeks we fly to England. We'll book you into a nice country hotel with our babies while I drive round with the estate agents looking for the perfect spot. When I find a couple I like you'll come and make the final decision. How about something with a thatched roof? Then we'll go looking for two cats, a male and a female. After that we'll find two dogs, a male and a female. Soon we'll have kittens and puppy dogs. Janey, it was so clever of you to give birth to a boy and a girl. It was such a lovely surprise. I wasn't sure until the second one, my new little son, came into his soon-to-be-lovely world. How does it feel to be the mother of twins?"

"And you didn't believe me even though I told you my aunt had twins. Can I have a kiss? Where are they?"

"You remember them being checked over first and then washed? After that, the nurse helped you feed them. It was then that you fell into an exhausted sleep. My poor Janey. The nurse took them to the nursery to be cared for."

"Where is she?"

"Who?"

"The nurse, idiot. Ask her to bring my babies, please."

"I'll be back in a tick. While you were in labour, I had a phone call from Manfred. You've topped the million mark in sales. Now there we are, kind nurse. Two squalling babies. Welcome to motherhood, Jane."

"Please, can I hold them? Don't cry, my little ones. It's your mommy. That's better now they're suckling again, even though it does hurt a bit. They've got such big eyes... What are you doing, Randall?"

"Popping the cork out of the champagne bottle. The doctor is coming just now to join us."

"Is that usual? I mean, having a party in a hospital?"

"It's the best French bubbly. Heidsieck Dry Monopole. There she goes. Thank you, nurse, for holding the tray. Four glasses of champagne. You're just in time, doctor. And thank you both from myself and Jane for making everything go without a problem. To Kimber and Raphael, everyone."

"To Kimber and Raphael! Welcome to the world!"

"And we're off to see the wizard, the wonderful wizard of oz."

"What are you doing, Randall?"

"Dancing."

"He's completely crackers. Come and give us all a kiss."

"Including the nurse!"

"Bonkers. What are we going to do with your father, my babies? Can we go home after the champagne, doctor?"

"In a few days. We need to make sure that you can manage with the feeding. You will need some help. Then we'll see about you going home. First time I've drunk French champagne in a hospital."

"There's always a first time."

"Celebrities live so differently to the rest of us. I enjoyed reading your books, Randall. Now my wife is reading Jane's. Must be a glorious life, being a writer. I envy both of you. Fame and fortune. What else can a person achieve in his life? Have I said something? Why are you looking at each other like that? Two healthy babies. Twins. A boy and a girl. Haven't had that for a while... Thank you for the glass of celebratory champagne, Mr Holiday, even though it was only a sip... Duty calls. Come along, Jessica. We have other patients to attend to."

"Can't I go home now? I feel just fine after my little sleep. A little sore maybe."

"I know you're eager to be off home, but you really need to stay with us for a few days more. When all three of you are discharged, Jessica or one of the other nurses will complete all the paperwork. You can pay the bill then, Randall. And I will keep checking on you, Miss Slater, as well as monitoring the babies."

"Is there something you're not telling us, doctor? Is there something wrong with the babies?"

"No, there's nothing wrong at all. You've just given birth to twins, and I can assure you, you will be grateful to have a few more days with us, getting all the help you will need from the nursing staff."

"Well, if you're sure, then. Randall, you will visit us, won't you?"

"I think we must listen to the good doctor here, and Janey, nothing will stop me coming in to see you and the children."

"I love working in a maternity hospital. Mostly the endings are happy. Like today. Cheers, everybody. Shame I'm not off duty as I would help you drink that bottle. And thank you, Randall. When's your next book due out?"

"We'll have to see when that will be."

"Must be fun having two surnames: Randall Holiday and Randall Crookshank. It must be a joy to write books. I love my work, but a doctor's day never ends. Jane's surname, Slater, will be on the birth certificates, not Crookshank. You are both aware of that? Anyway, it's none of my business."

Perfectly content for the first time in her life, with her babies back in the crib, Jane smiled at her new beginning. Like Tracey, having her own surname on the birth certificates would give her sole control of her babies. And a million copies! How quickly life changed. Would they really want to bury themselves in the English countryside? Only time and life itself would tell. Smiling at Randall, she wondered what Harvey was doing with her money. Not that it mattered. A million copies! She could afford it. Good luck to him. In the end, she had got what she wanted. Life, despite Randall's denial, was all about money. Money and procreation. All the sweet smiles and chatter were mostly a lot of selfish nonsense, people looking to get what they wanted from life.

FIVE DAYS LATER, Jane was ready to go home with her babies. The doctor was right, she had needed those days with the help of the nurses. Now she felt prepared with a bit of knowledge. Getting dressed, she waited for Randall, watching the babies in the cribs next to her, whilst he completed all the formalities of her discharge. A short while later, he came back into the room.

"Now there are four of us, Randall. Once it was just the three musketeers. Just take me home and put me to bed next to my little ones. I can't believe it's all over."

"They're fast asleep. It's a shame we will have to disturb them to get them in their car chairs. Whilst you've been here for the last couple of days, I've been running around New York, buying more bits and pieces for two babies, not just the one I thought we were having."

"I bet you enjoyed it! Thankfully my body is starting to feel normal. When do we leave for England?"

"In a few weeks' time. We need to get Kimber and Raphael onto your passport. Then we'll fly away, Jane. Leave all the noise behind. All the clamouring newspaper people."

"A million copies!"

"And still selling like hot cakes. People like a good story with a happy ending."

"Are we all fools?"

"I hope not, my Jane, or the world would have come to an end a long, long time ago. Right, let's be on our way... Careful as you get into the taxi. All strapped in. Back to the thirty-first floor. I've written the address down, driver... Just look at them. Eyes closed. Not a sound, and both of them look as if they are smiling in their sleep. They say the secret to having a successful life is to choose one's parents carefully, preferably rich and healthy. No one wants to be born poor. Our babies have chosen us well. Now all we have to do is keep them happy until they are old enough to fend for themselves."

With the babies secured safely next to them, they drove on through the streets of New York City; the streets teeming with people going about their daily business, Jane smiling at them through the side window of the cab. She had her babies; she had her money, and she had her freedom. Maybe life wasn't so bad after all.

PART 3

OCTOBER 1997 – "A JUG OF WINE, A LOAF
OF BREAD – AND THOU"

1

Three weeks later, telling himself he was hopefully never a man to sit around wasting his time, Randall found his perfect spot in the Surrey countryside, three miles from the small village of Cranleigh. The house was old, having been built in the previous century, paint peeling from the outside walls, the tiled roof red and solid, wooden windows rising up three storeys, the front door sheltered by a small entrance open on three sides. He had left Jane in The Running Horses with the babies and gone looking at properties with the local estate agent.

"How many acres, George?"

"Five and a half, Mr Crookshank."

"Please call me Randall. How much do they want for it?"

"Will you require a mortgage? We're so lucky to have such a beautiful day in October."

"I don't think so. First, my lady will have to look at it but this house looks just the ticket. You do take cheques?"

"For the deposit?"

"No, the whole house. I'm a man of the moment, George. No buggering around. I'll tell you what we'll do. You negotiate the best possible cash price with the owner while I look at other agents' houses... Just on the edge of those lovely woods. Very private. You can phone me the final price at The Running Horses."

"Don't you want to look at other properties?"

"Of course. Lead the way... How many bedrooms?"

"Six doubles and a large attic. In the old days, the servants slept in the attic. The house was built in 1839. Needs decorating. I can recommend local builders and house painters. You'll enjoy making it how you like it. The structure is solid. That's what counts. Where do you want to go now?"

"Lead on, Macduff. A nice, quiet place in the country. Do any artists live around here?"

"Not that I know of. They may rent property. Never sold a house to an artist."

"Fruit trees. A tennis court. A greenhouse with a coal-fired small boiler to heat it in the winter. Chicken run. Lots and lots of vegetable gardens. A man could be almost self-sufficient on five and a half acres. Our babies will love growing up in a place like this."

"There's a preparatory and a public school close to the village. I never know whether the school took the name from the village or the village took the name from the school. Day boys and boarders."

"Girls?"

"Yes. I believe so. Quite recent. The world has changed. Women's liberation, they called it."

"What is the name of the house?"

"It's been called the Woodlands for a century and a half."

"How appropriate so close to those big trees. What trees are they?"

"Oak trees. The woods behind the house are full of very old oak trees."

"Can you walk dogs in the woods?"

"Why ever not? The woods are public. Anyone can walk in the woods. There are fireplaces in every room. You'll be nice and cosy in the winter."

"Why are they selling?"

"Short of money, I suppose. No, his wife died. Poor man lives all on his own. You called your wife my lady. Does she have her own title?"

Randall laughed. "No, she's American. But don't go giving her any ideas!"

The chit-chat of a professional salesman went on for three hours before the man dropped Randall off at The Running Horses. Jane was sitting in the lounge with the carrycot next to her. The twins were fast asleep when Randall peeped at them, the girl's head at the top, the boy's head at the bottom, blankets covering them in the middle.

"I found the perfect spot. You'll love the Woodlands. What they called our new house."

"You bought it without showing it to me!"

"He's arguing the price. I need a drink."

"So do I. We always need a drink."

"Needs a lot of work on it. We'll go and have a look tomorrow when he comes up with the price."

"There's a message for you on the phone from Amanda. She wants to come and see you as soon as possible. Bit odd. How did she find out you are in England?"

"Is something wrong with James Oliver?"

"You better call her back. Here you are. I love these mobile phones. Then you can tell me about the house."

"Amanda. How are you? How's James Oliver?... I'm in England. In Surrey... When? Tomorrow! Why not? We're at The Running Horses at a place called Mickleham... Who's we? Jane and the twins. Jane had twins in New York four weeks ago. A boy and a girl. Can you believe it?... What's the matter, Amanda? Why are you crying? How's Evelina?... You're not together anymore. That's not so good... You'll give us a ring then. Preferably in the morning. We're looking for a house to buy. What's the matter, Amanda?... Okay. You'll tell me tomorrow... Of course, I'm excited at the thought of seeing James Oliver. Haven't seen my son in years. How you said you wanted it so the boy wouldn't fall between two stools. How strange you should find me in England... Yes, life is strange... Would Jane be prepared to look after James Oliver? What's gone wrong, Amanda?... Tomorrow then. Are you going to drive?... You don't drive anymore... A taxi will bring you. He can't miss The Running Horses... Now, look at that, Jane. The line's gone dead."

"What was that all about?"

"I have absolutely no idea. We'll have to wait until tomorrow morning. What a strange coincidence. The last person I expected to hear from was Amanda Hanscombe. She told me when she went to live with Evelina that it would be better for our son not to ask me questions about his mother sharing the bed with another woman. That he could never live two lives. I was to get in contact with my son when he'd grown up."

"How old is he?"

"Ten. Coming up for eleven. Tomorrow, I'm going to see my eldest son. Can you believe it? The last time I saw James Oliver was in 1989 at the Savoy Hotel. Amanda had seen me on television. He was two and a half. There's something very wrong. Why was Amanda crying? Life never stops twisting and turning. No point in panicking. Tomorrow will come tomorrow... So what do you want?"

"A nice pint of English draught beer."

"Sounds good to me... Waiter. Two pints of lager... My word. It's been quite a day. In this strange world, you never know what's going to happen next."

"How did she know your phone number?"

"Must have found out from someone. All will be revealed tomorrow. So, what do you think of England, my Janey?"

"Only time will tell. Sorry, that one's a bit hackneyed. Anyway, we're here. All four of us. I'll give you one thing, my love. You don't play around when you want something... Did Amanda know Manfred's phone number?"

"She knew Manfred Leon was my agent. Why? Did you give him our new phone number? We were meant to keep it secret... A couple of beers and then we'll go into supper. Are you still feeling tired?"

"Exhausted. How do you get a night's sleep next to crying babies?"

"Didn't hear a thing myself. Were they crying? Shame. Poor Jane. Some say life as a mother can be hell. Tonight, we'll put the cot in the bathroom and shut the door. Nice to have a room with its own bathroom... Now how does that look? Down the hatch, Jane. Another day. Another day."

Trying to enjoy his beer, Randall could not stop worrying about Amanda and his eldest son. The girl had had a horrible life with Evelina by the sound of it. Was Amanda hoping to come back to him? Or had she run out of money despite the substantial inheritance from her father that had freed her from relying on Evelina's money? Wondering what his son looked like, Randall tried to concentrate on Jane's conversation.

"What are we going to do with six bedrooms and a large attic? How do you get up to this attic?"

"There's a flight of stairs from the second floor. Three living rooms. A sitting room. A morning room. And a nice dining room with a hatch from the kitchen. You don't have to trail the food around the house. Open the hatch and pop it out. If we found the right person, like an artist without any money, we could have a cook. Give him the attic to live in and paint. We'd be best friends with the cook. Next to the kitchen is what

George called the maid's sitting room. In the old days, the servants must have lived separate lives from the owner and his family. Poor man lost his wife a few months ago. He's very old. Says he can't live in the house without his wife. Too many memories."

"What happened to his children and grandchildren?"

"He didn't mention them. Maybe he's running out of money. Spent his capital. Can happen if you live too long. Whoops. One of the babies has woken up. That's the strangest gurgling sound I ever heard. It sounds so happy."

"Should I go and look?"

"You'd better. All okay? Good... You'll like the house. In the garden, there are pear trees, plum trees, lots of different apples, a big walnut tree next to the grass tennis court. There were lots of small bushes with fruit on them George called gooseberry bushes and raspberry bushes. Never found them in Rhodesia on World's View. You think Dad will be pissed off we didn't call on him first? Never mind. When we buy the Woodlands they can come and stay with us for a couple of weeks. Be a change from the flat in Chelsea."

"I want to see the damn place first."

"Have a whisky, Jane. We've finished the beer."

"Why not?"

"Waiter!... Two double Vat 69 whiskies with lots of ice... He's still gurgling."

"How do you know it's Raphael? It's a lovely sound. I'm so proud of my newborns. I like this place. Those big wooden beams. I wonder why they called it The Running Horses?"

"We're not that far from Epsom racecourse. You know, if we buy the Woodlands we can go to the Epsom Derby. Most famous horse race in England. Probably the world. Do you like gambling, Jane?"

"Not particularly... Thank you. That was quick. A nice glass of whisky on lots of ice. Cheers, my love. To happiness."

"And the Woodlands."

"We'll see tomorrow. But it does sound nice."

"That's my girl."

"Are we really going to stick the babies in the bathroom? I won't be able to hear them."

"That's the whole idea. Cheers. To love and happiness." Randall chuckled.

"What's a morning room?"

"A place you sit in during the morning."

"Why can't you sit there in the afternoon?"

"I suppose the sun comes in during the morning. The English have weird habits."

"Oh, but what happens if the sun comes into the sitting room only in the afternoon? Why not call it the afternoon room? This place is going to take me a lot of getting used to."

With his mind wandering between James Oliver and Douglas, Randall wondered if he had done anything right in his life. Would his sons ever forgive him for walking out on them? Randall doubted it. If his own father had walked out on him so he never knew where he came from, he'd likely hate his own father. And now he had done it again. Not even bothering to marry the twins' mother. All he had done in his life was shout his mouth off through his books, making up stories to compensate for his own inadequacy. No wonder the wolves had howled in his head. No wonder he drank. Anything to escape from himself. Avoiding listening to Jane's chatter he let her go on and on, talking a good relaxation after the stress from having her babies. Poor kids. Little did they know what they had to look forward to. Or was the world of Randall Crookshank and Jane Slater any different to the rest of them?

When he carried the twins into the dining room, they were fast asleep in the carrycot. Jane had fed and changed them, and they were totally oblivious to the world they had come into. Maybe the Woodlands would give them peace. Randall hoped so. And if Jane didn't like the house he would go on searching for a place to hide from the turmoil and nastiness of humanity, with all its tricks and selfishness, the idea making him smile. He was trying, at the age of thirty-nine, to run away from himself. Making excuses for his own multitude of one-night stands. Tracey's daughter was going to be lucky never knowing her true father. And was he the father? Only a blood test would tell. Better for the girl to live her life in ignorance, happy to be brought up by her mother and whoever else came into her mother's hormone-screaming life.

"You're not listening to a word I'm saying... Roast beef. Looks good. Breastfeeding the babies makes me hungry."

"I was thinking of Tracey and Allegra."

"And trying to work out if she is your daughter. Leave it alone. Does it matter? The girl's alive. They've both got what they want. The rest doesn't matter. Oh, and you were probably thinking of your other two sons. What's done is done... On the phone, you said something about me being prepared to look after James Oliver? Why did she ask you? I presume she asked you, the way you replied."

"I don't know... The restaurant is filling up. A night at The Running Horses."

"Don't try to change the subject, my love."

"Would you?"

"What?"

"Look after James Oliver?"

"Oh, is that what you're up to? Six bedrooms. Now it all makes sense. I suppose your next move after James Oliver would be Douglas. Have you heard from Meredith? Is she sick of Clint living off your money? That nice divorce settlement where you were so generous. I remember your stories. When we drink, we tell each other everything. Pours out of our mouths. My word, that would be something."

"What, Jane? Thank you. Roast beef for both of us. Nice and rare."

"Can't I order my own food? Thank you. Roast beef it is... I go from no kids to four kids between the age of thirty-nine and forty. Next minute something can happen to Tracey and I'll have five of them. Just kidding. Nothing's going to let anyone get their hands on Allegra. I'm going to miss Tracey. I loved writing the script to *Lust* for her. Without Tracey Chapelle I'd still be working in that laundry for a pittance... You want a bottle of red wine with the beef? Don't grin like that, Randall. What's wrong with a bottle of wine? Though it does help them to sleep as I'm still feeding them."

"Nothing, I suppose."

"Where is Amanda coming from? Where does she live?"

"We'll find out tomorrow. I'll put the phone next to the bed. Not a sound from the little buggers. Your breast milk must be good. First, we'll sort out Amanda and then I'll take you to see the Woodlands. George says the old man wants to move out away from his memories as soon as possible. He'll likely sell his furniture. We can move in once I've paid. Have to sell some shares. Shouldn't take long. You're going to love the place. A bottle of French red wine, Mr Waiter. The best. Thank you, that one looks all right on the wine list. We'll find out what it tastes like when you bring us the bottle."

"You think she's dying?"

"Who?"

"Amanda. Beer, whisky and wine."

"You think she's sick?"

"Why else would she ask if I'd look after her son. Are we going to sit in the bar after supper?"

"We can't take babies into a bar."

"They're not going to drink."

"You're crazy."

"I like bars. I like people in bars. We can ask the barman if we can put the babies behind the bar counter."

"Now you really are crazy."

"You know I'm joking, Randall. I'm enjoying myself, aren't you?"

"I'm trying. Can't stop worrying about James Oliver... We drink too much."

"We've both done a lot of things too much in our lives, Randall. Not all of it bad. We could also put the carrycot on top of the bar counter. Easier to watch my babies. Oh, I do so love having twins."

"You know we are not going to do that."

"I know. Just teasing!"

By the time they went to bed all they wanted to do was sleep. Jane had left the bathroom door ajar. Randall fell quickly into a deep sleep that took him with his dreams right through to the morning. When he woke, Jane was lying next to him fast asleep. With both hands behind his head and looking through the now-open door into the small bathroom, Randall wondered why the parrots had not roosted in his mouth. Usually, red wine made his mouth feel like the bottom of a parrot cage. With one hand stretched out to the small side table, Randall picked up the mobile. There were no messages. The moment he had woken, the worry about James Oliver had instantly come into his head.

2

By ten-thirty, the phone had still not rung. There was no sign of Amanda.

"Stop looking at the phone, Randall. She's probably not coming. You never know in life what people are really up to. Give George a ring and tell him to pick us up. If the Woodlands is as nice as you say, there may be other buyers. People don't just give their property to one realtor. You got to move quick in this competitive world. You got a hangover? Mine's not too bad."

"How many times did you have to get up?"

"Twice. Those two are always hungry. Did you know, most mothers these days don't breastfeed their babies? They're both awake. Happy as a pair of crickets. Go in and look... Give him a ring, my love. I want to get us settled as soon as possible."

"George, Randall. Can you pick us up? So that's the price. An hour. We'll be waiting. That one was easy, Jane. Amazing how quick people are when they want to sell you something. We'd better get ready to go out. We'll have the phone with us should Amanda call. If she calls. I was getting all excited at the thought of seeing my eldest son."

"Are we going to have breakfast? I fancy a plate of bacon and eggs."

"It's a bit late, but very British."

"You've got to fit in, my love. Got to fit in."

"Not with that accent. At least a colonial Rhodesian accent is the same as the British. Public school, of course. Load of crap."

"What's that got to do with the price of cheese?"

"The way we pronounce our words. Tells a person which class you come from. In Dad's day, England was all about class. People at the top of the money ladder were snobs. And all the snobs went to public schools. In England, public schools are private schools and damn expensive. What I want most is a cup of tea. When do they stop serving food?"

"I have no idea. You should know."

"Can't remember. Feeding babies is the job of the mother."

"Like cleaning the house. I'll remember that."

"They call it being a housewife. Most women want to be a housewife. I wonder why she hasn't phoned?"

"Stop worrying. It's breakfast time. Come on. Then it's off to see the Woodlands. Don't forget your chequebook... How much am I going to make from a million copies?"

"You'll have to ask Manfred."

"If I like the place, make him an offer of ten per cent below his asking price. Are we going to split the cost? Joint ownership. Be the next best thing to a marriage to keep us together."

"Now you're worrying."

"A woman's always worrying about her man, my love."

"Okay. Half and half. You can pay me when the royalty is paid into your bank account."

"What's he asking?"

"Three-quarters of a million pounds. That's over a million US dollars."

"We're lucky to be rich."

"You can say that again."

Two hours later, Randall wrote out a cheque for ten thousand dollars, post-dated two weeks ahead to give his stockbroker time to sell enough shares and put the money in his British bank account. After ten minutes of negotiating and two phone calls from George to the owner, the furniture had been included in the seller's price.

"You can check with my bank that I'm good for the money. They hold my share certificates in a safety deposit box. When can we move in, George?"

"There's the key. The house has not been lived in for some time. The owner had already moved out. The place is yours. Consider your cheque as a rental fee until the property transfer goes through. We have everything we need. Poor man. Says he just can't live in this house without his wife. He must have really loved her. Says he's going to roam the world between their children. Families are so dispersed these days in the global village. Sad, really... Why do you keep looking at your phone?"

"I'm expecting a call. We'd better get back to The Running Horses. Nice doing business with you."

"If it's not rude, how did you make all that money to buy this little country estate?"

"Wouldn't you like to know... We're running away, George. We want to be just a couple of ordinary people."

"Did you inherit it?"

"Some of it. My grandfather was a famous Hollywood actor."

"What was his name?"

"If I told you that, George, you'd know who I am."

"You're Randall Crookshank, the new owner of the Woodlands."

"Some people have pseudonyms. Please. Back to The Running Horses. I'm in a hurry. My first wife says she has a problem."

"I'm sorry. I was asking too many questions. Most impolite. Enjoy living in your new house. A famous Hollywood actor. That's quite something. My wife and I love going to the cinema. Though these days you can watch it all on the box."

Still wondering why Amanda hadn't phoned, Randall sat pondering in the front seat of the estate agent's car. He was happy that Jane had loved the house, the garden and the setting next to the woods as much as himself. It had begun to rain when they got out of the car. Both ran with the babies towards the entrance. Inside The Running Horses, they walked into the main room off from the reception desk. An old woman dressed as a nurse was sitting on one of the big sofas with a boy on one side and Amanda on the other. Amanda's eyes when she looked at him were a terrible mix of fear and dread. She looked awful. The boy looked at him and looked away again, seeing just another guest.

"How long have you been here? Why didn't you phone? What's the matter with you, Amanda?"

"I have breast cancer. I'm dying. It was diagnosed too late. The doctor says I may be dead in a few weeks. And there's no one to look after James Oliver. This is my nurse. Claire has been so good to me. I'm going to have to leave him with you, Randall. Evelina can't cope with this. My poor son. He doesn't even recognise his own father. Give him a hug, Randall, please. He needs comfort. This has come as such a shock to James Oliver. He'll never be short of money. He's the sole heir to his grandfather's fortune. Claire will be driving me back to London. You must be Jane and those are your dear little ones. Please look after him, Jane. For me. I know it's difficult. We have to go. It has been a dreadful struggle for me to be here today. The nurse wants me back in the hospital. I don't want to die. Oh God, I don't want to die. I'm only forty-one years old. Look after him, Randall. Go to your father, James Oliver. I don't want to leave you, but it's the only place you have. Now we're all crying. I'm so sorry. What can you do when you're dying? How lucky for us you came to England. When I traced your agent and told Manfred of my illness, he told me what you two were doing. That you were living in England and that you wanted to live your lives out of the spotlight. I loved your books, Randall. Read every one of them. Thank you, Claire. Better to go while I can. Give Mummy a last hug. I love you so much, James Oliver. Never forget how much your mummy loved you. Goodbye, my darling boy. The car's outside. Stay with him, Randall. Don't come out. It's raining."

"I'm so sorry."

"Aren't we all? Death comes to all of us. Just some sooner than others. At least I found you. Goodbye, Randall. Everything's in his suitcases."

"Isn't there something I can do for you?"

"There's nothing. Absolutely nothing. It's all done."

Torn between staying with his son or following Amanda, Randall watched the nurse lead her away and out through the front door of The Running Horses, out into the cold and rain. She didn't look back. Her body was shuddering with sobs. When he stopped staring past the reception desk at the closed front door, he turned back to his son. Jane had her arm around the boy's shoulder. The boy looked bewildered. Under the front of the reception desk were three large suitcases. Breast cancer: the fear and curse of many women.

"I don't know what to say. This I never expected. Poor Amanda. How very awful. She must feel so alone. I'd better book James Oliver a room. We can't move into the Woodlands today."

"He'll sleep in our room. Ask reception to put in another bed. You don't want to be alone, do you?"

"Mummy's not coming back, is she?"

"No. I am so sorry, child. You're going to live with me and your father. Come and let me show you your little brother and sister."

"Do I have a brother and sister? Evelina wanted to have babies. Why didn't she want me to live with her now Mummy is going to die? Why do people have to die? Are you really my father? I do remember someone who was my father but he didn't look like you. Or I don't think he did. Your voice sounds familiar... You don't live here, do you?"

"No, I just bought a big house round the corner. Well, not quite around the corner. There's a prep school quite close to the house. Where were you at school?"

"I haven't been to school since Mummy got sick. I like playing football. Do they play football?"

"Come here, son, let me give you a proper hug. Are you hungry? We can have sandwiches with a cup of tea."

"Are they really my brother and sister?"

"Yes, James Oliver. Your half-brother and sister. That one is Kimber. She's a little girl. That's Raphael. He's your brother."

"I'm never going to see my mummy again, am I?"

"I understand you crying, James Oliver. This is awful for you. I am so sorry. Jane and I will do all we can to help you through the pain of losing your mother."

"I'm never going to stop crying. First, my daddy left me. Then Evelina. Now Mummy has gone away. What can I do but cry? And don't touch me! I just want my mummy!"

Feeling sick to his gut, Randall walked across to reception.

"We need an extra bed in our room. These bags here belong to my son. Please have them sent up to our room."

"Is there anything I can do for you, Mr Crookshank? That was the most awful thing I have ever seen. I'm afraid I heard every word."

"There's nothing anyone can do. Life goes wrong. It happens."

"That poor boy. What's going to happen to him?"

"He'll survive. He'll cope. He has us to help him."

"He'll be traumatised for the rest of his poor little life. I never had my own children. All I have ever wanted was a child of my own. Now I'm too old to have children. Life's so bare. I'm sorry. You have enough problems. Outside it's raining cats and dogs. The world can be so unkind. Unfortunately, there'll be an extra charge for the boy."

3

---

*T*he nurse phoned Randall the following Sunday to say that Amanda rapidly deteriorated and died.

"I'll need your address to send you the death certificate. What do you want me to do with her things? How is James Oliver?"

"Confused. Cries. Isn't hungry. Not interested in anything."

"Time heals all wounds. Just look after him for her."

"The Woodlands, Agates Lane, Cranleigh. Have her bills been paid?"

"The hospital has been paid. We'll have a courier deliver her belongings. She wanted to be cremated privately. No funeral. Do you wish me to send you her ashes? She was your wife."

"I'll scatter them in the woods. Thank you for being so good to Amanda."

"Just doing my job. Have a nice day."

"You too, Claire. Oh, you too."

Slowly approaching James Oliver, putting his arm around his son's shoulders, Randall said, "Your mother has died, James Oliver. She's gone forever. I am so sorry. I wish it wasn't this way but it is. I know it is hard for you. Tomorrow we're going to book you into a new school. You'll be a boarder and make lots of new friends. The school is close by. They play football. Don't walk away. Please. James Oliver. This is terrible for you, I know. And it is for me, too."

"Leave me alone. My life is horrible. I want to die like my mummy and go to heaven."

"Jane, do something."

"What?"

"I just don't know."

"What's a boarder?"

"You'll live at the school during term time and come here in the holidays, James Oliver."

"You're throwing me out again."

"It'll be better for you than being alone and crying. You cried all last night. Every night. You need new friends. I'm not throwing you out. I will never again walk away from you."

"Everyone tells lies. Why do people lie?"

"It's not a lie. It's a promise. The sun has come out and we're going to take out the dogs for a walk. You like dogs. The boy's name is Bob and the girl's Misty. Come on. Put on your overcoat, young man."

"I don't want to go for a walk. I don't want to do anything. I'm never going to have a mummy."

"I'm your mummy now, James Oliver."

"You're not my mummy. My mummy is dead and gone to heaven."

"Stop crying."

"Don't touch me. I hate you. I hate all of you."

"Do you hate me?"

"You left me when I was two-and-a-half. You disappeared. I hate you."

"What can we do with him, Jane?"

"Go for a walk with the dogs on your own. Time will heal. Leave him with me. And the babies are both crying. Motherhood. All hell's broken loose. Go on. Off you go. When you get back we'll both have a drink. Do we not need a drink? We'll have roast chicken for supper... Where are you going, James Oliver?"

"To my room. I want to be alone."

"There's no point in running after him, Randall... Are you really going to send him to boarding school?"

"I'm at my wits' end."

"We both are."

"Instead of walking the dogs, I'm going to have that drink. Raise my glass to Amanda. Being bi-sexual was a curse for the poor girl. But if you are born that way, there's little you can do."

"I'll get the ice and the glasses. I love our new home. He'll get over the loss of his mother. As I did. As you did. And you never even knew your mother. I'll be a Bergit to James Oliver. You don't know how lucky you were to have such an understanding stepmother. The pain will go. It must. Then he'll just have happy memories. When are we going to pick up the cats?"

"Tomorrow afternoon."

"A nice whisky around the fire on a Sunday afternoon. You must relax, Randall, or you'll do yourself an injury. Come and give me a hug. Stress causes the heart to pound. And that's not good for a man close to forty. He's ten years old. Not a baby. And at this moment he's better off without a nursemaid. He can't get out of the house without me seeing him. Get the whisky out of the cocktail cabinet. I love the old man's furniture. It's all so old. From another era. The British sure knew how to live comfortably. It's so quiet. Even the dogs are resting as they watch us with their chins on their paws. We were lucky to find two young, pedigree Border Collies. Expensive, but worth every penny. Sit. Relax. Pour the whisky. Why is life so difficult?"

"Always is. Always was. Sometimes in between, you get what you want. My poor son. I ruined his life when I walked out on him. All the nice words will never repair the damage. I'm a horrible person. Always selfish. Always only thinking of myself."

"Put on some Mozart and stop blaming yourself. We bought a medium grand piano with the furniture. We'll find a teacher for the boy. Turn him into an artist like his father. You always say it's in the genes. Poor little bugger. I still miss my mother all these years later. When are we going to ask Sophie and my father to visit us? They'll love this place. That log fire is just perfect. There's a fire burning in his room so he won't be cold. Cheers, my love. And here we are. Away from the crowd as you hoped. Tomorrow we're going to start writing. Leave it a week before you put him in school. We all need to calm down. Take it easy. Disappear into our books. I've missed Mozart these last few days. How's Shakespeare and his friend?"

"I have no idea. All I'm thinking of is James Oliver. Shouldn't we go up to his room?"

"Leave him alone. He'll come down when he wants us. At least she doesn't have to suffer anymore. Can you imagine having to suffer for all eternity? From that point of view, death isn't so bad. It ends everything.

And like a person, I doubt the world will last forever. Mozart. Beautiful Mozart."

"His Twenty-Fourth Concerto. You're right. We'll teach him to play the piano. Buy him a soccer ball. In England, football is soccer. How can one man write so much beautiful music? Give so much pleasure to so many people so long after his death? Now that's fame. Fame that will last with his music forever. Like Will Shakespeare. Are you sure I shouldn't go up?"

"Leave him alone, Randall. Sit down. The babies are settled again. For the moment, we have peace. So, where do we find our artists?"

"Probably nowhere. Thanks, Jane. I'm winding down. It was his wife who played the piano. Why he wanted to leave it behind, I suppose. There's a big difference between a performing artist like a pianist and a creative artist like a writer. Not that it matters. Just listen to that piano. You want another whisky? That one went down quickly."

"Why not? I wonder how many people are reading our books right at this moment? Makes you think. So far away and yet so close. They know who we are. We have no idea who they are. Thanks. Cheers. To happiness. Are we selling your apartment?"

"There's no hurry. My brother and Tracey will keep an eye on it. It's difficult to know where to invest your money. And who in this crazy life knows what's going to come next? A depression? A war? When the stock markets crash it's better to be in property. We'll see. My father and Bergit are going to love visiting this place. Maybe Phillip and Martha will come over. You know, we should go and see Douglas. That poor boy upstairs crying his eyes out has made me think. Have you put the chicken on? This place is so big we're going to need help. Especially now we have James Oliver. He can come home at the weekends, I suppose. Mozart. What would we do without Mozart, Jane? You think James Oliver can hear the music?"

"Put some more logs on the fire."

"At your service, my lady. When I told George I wasn't going to buy this place until it had been seen by my lady, he thought you had a title. So, here we are, Jane."

"The chicken is on. A nice slow roast. With spuds as you call them. It's so far from home."

"For both of us. We all still miss Rhodesia. Life is always changing. I like our new writing room. Two desks. Nice and cosy next to the fire. I hope they are enjoying themselves."

"Who?"

"The people reading our books. Giving millions of people pleasure is more important than money."

"You're off again. Without our money, we wouldn't be able to write our books. We'd have to earn a living. Just look at those two dogs. Their eyes are literally watering with happiness. You think they'll fight with the cats? And you still have Rabbit Farm on the Isle of Man. Property. Owning property. The game of being rich and holding on to your money."

"What are you up to now?"

"I want to look at my babies. They are so adorable when they're asleep. I wonder what kind of lives they will have?"

"Come back and sit down."

"Is life all about having kids, Randall?"

"Probably. Why I'm now worrying about Douglas. Have you ever played the piano?"

"Not one note. Won't servants interrupt our writing? Break our train of thought? Hoovering the carpets. Why we never break the rule and speak to each other when we're writing. I'll do the cleaning and you'll help me with the cooking. Rooms we don't use we'll keep shut. You can cut the lawn. The rest of the garden doesn't matter. You sit on the old man's lawnmower like sitting on a quad bike. You can drive it up and down the grass and still think of the characters in your book. We said we wanted to be away from people. I'll get James Oliver to help me in the house. Give us something to do together. Even your penniless artist stuck up in the attic will create unwanted distractions. We need peace and quiet to write. Friends, yes, when we want to be with friends. Otherwise, all we want is peace. Together. And all this happened to me in just one year. You think we'll have a real future together, my love? I'm so enjoying my drink. I know I shouldn't be drinking so much but who cares? A girl's got to enjoy herself. And we both like drinking."

"I've learned in life to take it one day at a time. No one can work out their future. We make plans like coming to England and buying this house. Let's just hope it all works out fine. A few plans in life have been known to work. You'll have fun trying to get that kid to help you with the cleaning. For the moment, you and I are as happy as pigs in shit. We've got what we want. A place to write. Twins. A son. There must be a local pub where we can go to meet the locals. See if there are any artists. I'm beginning to understand Shakespeare's friend more now I've run away from that awful thing they call fame. No wonder he didn't want to put his name on a play. The fun's in the writing. Not the aftermath."

"You still need the money."

"Shakespeare's friend was a rich aristocrat. He didn't need money. You're right, Jane. They look just lovely asleep. I'm going to look after these two. And that's a promise. No running away. She'll be beautiful just like her mother... Stop grinning. You are still beautiful. Misty, Bob, come here and talk to your father. We can eat on a tray in front of the fire. We'll open a bottle of wine. A new life in the English countryside. In the summer, the owls will hoot from the woods at night. We'll hear the call of a fox. See the old rabbit. Swallows in summer. We'll put out a couple of chaise longues on my well-cut lawn and lie in the sun. Once the babies can crawl, they'll be all over the lawn playing with the dogs. When they get big enough they can learn to ride horses, ride them through the woods. We'll have to get some. By then James Oliver and Douglas will be grown men. We'll gently move into our old age, you and I together."

"You make it all sound so romantic."

"We have to dream in this life, Jane. We have to dream."

"Now what are you up to?"

"Opening a bottle of red wine. Red wine should be allowed to breathe. We've found a true home. This time we are home. I feel so damn comfortable."

"Don't owls hoot in the winter?"

"Haven't heard them. Schubert. I think that's now Schubert on the music channel."

"You think he's gone to sleep?"

"I hope so. You have to look after yourself in this life whatever your age. Other people may help, but in the end, it comes down to yourself. When it comes down to it, we're all on our own. Fathers and mothers. Brothers and sisters. Wives and husbands. We live with them, argue with them, have fun together. But at the end of the day, it's still just ourselves. Our body and our thoughts. You can't be dependent on anyone. I'm going upstairs. I'm not going into his room. I just want to listen from the top of the stairs."

At the top of the flight of stairs, standing on the landing that led through to the bedrooms on one side and up the steep stairs to the attic on the other, Randall sat on the small bench under the window that looked out between the dip in the two joining roofs. The daylight had

gone, the garden shaped by the light from the rising moon. The door to
the boy's room was ajar at the end of the corridor. There was no sound.
No crying. No movement. Careful not to make any noise, Randall got up
from the cushioned bench and went down the dark corridor to the dim
light he could see through the open door of what George had called the
nursery. The boy was in his bed, the covers up to his ears, no movement,
no sound other than Schubert's music coming up the stairs from the
sitting room. Randall stood for a long while watching his son. Smiling,
hopeful, he walked back down the corridor, down the stairs and into the
sitting room.

"All is quiet upstairs for the moment. Still Schubert. Are we going to
eat? I'll get the wine glasses. He must have finally succumbed to
exhaustion after all the trauma. His door was ajar. Maybe Mozart had
lulled him to sleep. We can both relax, enjoy our food and the wine."

"What's next, Randall?"

"You tell me. A wind is coming up. Full moon tonight by the look of
it. Round and beautiful. The moon looking over him. She'll be in his
dreams. Alive and well. He's with his mother... Are the twins still asleep?
Don't you have to feed them?"

"Relax, my love. The night is still young. Pour yourself another
whisky before you carve the chicken. We're going to win. Come and sit
down by the fire. Why are wood fires so relaxing? Lovely flickering
flames. Tell me one of your stories. Become my favourite itinerant
storyteller again."

"Once upon a time in a place they called Rhodesia, a man arrived
from far away England to learn how to plant and grow tobacco on a
Crown Land farm that had been given to his English cousin, an ex-officer
and pilot in the Fleet Air Arm who, after twenty years of serving his
country, had gone out to the British colony of Rhodesia to make a new
life for himself as a farmer in the wilds of Africa."

Smiling to himself when the short story of love and happiness in
the wilds came to an end, and without saying another word, Randall
went through to the kitchen, took the chicken out of the oven and
carved the bird. With a plate of food in each hand, he walked back
through the cold entrance hall and put them down in front of the warm
fire.

"Did you turn off the oven?"

"Chicken. Roast potatoes and green vegetables. Good girl. You've
poured the wine and moved the armchairs next to the fireplace. There

you go, Jane. Supper. There's plenty left for James Oliver should he wake up. And I did turn off the oven."

"Was that the end of the story?"

"Oh, yes. Just a small tale to christen our new house."

"You forgot the trays."

"How silly of me. It's damn cold in the hallway. Let me have a sip of my wine. Oh, yes. That's good French wine."

"One of the pleasures of having money."

"Now you're having a go... And the music flows on. Must be freezing outside in the garden. Dad always said one of the great pleasures of living in Africa was never being cold."

"Get some food for the dogs or they'll eat our plates of chicken. Are there any ghosts in this house?"

"Hang on."

Back in the cold hallway at the foot of the stairs, Randall stood listening for any sound coming from upstairs. Satisfied, he went into the kitchen and did what he was told.

"There you are, my dogs. Tinned dog food. One tin each in your bowls... There. Is that better? Chicken on a tray. No. There are no ghosts. Not for a man from Africa and a lady from America. Ghosts only haunt the locals."

"How's my cooking?"

"Good as ever, Jane. How's the wine?"

"Perfect. What more can a couple want?"

"Is it long enough after giving birth to make love?"

"We can try. You've got that naughty look on your face... How do dogs eat their food so quickly? We'll have to put the cat food on a shelf or something, or the dogs will eat it. Home, sweet home."

"Go well, Amanda. Raise your glass to Amanda, Jane."

"Go well, Amanda. I'll look after your son as if he were my own."

Randall put his glass on the small table Jane had placed next to his comfortable armchair, got up and kissed Jane on her forehead. Neither of them spoke. The music flowed.

"Thank you, Randall."

"Thank you, Jane. It requires a woman to bring up a child. Supper on a tray on our laps. Peace and calm at last. There's nothing better than a plate of good food."

"And a glass of French wine... It's so nice, you and I. We don't squabble."

"What's there to squabble about?"

"So many people squabble. Argue. Use each other."

"Yes, they do. Why the world is in permanent turmoil. It's human nature to argue. People are rarely content."

When Randall looked up from his food, the sitting room door was open, James Oliver standing silently in the doorway.

"Can I have some supper?"

"Of course you can, darling. Come with Aunty Jane into the kitchen. Did you sleep well?"

"I had lots of dreams."

"Put another chair by the fire, Randall. Now we're all together. Do you like the music?"

"What is it? I could hear it from upstairs."

"It's called classical, son. Would you like to learn how to play that piano over there in the corner? Then you could play this music. Go with Aunty Jane and get your supper and we'll talk more about it. Football and learning the piano."

"I was dreaming about Mummy. She was so happy."

"I'm so pleased. You'd better close the door when you go to the kitchen."

"It's such a big house. The babies are fast asleep. When will they wake up? Do their toes touch? My baby brother and sister."

"Go on. Go get your supper."

"The dogs are following me. I like dogs."

"And tomorrow we'll have cats."

"Am I going to be happy again?"

"I hope so, James Oliver."

4

The day after the midterm school holiday, Randall placed his son into boarding school, having bought him a school uniform and a new pair of football boots. Leaving James Oliver looking lost among his fellow pupils in the big common room, Randall joined Miss Dixon, the boy's new housemistress in her small adjacent office to explain his son's predicament. A middle-aged spinster with a straight fringe above her glasses and wearing a skirt that dropped to her ankles. She listened diligently to Randall's story.

"He won't be the first of my pupils to lose one of his parents. You are right to put him into boarding school, Mr Crookshank. The worst that can happen to a child who loses a parent is to become a loner. Detached from life. He'll be sleeping in the boys' dormitory with twenty other boys from ages eight to thirteen. At thirteen, they go up to the senior school. I'll watch him for you. It's good he plays football and is eligible to play for the under-eleven side. If he gets in, he'll be part of a team which will stop him from becoming lonely. They'll accept him. Especially if he is good and helps them win against other school sides. Under the circumstances, I would say it is better for the boy not to go home over the weekends. You come to his football matches if he plays for the second side. Otherwise, he'll go home for Christmas. Good day to you, Mr Crookshank."

With a nod and a stare but no sign of a smile, the housemistress looked down at her desk. Not sure if he felt better or worse, Randall drove back to the Woodlands and took the dogs for their morning walk in the woods. Life went on. Had he done the right thing? Only time would tell. Friends. What the boy needed was friends.

"We'll just have to see... Misty! Bob! Stop chasing that poor rabbit. What a world. We're all chasing something."

Trying to get back into the head of Shakespeare's friend, he walked on down the path that wound between the oak trees, their trunks wider than a man's outstretched arms. Friends, that's what they all needed. Preferably artist friends for himself and Jane but life was never easy. They had tried the local pub three times and only talked to the barman.

An hour later, feeling sorry for himself and James Oliver, he went home. Jane was in the writing room with the door shut.

"Now what do we do, dogs? Can't write today and I don't want to sit and think. Better I sneak off alone and walk the mile to the pub. Don't look at me like that. You can't come to the pub. They don't allow dogs. Why's it always so cold in England? You're talking out loud again, you silly old bugger. Friends. We need friends. Off to the Jolly Farmer. You got to stand on your own two feet, James Oliver. How it works."

Twenty minutes later, Randall ordered his first pint of draught beer, sitting alone at the end of the long bar. In no time at all it was half past four by the clock behind Micky, the barman. A wood fire was burning in the grate, making the place warm and friendly. Micky pulled up the flap at the end of the bar and walked past the tables where he closed the curtains to cover the darkness outside. A man came in and sat at the opposite end of the bar to Randall. When Micky got back behind the counter, closing the flap behind him, the man ordered his drink. Randall drank at his beer and tried to stop thinking about his son lost and lonely among strangers.

"Are there any artists living in this neck of the woods, Micky?"

"What do you mean by an artist? A piano player? We don't have anyone playing that old piano over there. Not in my day, anyway."

"A painter. Writer. Someone creative."

"Never heard of anyone. Most people who live around here drive to the station in the morning and catch the seven-fifty to Waterloo. They work in London. In the City. Spend two to three hours a day travelling to and from work. Can a painter make a living? Doubt it. Unless he paints houses. It was beginning to rain outside."

"When I've had my drinks, can you call me a cab? Can't drink and drive. Maybe amateur artists. People who paint pictures for a hobby."

"You'll have to ask them yourself. Can't ask questions as a barman. Here we go. More customers. Did I ask you what you did for a living? None of a barman's business. You're new in the village. Sit around. You'll soon find out what's going on. What's your name, anyway?"

"Randall. I was born and grew up in Rhodesia."

"Oh. One of the old colonials. Don't meet too many of them these days. All the immigrants are from eastern Europe. Don't speak much English. They come here for the benefits when they can't get a job. You can live off benefits. Must have been nice in the colonies in the good old days. What did you do?"

"My father was a tobacco farmer. Now lives in London."

"Anyone left in Africa?"

"A few. Anyone with money or an opportunity in England has left. All part of the history of the British Empire. Empires start and empires end. Life goes on."

"Hello, Reggie. Your usual? Meet Randall. He was from Rhodesia."

"Where's Rhodesia?"

"They now call it Zimbabwe. Nice to meet you, Reggie. Can I buy you a drink?"

"Anyone can buy me a drink. Africa. Thanks, Micky. Nothing better than a barman who knows what you drink. The bugger fired me. When I got to work this morning he had cleaned out my desk. Thought he was a friend. He was the one who talked me into joining his company. They make tea and sell it in teabags in the supermarkets. My job as the salesman was to get their product into the supermarkets. I had contacts from my old job selling branded toothpaste. Knew all the buyers. Took me a year to get tea from Sri Lanka into eighty per cent of the big shops. Once the tea was on the shelves I was no longer so important. I think my friend thought I was a threat to his job. The directors of the three outside shareholders who owned the majority share in the company had patted me on the back. I was so naïve. Once the tea was selling so well there was no way the stores would stop buying our product. Now I'm out of a job. I never had an employment contract. Not in writing anyway. I hadn't thought you needed to put a deal with a friend in writing. All I got was one month's salary in lieu of notice and a kick up the arse out the door. Why are people such crooks? Thanks, Randall, for the drink. You know, the bastard wouldn't even give me a reference. My old company won't give me my job back. They'll say I hadn't been loyal to them when I decided to leave. They were right probably. I was thinking of my one big opportunity instead of dedicated hard work climbing the corporate ladder. You reap what you sow, I suppose. The beer tastes good. Tonight, I'm going to get myself well and truly drunk. Drown my sorrows. Lucky, I don't have a wife. I like women, not marriage. Do you have a wife, Randall?"

"A live-in lady, the mother of our twins."

"And what do you do for a living? You don't by any luck have a job for me? That would be nice. One minute down. The next minute up."

"I don't work. Made some money in America. Jane and I grew sick of people."

"Join the club. What do you do with yourself?"

"I write books to myself for a hobby. So does Jane. Just bought a house on five and a half acres."

"Shit. You must have money. Are you going to publish your book?"

"That depends."

"On finding a publisher?"

"That sort of thing."

"I've been writing songs for years. Never got one of them recorded. First you need a singer. Then a label."

"Where do you live around here?"

"With Mrs Garraway. She's an old lonely lady. Rents out three of her rooms to young people. The rent's not too bad... Now it's my turn. What are you having, Randall? When I've spent my last month's salary, I'll apply for the dole. Do you like music?"

"Preferably Mozart."

The name Mozart hung in the air as the man called Reggie looked around the pub.

"Excuse me. A friend's just come in. Buy you a drink next time... Luke. How are you, you old bugger? Are you going to buy me a drink?"

The world never changed. People were the same wherever you were. Randall smiled ruefully into his beer and turned away. Had Reggie just been fired or was the story a ploy to avoid his round of drinks?

"What do you think, Micky?"

"You tell me."

"Has he done it before?"

"Lots of times."

"Was he fired?"

"Probably for cheating. You meet all sorts serving in a bar. You want another beer?"

"Why not?... Maybe his friend was the cheat. Or the friend genuinely became nervous of losing his job. That lonely world of money and business. They don't give a damn what's right or wrong. They just want the profits. Anyway. I offered to buy him a drink before he told his story. Not good losing your job. The older I get, the more I hate the modern world. How do they live with themselves? You ever been fired, Micky? Sorry. You have work to do. Don't worry about me. I like drinking alone in pubs and watching the world go around."

The pub began to fill, people standing with their backs to the fire before walking across to the bar, picking free potato crisps from the bowls on the bar as they waited for their drinks. Most of the people seemed to know each other. Did Randall want to become part of the community? He wasn't sure. Finishing the beer, he ordered himself a double whisky, wondering if drinking at home wouldn't have been better than coming to the pub. Reggie had moved off from talking to Luke as he worked his way down the bar. In Randall's experience of life, it was usually about the money than genuine friendship. Was a songwriter an artist? Was young Reggie an artist or was it just part of his story, the chatter of people drinking in public? Two young girls came in, both of them giggling as they walked up to the bar, both of them looking for men. One glanced at Randall sitting up on his stool and looked away uninterested, making Randall feel he was getting old. Before Micky asked the girls what they wanted, two men offered to buy them a drink. The game was on.

"It's cheaper to get yourself a whore."

"I'm sorry. What did you say?"

"You were watching those two girls. To get into their pants will need a dinner or two in a fancy restaurant. Whores are cheaper. You just pay for what you get. Are you new in the village or just visiting? Never seen you before. I'm Clive Hall. We've been living in these parts for a couple of hundred years. Still have Croswell Hall, though the old house is falling apart. Can't afford the upkeep. All I inherited was the Hall. I have to make a living unlike some of my lucky ancestors. My wife only married me because she likes being the lady of the manor. Worked for me. No one took much notice of me before I inherited the manor house. She didn't have any money. We're all so naïve when it comes to women. All we really want is their bodies. You going to introduce yourself?"

"Hall of Croswell Hall. Was the manor house named after your family?"

"It actually wasn't. Just a coincidence. A lot of big houses in those days were called Halls. Can I buy you a drink? My wife doesn't like drinking. Doesn't like me as a matter of fact. There's something wrong with my sperm so we couldn't have children. You got any kids? Wish I'd had kids. So, what's it to be?"

"A whisky. I'm Randall."

"You have a weird accent. Where you from?"

"America. Before, I lived here in England for a while. I grew up in Rhodesia. I can't stay long or Jane will be upset. She's just had twins."

"Blimey. Micky. Give us a round. I hate commuting to work every day. Work in the city for a firm of stockbrokers. So, what do you do for a living, Randall?"

"I don't work."

"You live on the dole?"

"Not yet. I just bought a place called the Woodlands. Does the name of the house mean anything to you?"

"About a million pounds. So, you made your fortune in America."

"Something like that. Thank you, Micky. Cheers, Clive. To happy times. Doesn't your wife like coming to the pub?"

"She doesn't drink. Does your wife drink?"

"We're both practising alcoholics."

"I can't drink much when I'm working the next day. Can't cloud your brain and make mistakes in a stockbroker's office. You think they are going to score?"

"Who?"

"Those two men chatting up the girls. It was fun being single. Always on the lookout for a bit of fun. I was lucky, I suppose. My wife has never cheated on me. As far as I know. She might have done it to have a kid. Make a child of hers heir to the manor house. She's a snob, is my wife. What makes her think people are different is beyond my comprehension. Does saying you are lady of the manor make you a better person? So, you bought the Woodlands. The old man's wife died. Can you pass me that bowl of crisps? No. Better go."

"Have one on me?"

"I have the car outside. Drink and drive and they lock you up. What a world. Someone is always controlling your life. Telling you what to do.

Nice meeting you, Randall. Enjoy your new house. Don't do anything I wouldn't. What did you do in England?"

"Went to school. The London School of Economics. And worked for my Uncle Paul. He part-owns Brigandshaw Limited. You heard of it?"

"Everyone's heard of Brigandshaw Limited! So you made your money on the stock market?"

"Not really. Thanks for the drink."

"My pleasure. If you want any investment help you know where to come. My boss likes me to find him clients."

"I'll remember that Clive of Croswell Hall."

"On the way home I'm going to buy myself a bottle of whisky."

"Careful. Clear head tomorrow. Don't break the rules."

Feeling bored, Randall picked a salty crisp from the bowl and put it in his mouth. There was nothing really free in life. A bowl of crisps made a customer thirsty. Another twist in the game of life.

"It's always about the money."

"You want another drink, Randall?"

"Why not, Micky? What do you do in life when you're a bit bored? Jane didn't want to be disturbed, nor disturb the babies."

"Get drunk. What everyone else does. Double whisky coming up. You want some more crisps?"

"Why not? Don't you get bored being a barman? Hearing the same old crap night after night."

"The tips are good."

"Of course. How silly of me. It's all about the tips. A man has to make a living. When I leave, add ten per cent to my tab as your tip, Micky. Can't break the rules."

"What rules?"

"Never mind."

When the drink came, Micky gave him a look, saying nothing. Randall took a sip of his whisky, as his mind began to wander around the world, from place to place as he looked at his past, each place vivid as if he had never left. From the bush of Africa to all those people in the big city of New York. People came and went. Old friends. Old memories.

"Do you mind if I sit next to you? The place is so crowded. This one is the last empty stool in the bar."

"What did you say? Sorry. Miles away. Living in the past. It's a public bar. You can sit where you like."

"Why are you being rude?"

"Am I? I'm so sorry. Her name was Amanda. My very first. Memories of the past. Most of them good."

"And what happened to Amanda?"

"She died of breast cancer. What is a young, pretty girl doing in a bar on her own? Or am I being rude again?"

"Did you love her?"

"She went off with a woman."

"To answer your question, I was bored out of my mind in my bachelor flat all on my own. I'd just finished my book."

"You can always find another one to read."

"It's my second book. The first one was rejected by eleven publishers. The worst thing in life is rejection. Thank you, Micky. Give me a gin and tonic. I've always wanted to be popular. I was never popular at school. The other girls laughed at me for not being able to play sport. The only thing I was ever good at was English. I so wish I could become a famous writer."

"Careful what you wish, lady. Popularity creates jealousy with all its consequences. Better to live a life out of the limelight or people destroy you. Is the new book any good? Fiction or fact? You don't have to tell me."

"But I do. You have to get people to read. Would you like to read my manuscript? It's all neatly typed. I write on a computer. Grammar check. Spell check. There's nothing wrong with the English. It's the story I worry about. Where you from? You're not from these parts."

"I am now. I've lived from pillar to post. So, what's it about?"

"It's a love story. A girl and a boy wanting to find a new life away from their parents and their brothers and sisters. A life of love instead of constantly arguing, of people putting you down. I don't think my mother has ever paid me a compliment in her life. Dad just sits and smokes his pipe."

"I'll read it."

"Will you really?"

"But be careful. If it is no good, I'm going to tell you. No being nice. The truth."

"Wait here."

"Where are you going?"

"My flat's just down the road. Look after my drink. It's so wonderful. Someone wants to read my book. All I want's the truth. I hate people saying nice things just to be nice."

"Has it got a title?"

"*Boys and Girls Go Out to Play!*"

"A bit long for a book. They're normally five words or less. How big is the book? How many words?"

"About eighty thousand."

"That's about right for a first book. Publishers don't like voluminous books the first time round."

"Please don't go away while I'm fetching my book."

"I might just drink your gin and tonic."

"Now you're smiling. Back in a tick. What's your name, by the way?"

"Randall."

"I'm Mary."

Wondering what he had got himself into, Randall watched the girl rush out of the pub. He put her drink with the bottle of tonic next to his glass of whisky and stared back into space, ignoring the people and the blaring music. Around him, the six o'clock swill went on unnoticed. *Boys and Girls Go Out to Play*. How it was. How it is. How it always will be. Tossing back the last of his whisky, Randall caught Micky the barman's eye. When he got home, he and Jane were going to get themselves well and truly drunk, playing the game of life with all its consequences. At least reading Mary's book would give him something to do. Even *Shakespeare's Ghost* was no longer drawing him back to his desk. Had he written himself out? He hoped not. If he had, there would be nothing to do of any consequence for the rest of his life. With his mind off on its travels, a man took Mary's empty barstool. At least Jane had something to write; living with Margaret Neville would give her something to do. Maybe *Shakespeare's Ghost* was finally finished. Randall needed a new story. Something else to tell. Feeling better at the idea of dreaming up another story he stirred the ice and whisky in his glass with his finger and took a swig... Time passed.

"Someone's taken my seat. Here you are. Please don't lose it. I only have two copies. How long will it take you to read?"

"You can sit on my stool. A day or two. Depends how good it is, Mary. Good books don't let you put them down."

"The front cover has my address and phone number in the bottom right corner. I'm so excited someone finally wants to read one of my books. Oh, good. At least you saved my gin and tonic. Cheers and beers, Randall. My friends didn't want to read my stuff; not interested. As for my parents and my brothers and sisters, they are not in the slightest bit interested. They think I'm wasting my time. Can I have your phone number?"

"You don't trust people, do you?"

"I try to. But it rarely works. So, what does my first reader do for a living? Why are you smiling like that? You must be married by now. Please don't say that's your motive. Men just want to get in my knickers."

"Relax, Mary. I'm not after your body. My partner in crime just had twins but we did not marry. If your book is good, I'll ask Jane for a second opinion. How did you know I'm not a tourist who will run away with your manuscript?"

"Hope. I just hope your offer to read it is genuine."

"Well, Mary, that's my drinking day in the pub over. With luck, Jane will have finished her work and we can get down to some serious drinking. What do you do for a living to have time to write a book?"

"I'm a caregiver. I look after old people who can't fend for themselves. Do their shopping. Nurse them when they get sick. I did a six-month course in looking after old people at the local college. Pays the bills. But most important, it has given me time to write my books. Two of my old people are being visited by relatives. Why I'm here in the pub. I checked on the other one at lunchtime. She has my mobile phone number if she needs any help... What's your last name?"

"Just maybe one day you'll find out. Be talking to you, Mary Poppins."

"My surname is Wilson. It's there on the corner of my book."

"Just kidding. Don't get too excited. Half the world wants to write books. Very few of us have the luck, talent or a story to tell."

"You do live around here?"

"We just bought a house called the Woodlands to get away from the world of people and live in peace on our five and a half acres."

"You must be rich."

"We were lucky. Both of us."

"Twins."

"A boy and a girl."

"Don't you want to read a page?"

"Not when I've been drinking. Patience, Mary."

"Hope springs eternal."

"I hope your book is good. I really do. For your sake. And all the rest of your readers. Writing shouldn't be about fame and fortune but about giving people a chance to find another world. Where they are happy. It's called good entertainment without which most people would go nuts."

"You're a strange man."

"We all get a bit strange as we get older."

"Is Jane much younger than you?"

"We're both pushing forty."

"Twins at nearly forty!"

"She was lucky. We both are. In life, you never know what's going to happen... Micky, can you order me that taxi?"

"There are three of them right outside waiting for customers. There we go, Randall. Your tab. Plus ten per cent. Thanks for the tip."

"My pleasure."

"Enjoy your reading."

"You really do pick up on what we all say."

"I'm a barman. Thank you. All paid for by cash."

"You can put the tip in your pocket without worrying about the taxman."

With the girl's manuscript, Randall walked out of the pub. At the door, he looked back. The man who had taken her barstool was chatting up Mary. Outside it was raining, the wind pushing the rain into Randall's face. Next to the kerb, in front of the pub, was a line of four taxis, the last one discharging its passengers.

"Do you know where to find the Woodlands in Agates Lane?"

"No problem. Been driving a cab in these parts for ten years. I know the road. You'll have to point out the house."

"You'll have to drive me right to my front door."

"My pleasure."

When Randall got out having paid the man the amount showing on the meter with his tip, the rain was coming down in buckets. Inside, the door to the writing room was open, music playing from the sitting room as Randall took off his wet coat and hung it on the stand next to the front door before walking across the hall.

"What's in that plastic bag?"

"A girl in the pub gave me her book to read."

"Was she pretty?"

"Oh, she'd have to be pretty. Good girl, you've got the whisky out. How was today's writing? After walking the dogs I didn't want to disturb you so I walked to the Jolly Farmer. Full of people. Same old stories. There's something the matter with me, Jane. Why am I bored? It's nothing to do with you or the twins. I'm going to have to try a new book. How was Margaret Neville?"

"A lot of fun. Brought back many memories. Kimber and Raphael are settled, for now."

"The fire is nice. Are we going to eat or just drink? I've had a few. What's the matter now?"

"I don't like you being bored. The two of us are meant to be in paradise away from all the attention. We're never satisfied, Randall... I made a stew. We can eat in front of the fire when we are hungry."

"What are you doing now?"

"Reading a page. Pour yourself a drink. How did you meet this Mary Wilson?"

"She sat up at the bar next to me."

"Men. They never fail to amaze me."

Sitting in the armchair in front of the fire with his glass of whisky, Randall tried to make himself feel comfortable while the cats climbed up onto his lap watched by the dogs lying on the carpet, the music playing, his boredom going as he smiled at Jane reading from the manuscript. He was home away from the noise and chatter of other people, people who in the past he would have found amusing. Jane put the manuscript back on the coffee table without saying a word.

"Any good?"

"You tell me. She can write. English is good. Who else did you meet? Anyone interesting?"

"Not really. I prefer being here with you."

"You think he's enjoying his new school?"

"I hope so. I'm going to ask Miss Dixon, the housemistress, to find him a piano teacher."

"Makes sense. The cats look comfortable, at ease with us even though we've only just got them. It was good to get them from the cats protection place. I think we should keep their given names, don't you? Luna and Jasper. Good names. Are you really bored?"

"I'm without a story to write. One will come. *Shakespeare's Ghost* is finished. I've come to the end of their story. I hate it when I finish a book. Maybe we should watch some television."

"Whatever for? The news is always negative. Wherever in the world there's a problem they put it on the news."

"We might find a nice movie."

"And we might not. I hate watching for ten minutes and turning it off because it's no damn good. Better to listen to beautiful music."

By the time they went to bed having eaten some of the stew out of the large pot, Randall was happily plastered, falling quickly into a deep sleep. When he woke in the morning and opened the bedroom curtains it was still raining outside.

"Did the little buggers wake you during the night, Jane?"

"A couple of times for a feed. They really are so good. You want some tea?"

"Are you going to write today?"

"We'll see how things are after breakfast. Maybe write. What's on the agenda?"

"Reading Mary's book, I suppose."

"Just look at them lying in their cot. Just the look of them makes me feel content. I'm so happy. Thought I'd never have kids."

"I'll cook breakfast. Looks like it's going to rain all day. You know, in Rhodesia it didn't rain for six months. Then came the rain. My mouth feels like the bottom of a parrot cage. Oh well, no pleasure without pain. Are you really going to make the tea? Poor girl. She must be sitting on pins and needles wondering what I think of her book. I'm going to stay in bed and read her book while you write when the children are sleeping. At least the phone doesn't ring. Give me a good morning kiss. There you are. Another day, Jane. Another day."

"I'll bring up the manuscript with the tea. There's a howling wind outside instead of the noise of traffic. Did the wind blow in Rhodesia?"

"Sometimes."

After Jane went down to write in the morning room they had converted into their writing room, having eaten their breakfast in the warm kitchen, Randall took himself back to bed, wondering what a man did when he finally had everything he wanted: there was no challenge; nothing to get excited about; nothing to strive for. Feeling envious of Mary Wilson, Randall picked up her book and began to read, the pages quickly turning.

When Randall finished the third chapter propped up against the cushions, the fire had burned down in the grate. He was smiling. Not only could the girl write, she had a good story, a story of two young people enjoying their lives together. Having put more wood on the fire, Randall climbed back into bed and went back to the story, quickly oblivious of the wind and rain outside the bedroom window as he went down into Mary's rabbit hole. When Randall finished the book the only thing he could find wrong was the title. There was far more in the minds of the two leading characters than just boys and girls going out to play: they understood life with all its problems; they told each other the truth; never hid things from each other; always tried to help each other, making both of their lives worth living. Mary's book was an example for all of them to find happiness; whether people were able to behave like the characters in her book was another story. It was easier to write what they wanted but not so easy to live it.

When Jane came into the bedroom with a bowl of last night's stew, Randall was still thinking of Mary's book.

"Lunchtime, my love. Hangovers make you hungry, don't they? Did you hear Kimber crying? No? I didn't think so. It started Raphael off too. They both needed changing and feeding. Poor loves. But I managed to finish another chapter. My book is writing itself. I love being Margaret Neville. It's not too hot. Heated up just enough. Still raining. England must have the worst climate on earth. At least you kept the fire burning."

"Can you do me a favour?"

"Ask and ye shall have. Seek and ye shall find. What's the favour?"

"Read this book and tell me what you think."

"Is it any good?"

"I'm not saying a word until you've read it. Glad your book went well today. There's nothing better than a good write even though the howling disrupted you, but you would have been prepared for that. Lunch in bed. Now that's something. I'm hungry. Nothing wrong with a good stew. Good. You're smiling. Poor James Oliver. Always hell, the first days in a new school."

"How's your boredom feeling?"

"A lot better. I've been searching my mind for a new story to write."

"Anything coming?"

"Not yet. Maybe. You never know till it hits. This stew is good. Did you eat? Come and sit on the bed. I'm feeling horny. Do you mind? We must never let the twins interfere with our sex lives. I drank too much last night. You were sensible."

"Eat your lunch. Then we'll see how we go... Why do you want me to read a book written by a pretty young girl? Or is that a stupid question to ask a man?"

"We need to help other aspiring writers, Jane. And not be selfish."

"Are you after her?"

"Don't be bloody ridiculous. She wants to be famous. What is it in all of us that want to be famous? Sport. Music of all sorts. Actors. Being rich."

"We all like to show off, Randall."

"Just tell me what you really think of the book. I don't want to waste Manfred's time."

"That good?"

"See for yourself."

"And what's going to be in it for you and me? Are you really horny? Silly of me. Men are always horny. Especially when they've just met a pretty girl."

"Why do women always worry about their men? I'm not going anywhere. I've done all the running around I want to do in my life. We're a middle-aged couple, for goodness sake. Young girls aren't interested in an old goat."

"You're not an old goat. Not yet. We haven't had sex for a long time. Babies. How it works. Then nature says have another one and you're off again."

"You want another baby?"

"Why not? Now I know that I can. Just let's take it gently. When we go again it's got to be good. You want some more of that stew? Don't look at me like that. The twins are only five weeks old. Give a girl a chance. The little sweethearts tore my guts apart trying to get out. Pain, glorious pain. The pain from giving birth is the only pain worth having in life. Men never understand what us mothers go through. Give me the book. I'll read it. Manfred's always after new authors. New York seems so far away."

"Are you still hurting down there?"

"What a question, but no, it is getting better, my love. Finish your stew and give me the bowl. What are you going to do this afternoon?"

"Nothing. Absolutely nothing. That's my problem. I've done everything I ever wanted to do in life. And now we have the perfect home. What's there left to do?"

"Write another book, Randall. That's our future. Write books for the love of writing. Escape into our rabbit hole and give our readers fun. That's our future. We're writers. And always will be writers. Writers don't have to worry about getting old like sportsmen and pop stars. We flaunt our minds, not our bodies. All we need are the memories in our minds to bring our characters alive and keep our readers captivated. Strange you should find another writer in the pub. Maybe all those artists are here. Are you going to stay in bed all day or are you coming downstairs? The cats and dogs miss you. As do the children. And you could do a bit of tidying around the house."

Randall finished his stew and decided to have a nap. It was nap time. If Jane needed help cleaning the house he would leave it for another day. What was a bit of dust on the furniture anyway? No one went outside and dusted the trees. What was the difference? The trick was to lie thinking up a new book to write, in between cat naps and keep the fire in the grate burning. His mind wandered back to World's View which made him think of his father. Would his father and Bergit enjoy staying with them or would they prefer to be left alone in their own home? Randall needed more time to let his mind settle, away from other people and their problems. He wanted his mind free of the memory of other people's chatter. Was going to the Jolly Farmer such a good idea? Randall wasn't sure. Like so many other things. Did women lose interest in sex when they had babies? Only time would tell. Slowly, thankfully, Randall drifted into sleep.

When he woke, all he could remember from his dream was running through the African bush, never reaching where he wanted to go. A hope dawned in his mind. Why not write another book about Africa? Instead of living back in history with Lawrence Templeton-Smythe, he could write a modern saga. Or would his political view of today's Africa make his book politically incorrect and therefore unacceptable in today's thinking? What a life. Who was right and who was wrong? What form of government was best for the people? If you discouraged the competent with exorbitant taxes they wouldn't create a thriving economy, putting large numbers of people at the bottom of the wealth ladder out of work, making their poor lives even more miserable. So many great men, or men that people thought were great from their political rhetoric, had tried to help, few of them ever succeeding. There was always a part of society exploiting a system. Rhodesia, once considered the breadbasket of Africa, was now short of food, large numbers of its indigenous people permanently hungry, something that had never occurred when Ian Smith ran the country in the same way the British had run it as a colony. No foreigners were now interested in investing in Zimbabwe with a quasi-capitalist, indigenous-orientated government and a currency depreciating daily, making bringing hard currency into the country financial suicide. His old country was going down the financial drain and would stay down the drain despite all the talk of democracy and all its benefits. Only a few people in a country were sufficiently educated and sufficiently capable of running a successful business that created wealth for everyone. Everyone suffered when the brains were chased out of the country. Talk was talk, but talk never helped anyone. Or was his mind making excuses for the good old days of British colonialism?

The more Randall thought, the more he concluded there were few if any, solutions for the masses. That only the few grew rich in a world of greed, materialism and corruption. It made him sad. Instead of getting up and putting more wood on the fire, Randall tried to imagine what it must be like to go hungry as he drifted back into sleep, the rain still pouring down outside as the light began to fade. When Randall woke the room was dark, mirroring the turmoil of his dreams. As he lay in the dark with his hands behind his head he could think of nothing else to do other than get himself drunk. The last thing he wanted to do was write a book that got him involved in politics, making himself and his family a target for retribution. Everyone had their opinions. There was no point in shouting his mouth off. Let the Africans of Africa sort out their own problems. Who was he to tell them what to do? The world was full of politicians seeking self-gratification and always had been.

After getting up and putting on his clothes he went downstairs and into the sitting room. Jane was in her armchair in front of the fire reading the girl's manuscript. There was no music playing, no sign of the cats and dogs. Randall sat down in his armchair and stared into the fire, bored out of his tree, asking himself what the hell was the matter with him.

"Oh, what the hell."

He got up and went through to the freezer in the kitchen and filled up the ice bucket. The dogs and cats were under the kitchen table looking hungry. Randall fed the animals, and with the ice bucket, two glasses and a bottle of whisky went back into the sitting room. Jane was still absorbed in the book, not looking up. Randall poured whisky over a glass filled with ice, said cheers in his head to himself, and sat back in front of the fire. He was an old goat with a drinking problem and little else. Keeping quiet, Randall drank his whisky. Outside the wind had gone down. He looked up at the old ceiling and around the walls. Another night of drinking. Another day with a hangover.

"Better than being starving hungry."

"What did you say, Randall?"

"Nothing. Just thinking. Can I pour you a drink?"

"Why not? I'll finish her book tomorrow."

"You like it?"

"So far. She's a lucky girl."

"Aren't we all? Money, food and a nice Scotch whisky. There you go. And here we go again. What's for supper?"

"Stew, if we ever get round to it. Put on the music. Let's get comfortable."

"Did you feed them?"

"Twice. They are always hungry. Their sucking power is phenomenal. Enjoy yourself, Randall. We've got it all. We have a perfect life ahead of us. We'll never have to worry about money or other people. I made a big stew to last a few days. Who wants to cook every night? Relax, my love. The cats and dogs are happy. The twins are fast asleep. I'm happy. And nobody knows where we are so they can bug us. We can let our books talk, we don't have to shout and scream how good we are. Sure, the sales would stay high if we did but we don't need any more money. Too much money can become a burden. Even a tiny cottage somewhere in the Rocky Mountains would be just as comfortable. Peace and quiet and a companion. Now you're smiling. Put on some Mozart. A Haydn symphony. Let the music flow over us. Stop worrying about what you are going to do next. Things happen. Let your life flow... That's better. Lovely music. What's better than a warm fire, Mozart and a glass of whisky, with a meal ready if you want to eat? And later, a comfortable bed for two. You can write a book about the lucky ones like ourselves. Make life look like it's worth living. Take as long as you like to write a book. There's no hurry. Take it easy greasy you've got a long way to slide. And that's one of yours, not one of mine. Easy greasy. Where do you get them from? Mind you, you always were nuts."

"The animals will have finished their food. I'll let them in. There's something so nice about a cat asleep on your lap... I should phone Mary and tell her I've read her book."

"Leave her alone. Another day won't hurt. We've all been through it. And even if the end is as good as the beginning it doesn't mean a publisher will buy the book. The only question they ever ask themselves is whether it will sell. She's got a job as a caregiver. She has a home of her own. Let the book take its course without getting the girl over-excited."

"You always talk sense."

"Of course I do. I'm a woman. Go get the dogs. Tomorrow, with luck, you can take them for a proper long walk."

"Where are we, Jane?"

"Here. Right here. In good old England. Back to our roots. Where we came from before our families migrated to Africa and good old America."

"Some say we all migrated from Africa. That Homo sapiens evolved first in Africa."

"Does any of that matter? It's you, me, Kimber, Raphael and James Oliver."

"And the dogs."

"And the cats. Don't forget Luna and Jasper."

Randall walked to the door of the sitting room, turned the handle and whistled through the open door, bringing the dogs running. There was no sign of the cats.

"The cats are probably fast asleep under the kitchen table... Bob! Misty, stop jumping all over me... Despite what you say, I'm going to phone Mary. Can't leave the poor girl on tenterhooks. By now her mind will be going around in circles, one minute up, the next minute down, wondering what I think of her book. Can I invite her around, Jane? Not tonight. Tomorrow. Good."

Picking up his mobile, he dialled the number written on the front of the manuscript.

"Hello, Mary. It's Randall. Would you like to come round tomorrow for a cup of tea about five o'clock? The Woodlands, Agates Lane... Good. You do have a map... No, I'm not saying anything on the phone except you can relax... Okay. If that's what you want. Tomorrow at five."

"Go and get Luna and Jasper, Randall."

"She wants a drink, not a cup of tea."

"Don't we all?"

"You'll have finished her book by five o'clock tomorrow. Pussy cats. Why do they call them pussy cats?"

"Because they are covered in fur. I'll write tomorrow and then finish her book. Are you going to try and write? When you're not there your desk looks so empty."

"Would a modern, political book on Africa create a problem?"

"Why should it? We're living in England. You can say what you like. Give those new politicians a blast. All they want is power and money. Put yourself in the mind of your main character and make him live his life as a white man in South Africa after the end of apartheid. What did it mean, apartheid?"

"Separate development. The Dutch settlers who controlled the government until Mandela took over wanted the races to grow and live separately in their own communities. Now they want a rainbow nation with everyone mixed up together. The new government of Nelson Mandela can't afford to antagonise the whites as they produce ninety per cent of the government's revenue. It's a catch-22 for all of them."

"Sounds interesting. Make it into a personal story of individual people going through the change. Tell your story from both sides. You'll need black and white characters."

"Are you writing my book?"

"Just trying to help. Pour my whisky first and then go get the cats."

"Will it work?"

"What?"

"A book about today's South Africa."

"Who knows? By the time you've finished the book who knows what they will be up to? Wouldn't have been a good idea to write it if we were living in South Africa. Politics. I hate politics. I'll stick to writing about a nineteen-year-old called Margaret Neville in her search for lasting love. That's my boy. Now you've drowned the ice nicely with whisky. Tastes perfect, my love."

"Then I'll write tomorrow."

"You see? Now you have something to do. All you need in this life is a little help from your friends."

Thinking of Mary Wilson's pent-up excitement, Randall walked to the kitchen, the music flowing through the old house. The music channel had changed to Haydn, his Twenty-Eighth Symphony, one of Randall's favourites.

"Wake up, pussy cats. Come here. There we are. Do you like the music? Of course you do, you're purring. You want a bit of cold stew? Tastes nice out of the pot. You can lick my fingers. Did I tell you I'm going to write tomorrow? I'm going back to Africa. A cat on each arm. I can feel your bodies vibrate as you purr."

"What are you up to, Randall?"

"Talking to the cats."

"Put them on the carpet in front of the fire and close the damn door. There's a cold draught coming through with the door open."

"Haydn's Twenty-Eighth. I love his slow movement... Is that better? England's so cold in the winter. I'm going to enjoy living back in Africa, even if it's only in my head. I'm going to start the book at the time of Nelson Mandela's inauguration as the first democratically elected president of South Africa. You think all those people knew who they were voting for, or do they just do what they are told by the party promising them everything from free houses to free electricity? The catch is going to be delivering on all the promises. Democracy. Take from the rich and give to the poor. Nothing wrong with it. Gets heroes elected along with all their cronies. Power and money changes hands. So long as the poor benefit, it's good. Gordon Appleton, my main character, starts off the book when he has just turned forty. He can't make up his mind whether to stay in South Africa and continue running his business or take his family to England. His father was born in England so he has the right of residence. He won't be able to get his money out of South Africa because of exchange control but thinks he's still young enough to start all over again. What you think of it, Jane?"

"Write your own book. Don't ask me. How's she going to get here tomorrow?"

"Must have her own transport or she wouldn't be able to look after three old people at the same time. Are you hungry?"

"Not yet. The whisky is going down so nicely... Now, look at that. You've got a cat on your lap. I'm so enjoying this house. Wood fires in the sitting room and our bedroom... Here comes the other one... And the babies are still asleep... How did I get so lucky?"

"You got pregnant with a little help from your friend."

"Don't let your book get too involved in the politics. And never so much as think of criticising democracy or they'll nail you to the cross."

"There's nothing nicer than eating a bit of cold stew in your fingers. Cheers again. To happiness."

"To happiness, my love. And to the most beautiful thing in life: peace and quiet."

"Haydn mingling with the purr of the cats. How did we get so lucky? I wonder what they'll do with their lives? Before you can say Jack Robinson they'll be running around this very room chasing the cats and the dogs. Kids grow up so quickly. In ten years, James Oliver will be on his own way in life, the past forgotten."

"We all have to make our own lives."

"You can say that again... You want a drop more whisky?"

"Why not? Why ever not?... Can I have a cat?"

"Of course you can have a cat... There you go, my pussy cat. Purr on your mother's lap... Every country in Africa descended into turmoil at the end of colonial rule. Most ended in civil war. Their economies tanked. Let's just hope it doesn't happen to South Africa. Wouldn't like

Mandela's job for all the tea in China. Has he got the people who can help him run the country properly? Have any of them had any experience other than in politics? What can they know about the power of the financial markets; the stock markets and the currency markets? And even if they do, can they control the markets as they affect South Africa? The markets ruined Zimbabwe. My fear for South Africa is ending up the same way as Zimbabwe. Mugabe made himself popular by threatening to expropriate without compensation all the white-owned farms. But think of all those poor sods who'll end up without jobs. Running a tobacco farm requires considerable skills and experience. Ask my father. Since he left World's View, the farm has virtually collapsed. Management. Can't do anything without competent management. It's management that creates the income and pays the wages. What experience have any of the new South African cabinet had other than years in a white man's jail drumming up the anti-apartheid movement and gaining the support of overseas politicians trumpeting democracy? Will democracy last forever? Didn't last long for Oliver Cromwell, or was destroying the monarchy democracy? Is communism better? Ask the Russians. Even they say they've tossed it out of the window. Will civilisation last? I doubt it. We'll blow ourselves to pieces."

"Put it down in a book. Just don't make it boring. All people care about is themselves. Isn't that right, pussy cat? The trick now for us is not to show off our fortunes. To keep away from fame. When you've got enough, enough is enough. Maybe we should have bought a smaller house. But if we had, we'd have had other people on top of us. We wouldn't be able to hear the call of the night owls. You know what, my love? We've found paradise, away from the crowd with our kids... I need another drink. I'm pontificating. And I'm drinking too fast."

"What do you mean by pontificating?"

"Talking a load of rubbish, I suppose. The booze is talking. I'm happy. So's the cat. That's what matters. We don't need the other world anymore. That world where they tear at each other's throats to get what they want... Thank you, Randall. For everything. For the first time, I have a life... Cheers, again. To you, me and our new wonderful family... Just look at those dogs. Their eyes are smiling."

"You need some cold stew. You know the old truism: never drink on an empty stomach."

"Then it's my turn to go to the kitchen."

"We got away from the whole damn lot of them."

"That we did. It happens when you've the money. You don't need people anymore. Why are we all so damn selfish? All we ever think about is ourselves. And don't forget, I'm paying for half of this house so there's no misunderstanding as to whose place it is... You think James Oliver will learn to play the piano over there? You can hold the cat while I get the stew. Tonight is lovers' night. We're going to make another baby."

"Are you crazy?"

"You never know your luck. Got to keep my hand on the helm."

"You want to get married, don't you?"

"Whatever for? Half the marriages end in divorce, anyway. Give each other what we want. That's the way to maintain a successful relationship. You said you were horny, my love. So we'll make love. Now you really are smiling. There you go, my cat. You can both sit on his lap."

"What's the world all about, Jane?"

"You tell me. Let's just enjoy what we've got while we've still got it."

PART 4

OCTOBER TO 29TH DECEMBER 1997 – IN THE WOODS

1

---

*J*ane answered the front door at half past four, an hour after finishing Mary's book. Randall was still walking the dogs in the woods. Behind the young girl stood a yellow three-wheel scooter with a crash helmet propped on the seat.

"I'm sorry. Have I found the right place? I'm looking for Randall. Don't know his surname."

"I'm Jane. Come in. You can hang your coat on the hat stand over there. Randall's still walking the dogs."

"I'm early. Couldn't wait. I'm so jittery. Did he say anything about my book? When's he coming back? My whole mind is in a turmoil."

"Let's have a cup of tea."

"Can I have a drink? Oh, do I need a drink. Didn't sleep a wink last night wondering what he thinks. I'm sorry. Asking for a drink is rude."

"I also read your book, Mary. Just finished it in fact."

"What did you think? Is it any good? Please tell me. If it's no good just give me the manuscript and I'll go home and kill myself. I can't handle another rejection."

"We'll wait for Randall. We try not to open the bar until six o'clock. We'll go into the sitting room where the fire's burning nicely. Your manuscript is on the coffee table. Why don't we break the rules? Rules are to be broken. You drink whisky?"

"I'll drink anything at the moment. No one wants to read my books. Friends or family."

"What drives you to write, Mary?"

"An urge deep inside of me. I want to use my words to understand life. I love living in my books. The first one was rejected by eleven publishers. I hate rejection. Why I need a drink. The suspense is killing me... Why are you smiling?"

"I know how you feel, Mary Wilson."

"So you read my name!"

"That I did... They call it going down the rabbit hole. Writing and reading books. I went down your rabbit hole and know all about you. Writers tell their own story through their characters. We call it fiction. But is it? I'll get the ice and a bottle of whisky. Randall shouldn't be too long. He said you were coming at five. Are your old people cared for tonight? Randall told me how you make your money. Do you like being a caregiver?"

"It works. Gives me the time to write... Why do so many children leave their old parents on their own? They get so lonely. What they like best is telling their stories. Having someone who will listen. Sad when you have to pay to have someone listen to your stories. I love it. Gives me material for my books. That insight into human nature if you understand what I'm talking about. You don't mind my following you? I'm so jittery. Will he be long? You're smiling again."

"You'll have fun digging into human nature with all its quirks. I know just what you're talking about."

"What do you do, Jane, apart from looking after your twins and the house? Randall said you just had twins. Where are they?"

"In the writing room fast asleep. I'd just fed and changed them when you rang the bell. They're very good babies. I'm incredibly lucky from what I've been told. They should sleep for a couple of hours and then I'll start all over again."

"You have a writing room? How exciting. Can I see your twins? I'd so love to have a baby. The trouble is finding the right man."

"Don't tell me. Took me twenty years. We keep them in a carrycot so we can move them around with us. There they are. My little Raphael and my little Kimber. Be very quiet. They're sound asleep. Why I didn't move them into the sitting room."

"Two writing desks. What are those piles of pages on both of the desks? Sorry. None of my business... Oh, just look at them. They're so cute."

"Do you have a boyfriend?"

"Just transient lovers. They come and they go. Men. All they want is sex."

"We'd better get the ice from the kitchen."

"What's that noise?"

"The dogs barking. Must be Randall... Did you try and pick up Randall in the pub? He's thirty-nine, you know."

"I had no idea he was that old. Looks much younger. Of course, now I know he has you and the twins I'll look at him differently."

"Keep looking that different way, Mary. Despite what he says or does with your book."

"Is he going to do something?"

"We'll have to see."

"But what can he do other than comment on my book?"

"We have friends. Friends in America. That's the outside kitchen door... Randall. Is that you?"

"Who else is it? Misty! Bob, stop jumping all over me. You'll get fed in just a minute."

"Mary's here. We're opening the bar early. Ah, there you are. Pass me the ice bucket."

"Hello, Mary."

"What did you think of my book?"

"Let's get the drinks ready and sit by the fire in the sitting room."

"You're making me want to burst I'm so tensed up."

"Tense as a turkey on Christmas Eve. Relax, Mary. Your book is good. Why don't you ask Jane? What did you think of it, Jane?"

"Needs editing. The rest shouldn't be a problem. A bucket full of ice. Come on. The bar's opening. Let's get started."

"Where are the twins?"

"In the writing room, Randall. Fast asleep."

Not sure if a snake hadn't come into the house making Jane feel sick to her stomach, she watched them flirting with each other, Mary oozing her sex appeal. How could a woman in her fortieth year compete with a girl in her twenties? And when Mary found out who she had picked up in the pub, the game would be on. A good-looking writer desperate for a publisher would do anything to get what she wanted. Mary Wilson had the same sexual pull for men as Tracey Chapelle. Tracey had seduced Manfred Leon to get herself an agent before screwing Godfrey Merchant after keeping him on the hook to make sure he published her book. Men were so easily manipulated by sex. If what was happening right in front of her wasn't a threat to Jane's happiness it would have made her laugh. Tempted to lie and say the book was lousy, Jane sat herself down in front of the fire.

"So, did you finish reading Mary's book?"

"I did."

"And what did you think of it, Jane?"

"You go first, Randall. I'm sure your opinion is more important than mine... Thank you. A bit early in the day. But who cares? How was your walk? You'd better tell Mary who you are before the whole thing becomes ridiculous. Mary Wilson, have you heard of the writer Randall Holiday?"

"Of course I have. Is that important?"

"He's sitting next to you."

"And sitting next to you on the other side is the mother of my twins and the bestselling author of *Love in the Spring of Life* that has sold a million copies since it was launched in New York City last month. We came to England to get away from the constant attention of fame. Fame is a pain in the backside. Here, we want to live privately without anyone knowing who we are. Jane also wrote the film script for Tracey Chapelle's novel *Lust*. Why we could afford this house. If we help you with your book, please don't take advantage of us. We want to write our books in peace without the constant attention of the media. I told you in the pub beware of the fame. And yes, your book is good. You create pictures with your words that come alive to the reader. It's a strange gift that Manfred Leon will recognise immediately. You create real pictures instantly in the reader's head. Manfred is our literary agent in New York, the only person in America who knows Jane's new phone number. How Amanda found us here before she died of breast cancer, leaving behind my son James Oliver who I've put into boarding school. If you so wish, I can send Manfred a copy of your book."

"You're both kidding me. This is totally ridiculous. Give me back my manuscript and I'll get the hell out of the way. Getting my leg pulled like this is worse than eleven rejection letters. The chances of chatting up Randall Holiday in the Jolly Farmer are the same as being struck by lightning and attacked by a white shark all at the same time. Why are you both making fun of me? All I wanted you to do was read my book and tell me honestly what you thought of it. Why do people always lie? I hate people who lie."

"Your manuscript is right in front of you on the coffee table if you want to go. Luck sometimes comes to us, Mary. We're not lying. Jane, what did you think of her book? Am I wrong? I don't think so. You're smiling. Tells me you agree."

"Do you have a copy of one of your books with your face on the back cover?"

"No, I don't, Mary. I avoided putting my face on the back cover."

"How can I be certain this isn't a joke?"

"I tell you what. Jane, take Mary to our writing room and turn over the pages I wrote this morning and let her read. Have you read any of my books, Mary?"

"I've read most of Randall Holiday's books."

"Then read in my handwriting what I wrote before I walked the dogs. You'll see. All writers have their own signature. Take her through while I enjoy my whisky."

"It's bizarre."

"Life's bizarre, Mary. Go on. Tell me what you think of the first four pages of my new book. And when you've done that, you can read what Jane wrote today. It's all on our desks... Oh, I've got it. You think I'm after you. Well, I'm not. Jane and I are happy for the first time in our lives. If we help you, Mary, I want one promise that you must always keep. Don't mention our surnames ever again. Forget this house and who lives in it. Have you got the message?"

"I'll bet neither of you write books."

"Go and have a look while I turn on the classical music channel. You can trust us with your book if we can trust you to keep our privacy. Read, Mary. Let our writing prove to you who we are. And when you go out of the room, shut the door. The draught is freezing. And don't wake the twins. Cheers, Mary Poppins. Your luck is in. The best books in the world often don't get published because it is impossible for an unknown author to find a publisher. And don't swallow your whisky like that all at once. Off you go. Have fun. This morning was a good start to my new book, of that I'm certain."

"Don't you have a passport?"

"I do. But it says I'm Randall Crookshank. Holiday is the name I write under. Go and read. Let my writing talk, not my name. It's a strange, strange world, Mary Poppins. You never know what's coming next. Oh, and you might have to go to America. To use your good looks to promote your book. As Manfred says: it's all in the marketing once you've found a good book. There are always tricks when it comes to making money."

"I'm beginning to believe you."

"Why on earth would I bother to lie to you? I'm not looking to seduce a pretty young girl. I have my life partner in Jane. For the first time in both our lives, we have found happiness. And peace. This new home next to the woods is our paradise. I have no wish to destroy it. Both Jane and I have been through all that crap. Every now and then in life, we have that piece of luck that changes everything for the better. Monday in the pub was your lucky day if Manfred likes your book, finds you a publisher and the book sells."

Giving Randall a smile of relief, Jane walked Mary through to the writing room and watched her sit down at Randall's desk and turn over the written pages. The fire had gone down. Carefully, Jane picked up the carrycot and took her babies back to join Randall.

"She's reading."

"Don't worry about her, Jane. I'm not after her."

"You were flirting."

"All men smile at pretty girls. What did you really think of her book?"

"It's good. Very good."

"What I thought. Can't waste that kind of stuff by throwing it down the drain. Have a drink, Jane. Relax. I'm cooking tonight. A nice sauce on a pile of spaghetti."

"Are we inviting her to supper?"

"No, we are not. If she wants, I'll give her Manfred's address so she can send him a copy of her manuscript and mention my name. That's the easier way. It's you and me around the fire with a nice couple of whiskies. If she goes to America she can stay with Tracey."

"You think Manfred will go for it?"

"Who knows? I'll tell her to send him her photograph. That should help. Why are you grinning?"

"Men. They never change."

"Worked for Tracey. And for Manfred. In the end, he made a bloody fortune out of Tracey Chapelle. And as we say, in the end, it's always about the money."

"There's still some of Monday's stew left. You don't have to cook."

"Marvellous. The runaway couple."

"Did you enjoy writing today?"

"Never been happier... What happened to the cats and the dogs? Never mind... And the music plays. You think Mary can play the piano? She could teach James Oliver during the school holidays. I enjoyed my write, enjoyed my walk and I'm enjoying my drink. What more can an old goat like me ask for? And best of all, the wolves have stopped howling."

"Be careful with her."

"Always be careful, Jane. Maybe half a dozen photographs for Manfred. That should get his full attention."

"You think he'll want to sleep with her?"

"Who knows? Probably. Probably not. But what he'll see from the photographs is an opportunity to promote the book. Put her on talk shows. Let her smile at the people. Then they'll buy her book."

Relaxed for the first time since opening the door to Mary, Jane sat back with her drink and listened to the music, time slipping gently by. When Mary opened the door, the dogs pushed past her into the room.

"Wow. Can you two write. Makes me realise I'm not as good as I think I am. I believe you. You're telling me the truth. Can't have two manuscripts in different handwriting in the same room as good as what I just read without it being the truth. That would be just as crazy... Oh, look at that. A piano. Didn't see it before, I was so tense. Do you mind if I play? If you don't like how I play you can turn up the volume on your music channel. So, where do I go from here? We'll need to copy the book. I can do the posting once I know where to send it. It's my lucky day. I love a big grand piano. Do either of you play? How does that sound? Johann Sebastian Bach. My grandmother was a music teacher. She gave me my passion for the arts. Sorry. Better stop. Can't compete with a symphony orchestra. Thank you, Randall Holiday. This is my last drink or I won't be able to drive myself home. Can't afford to be picked up for drinking over the limit and lose my driver's licence. Those poor old people would be devastated. Thank you. Cheers, both of you. You make South Africa sound so wonderful. Africa. I'd love to visit Africa. And Jane, your Margaret Neville is a very lucky girl to find love so young. Never found it myself. All the men ever wanted from me was sex."

"Is your grandmother still alive?"

"No, Randall. She died last year. I miss her so. She was my inspiration. Why do you ask?"

"We need a piano teacher for James Oliver. To hopefully take his mind off the death of his mother."

"I can teach him! How old is he? It'll be a little payback for helping me to find a publisher. You really think this agent of yours will do the trick? All that waiting. Down the hatch. Got to go. Love the dogs. Thank you, both of you. What are you writing down, Randall?"

"There you are. Manfred's address. Mention my name. I'll write him a separate letter. Now, make the promise to never mention who we are."

"I promise. Cross my heart and hope to die... How long will it all take?"

"We'll just have to see. Patience, Mary. Good luck. If James Oliver wants to learn how to play piano, I'll come back to you. I've written down your phone number. Ride your scooter home safely. I'll see you to the front door. My word, you certainly know how to play the piano. Your grandmother must have been good."

"She was. It's so sad when people die. Your poor son. Goodnight, Jane. Enjoy the rest of your whiskies around that lovely fire. I envy your peace as much as the fame you've run away from. What a strange life we all lead. When you don't have it you want to be rich and famous. Then you get what you want and it drives you crackers. I'm going to try and love being famous. I can feel it."

"First you have to get famous."

"That's true, Jane. Keep my fingers crossed. Tonight has been quite an experience. Anyway, my old people are fine. Not a beep. What would we do without these new-fangled mobile phones? Can I pat the dogs? From the bottom of my heart, I thank both of you. Now it's life in the fast lane. I can feel it coming."

"Close the door behind you, Randall."

Alone with only the music, the dogs and the fire and the sleeping twins, Jane sipped at her whisky as she looked across the room at the piano. Would good-looking Mary teaching James Oliver be a good thing? Only time would tell. The idea had put her nerves back on edge as the minutes ticked by.

When Randall returned he was smiling.

"Did you tell her to send the photographs?"

"Of course. Either do a job properly or don't do it at all. When I write to Manfred, will you add a note saying you also like the book?"

"Why don't we phone him? You can tell him you've finished writing *Shakespeare's Ghost*. That you've started another book: we both owe a lot to Manfred Leon. Come and sit down. Let's sit quietly and enjoy our drinks. Just the two of us. What's the weather like outside?"

"It's drizzling. The English climate is lousy."

"We should have gone to live in your beautiful Africa."

"And ended up tortured by politics? I'll be in Africa in my book. What's the matter, Jane?"

"That girl's far too good-looking."

"Stop worrying. I'm not after her. Sure, she flashed it a bit. All women flash it when they want something."

"That's what worries me. We're not even married, for goodness sake."

"But we're happy. That's what counts. There are many girls like Mary. I've been through far too many of them. Done all that. It's brief, sexual satisfaction and then nothing. You and I have a life together in our house by the woods. Who wrote *A House by the Lake*? After you've finished with Margaret Neville you can write *A House by the Woods*. How does that idea sound? It's so nice sitting together in the same room writing our books. How's your whisky? A little more ice and a little more whisky. Forget Mary Poppins. We have a perfect evening ahead of us even if we do eat cold stew. Why cook when you don't have to?... Who's the composer of this lovely music?"

"I have absolutely no idea. You'd better check the TV set. I like the way we don't have the TV set staring at us all the time."

"Schubert. It's Schubert. I love the music channels. I've learned to love so many composers. Listening to music is far more rewarding than watching a movie... Are you glad she's gone home?"

"I'm afraid I am."

"Not only can the girl write, she can play the piano. She'll be home by now. She's only around the corner. It's going to change her life finding a publisher. Let's hope it's for the better. Oh, how I'd love to go outside again on World's View and look up at the stars. You could see three layers of stars. Follow the direction of the Southern Cross. Good old Africa as it was for those good old colonial masters who lived like feudal barons in the last gasp of the British Empire. Feudal barons. That's what we were. And then they kicked us out for stealing their country. But as they say in the classics: nothing lasts forever. Are they better off without us? Probably. Who wants some white foreigner telling you what to do? Oh, but was it good while it lasted, Jane. But never mind. There's nothing wrong with what we have at the moment."

"Except the weather."

"Doesn't matter when we sit in front of that lovely log fire away from the television. It can rain all night outside for all I care. At least it didn't rain when I walked the dogs."

"What did you two talk about? You were gone a good ten minutes."

"Are you back again worrying about me and Mary Poppins? We talked about her book. All writers have no idea how good their books are. They have to be told by their readers. She wanted self-assurance and I gave it to her."

"How old is she?"

"Twenty-four. I asked her."

"Oh, you did, didn't you?"

"Please don't write a sentence like that in your book... The previous owners knew how to live in this house we love so much. Even put the TV on a trolley. TV on wheels."

"Did you talk about anything else?"

"We did, as a matter of fact. She wanted to know why you weren't wearing a wedding ring. I told her about my two previous failed marriages. When we settle down I'm going to bring Douglas here for a holiday. To join his half-brother and the twins. I don't care what Meredith does. He's my son and I have the right to see him."

"Maybe he'll want to leave his mother and the money-grabbing Clint and come and live with us. That would be fun. How old is Douglas?"

"He's four. Next year he'll go into school. We could put him into the Cranleigh Prep School as a dayboy. The two of them at the same school. Give James Oliver a brother to look after. Would you really like to look after four of them?"

"Why ever not? The more the merrier. Who knows, I might have got myself pregnant last night. You really were horny."

"Are we doing it again tonight?"

"And tomorrow. And the next day. This is Camelot where everything is perfect. How did she react to us not being married?"

"Gave me an odd look and changed the subject back to her book... He'd love the cats and the dogs. I don't like that Clint. All he wanted was my money when he found out Meredith and I were married in community of property; that there was no prenuptial contract. She was a fool to fall for him. But he was young. Some women prefer young, good-looking men. Not an old goat pushing forty. All I worry about is Douglas. Clint's influence on Douglas. If your stepfather got his money without working for it himself it sets a bad example. I'm going to write to Manfred. Put my review of Mary's book in writing. You can talk to your wonderful agent on the phone. Ask him to pay you a fat royalty cheque before someone runs off with your money. You must remind Manfred to have your sales audited every six months, to keep your publishers on the straight and narrow. You have to make people stay honest in this crooked world. Only the publishers know the exact number of sales. Many of them cheat their authors so they can also cheat the tax man and keep overseas sales in an offshore bank account. If it wasn't for Manfred we'd never be certain how many books we have sold. It's in the agent's interest to make sure his authors get paid properly. Everyone is after the money. They'd steal their grandmother's pension if they got the chance. Heard about that once. What a lovely world. I need another slosh of whisky to cover the ice in my glass. Stop worrying, Jane. We're past all that crap. It's just you and me, and peace and quiet. You want another slosh of whisky? No. I'm having another. Why not have one later then?"

"I do have to be careful, Randall, the babies."

"I know but we can still enjoy a few. Cheers, Janey. To many more happy days. Let the world go round without us. Let's not bother to watch the news and worry about other people's problems. We are so lucky to be financially secure. We'll always be able to pay the bills, thanks to our readers. And if readers get pleasure from reading what we write for them it's a fair exchange. Do you miss America?"

"Of course I do. It was my home not even a month ago. But I'll go where you want to go, my love. And yes, I'm glad we're away from the constant prying of the media. Being pushed at them by my publicist. Like you, it drove me crackers constantly having to smile at people. You called it arse creeping whatever arse creeping means."

"Just doing their jobs. You can't blame them. All you can do is get the hell out of their way. I hate interviews and talk shows. But that's life. How it works. Readers like to know their authors. Who wrote them their stories... It's Schubert's 'Rosamunde'. So beautiful. I'd love to thank Schubert for giving me his music. But he's long dead, so he doesn't have to worry about me interfering in his life along with a million other people."

"I'm going to phone Miss Dixon and ask her to find James Oliver a music teacher."

"You do that, Jane."

"Then we don't need Mary coming into this house."

"Probably. School holidays are long. What's James Oliver going to do when it's raining?"

"Watch television. Read a book. There are lots of lovely kids' books for a boy almost eleven. Let him live in their fantasy world. Don't they play sports in the school holidays?"

"I don't think so."

"When did you last speak to Meredith, Randall?"

"Not since we broke up. We could get Mary to play Johann Sebastian Bach."

"Shut up, my love. You're teasing me... Are we ready for the stew?"

"I don't think so. This whisky is finding just the spot... We could have a bottle of wine with the stew."

"We should really watch our drinking."

"Whatever for? Provided it doesn't interfere with tomorrow's writing. Gordon Appleton is talking to me right now in the book in the back of my head."

"Margaret Neville chirps every now and again. You know we are nuts."

"Stark raving bonkers. It's a writer's paradise, this house by the woods... Thank you, Schubert. What a lovely ending. I'll listen for that piece of music time and again... Red or white? If it's red I'd better open the bottle to let the wine breathe. Red it is."

Smiling happily, Randall walked across to the cocktail cabinet. There he took out a bottle, fitted the corkscrew and popped the cork out of the neck.

"There's nothing more satisfying than the sound of a cork coming out of a bottle, Jane. I love pulling corks... More lovely music. And the night goes on... Are we really going to make love tonight? Making love is as beautiful as listening to music. More beautiful. The ultimate pleasure in paradise, my lovely Jane. I'm so happy when you smile at me like that. Makes me all warm inside... Do I hear the sound of a baby? They're awake. It's a happy gurgle mingling with the music. They'll grow up to have our same love and passion for classical music. I'll bring them closer to the fire so I can smile at them."

"Everything has happened so quickly. My life has completely changed. From an apartment in Manhattan, chasing the launch of my book to giving birth, to being here with my children in the quiet of the English countryside. All in the blink of an eye... Whilst you keep an eye on them, I'll pop the stew in the microwave and when it's ready, place the pot on the coffee table next to that nice bottle of wine with those beautiful crystal wine glasses. A couple of bowls and a couple of spoons.

And there's some crusty bread to go with it. I like having everything ready. Love and companionship without any stress or argument. Every girl's hope. Every girl's dream. Will we always be happy?"

"Of course we will. You girls worry too much. Sit where you are. I'll go and get it all ready." A short while later, Randall returned with everything on a tray, the stew pot steaming, and added another log to the fire.

"We were so lucky to get the house with everything in it. Don't have to go out and buy anything. Those wine glasses look expensive. Poor man. Wanted to walk away from his happy memories. You pick up a wine glass your dead wife once drank from and it makes you desperately lonely. You think he's happier being away from this house? Makes you think about life. At least he was lucky to be one of the few with a truly happy marriage. Third time lucky, Randall, not that we're going to be married. He even left behind all those trinkets on the shelves. I'm so looking forward to writing tomorrow."

"Hold your horses, Jane. Back in a minute. Just getting the salt and pepper pot. And I'll close the door. You know, it never got cold on World's View."

With the door shut and left alone with her babies, Jane wondered how long it would really last. Were they fooling themselves? Trying to convince themselves? Trying to believe there was such a thing as permanent happiness? As she stared into the fire, Jane's mind drifted far away. She was alone in the clouds. Nothing more than herself. Lost in her spirit as she drifted further and further up into the ether to that place of permanent loneliness. She struggled desperately to hold back the tears.

"Are you all right, Jane? You look weird."

"I was far away above the clouds."

"You were up in heaven!"

"It didn't feel like heaven."

"You're shuddering. You want me to hug you?"

"I'll be fine. I'm back here again. Back with you and my babies."

"And a nice pot of your stew. I'll dish it out and pour us each a glass of wine. Then maybe we'll drink a whisky or two... How does that feel?"

"Much better. There's nothing more comforting than the hug of a lover."

"The only way to enjoy life is to live in the present. Don't let your mind drift away into the universe where we may not have come from. I always wonder where life began. People who believe in religion say God made man: there we weren't and there we were. The scientists say we evolved and came out of the sea. But nobody is really certain. One of my old school friends was convinced we arrived in a spacecraft from another planet. There's so much confusion. Will we ever know? Does it matter? All we really do is pass our genes down from generation to generation. Maybe some disease will wipe us out. A deadly virus. But now, here, on our couch in front of that fire with a nice glass of wine, food in front of us on the table, our job in life is to enjoy our lives and leave tomorrow to take care of tomorrow. You mustn't worry, Jane, about what might happen. All you do is get yourself worked up for no real reason. I have no idea what kind of lives Kimber and Raphael are going to have. They'll have to find out for themselves. Yes, because of our money, they'll each have a good private education and know that when their parents die they will inherit lots of money, provided someone in the meantime hasn't stolen it. But will they be happy? That's up to them. Like the two of us now. Stop worrying about the future where neither of us can be certain of what's coming and just enjoy our evening together."

"She'll do anything to get what she wants."

"It's Manfred she must go after, not me. I've done my part. Or will have done when I post Manfred my letter. After that, there's nothing more I can do for the girl and she'll know it. If Manfred responds positively, they'll have to take it to the next level which will have nothing to do with me. If she teaches James Oliver to play that piano over there all she will have done is return a favour. I know you went through a lot in your life. More than most people. Relax now and enjoy. Are you feeling better?"

"Will they leave us alone?"

"Probably not. The press have a habit of finding what they want. For now, we're out of their way. Incognito as they say."

"Why is life always so transient?"

"How it works. One minute New York City, the next minute, if you're lucky, a house by the woods."

"And the same goes on."

"Hopefully. We have to hope. If we didn't hope there would be little point in life. Peace and hope. Let's hope they grow up strong and healthy. We must hope for our babies, Jane. Not worry about things that may never happen. Just look at those little eyes smiling up at us. They are so beautiful."

Instead of drinking the wine sitting in front of them, Randall topped up his glass with more whisky and silently raised his whisky glass to the heavens. An hour later, the twins began to grizzle. Going to the kitchen to heat up bottles she had previously prepared with expressed milk, Jane returned, each of them feeding a baby. Finally, both babies were changed and settled back in their carrycot next to the coffee table. The music played on. The drinking went on for Randall, for Jane more slowly. When Randall got up to put more wood on the fire, he tripped over the carpet, making them both giggle. By the time they took the babies with them and went up to bed they were tiddly. Both holding a side of the carrycot, when they reached the stairs they went up sideways, concentrating on not dropping the twins. Safely in their bedroom, Jane tucked up the sleeping babies in the cot in the corner of the room and climbed up into the big double bed. Remembering her promise, Jane tried to arouse Randall by gently feeling the back of his neck. Instead of turning to her, Randall fell fast asleep, any thought of lovemaking destroyed by the drink.

On her back in the dark, Jane listened to the wind howling outside the bedroom window, a branch of a tree just touching the panes of glass. She couldn't sleep despite the wine and whisky. All they had done was talk and drink as Randall tried to convince her they were having a perfect evening. Was her life going to be a permanent game of writing in the morning and drinking in the evening? As the alcohol seeped out of her system, the worry returned. She would phone Manfred in New York when she finished her writing, by which time Manfred would have gone to his office. Randall was right: she wanted that royalty money in her American bank account so that whatever happened with Randall she would not have to worry about money. She would pay Randall half the price of the house and invest in a mix of equity funds to make sure she held on to her money, the thought of having her own money calming Jane's nerves. He was right: in the end, it was all about the money, never running out of money, never having to rely on other people. Slowly, quietly, with Randall snoring gently beside her, Jane fell asleep and went into her dreams, happy dreams that lasted into the morning when she woke with the first sign of daylight coming through from behind the drawn curtains over the windows. The wind had gone down, the branch of the tree no longer tapping on the outside of the window. Next to her, with his back to Jane, Randall was silently fast asleep. Jane got out of bed and checked on her babies. It was cold in the room, the fire having long gone out. Stacking a pile of newspaper and small pieces of wood in the grate, Jane relit the fire. Luckily for the day's writing she was thinking of Margaret Neville's story, which eased her worries. Jane got back into bed and tried to sleep. If her babies had been awake, she would have brought them into the bed and fed them from her breasts. There was plenty of milk. When she woke there was no sign of Randall, and then she heard the toilet flushing. Both babies were awake. Jane brought them up into the bed one at a time and began feeding them, exquisitely happy with the suckling feeling on both of her breasts.

"You want some tea? How long have you been feeding them? I was as sick as a dog in the toilet. What dreams. I was in a spacecraft among the planets staring at the great universe. How are you feeling? I drank too much last night... Did we make love?"

"No, we didn't."

"Better give the booze a break for a couple of days. I'm not going to write today. Too hungover. Oh, well. Can't win all the time. Did we leave the dogs in the sitting room? They'll crap on the carpet. Never mind. All part of the game. I'd better go downstairs and let them out, including the cats... Now look at that. I draw the curtains and outside the sun is shining. Good girl, Jane. You relit the fire. And here we are again."

2

*B*y Christmas Eve Jane was so tense she was about to explode. Whenever she told James Oliver what to do he gave her a loveless look and said, "You are not my mother." Douglas cried most of the time and was permanently miserable. Trying to be a surrogate mother just did not work. The pleasure of suckling her babies had gone now the twins drank from milk bottles. Margaret Neville had long run out of her head and would not come back again: her second book was dead in its track. And to make her day, as she tried to prepare for Christmas with little or no help from anyone, and despite initially saying they wouldn't engage Mary Wilson, she arrived to give James Oliver his music lesson. The two of them together were as happy as a pair of crickets. Randall was out walking the dogs, and the fun had not yet begun. All Jane ever seemed to do was cook the food, make the beds and clean the rooms. For all intents and purposes, she was a skivvy looking after Randall and his family. Jane's only consolation was the royalty cheques pouring into her New York bank account. Should she invest in half of the Woodlands? Jane was no longer certain, despite Randall's constant assertion that everything in their relationship was perfect. With the sound of the dogs barking and the discords from the piano putting her teeth on edge, Jane tried to face up to the new day. What else could she do? What was the alternative? Next February she was turning forty and no one other than Randall gave a damn about her life. For two months they had both stopped drinking to avoid damaging their systems and jeopardising the children, making Jane feel worse in herself rather than better.

"Dogs! Come here. Stop jumping all over the furniture. They loved their walk in the woods, Jane. Is something wrong? You look flustered. How's the music lesson going? Hello, Mary Poppins. Happy Christmas for tomorrow. Hit the right bloody note, James Oliver. I know, I know, you're learning. Have you heard from Manfred? By the look, the answer is no. Patience, Mary. If he wasn't trying something with your book he would have sent you back the manuscript. I love that Christmas tree. All the tinsel and decorations. I'm so excited Dad and Bergit are coming for Christmas. We're going to be one big family. Lucky I wrote early this morning before the piano lesson started. What's for lunch? I'm starving. Saw the squirrels and a rabbit. You should have come with me, Jane."

"And you would have done the housework."

"I've told you we can employ servants. As many as it takes."

"We wanted our privacy. That was the whole idea of coming to England."

"Sometimes you have to change your ideas. Today is Christmas Eve. Tonight I'm going to have a drink. You want to stay for a drink, Mary? Good, Jane, now you're smiling. Tonight is whisky night. Where's Douglas?"

"In his room sulking."

"What did you say to him this time?"

"I told him to cheer up. Did more harm than good. There's something wrong with that boy."

"He must miss his mother."

"I don't think so. He doesn't want to go home."

"Then what's his problem?"

"I have absolutely no idea. Three months ago I didn't have children to look after. Now I've got four of them. Dogs, stop jumping on the furniture. It's going to rain."

"It always rains in England. Come and give the old goat a kiss. Already forty! Time marches on. Anyone want some tea? I'll make the tea. How's that for a kiss, Jane? Are you feeling better? Christmas in good old England. I can't believe it. Africa's a million miles away were it not for Gordon Appleton. You must start writing again, Jane. James Oliver. Hit the right key for once. Don't you like learning to play the piano?"

"Sometimes I don't, Dad!"

"Kids. They're worse than my publicist for driving me nuts. Jane, sit by the fire while I go to the kitchen and make us some tea."

"Can I stop playing?"

"You can do what you like for all I'm concerned. I'm just your father."

"James Oliver, you are doing just fine. I'm a good teacher. A moment ago, we were having fun. Try to enjoy yourself. When you get through the gap and find how easy it really is you'll be over the moon. I had your same problem to start with. Were it not for my grandmother's constant encouragement I wouldn't be able to play Chopin and Bach. It's such a thrill getting it right. All I hope at the moment is I got it right with my book. The suspense is killing me. Now, young man, let's try again. Both hands on the keyboard... There you go. You got it. You hit the right key."

Not sure if Mary Wilson the aspiring author wasn't pandering to Randall rather than James Oliver, Jane plonked herself down in her chair in front of the fire and tried not to think. A cat climbed up on her lap making her stroke the animal's fur. Away to the side, the piano lesson went on. With her foot, Jane pulled the small trolley with the TV towards the fire and turned on the set, bringing up the same old rubbish on the daily news. With Mary frowning at her across the sitting room, Jane turned off the television, her mind racing again, the idea of getting drunk making her smile. In her mind she went through the menu for tomorrow's Christmas lunch, telling herself to stuff the turkey first thing in the morning. Maybe a servant would help if she could find someone who didn't get on her nerves. But now being now, she'd ask Randall to peel the potatoes and cut up the vegetables. For a brief second, Margaret Neville flashed through her mind, making Jane sit up with excitement, a flow of pleasure calming her down, the piano no longer quite so annoying. She was the reason for feeling unhappy, not Randall or his two sons. With the same foot, Jane pushed away the television and smiled at the flickering flames of the fire.

When the tea arrived, the piano lesson stopped. Jane went upstairs and asked Douglas to come down and have his tea. The small boy took her hand as they walked down the stairs. Back in the sitting room, in front of the fire, Jane drank her tea and watched the two of them flirting as her mind wandered back into her book and the mind of Margaret Neville. Maybe she would buy half of the house after all. It is what she said she would do. Were they flirting or was it the usual prattle of light conversation, trivial talk without any meaning? Maybe the day after tomorrow, with Randall happy talking to his father and stepmother, she'd sneak into the writing room, close the door against the sound of people's voices, read back the beginning of her last chapter and find herself back in her book, the only place where she found true entertainment free from her worries. When the phone rang it brought her back into the room, Randall looking at her with a question mark written on his face.

"Who the hell can that be, Jane, on your mobile?"

"Must be Manfred wishing us a happy Christmas. He's the only one I know with the number... Hello, Jane Slater speaking... And a happy Christmas to you, Manfred... I'll tell Randall. He's waving. Mouthing you a happy Christmas. How's New York?... Oh, we're loving England. Had a bit of a writing block the last few weeks but today there was a glimmer of hope. The main character came back into my head. And thank you, Manfred, for paying all that money into my bank account. You did take your commission?... Of course you did... Thanks for the call... A merry Christmas to you and a happy new year... Yes, I'll send you the manuscript when I've finished the book... No, Randall's not been having a problem. His new book is writing well... What did you think of Mary Wilson's book?... You did, didn't you? Sounds good. What kind of an advance are they talking about?... Sounds reasonable. How's my book selling?... Wow. And the money flows in... Of course you can come here for a visit. You're our literary agent... Bye."

When Jane put down her phone she had hope that life wasn't as bad after all as she thought it was. Mary was looking at her with popping eyes. They were all silent.

"Go on then. What did he say?"

"A fifty-thousand-dollar advance, Randall, but he's asking for a hundred thousand."

"Is the publishing certain?"

"Nothing's certain until it happens, Mary. You know that. But it looks good for you. Come and sit by the fire. Randall, let's open the bar. Life's not all bad. And yes, let's look for a house servant, someone who's quiet. She can live in the attic and relieve me of my daily chores. I'll go and get the ice and the glasses from the kitchen. Douglas, come here. Give Aunty Jane a hug. There we are. Why don't I turn on the music channel?"

"Or I can play the piano. I'm so excited. It worked. I'm going to be a famous author. Well, at least I hope so. My poor old people. They are going to miss my daily check-ups. Chopin. I'm going to play you a Chopin nocturne. His music is so dreamy. My grandmother would be over the moon for me. Maybe she knows. What a lovely thought. How does that sound?"

Jane watched the back of the girl as Mary sat at the piano playing her music, the notes gentle against the crackling sound of the fire. To Jane's amazement, Douglas was smiling, no longer looking his miserable self. She felt joy for Mary about to become a published author, a privilege that came to so few of them. When the nocturne came to an end everyone in the room was smiling. Randall got up and went to the cocktail cabinet as Mary stood up from the piano stool and came over to sit in front of the fire. Jane went through to the kitchen and brought back the ice bucket full of ice with three whisky glasses she kept with the others in the kitchen cupboard, along with two glasses of juice for the boys. Randall smiled at her and held up the whisky bottle.

"Let the bar be open. Whisky on the rocks. Cheers Jane. Cheers, Mary. And to your future success. And to James Oliver's future success as a pianist."

"And me, Dad. What am I going to be?"

"For the moment a small boy, Douglas."

"I want to be a writer. How much is a hundred thousand dollars?"

"You're too young, son, to know about money... There we go. The music channel. Beethoven's Third Symphony. Three o'clock is a bit early to open the bar. We can call a taxi to take you home, Mary, so you won't have to drive your three-wheel scooter. To your book, young lady. Down the hatch... Now let's have another one. James Oliver, why don't you take your brother for a walk in the woods after you've finished your drink? The dogs would love it. Make sure you both wrap up warmly and take an umbrella. So far it hasn't started to rain. Tomorrow you're going to see your grandfather. We're a family again. One big family... Misty. Bob, go with the boys. Up you get. Off that carpet. The cats can stay."

"When will I get my advance from Manfred Leon?"

"As soon as possible, hopefully. Who knows? Before you know it you'll be running around America doing a book tour and giving yourself that fame you crave for. Just be careful. Life is never a bed of roses. There are always consequences. Good and bad... When we get hungry, we can all eat in the kitchen where it's warm. The fire's not burning in the dining room. We're at it again, Jane. We're back on the booze. How's your whisky going down?"

"Like nectar. The drink of the Gods. The twins will need their next feed in an hour or two, so we're good for now."

"And it all started for you, Mary, by walking into the Jolly Farmer. Let's all drink to the luck of life. Good old Manfred. I told him your book was good. So did Jane. You never know. The next minute you'll be living in America."

"In the fast lane."

"The very fast lane. But you're young. At twenty-four, they enjoy the fast and the furious. I'm forty. I can barely believe it. Life goes by so quickly once you turn thirty. To many more books, Mary Wilson. May you never stop writing. May none of us here ever stop writing. May we never find that void. To the fast and the furious and the runaway couple. Jane and I both remember all that running around. Enjoy it while you can. Be careful with your money when you make it. Invest and give yourself a lifetime of financial security so that writing becomes a pleasure rather than a necessity. Life can be cruel if you don't have money to buy yourself out of the shit. Get yourself packed and ready to fly yourself to America."

"I must look for another caregiver for my old people. I'm going to miss them. I'd hate to get old. Must be sad to slowly grind to a halt. No one cares about old people unless they are paid to do so. In my next book, I'm going to include an old woman as one of my characters and tell what I learned from my old people. This whisky is tasting so good. I'm so happy. I could have spent my entire life looking after old people and just making a living. Exciting men wouldn't have looked at me. Now I have a chance to find a husband with something to show for his life, not someone you struggle with to pay the bills for yourselves and your children. I will never forget either of you for as long as I live. I will always remember that night I went into the Jolly Farmer. Eleven rejection letters for the first book and then this. What's America like? It always sounds so big. Those great big cities. Do you mind if I have another whisky? I want to celebrate. My life has started, thanks to you, Randall."

"It wasn't all about me. First, you had to write a good book. James Oliver can still learn the piano at school. Or we'll find him another teacher in the village. I look forward to watching your fame blossom. Just one thing, Mary. Please do me a favour and change the name of your book."

"How about *Go Get It, Sheila*. Short and sharp as you suggested. A bit Australian. Anyway, we'll see. Your Manfred will guide me. What's he like?"

"He likes good-looking young girls."

"Does he, Jane? Why doesn't that surprise me? Thank you, Randall. Happy days are here again. And having to pay for a taxi to get me home doesn't bother me anymore. I'm rich.

How do they pay you?"

"Straight into your bank account."

"I can't believe it. Gets better and better. Give me a moment. I want to phone my old people and check on them before I get myself drunk. You're so lucky, Jane, to have someone to love you. To have those beautiful twins. I hope I'll be so lucky... Hello, Mrs Scott. How are you?... That's fine. Sleep well tonight... One down. Two to go... Mr Collander. It's me. Is everything well?... Have a happy Christmas. I'll be thinking of you... Mrs Barker. It's Mary. Just checking on you... You're fine?... Love to you as well... There we are, folks. No problems. Must be Christmas. It's so easy to dial when you have their numbers on your mobile. I love this music. Beethoven. And all my dreams have come true. Everything in my world is rosy."

When the Beethoven symphony finished Randall turned off the music channel on the television and nodded to Mary. The boys were still walking the dogs in the light rain. The twins were lying in their bouncy cradles, the cats asleep on the floor next to them. Jane watched Mary adjust herself on the piano stool, her foot close to the pedals, her hands above the ivory keys. Quietly, the music began. No one said a word as they listened to the music.

Later, when James Oliver and Douglas came back from their walk, it was five o'clock in the evening, time for Jane to prepare the evening meal and feed the animals. She was content, no longer worried that Mary was interested in Randall other than as a friend. Life made Jane smile: when they had what they wanted there was no point in using people anymore to achieve their ends. The way Mary now looked at Randall had nothing to do with sex appeal. With a bit of luck, Mary Wilson would soon be in America and no longer a threat to Jane's peace and tranquillity in their house by the woods.

When the taxi arrived to take Mary home, Randall and Mary were happily tipsy, the boys fast asleep upstairs in their bedroom.

"I'll come back tomorrow and pick up my scooter but I won't come in. Thank you all for a lovely evening. You think Manfred will phone me for my bank account number? Good. I can't wait to go to America."

Alone around the fire with the cats, the dogs and the twins, Jane's life of perfection came back to her. Randall topped up his glass and touched her gently on the cheek with the back of his hand.

"We got it right, Jane. No worries, as the Australians like to say. Maybe Manfred can think up the right title for Mary's book... Would you like to be that young again?"

"And repeat my drunken debauchery and end up working in a laundry? No, thank you. From now on I'm going to live in the present with you, my love, and forget about the past and worrying about the future. I have a better idea than a full-time servant under my feet all the time. We'll get someone from the village to come in once or twice a week to do the housework and the laundry. Tomorrow's Christmas Day. The new year is about to begin. And the day after Christmas I'm going back to writing the story of Margaret Neville. All evening she's been living in the back of my mind. How's Gordon Appleton going? Is your mind still in the old Africa? Do you want to go to bed?"

"I rather think I do, the way you are looking at me. I'll carry the twins up to the bedroom. We're back on the booze but who cares? Well, I am at least. The trick is to eat well and not drink the whisky too fast... You see, she wasn't after me."

"Not anymore. Put the guard in front of the fire and turn off the music channel. Tomorrow's a big day. You know what they say: early to bed, early to rise."

"There you go. Everything is now so quiet. You know, Jane, I'm more content now than I've ever been in my life. Thanks to you and the twins. Just look at them... And up we go to bed. What more can a man ever want?"

With the lights out, they made love, falling asleep in each other's arms. Jane dreamed of her father talking to Sophie about their early lives together, that brief meeting of innocent youth. In the dream, they were old, happy, both caring for each other.

3

---

*W*hen Jane woke for the second time, having attended to the twins during the night, it was Christmas Day.

"Can't sit around today, my love. All that work to do. Luncheon for six around the dining room table. We're going to have to put the twins in the pram. They're getting too heavy to cart around together. Oh, my goodness. That's the doorbell. It's later than I thought. Wake up, Randall. Get dressed."

"What's the hurry?"

"Your father and stepmother have arrived. I'm nervous. What will they think of me? He'll think it wrong we're not married. Oh, well. Four grandchildren for Christmas. Not a bad present. Hurry. That's the front doorbell again... What are you doing?"

"Morning, Dad, happy Christmas to both of you. Down in a minute. What's going on?"

"James Oliver opened the door. Happy Christmas."

"Happy Christmas, Randall."

"Happy Christmas, Mother. It's cold down there. We'll get the fire going in the sitting room."

Jane watched Randall close the window and started to giggle. It was going to be a happy Christmas. One big family Christmas.

"No time for the cook to bathe. Let the day begin."

"I'm going to bathe. Go down and introduce yourself. Take the twins.

There's no great hurry. The boys will be all over them. They must have driven down from Chelsea at the crack of dawn unless there isn't much traffic on Christmas Day."

"What do I call him?"

"Jeremy. It's his name. Jeremy and Bergit."

"That's odd, seeing he's my baby's grandfather. Does he like Americans?"

"Go down and find out. Of course he does. His sons lived in New York for goodness sake. Phillip still does. And there is my half-sister, Myra, who is married to the American actor Julian Becker. Stop getting yourself into a fluster. Put the kettle on when you've met them and make us some tea. They are both easy to talk to if you don't mind them reminiscing about the good old days in colonial Rhodesia. Tell them about yourself. Your books. Maybe leave out the debauchery and the laundry. What time do we open the bar?"

"You're at it again."

"You know what they say: once you start, you can't stop. We'll just drink nice and slowly. See if the boys have made themselves breakfast."

"At your service, sir. Anything you say. Tea and biscuits with your relatives. Maybe Bergit can help give the twins their bottles."

"She'll love that."

"Do I look all right?"

"You're wearing a dress and a pair of shoes. Why is it always so cold in England? Now listen to that. The dogs are barking. Dad loves dogs."

"Don't soak in the bath too long."

"I'll try not to. The scooter has gone. Mary must have come round in a taxi when we were fast asleep."

"What's she doing for Christmas?"

"She never said. Maybe spending it with her family. If they're not interested in her books, a hundred thousand dollars should make them sit up and think. At least I stoked the boiler last night. The bath water is boiling hot... I'll try not to be too long."

With a slight feeling of trepidation, Jane carried the twins in her arms down the stairs. Two old people were playing with the dogs in the hall, watched with smiles on their faces by James Oliver and Douglas. The front door was closed.

"Hello, I'm Jane. You must be Jeremy and Bergit. I've been so looking forward to meeting you. Let me help you with those bags. Oh no, I can't. Got my hands full. You can hang your coats on the hat stand over there.

First, I'll show you your bedroom and then we'll have tea in the kitchen. The kitchen boiler makes the kitchen warm. I'll light the fires in the sitting room and the dining room. Old house. No central heating. Good morning, James Oliver and Douglas. Did you sleep well? How was the traffic on the road? Sorry, can't stop talking. I'm nervous. This is Kimber and Raphael. I have a better idea. James Oliver, show your grandparents the bedroom next to yours. The bed is made up. You can put a match to the fire if you want to. Oh, and when you come down, you can help bottle-feed the twins, Bergit."

"Can I get a word in edgeways? It's so much fun to be a grandfather. Give the old man a hug, Jane. Where's Randall?"

"In the bath. We only just woke up."

"Do you have a garage where I can park my car?"

"Randall will show you. Happy Christmas, everyone."

"Happy Christmas."

"Don't stand there, James Oliver. Show your grandparents up to their bedroom. I'll put the turkey in the oven. It's all pre-prepared. You all must be hungry. Always slow-cook a turkey. What my mother said."

In the kitchen on her own with the twins lying in their bouncy chairs near to the kitchen table, Jane began running around in circles as she prepared the Christmas dinner of roast turkey to be followed by a nice apple pie. She would put the pie in the oven an hour before she served the turkey. Standing next to the sink, Jane began to peel the potatoes. The kettle boiled and whistled, making Jane put down the potato peeler so she had hands to make the tea.

"You need some help? Give me the potato peeler. Such a nice old house. James Oliver is showing his grandfather the garage. So, you're American. Where did your ancestors come from?"

"Right here in England. I'm a Slater."

"Then you must feel at home."

"Where's Douglas? Keeping track of the kids and animals drives me crazy. Nice crazy. But you know what I mean. You've been through it all yourself. Kids. We'll let the tea stand for five minutes. Tastes better. So, tell me all about your life in Africa. Randall's writing a new book about his lovely Africa."

"Well, where shall I start, Jane? World's View. We both miss the farm so much..."

By the time Jeremy joined them, Bergit had still not stopped talking as she stood peeling the potatoes while Jane rolled the pastry on a wooden board covered in flour. The African story went on, Jane only half listening as her mind raced from job to job. Randall came down after she poured the tea into the cups standing next to the jug of milk and the bowl of sugar, spoons ready in the saucers. Despite the panic, Jane knew she was organised.

"Well, here we all are. Happy Christmas again to you all. Dogs and cats. This place is chaos. How are you, Dad? How are you, Mother? How do you like our twins? That one is Kimber. That one Raphael. You can feed them their bottles. Now, what do you want me to do, Jane?"

"You can light the fires."

"Come, Dad. Then we'll drink our tea."

"James Oliver showed me the garage. Good to see you. How's Phillip and Martha? We're going to America in April for a visit. I miss my sons. We plan to see Myra and Julian and the children as well. So sad when children live so far apart from their parents. But we're grateful to have Craig and Jojo nearby. Be back in a jiffy, Jane. Can't let the tea go cold. Have you sold your apartment in Manhattan?"

"Not yet."

Trying to concentrate on what she was doing, Jane kept quiet. From the sitting room came the sound of a Beethoven symphony Randall had found on the music channel. Under the kitchen table, Douglas was sitting on the floor playing with Jasper and Luna. Jane put the stuffed turkey in the preheated oven lit by gas. The bird would be cooked in three hours and Jane wrote down the times on a piece of paper to tell her when to put the potatoes in the roasting pan and when to take the food out of the oven. Jane drank her tea as she smiled at Bergit, trying to show interest in the old woman's story. Randall and his father came back and sat down round the kitchen table.

"That's a big tree in the hall, Jane. Goes halfway up the side of the stairs. All those presents under the tree. What's that big open drum next to the tree?"

"Works like a gong. When Randall hits the drum it'll be time to open the Christmas presents."

"I wondered what a drumstick was doing in the drum. Nice, fancy artwork on the outside. Where'd you get it from?"

"Came with the house. All the furniture came with the house."

"When are we getting our presents, Dad?"

"Any minute, James Oliver. First, let's finish our tea. Jane, do you need my help?"

"I'm organised."

"We'll open the bar when lunch is served. All right, boys. Let's go. Time to hit the gong. Are you coming, Jane?"

"You go ahead with the presents. The cook's staying in the kitchen. Later, you can help me lay the table in the dining room. How are the fires burning? Off you go, all of you."

Listening to the music and the excitement of the boys as they opened their Christmas presents, Jane tried to relax and enjoy herself. What she needed was a drink. Was it all fun? Jane wasn't sure. Were they interested in some stranger who had got herself impregnated by their son? Why should they be? All the attention was centred on Randall and the boys, the twins too small to hold their attention. Quietly, Jane bottle-fed her babies, bringing a soft, warm smile to her face. At least she had the twins. They were hers. Did the rest really matter?

And the day went on, Jane on the sidelines doing most of the work as the Crookshank family chattered among themselves, Jane looking forward to the next morning when she would disappear into the writing room and join Margaret Neville. She was a stranger in her own house. Or was it her house? She had still not paid Randall her half. By the time the long day finally came to an end, Jane was not sure what her life was all about. Where would it go? Where would it end? An unmarried, thirty-nine-year-old American living in England.

Finally in bed, exhausted, with the lights out, Jane rolled over on her side of the bed and fell asleep, the night a void, nothing to dream. When she woke in the morning, Randall was still fast asleep. Gently, Jane got out of bed and put on her clothes. Outside the bedroom, all was quiet. Jane walked down the stairs on her own leaving the twins with Randall. In the writing room, she lit the fire and warmed her hands. When she was ready, she went to her desk and began writing Margaret Neville's story, far away in the other world.

THREE DAYS LATER, when the guests left to drive back to their apartment in Chelsea, close to the Thames River, Jane gave a big sigh of relief.

"You mind if I take the dogs for a walk on my own, Randall?"

"Do what you like... That was so much fun having them. The boys enjoyed every moment of it. I'm going to have a drink. You want a drink, Jane? You deserve it."

"Maybe the walk can wait."

"That's my girl. Peace again in the Garden of Eden. How's the book coming along? It must be so nice being back in your book."

"You can say that again... Damn. That's my phone. Who can it be?... Hello, Jane Slater speaking... Manfred!... Where are you?... At Heathrow Airport! What are you doing in England? Have you got a piece of paper? I'll give you directions to give to the taxi driver... See you in an hour, Manfred."

With the phone back on the table, shaking her head, Jane looked at Randall.

"No peace for the wicked, my love. At least this time there is only one of them. No offence to your parents. Now I've got to remake the bed in the spare bedroom. I wonder what he wants?"

"Mary Wilson. You can bet on it. Those photographs were quite enticing."

"You men all have dirty minds. He'll want her to sign an agent's contract. That's what he's come for."

"You want to bet?"

"When does Douglas go back to his mother?"

"I have no idea. Why don't you give her a ring?"

"She was your wife."

"All right. I'll ask her."

"He won't want to go."

"Not his decision."

"Where are they?"

"In their bedroom, playing with their Christmas presents... Manfred Leon in England. I can't believe it. Now I do need a drink."

Not sure if Manfred wasn't after them, not Mary, Jane sank her whisky without taking a sip, offering Randall her glass for a refill. Smiling at her, Randall covered the ice in her glass with whisky. They were both on tenterhooks, not knowing what to expect from their agent. In Jane's experience, successful businessmen did not cross the Atlantic to meet a new client, whatever they looked like. There were plenty more women in New York happy to oblige a rich literary agent with whatever he desired. Every young, pretty girl in America dreamed of becoming famous or marrying a man with money. When the doorbell rang, they both jumped.

"Put more wood on the fire, Randall, while I answer the door. Give Mary a ring and tell her to come over... Good afternoon, Manfred. Or is it evening? It gets dark so quickly in England. Raining again. Come in.

Randall's making up the fire in the sitting room and phoning Mary Wilson to come over. You can let the cab go."

"I've paid him."

"You don't have much luggage."

"Only staying in England a couple of days. Any chance of a bed for the night?"

"Just have to make up a bed. Why are you here?"

"To see you and Randall."

"I thought as much. We don't have help in the house. We like to be left on our own. Why we came to England. To get away from all the attention. Now there's something. Randall's put on the music channel. Did you know Mary is a lovely pianist? She'll be joining us shortly. I'll make us all a casserole for supper. There you go. Leave your bag in the hall. How do you like our Christmas tree?"

"Hello, Randall."

"Hello, Manfred. Mary's on her way. Glad you loved her book."

"There aren't many authors who can get into the heads of their characters and bring them alive. Most books I get sent read like newspaper reporting. They don't have that third dimension."

"This is a surprise."

"Not really. You can't run away from the people who made both of you famous. Books don't sell themselves. They have to be promoted. Authors require constant media attention or the public forget about them. When are you both coming back to America?"

"We're not. You want a drink?"

"You can't just run away, Randall. A few weeks away maybe. A couple of months maximum. You both have obligations to your publisher and your publicist. Let alone your agent. They've sent me over to bring you back. You have to honour your obligations in life. You should know that. We have our expenses to pay. Our salaries. And we can't do the marketing without the author. Be realistic, Randall. And yes, I'd love a whisky... You two must remember what we've done for you. We don't just do it for fun. We do it to make money. All that time and money I spent building up your name, Randall. You can't just let it go to waste. That's being selfish. Every artist has to promote his work. Johann Strauss visited England and Queen Victoria to make them waltz. There's more to success than writing the music. The Queen danced the Viennese Waltz to Johann Strauss's music until four in the morning, and England followed suit. You have to think of other people, not just yourself. I want you on the Jay Leno show next week. You've got to talk to the public to get readers. The public like to read the work of celebrities. Fame is hard to get and easy to lose. Be realistic. You can't just run off into the English countryside and let us all down. I have another seven interviews lined up for you. Making money is hard work. For all of us. You two have to do your part. You can't be selfish. Does it sound as if I'm giving you a lecture? Because if it does, it's exactly what I'm doing. You have to think of other people, Randall and Jane. It's a hard, nasty world out there. You have to have money to survive. If anyone knows that, it's you, Jane. From working in a laundry to fame and fortune all because of me. Now you must pay me back. I want you to do a book tour of thirty-four countries I've lined up. You'll be on the road for five months. Bookshops. Talk shows on radio and television. The money from the sale of your books must continue to flow."

"And what do I do with my babies?"

"Get someone else to look after them. Like any other rich parent. And who's that, Randall?"

"James Oliver. My son. His mother died of breast cancer. Where's Douglas, James Oliver?"

"In the bedroom sulking now Gran and Grandad have gone. I'm hungry. What's happening?... Who are you?"

"Don't be rude, James Oliver. Aunty Jane doesn't like you being rude. This is Manfred. Our literary agent from America."

"What does he want?"

"That's a big question. Come and sit by the fire. You'll have to wait until supper time for your food."

"When's supper time?"

"In two hours. I have to make the casserole. All right. You can have some cake in the meantime."

Wondering what was going to happen next in her life, Jane decided to go off to the kitchen, leaving Randall to sort out Manfred. All she thought she had had to do was write a good book. The vultures were back again. For both of them. However hard they tried, there was no getting away from the constant greed of people. Feeling her life about to collapse, she picked up the half-empty whisky bottle on the table as she passed and took it with her to the kitchen with her half-empty glass.

"You're following me, James Oliver."

"I want my cake."

"Of course you do. How silly of me."

How Manfred thought his authors wrote their books was beyond her. Writing was a full-time job that did not work with constant interruptions, with her mind cluttered up with interviews and being nice to the public to make them buy her books. She had to stay in Margaret Neville's mind for as long as it took her to write the book; the story would not flow if it was constantly being interrupted. But all that money Manfred had paid into her bank account had a price. Instead of being able to live in peace in their house by the woods and write books with stories that flowed from chapter to chapter as the words played through their minds, minds that remembered exactly what they had written, it would all become a jumble. But did she tell Manfred to shove it? She didn't think so. And back in the jungle of life, would her relationship with Randall continue? She doubted it. No longer the runaway couple writing in the same room and enjoying a whisky or two in the evenings around a roaring log fire, they would start arguing with each other like the rest of them. And what was the point in having children if they were brought up by a paid employee, giving their love to a woman who wasn't their mother? She only had to look at James Oliver and Douglas to see the confusion. But life was life with all its warts and there was no getting away from it. From her place by the table in the kitchen as she cut up the meat and the vegetables, she could hear them arguing over the sound of the music as she watched James Oliver stuff his face with Christmas cake to the point where he wouldn't want any supper. The big losers from the argument coming from the sitting room with the door still open would be Kimber and Raphael. But a life of poverty working in a laundry hadn't been that much fun either.

"Go and check your brother. Tell him to join us in the kitchen. And stop stuffing your face with cake or it will ruin your supper."

Half an hour later, when the front doorbell rang for the second time, the casserole was ready to go in the oven. James Oliver had wandered off with the dogs, the dogs following him as was their habit. She heard Randall go to the door and welcome Mary Wilson. With the third whisky half finished in her glass, Jane walked back to the sitting room, giving Manfred what she hoped looked like a smile. Instead of looking at her, his eyes were fixed on Mary in a dress that showed off everything. Maybe the snake from the pub was going to do her a favour by seducing Manfred. Instead of shaking Manfred's hand, Mary gave him a kiss right on his lips.

"Thank you so much, Manfred. I owe you everything. I'm so happy you loved my book. Oh, what joy. Randall, please give me a drink. Are we all going out to supper?"

"Why don't you and Manfred go out to dinner and talk about your book? Randall and I need to stay at home with the children."

"Would you mind, Jane?"

"I'd be very happy for you both. You can get to know your agent. Randall can order you a taxi."

"Where are you spending the night, Manfred?"

"I'm not sure, Mary. Would you two mind if I took my new author out to dinner?"

"It would be our pleasure, Manfred. I'm afraid next week Jay Leno is out of the question but we can talk about that later. And the twins are far too young to be separated from their mother. You two go and have a lovely evening. How's the casserole coming along, Jane?"

"Give it an hour and a half."

"Good. Plenty of time to drink. That fire is so nice. Just look at the Collies on the floor in front of the fire and the cats on the sofa. And Mozart. That's all we need, Manfred. When I've finished the new book on Africa, I'll send it to you. My old readers will love it. And you'll make lots of money. Come. I'll show you both to the door. Have you ever ridden on the back of a three-wheel scooter, Manfred? Because you are about to try. You can hang your bag on the back."

"Are you going to do the book tour, Jane?"

"That depends on Randall. We'll talk to you later. Enjoy your evening with Mary. Why don't you take him to the Jolly Farmer, Mary? Where it all began. It's nice and close to your home and there are always taxis, as you call them in England, if you've had a couple of drinks. Leave the swank restaurants for later in Manhattan. How's Tracey, Manfred?"

"She's just fine."

"I'm sure she would be. Lovely seeing you, Manfred. And I thank you from the bottom of my heart for everything. Did you have a look at my babies? Aren't they sweet? Twins. I was blessed with the best literary agent in America and twins. Mozart. Just listen to that beautiful music of Mozart. It's the music that counts in the end, Manfred. Good music lasts forever. Hopefully, like a good book. Must be two hundred years ago that Mozart wrote this music."

They both stood at the front door and watched Manfred climb on the motorcycle behind Mary, his overnight bag clutched in his right hand. When the sound of the bike's engine was lost, they turned back and walked through the hall past the Christmas tree into the sitting room and their waiting glasses of whisky.

"That worked."

"What do you mean, Jane?"

"He won't come back tonight. Do I really have to give up everything for five months and go on a book tour?"

"No more than I have to go on the Jay Leno show. Why are people always so greedy? Both of us have made Manfred lots of money he would never have had without our books. Let alone the publisher. The publisher makes five times the amount of the author. Writing good books needs concentration. Not all the promotion and celebrity crap. You and I have an addiction to alcohol. We are lucky we don't have that worse addiction, the addiction to fame and the constant need of other people's praise. There are lots of ways for them to keep our names and books in the public eye without the need for our presence. Not every successful artist has to shout and scream. Let our books do the talking for us, Jane. Word of mouth is the best promoter of our books. People telling their friends they've read a book they really enjoyed. Forget about the book tour. He says we are being selfish. What about him? Let's drink to the runaway couple... Now who the hell is that? The front doorbell again. I hate the sound of that bloody doorbell... I'll go. Have you fed the twins? Cheers. To peace and quiet on our own... All right! I'm coming!"

Smiling as she sipped at her whisky, Jane watched Randall walk out of the room. With the sitting room door left open to the cold draught, she heard the front door being opened on the side of the hall.

"Hello, Randall. Where is he?"

"Hello, Meredith. There must be telepathy. I was about to phone you. He's upstairs with James Oliver in their bedroom."

"Well, go and get him. He's my son and I've come to take him home."

"He's also mine, don't you remember?"

Jane got up and closed the door to the sitting room. Shaking her head, she went back and sat around the fire, no longer able to hear the argument. When Randall came back to join her around the fire ten minutes later, he was smiling.

"At least Douglas ran into his mother's arms. You know, Jane, there really must be a thing called telepathy. Now it's just you, me, James Oliver and the twins. What a world. And guess who paid the bills?"

Two hours later, when James Oliver had eaten his bowl of casserole and gone back up to his lonely bedroom, there was still no sign of

Manfred. Trying to avoid the five-month book tour had made her feel guilty. But would a long separation from Randall do their relationship any good? Jane doubted it. And the idea of some stranger feeding her babies made her feel sick. They were hers. Her whole future. They had grown inside of her, making her love for them overwhelming. Her whole future depended on her babies. If she lost the twins by not caring for them herself she would lose her life. Men were fickle, taking what they wanted. Only the twins would be there for the rest of her life, growing with the years and becoming two individuals who would always be her babies, wherever they were or wherever they went in their long journey through life. However much she hoped she now loved Randall, there had been more women in his life than even he could count, from the boys' mothers to Tracey and all the rest of them. For women, Randall was still young. Especially with his fame and fortune. She was getting old for men and had lost most of her pull. Without the twins, the future would be loneliness despite her new-found wealth. A person could buy company but never love or friendship.

"Funny how when you've had a nice big bowl of casserole you don't want to drink so much. Are you waiting up for Manfred?"

"Have a last one, Jane, and then we'll take ourselves and the twins up to bed. I love sitting around the fire with the cats and the dogs. And don't be silly. Manfred won't come back to sleep here tonight. They both have what the other one wants. She'll seduce him to make sure he does what she wants. With luck, she'll take Manfred's mind off the Jay Leno show and your book tour. It's the publisher pushing him. If an agent doesn't do what the publisher wants, they won't take his next authors. Literary agents have to climb up the publisher's arse to keep themselves in favour. Tracey seduced Manfred first and then her publisher Godfrey Merchant to get what she wanted. When Manfred brings back a girl with Mary's power of seduction, Godfrey will be as happy as a pig in shit and will be all over Manfred for doing him the favour."

"You men. You just never stop."

"How does your drink look now?"

"Cheers, my love."

"Cheers, my Janey. To many years in the peace of our new home."

"I'll drink to that."

When they went to bed at midnight, both of them happily drunk, the doorbell had not rung. The snake was no longer a snake. No longer a threat to Jane. Instead of ruining her life as Jane had feared, Mary Wilson had done her a favour.

"Help me with the carrycot, Randall."

"I'll go up backwards, stair by stair, sitting on my arse pulling the cot... Now you've got the giggles. I can't believe they're still fast asleep... To bed, to sleep, perchance to dream. Good old Will Shakespeare."

"Are you going to send Manfred *Shakespeare's Ghost*?"

"Why not? It's as good as finished. There never was a definite answer to whether Shakespeare had help writing his plays... Me on my arse. You on your knees. The twins asleep in their cot in the middle. And you've still got the giggles."

"They won't sleep so well with a nanny."

4

*E*ight hours later, having only got up once to see to the babies, Jane woke feeling better than she might have expected. The trick had been in eating the casserole in the middle of their drinking session. She got up and went to the window where she pulled back the curtain. Outside, the sun was shining, no sign of the rain. When she opened the window, she could hear the birds singing.

"What are you doing?"

"Listening to the birds. They sound so happy now the sun is shining. The poor birds must hate the rain."

"Come back to bed... Have the twins woken?"

"Not yet."

"Close the window. You've let in a cold draught. Oh, how I miss my Africa. Despite all the booze last night I slept well enough to write today. Are you going to write with me?"

"What about Manfred?"

"He'll be far too busy to worry us. Anyway, he's given us his lecture. He can't force you to go on the book tour. He'll tell Godfrey Merchant he did his best. What the hell was that?"

"The back door slamming. There they go. Good morning, James Oliver. Did you sleep well? Enjoy your walk with the dogs. The sun is shining. Can you believe it? Douglas has gone back to his mother. You have your bedroom all to yourself again. Bacon and eggs for breakfast."

"Close the window. It's freezing even under the bedclothes... Why don't we make love?"

"We can have a cuddle and see what happens."

"Oh, I know what will happen."

"You're horny."

"What's wrong with being horny?"

"So what do I tell Manfred?"

"That you are not going on his book tour. But leave the arguing to me. That's better. We're happy, Jane. That's all that matters. Happy away from the crowd. And so it shall be. Let Manfred and Godfrey chase the money. They need our next books more than we do. When you have enough money to live comfortably, what's the point in making more? Our joy is in the writing. Not in the fame and fortune... How does that feel?"

"Oh, shit. Please take me, my love."

And the physical love went on and on to their perfect, simultaneous climax. Exhausted, they lay back, their heads on their pillows, still no sound from the twins.

Half an hour later, with the sun still shining through the window, Jane and Randall woke to the sound of crying babies.

"You're hungry, my darlings. Of course you are. Mommy will be back shortly with your bottles."

Quickly getting up, she trod down the stairs to the kitchen, and made up their bottles as fast as she could. Back in the bedroom she picked up Kimber and gave her to Randall with a bottle. Then with Raphael she climbed back into bed.

"There we go. Suck the milk bottles to your hearts' content. When you've finished, I'll make your daddy some tea. Then we are all going down to the writing room after Mommy and Daddy have drunk their pot of tea... Wow, that was quick, Raphael. I'll bring you some more from the kitchen while the kettle's boiling. What a perfect day. Can you hear the birds singing, my darlings? And just look at that. Kimber has also sucked her bottle dry. No wonder you were both crying. You were hungry. And you've both got wet diapers. Mommy's not going to leave you to be looked after by some stranger. You both want your mommy. In a few weeks' time you'll be four months old. You're going to have lovely lives, both of you. The whole wide world is in front of you... First I'd better change your diapers. There you go. Didn't take long, did it? Dry as a bone. And now you are smiling, my little darlings."

"Are you talking to yourself or the twins?"

"Both Randall. Today's a writing day unless Manfred interrupts us. A pot of tea and some buttered toast and down to the morning room we converted so nicely into our two-desk writing room. Are you happy, Randall?"

"Happy as a cricket. Has James Oliver come back from walking Misty and Bob?"

"I have absolutely no idea... I dreamed of a strange world where there was just you, me and the twins. I love dreaming when I'm asleep. Did you fall asleep after we made love?"

"Briefly."

"Did you dream?"

"I always dream when I sleep content. I was on a boat on Lake Kariba all on my own and then a large fish eagle came crying from the shore and landed on the bow of the yacht. Then I woke to the sound of the twins crying and I was back here in the house by the woods. The dream has made me even more determined to write my new book on Africa."

"Let's slowly wake from our dreams and then join our characters down the rabbit hole where we will both live in our separate stories. We are so lucky being writers. We can always escape from reality. Let's just hope we don't get disturbed down our rabbit holes until we've finished our writing. You want me to put the babies in the bed with you? I've changed their diapers."

"I'm hungry."

"We're all hungry. It's breakfast time. How old is Manfred?"

"He's a forty-nine-year-old with a large paunch."

"Bit old for a pretty twenty-four-year-old girl. But that's life, Randall. How it works. We'll just have to see. Don't forget we both have good imaginations. You never really know what people are up to."

AN HOUR LATER, with the twins full of milk, there was still no sign of James Oliver or the dogs.

"Did he eat before he walked? Tea and toast. Down we go, Jane. Writing time. I want to live in my Africa even if it's only in my mind. Is Margaret Neville calling you?"

"She's been calling since I woke from my dream. I lit the fire in the writing room. I feel calm and at peace with the world. Ready to write."

Within a minute of sitting at her desk, rereading her last words, Jane left the real world and joined Margaret Neville, the story flowing, Jane unaware of the passing time.

When the front doorbell rang, making them both jump, she had written four pages in her handwriting on long sheets of clean white foolscap paper.

"What time is it, Randall?"

"Half-past two in the afternoon. I hate that doorbell. I'll go. I see the twins are stirring, needing their next feed."

"I'd better do their bottles before they both start yelling. I lost it the moment the bell rang. I was in mid-sentence. But what are we going to do?"

"Let me argue ourselves out of the problem."

"Be careful."

"I'm always careful with Manfred. He's my agent. Without him I would never have published a book."

When Randall opened the front door with Jane just behind him they found Manfred standing on the steps with a satisfied grin on his face.

"Where's Mary?"

"Back at her flat, Randall. She will be coming to America. The taxi is coming back for me in an hour. We three still have some business to do."

"Come in. We were writing at our desks. Jane is now feeding the babies. Never mind. Hopefully, our stories can wait until tomorrow. But whatever you say, I'm not going on the Jay Leno show and Jane isn't going on a five-month book tour."

"Your grandfather wouldn't approve of your attitude, Randall. Ben Crossley, were he alive, would have some words for you."

"My grandfather was a famous Hollywood actor. Actors are very different to writers. Actors are performing artists. Writers are creative artists. Actors are always in the public eye when they are successful. That's their business. They spend their working lives in front of a camera. You were his movie agent, not his literary agent. Don't you understand the difference? Come in, for goodness sake. Despite the sun, it's freezing cold. Come and join us in our writing room where there's a nice fire burning and we'll show you what we mean. It's wonderful to see you in England but the moment you rang the bell we both lost our stories. And without these stories written properly so they flow, you wouldn't have a product to sell. I know Godfrey Merchant has to find the right books and sell as many copies as possible to satisfy his shareholders. That authors promoting their own work can help increase the sales. But an author can't do both, Manfred. Can't write and at the same time have the world chasing after him. We can't be celebrities as you like to call them, permanently in the public eye promoting our books, and write them at the same time. I don't envy Godfrey's job having to constantly chase sales to maximise the profit for his shareholders."

"The shareholders invested their money in you, Randall."

"And we wrote the books for them or they wouldn't have had anything to invest in... How did you enjoy your evening with Mary?"

"She's happy to become a celebrity. What she wants more than anything else in life."

"She's young. Ask her again in ten years' time."

"So you are not coming over, Jane?" as she came into the room with two bottles.

"No. I'm sorry. And I feel as guilty as hell. But my babies come first. I don't want them looked after by strangers. I'm so sorry... There we go, Kimber, then your brother. Would you like to read what we've both just written? How about some Christmas cake? There's still a bit left. I want to be happy, Manfred. I don't want to be torn to pieces. Here is our world. Our creative world. Where the story begins and finishes. Right at that desk."

"You can tell Godfrey you tried your best. I'll phone him if you like and explain my side and Jane's side of the story."

"Will you, Randall? That will help."

"And I've a new book for you. It's called *Shakespeare's Ghost*. All about a man who wanted to stay anonymous despite his love for helping Will to write his plays. Does that sound familiar? When you and Godfrey read my book, you'll understand what I'm on about. All we two here want is the peace in which to write our books and go on making Godfrey's shareholders money, that money that everyone shouts about and that controls the world. The driving force of most people's lives where money is king. Put that cat on the floor and sit in that comfortable armchair and warm your hands by the fire while I go to the kitchen. She bakes the best Christmas cake in the world."

"So that's it," Manfred said when Randall returned.

"'Fraid so. And don't forget who introduced you to Mary Wilson. Smile, Manfred. Godfrey's going to love meeting Mary as much as he loved meeting Tracey. And give Tracey and Allegra both our love when you see her."

"She still won't say who is Allegra's father."

"That's her prerogative. The child is born. That's what she wanted. What all women want. They all want to be mothers, am I not right, Jane? What's the most important thing in your life right now, Jane? Not your books. Not me. It's your babies. You don't have children, Manfred, so you don't understand what it means to be a parent. And you did tell me your problem."

"I'm infertile."

"I know. And both Jane and I are sadly sorry for you."

"Would you like to be one of the twins' godparents? Probably Raphael?"

"I'd love to be, Jane. I'd have a child to think about. A child in my life."

"Then we all are happy. Let me go get you a cup of coffee to go with the cake, and Randall and I some tea. Randall, can you feed Raphael, please?"

In the kitchen, with still no sign of James Oliver and the dogs, Jane stood thinking. Had she done the right thing by asking a man with Manfred's morals to become a part in Raphael's upbringing? She wasn't sure what faith Manfred belonged to. She knew the name Leon had originated in some part of Russia but never once had they discussed religion. She wasn't even sure if Manfred was a Christian.

"Anyway, stop flustering yourself, Jane Slater. The whole thing's a muddle. They don't even have legitimate parents. Will the local Church of England even christen my children?"

With a tray of cups and saucers, Jane went back to the sitting room.

"A lovely offer, Jane. And a lovely thought. One I will always cherish. I'm Jewish, so it won't work as both of you are Christian and the godparent's job is to make sure the child stays a Christian. It's one big crazy world we live in. Despite believing in the same God, Jews and Christians have been arguing about religion for two thousand years... They are so cute. They've been gurgling at me between their feeds. You are so lucky. Once I'm dead I'm gone. You'll both leave your children behind. My life will have had no purpose... You're right, Randall. Jane makes the best Christmas cake in the world. It's quite delicious. I'm going to stop pestering you. Suddenly, my life feels so empty. What else do you want to talk about?"

"'Raindrops and roses, whiskers on kittens, warm woollen mittens, these are a few of my favourite things."

"Stop singing, Randall. You can't sing... And neither can you,

Manfred... Why don't we all have a drink while we are waiting for Manfred's taxi to return?"

"It's a bit early in the day to open the bar."

"Who cares, Randall? It is mid-afternoon and we've both finished writing for the day. Would you like me to sing to you?"

"Don't be ridiculous."

"You see, Manfred? The perfect couple. Always telling each other what to do and what not to do. We like to call ourselves the runaway couple. We live in the woods on our ownsome with James Oliver and the twins, writing books and drinking bottles of whisky. Thanks to you and Ben Crossley we have more than enough money to see ourselves and our children through life. We are among the lucky ones that don't have to worry about money."

"Don't you want more? A book tour would greatly increase your sales."

"Randall says that when you have enough money, what's the point of making more? I have lots of lovely money. Randall owns three properties, one here, Rabbit Farm on the Isle of Man and his apartment in Manhattan. What more could we ever want?... Well done, Randall. Here comes the ice, Manfred... There you go... To a happy life for all of us. And best of luck to Mary Wilson and her books... Now, doesn't that whisky taste absolutely delicious? We drink too much but who cares? We're happy. Being happy in life is all that matters... And to a safe journey back to America. Thank you for everything you have done for us, Manfred. And there are lots more books to come. Now listen to that. The Collies are back with James Oliver. We're in the writing room! How was your long walk? You must be starving hungry."

"I came back earlier and thought you and Dad were writing so I made myself some sandwiches, fed the dogs and went back into the woods. Now it's clouded over and has begun to snow. There's a car outside the front door with a man behind the wheel."

"Time to go, Jane and Randall. I'm looking forward to reading *Shakespeare's Ghost*. Maybe one last drink together. To many more books from both of you in the future. You're right, Randall. Without good books we'd be out of business. There would be no publishing companies making fortunes for their shareholders. I envy you your happy lives more than either of you can imagine."

PART 5

JANUARY TO FEBRUARY 1998 — DILEMMA

1

Two weeks into the new year, Randall sent Manfred a photocopy of the handwritten manuscript of *Shakespeare's Ghost*, asking him to have it typed and for three people to read the typescript alongside the hand scripts to remove any errors in the typing.

"There she goes, Jane. Registered. From what I read, everything will be sent at the press of a button in the future. Not packaged and posted at the counter in a post office, like we've just done. Some say the Royal Mail will be extinct in thirty years' time. Do you know the Royal Mail is nearly five hundred years old? The English were always ahead of the game. All we need now is three pairs of fresh eyes to make sure I haven't made any grammatical mistakes and the book can go to the printers."

"And if they don't like it, Godfrey and his crew?"

"They can throw it in the waste paper basket for all I care. My joy is in writing the books, not reading reviews. I just hope people will enjoy reading that book as much as I enjoyed writing it. So, what's on the agenda this morning, on this day of the first month of the year? How quickly the years fly by. I loved those years as a kid in Rhodesia riding my bicycle around the farm, having fun with the animals. When the winter's gone, you and I are going to take the kids to Rabbit Farm for a holiday. My neighbour's growing crops on my land but the house has been long empty. They'll clean it up for us as thanks for using my land. That was the agreement."

"Why did you call it Rabbit Farm? Was it a way of describing writing down the rabbit hole?"

"No, silly. That part of the Isle of Man is teeming with wild rabbits. Two weeks on a farm. How does that seem?"

"When are we visiting your place in New York?"

"Probably when they launch that book. Go well, *Shakespeare's Ghost*. May you give many people enjoyment. Many people who I will talk to for hours without so much as meeting them. Enjoy my rabbit hole, all of you."

"What are we doing tomorrow to belatedly celebrate your birthday?"

"Now that's a surprise."

"Tell me. I hate surprises."

"We're going up to London and the Royal Albert Hall to listen to Mahler's Second Symphony. Pity James Oliver is in boarding school. It would be wonderful to give him the experience of a full symphony orchestra. We'll have a babysitter for the twins."

"Let's go home. It's still pouring with rain. I'll get the fire going. Make us a nice supper with the fresh fish we are going to buy from the fish shop two doors away. Then we'll open the bar and raise our glasses again to your fortieth birthday and wish for many more good years to come... Is it just Mahler?"

"No, the concert starts with Mozart's Twenty-Fourth Piano Concerto. It's going to be exciting listening to an orchestra and watching them play at the same time."

"I can't wait."

"Neither can I."

"First the fish, then 'home, James, and don't spare the horses' as you like to say. Where do you find all those old sayings?"

"Books, Jane. Everything comes from books and plays. From people's writing... We could also go to the pub after getting our fish. Two beers only for me and with luck they won't arrest me for drunken driving."

"You ought to be careful, but you can have more when we get home."

"Why not? Tomorrow we're celebrating my fortieth birthday. I know I have already turned forty last month, but it'll be my last binge of my thirties."

"Do you need an excuse to drink?"

"Not really. We can fry up the fish and eat sitting in our armchairs in front of the fire. The new books are going well. The kids are well. What's wrong with a little celebration, Jane? Tell you what, I have a better idea.

We'll go to the Jolly Farmer and eat their food. Save you having to cook. We've plenty of money. Let's spend a bit of it. We'll get the fish next time. Come on. To the pub."

Smiling, free from people and their problems, Randall drove to the Jolly Farmer, parking the car close to the small rank of taxis that gave the drivers freedom from the wrath of the law and its drinking regulations. Inside the pub they sat up at the counter, the pub surprisingly full for a wet afternoon. Randall ordered himself a pint of draught beer and a glass of cider for Jane. They raised their glasses to each other in silence, both of them smiling.

"It's so wonderful to at last have a purpose in my life, my love. You think Kirsty will be able to look after the twins? It's so nice doing the shopping together."

"Of course she will. She's seventeen years old. Relax. She'll call you if anything goes wrong. Poor girl. Left school and has no idea what to do with her life. I love pubs. They have a nice, closed feeling of mutual warmth."

"When are you going to phone Godfrey Merchant?"

"I phoned him this morning when you took the dogs for a walk in the woods."

"I wondered why you didn't want to come with me. What did he say? You've gone silent, Randall. The smile's gone off your face."

"You don't want to know."

"Come on. Out with it."

"He told me that after all the money they had spent on marketing my books and making my name recognisable to the reading public, I had no right to refuse to go on the Jay Leno show. That snubbing the *Tonight Show* with the biggest audience in television was totally unacceptable. He said he thought I should know better. I'm not sure if he'll publish *Shakespeare's Ghost*. He went on and on and was downright rude. Then he cut me off without so much as saying goodbye."

"Did he mention the cancellation of my book tour?"

"He did. And he blamed me. I didn't argue with him."

"Will they publish my next book? Margaret Neville has such a beautiful story to tell."

"Who knows? We're not publishers. We're writers. Provided we make sure we have paid our taxes properly I can't see us having any financial problems whether they sell more of our books or not."

"But people won't be able to join us down our rabbit holes."

"That's true. You never win in life. You took a decision, Jane. Put the twins ahead of your books. Are you sorry?"

"Definitely not. Then cheers. To two successful authors who will likely never be published again. Does it bother you, Randall?"

"I don't think so. When you've done it, what's the point of doing it again and again?"

"Manfred can find us another publisher."

"Can he?"

"Is there any point in writing a book that isn't going to be published? It's like writing a letter to yourself. It'll knock the wind out of me. Oh, dear. I blew it. After all the excitement, I blew it. Can't you phone him again?"

"And tell him we'll do anything he tells us? They'll chew us to pieces. Do you have any idea how many people have killed themselves after becoming celebrities? It isn't worth it. He'd never leave us alone. We'd be back among the screaming crowd again living in a city. We want peace on this earth. Hemingway refused to go to Norway to pick up his Nobel Prize for literature. And not long after, he put both barrels of a shotgun in his mouth and pulled both triggers. It's not worth it, Jane. Fame is not worth it. If worse comes to the worst, we can pay someone to publish our next books. Oh, and remind me to ask Miss Dixon to find James Oliver a piano teacher now Mary Wilson has gone off on the hunt. We made it, Jane. We achieved our goals. We don't need them."

"Are you sure?"

"Nobody's ever really sure of anything. Except we are happy. Let's stay away from the howling wolves. I don't want those wolves back screaming in my head."

"I'd better phone Kirsty and tell her we are going to be late."

"She's quite happy watching television. Tell her we'll double her pay. That'll make her happy. You see, Jane, it's all about money. It's always about money. Good. Now you're smiling again. Let's have a look what's on the menu. Look at that. Chicken wings and chips again. We can have a whole basket of chicken wings and legs all to ourselves. Eat supper with our fingers. And drink. What else can we ever want? You know who will be the real losers?"

"Who?"

"Our readers. They'll never meet Margaret Neville or Shakespeare's friend. Sad but true. Oh, don't look like that. Who the hell knows what happens in this life? You think they get the chicken from the fast food down the road?"

Drinking his beer in silence, Randall looked away from Jane's panic-stricken face. He had been a published author for a lot longer than Jane, all the excitement long lost in the mire of interviews and people bowing and scraping to him just because they thought he was famous.

"I suppose I could go on the book tour. Could Kirsty help you look after the twins? Oh, it's all so horrible. Five months is a lifetime to be away from my babies. I'm torn. I loved having my book published. It made me feel so good. It gave me the high of all highs. Nothing can give you such a high as being successful. We all want to be a success in life, Randall. And if I don't go it will all disappear. I'll be that old, unimportant Jane again with nothing to do. And money goes as quickly as it comes."

"Not if you properly invest your after-tax royalty income that's in your New York bank account right now and only append the after-tax dividends and interest. You'll never be short of money. Put it in a global equity fund and spread the risk around the world. Half in shares, and half in cash and government bonds. You don't have to buy property unless you want to."

"One minute you have what you want and the next minute it flies out the window."

"You can't have both worlds, Jane. You either want to be a mother and bring up your children or be a famous author everyone likes to talk about."

"Can you imagine working in a laundry?"

"Not really. But it's all changed since then. You have the security of your own money and you have the twins. Have another cider while I have another beer whilst we wait for our food. Then we'll start on the whisky. We'll take a cab home. Kirsty can still pedal herself home in the dark. Her parents don't live far from us."

"My mind is in turmoil."

"Let's wait and see. Godfrey will also have a problem if he stops our books having gone this far building our names. You better phone Kirsty and tell her we're going to be late."

"Would you miss me?"

"Of course I would. You're my lover. My friend. My drinking companion. What on earth would I do on my own for five months?"

"That's what worries me. You think he'll simmer down?"

"Who?"

"Godfrey Merchant."

"Maybe with a bit of luck, Mary Wilson will take his mind off it. Let's hope she screws his brains out."

"Who paid her airfare to America?"

"Manfred, silly. The girl didn't have any money. She was a caregiver. Not much different to a babysitter. Manfred hadn't actually sold her book. It's only sold when she gets paid the advance."

"But if I leave it any longer it will be too late."

"Are you phoning Kirsty?"

"No. I'm phoning Manfred to tell him to phone Godfrey. I'm going on the book tour. I'm too scared not to. I don't want to regret not going. I'm going to take the twins and Kirsty on the tour. Why don't you join us instead of being on your own?"

"That's a thought. Please, Jane, don't phone him now. Let's sleep on it for a couple of days. Then make a decision. You're panicking. Never pays to panic."

"There's no answer. It's gone to voicemail. Hi, Manfred. It's Jane. Phoned to keep in touch. Talk to you later... Now I feel better... Hello, Kirsty. We're going to be home late. How are my babies? Lovely. Double pay for double stay... Now, what's the matter, Randall?"

"What about James Oliver? I promised to go to his school on Sundays and watch him play sport, or take him to lunch in a restaurant. Then there's the Easter school holidays. If I'm off with you in some faraway country he'll think he's been abandoned. He's only just lost his mother. And what about the cats and dogs? They'd hate living in kennels. I'm not sure if there are even cat kennels nearby. Anyway, what am I going to do with myself while you're promoting your book? I'd be surrounded by strangers."

"Then I'll take the twins on my own if you don't want to help me."

"You'd have to carry them around with you from one airport to the next. Where do they sleep on the plane? You can't push a pram up the steps onto an aircraft. And when you're doing the job for Godfrey Merchant that'll take hours at a time, will a seventeen-year-old be responsible enough to look after them? No, if you're going, leave the twins here with me. We'll speak to each other on the phone every day. Instead of Kirsty, I'll find a trained nurse to look after them. A middle-aged or older professional who's brought up her own children and knows what to do. It'll cost, but a lot less than what you'll bring in from extra sales. Maybe you do need more backup money in this crazy, volatile world. They're only just three months old. They won't remember missing you."

"You won't have an affair while I'm gone? Remember, we're not married. Oh, hell. No longer the runaway couple. Maybe for the sake of my twins, I'd better make as much money as possible. I'm also nearly forty. It's not as though we've been together for a lifetime."

"Sleep on it."

"I won't be able to sleep a wink."

"Your phone is ringing."

"It's Manfred. Hello, Manfred. You can tell Godfrey, I'm going on the book tour. Where do I have to be and when?... New York next Thursday... You'll have one of your staff pick me up at the airport. I'll phone you my arrival time... And she's going with me on the tour? That's wonderful. I wondered how I'd know where to go. How are the film rights coming along?... Splendid. Everything sounds organised... Yes, my passport is valid for three more years... She'll arrange visas where necessary. You're a wonderful agent, Manfred... Yes, I will. Have yourself a lovely day. How's Mary Wilson enjoying New York?... Thursday, Manfred. See you Thursday... He sent his regards, Randall."

"I'm sure he did. Tomorrow, I'll start looking for a registered nurse."

"I'm so sorry."

"So am I."

"Here's our food."

"Let's tuck in and then go home. Tonight I'm going to get myself well and truly drunk. It never stops, Jane. The game of life never stops. You can never keep away from them. Just when we thought we'd found our perfect sanctuary away from the crowd."

"I can't change my mind again."

"I'm not asking you to. Let's go home. Thirty-four countries. I didn't think thirty-four countries spoke English."

"The book tour is thirty-four countries and states. I'll spend most of the five months in the United States."

"You'll be able to see your father and Sophie."

"But he won't be able to see his grandchildren. The thought of you coming to this pub on your own is going to drive me crazy. I've counted six girls without male escorts. You'll meet another Mary Wilson."

"I'll drink here, yes. But I won't chase young girls."

"You promise?"

"I promise, Jane. How are Jim and Sophie getting on these days?"

"I have no idea. We don't speak much. Anyway, at least he has a companion."

"What are we going to do with ourselves? You go from pillar to post and financially find what you want and then it explodes. I hate drinking on my own. Drink up your cider and let's go."

"If you get blind drunk tonight you won't enjoy tomorrow's symphony concert. Why don't we sit over there at one of those tables and enjoy our chicken? Fried chicken is bad for your health but it tastes so good."

"Poor, Jane. Life was never easy. I'm just glad it isn't me. They'll push your face and book at every opportunity into the public eye. I hated sitting at a table in a bookshop signing copies of my books, smiling at strangers, asking their names. Putting their name inside in my handwriting. Why do they even want to meet the author? It's the book they want to read. I just never understand people. And we think the human race is so damn important which it isn't. We're just animals who live and die like the rest of them. I'm not important. Why do they think authors are important? I want to hide away for the rest of my life. Yes, we love giving other people joy when they read our book but that's it. Godfrey Merchant is never going to leave us alone. We're a marketing tool. You're right. Let's go sit at that empty table and drink a bottle of wine with our supper. Why the hell did I phone Godfrey this morning? He's driven us to drink. Now why are you smiling?"

"We don't need too much encouragement when it comes to drinking."

2

The week went by, and with it, Jane, leaving Randall alone with the twins and an old lady, Randall having no idea about the point of his life. He was forty, rich, famous and lost on his own with nothing to do with his future.

"What the hell am I doing in a bloody great house like this and no one to even talk to?"

Sitting in front of the fire on his own with his bottle of whisky, Randall began to drink.

THE NEXT DAY, after a bad night's sleep, Randall lit the fire in the converted morning room and tried to get back into his book. Nothing happened. His mind stayed blank, empty of story, as empty as Jane's chair on the other side of their writing room. In one terrible moment, Randall understood: there was nothing left to do in his life. He put down the pen, wondering if he would ever pick it up again and left the room, the house no longer giving him that feeling of warmth and pleasure. Three homes and he didn't want to live in any of them. He found the old nurse in the sitting room reading a book in front of the fire, the twins in their new pram next to her.

"I'm going to the pub, Mrs Fortescue."

"You should be careful of drinking so early in the day, Mr Holiday."

"My real name is Crookshank."

"I know it is. How do you write books, Mr Holiday?"

"Today, I have no idea."

"I don't understand people. They have two lovely babies and run away from them. Anyway, they're now in my care. Go and drink if that's what you want. It's none of my business."

"What are you reading?"

"Does it matter?"

"Will you cook supper?"

"It's part of my job. What you pay me for. A job is a job, Mr Holiday. Will she come back again?"

"Who knows, Mrs Fortescue?"

"Good, well-paid jobs are difficult to come by. Would you like me to drive you to the pub? You can phone me when you are finished."

"I'm finished already."

"What do you mean?"

"Life. My life is finished. And thank you, you can drive me to the Jolly Farmer. You can return and drive me back when I'm drunk."

"Bad as that?"

"It's worse. Far worse. They've all gone. We meet, we mate, we cheat and we go on our way. Or we spend our lives chasing rainbows. And when you have all the money you can ever want, the chase is over. Everything is boring. Boring, boring, boring... I need a drink... Why are you looking at me like that?"

With the old nurse shaking her head Randall went to fetch his coat. There was nothing left in his life other than alcohol. Would too much alcohol kill him in the end? He rather hoped so.

"How the hell do I bring up three kids on my own?"

BY THE TIME they reached the Jolly Farmer, it was half past four in the afternoon. The old lady dropped him off without saying a word. Inside the pub it was warm, letting Randall unbutton the front of his overcoat as he took a seat up at the bar, the heels of his shoes down on the bottom front rung of the chair. With a double whisky, he looked around, trying to enjoy himself. An old man was sitting alone opposite Randall staring into his pint of beer, unaware of his surroundings. Two groups of young men on opposite sides of the pub were talking loudly amongst themselves, all of them talking at once. There were no young girls on their own. Feeling like a lost fart in a haunted shithouse, Randall wondered why he hadn't stayed at home. Either way, he was drinking alone, a habit he hated as much as his boredom. By the fourth double whisky, the haunted shithouse had gone, the alcohol making him feel life wasn't so bad after all. As people came and went, no one took any notice of him or the old man on the other side of the bar. One of the lads in the noisy group to Randall's right was trying to play the pub's upright piano. One of his friends closed the lid of the keyboard on his fingers making them hurt, the two going into a fight. By seven o'clock Randall had spoken to no one other than the barman to order his drink.

"Hello, Mrs Fortescue. Can you come and pick me up?... No, I haven't eaten... Thank you. Ten minutes."

With the mobile on the bar staring up at him he sat and waited. And if Jane decided to stay home in America what else was there to do for the rest of his miserable life? And if she came back should he marry her? Would marriage make it permanent? They had had casual sex the night Jane got herself pregnant. There had been no great affair, let alone love. Just convenient sex for both of them. Kids from all these women and now look at him: alone, half drunk and bored to tears with no idea what to do with the rest of his life.

"Ah, there you are. Would you like a drink, Mrs Fortescue?"

"I don't drink, and the children are in the car. Come. Do you want some help getting off that barstool?... Why are those boys shouting at each other? And who's that old man staring at me? He must be in his eighties. What's he doing in a bar? Men, I never understand them. Thank goodness I never married again after my husband died. And the children aren't interested in me. Come along now, Mr Holiday. I have your supper in the oven. The fire's lit in the sitting room."

"Do you ever see your children?"

"Not very often. They are more interested in their own lives than mine. Quite rightly. At sixty-five, I am of no interest to anyone... Why does that old man keep looking at me?"

"Maybe he needs some company."

"Well, he's not getting mine. Come along. Can't wait around. Put on your overcoat. It's cold outside... Boys, behave yourselves and please move out of my way... Why do people get themselves drunk, Mr Holiday?"

"To escape."

"No one ever escapes life."

"They do when they die... I should buy myself a shotgun."

"What for, may I ask? You're not going to start shooting the poor pigeons, I hope... Put on your seatbelt, Mr Holiday. Rules. Always obey the rules."

The car lurched forward, Mrs Fortescue grinding the gears as they drove on back to the Woodlands in silence.

Five minutes later Randall sat in front of the sitting room fire with a full bottle of whisky and turned on the music channel, the music taking away his loneliness. When Mrs Fortescue handed him a tray with a plate of roast chicken he was feeling much better than he had felt in the pub.

"Are you eating with me, Mrs Fortescue? You're quite welcome."

"I eat in the kitchen with the twins."

"Thank you. The food looks good. Lots of nice vegetables."

When the elderly lady closed the door behind her, Randall put the tray of food on the carpet by the fire and picked up his glass of whisky. Was he really going to buy himself a shotgun and kill himself? What about the twins? What about James Oliver? Picking up the mobile, Randall tried again to phone Jane in America, the phone ringing for a while before it went to the answering service.

"Why don't you pick it up, Jane, when I call? Why don't you phone me? Oh, what the hell. They've got her running around like a blue-arsed fly. Now look at that for luck. Mozart. Wolfgang Amadeus Mozart."

Smiling, Randall drank his whisky, put down the empty glass and picked up the tray and began to enjoy his dinner, the notes of Mozart's music making him feel happy. Was the answer to write a book about today's South Africa with all its dramas, each side wanting control of a country with its multiple competing tribes and different races that had no wish to see the other side's point of view? Would they ever become one community living in harmony? All the people could do was hope. Would writing such a book make a middle-aged man living on his own happy? Or should he go back to Lawrence Templeton-Smythe, the first white hunter in the country that was to become Rhodesia, and create a fictional world he could make seem like happiness? He could take Lawrence on through his life and bring him back to Africa, the place he loved and cherished, a new home far away from the meanness and manipulation of other people. Would living in Lawrence's mind make Randall content with his own life? Listening to the beautiful music of Mozart and Mahler took Randall back a week to their wonderful night in the Royal Albert Hall where they had listened in ecstasy to Mahler's

Second Symphony and Mozart's Twenty-Fourth Piano Concerto. The memory made him smile as he finished his dinner. After putting down the tray, he picked up his phone and tried to phone Jane without any reply.

"Drink, old boy. All you've got is booze, music and, with luck, the story of Lawrence to take you through what's left of your life. Cheers, Jane. Enjoy your new life back in America if that's what you want. I'll be the single father and bring up the twins. What the hell am I talking about? Of course she'll come back to her children. Just answer the bloody phone or it's going to drive me nuts not knowing what the hell is going on."

And the night went on as Randall drank down his bottle of whisky with the music playing and soothing his nerves until, alone and drunk, he managed to climb up the stairs to their bedroom where he fell into bed and a drunken sleep without a dream.

The following morning, with a splitting headache and a mouth that felt like the bottom of a parrot cage, Randall went downstairs and back into the sitting room. The fire had gone out, the tray was still on the floor and the whisky bottle was empty. Randall picked up his discarded phone and smiled through his self-inflicted misery. When he played the one message 'Why the hell don't you pick up your phone', he again phoned Jane and got her answering service.

"Sometimes, you just can't win."

Feeling better, Randall went to the kitchen to make himself some breakfast, no sign of Mrs Fortescue or the twins. Outside, the sun was shining on the wet leaves of the trees.

"Must have gone for a walk. It's just another day. Another day 'when all our yesterdays have lighted fools the way to dusty death'."

"Did you say something, Mr Holiday?"

"I was quoting Will Shakespeare. Thought you'd gone for a walk. Never mind. Don't worry. I'm making my own breakfast. How are the twins? Good. You're smiling, Mrs Fortescue. Did you sleep well?"

"I always sleep well."

"You're very fortunate."

"You need some servants in this big house, Mr Holiday. We can't have the furniture collecting dust. My job is to look after the twins and cook your food. I am not a cleaner. The house is a mess. To say nothing of the garden. When was the lawn last cut? The place is overgrown."

"I don't like people on top of me."

"Then why did you buy a big house with acres of garden?"

"To be away from people's noise. Oh, well, if you say so. Can you find me a cleaner and a gardener? You've lived in this village a long time. You must know people. Oh, hell. Now I'm going to get the noise of vacuum cleaners and lawnmowers; people getting into my mind and leaving their problems."

"What are you going to be doing today, Mr Holiday?"

"Nothing much. Can't write on this kind of hangover. Not that I have anything to write. When books won't tell you their story you leave them alone. A book has to write itself. Later, I'll go to the pub if you will help me."

"I have a friend who needs money. She's on welfare. Barely covers her costs."

"Then you'll have a companion."

"What will you pay Mrs Grainger?"

"Whatever she asks... Now, let me see about my breakfast. The only thing to do with a hangover is feed it."

"Can she come today?"

"She can come right now, for all I care. Sorry. That sounded rude. Why won't Jane answer her phone? I hate answering services. They're so impersonal. The modern world is becoming a very impersonal place with all the new technology. Have you heard of the internet?"

"What's that?"

"You don't use a computer?"

"What's that? When do you wish me to drive you to the pub?"

"Four o'clock. I'll have a late lunch and then you can drive me to the pub."

"You're a strange man."

"You can say that again."

"Give me that frying pan. The kitchen is in a big enough mess as it is. Bacon and eggs? Toast? Go and sit in the sitting room and I'll bring your breakfast to you on the tray."

"How are the twins?"

"Don't you ever pick them up?"

"Not really. I'm scared of dropping them. They look fast asleep. I'll take my tea to the sitting room and light the fire. You are most kind, Mrs Fortescue. Most kind. Dogs! Stay where you are. And no, I'm not taking you for a walk. The cats look comfortable, Mrs Fortescue. At least someone is happy. Voicemail. Still the same message. Why doesn't Jane pick up her phone?"

"Leave her a message."

"I don't want to talk to a machine. I want to talk to Jane. Why are you looking at me like that?"

The silent look moved away to the frying pan, Randall's frustration reaching boiling point. In the sitting room, he put on the music channel and tried to calm himself down, all the time conscious of the silent telephone on the side table beside the armchair he had moved in front of the fire.

"What am I doing in a country without sunshine? What am I doing, period? And you can't start drinking until you go to the pub, you silly old goat."

By the time Mrs Fortescue brought him his breakfast, he was bored out of his mind with nothing to do.

"Mrs Grainger will be coming tomorrow. You don't mind if she moves into the small bedroom in the attic? That way she will not have to pay her rent."

"Oh, go and find a butler and a head gardener and tell them to employ whoever they need. Fill the house up with people and drive me nuts."

"A gardener, yes, though I'm not sure about the butler."

"Do I detect the glimmer of a smile? Four o'clock on the dot. It's Friday. The pub should be full of people."

"I thought you said you did not like people."

"People in pubs are drinking companions. That's different."

"Forgive me for my ignorance."

"Why does time go so slowly when you're living on your own?"

"You confuse me, Mr Holiday. Enjoy your breakfast... Isn't the music a little loud? Those poor dogs need a walk. You'll discuss Mrs Grainger's wages with her tomorrow. You don't mind her living in the attic?"

"She can live on the moon."

"They do say too much alcohol is bad for people. You should stop drinking, Mr Holiday."

"Now that's just perfect. I employed you to look after the twins, not to tell me what to do."

"Then I'll leave you alone in peace."

"Now you are smiling."

"Not really... Now, what's the problem? One of the twins is crying. They miss their mother."

By the time Mrs Fortescue drove with him to the pub, dropping him at the door, Randall had phoned Jane a dozen times, not once getting her to answer her phone. Ducking from the rain, Randall walked inside the pub, the place empty, just the old man up at the bar. The time on the round clock over the bar read ten minutes past four. It was too early for people to have left work. He walked through and took the barstool next to the old man.

"We've got the place to ourselves. You mind if I sit here? I'm Randall."

"Jake. Jake Crawley."

"You want another drink, Jake?"

"Why not? Didn't I see you here yesterday? You must have left work early."

"I don't work."

"I'm too old to work. What do you do for money?"

"I inherited from my maternal grandfather. Have you heard of Ben Crossley?"

"Who hasn't? He was one of my favourite film stars. Lucky man. I wish my ancestors had been wealthy. Anyway, I have a pension from the railways."

"You drove trains?"

"Most of the time. Thank you, Randall. Cheers. That barman is good. You didn't have to tell him what we drink. It's nice to talk to someone. You have an odd accent. Where are you from? Not these parts."

"I grew up in Rhodesia. On a tobacco farm. Cheers. Nice meeting you, Jake. I hate drinking on my own."

"Don't we all? I've been drinking a lot on my own for years waiting for God to let me die."

"You don't have a wife?"

"Never have married. There was only one true love in my life."

"Why didn't you marry her?"

"We were four years old when we met. Penny was my next-door neighbour's daughter. We were closer than brother and sister though we weren't. When we were ten years old we were caught with our pants down behind the bushes at the top of their garden by her father. He told me never to step foot in their house again. We were so young and innocent we had no idea we were doing anything wrong. Curiosity had made us want to look at why our bodies were different... But why am I telling you this story? I hate talking about myself. It's so boring for other people."

"Go on. What happened?"

"I made the sound of an owl calling from the open bathroom window that looked out over the shed to the house next door. When Penny heard, she opened their landing window so we could just look across at each other. When her father caught her he slapped her around. I could hear her crying. After her third beating, we had to stop. We were never allowed to communicate again. Neither of us were ever the same again. I had lost my love. Penny had lost hers. There was no sex in it. At that age, there was no sexual attraction. No impulse. Our mistake had been innocent curiosity. Strange how something so small can change a person's life forever."

"What happened to her?"

"Our lives went on. She became a lesbian. So far as I know, she never had a male lover. She went into the theatre in London's West End. By the time we were old enough to make our own decisions, she was not interested in me or men. I'm sorry. Thank you for the drink. Went down very nicely. I must be boring you."

"Not at all. Would you mind if I put your story in a book? Not using your names of course."

"Do you know how to write a book?"

"People say so."

"Are you a writer? What's your name? I don't read books, I'm afraid."

"Randall Holiday."

"Doesn't ring a bell. And all these years because of that one disastrous moment on a summer Sunday afternoon I've lived on my own. There's been no point to my life. If we married, we'd likely have great-grandchildren by now. Now it's my turn. Same again? Micky, give us the same again Now, Randall, tell me a bit about your life. It's so nice to talk to someone. Ben Crossley's grandson. Now that's something. What's a Rhodesian or whatever they call themselves these days, doing in a place like Cranleigh in the English countryside? Two nice pints of beer. Down the hatch. In an hour, this place will start filling up."

"When he caught you, were you touching each other?"

"She was tickling my bare bottom and giggling. We were always giggling together. Years later, the war came along, I volunteered to join the army, hoping I'd get myself killed. They'd spent money training me to drive trains. There weren't any trains in the army. The army drove trucks. All I could do was join the Home Guard and stay in England. We were bombed twice in the railway yard. Missed me both times. Are you married, Randall?"

"A couple of times. Four children, from three different women. But now I have three of the kids to bring up on my own. Life is full of shit. Is your Penny still alive?"

"I don't know."

"Then you should find out. You'd have lots to talk about. If she was in the theatre it shouldn't be too difficult to trace her. I can help if you want. Lots of contacts in the theatre through my grandfather."

"Would you really?"

"Why not? It would be fun. What was her surname?"

"Long. Penny Long."

"I can only try. You're right. People are starting to come in. Damn, I left my phone in the car. Anyway, there's a payphone in the corner over there. The old woman who looks after my kids drives me to and from the pub. Have to phone her to pick me up. It's a strange world, Jake. A strange old world. What it was all about I have absolutely no idea."

By the time they had finished their drink, both of them sitting comfortably on their barstools in silence, two young girls came into the pub, looked around and sat themselves up at the bar, one of them looking suggestively at Randall.

"Where are you going, Jake?"

"Home. Talking about Penny has upset me terribly."

"Have another drink."

"That girl's giving you the eye."

"The last thing I need in my life at this moment is another woman."

"I want to go and feel sorry for myself on my own."

"Do you drive or take a taxi?"

"Walk. My lonely little flat is just around the corner."

"You don't have brothers or sisters?"

"They're all dead. Will you excuse me?"

"I'm sorry I've upset you."

"My own fault talking about myself. Enjoy your evening."

"We'll chat again."

"Maybe. Please don't look for Penny. If she is alive after all them years, what would she want to do with me? Likely, she wouldn't even remember me. Kids have lots of friends. Why would she remember one out of so many friends? It was all a long, long time ago. Back then, we

British still had an empire. Now everything has gone. Let me go before I make a fool of myself."

"How old are you, Jake, if you don't mind my asking?"

"Eighty-three. Not long now to go."

"How's your health?"

"There's nothing wrong with me. That's the trouble. I've just lived too long. There you go, Micky. Everything paid for. At least I have a good pension. Four kids. You just don't know how lucky you've been. There will always be someone to take an interest in you. And your genes will go on forever. Keep the change, Micky. We all need money to live. They say money is the root of all evil. But they were wrong. My railway job and its pension were, and are, my only saving grace. And there I go again talking about myself."

"But if she is alive?"

"Please, Randall. Now I'm crying. There's nothing more pathetic than an old man with tears in his eyes. Goodnight."

"Walk home safely."

"I hope not."

Randall watched the old man walk slowly out of the bar, himself feeling the old man's dejection. For a long while Randall stared at his beer thinking of Jake Crawley's story, a story as clear to Jake today as it had been when he was ten years old. Was she really tickling his bottom when the girl's father looked over the top of the bushes, or was she tickling him somewhere else, provoking the father's wrath? Or was young Jake touching the girl? There were always two sides to a story. Not that it mattered for Jake and the girl: their lives had been changed forever, everyone a loser including the girl's father who would have known as the years went by that his action that day had turned his daughter into a lesbian, a woman who hated men. Had the father asked for forgiveness or did he still think he had done the right thing? Hot tempers had never helped anyone, whether they rationalised with themselves afterwards or not. Finding Penny Long was worth a try if it stopped the old man wanting to die.

"She's probably dead. Micky, give me a double whisky and let me drown the poor old man's sorrows."

"That was quite a story he told you."

"You were listening?"

"Couldn't help myself. Made me realise how lucky I am. I may not have a job with a great financial future but I have a girlfriend who also works in a bar. The tips are good. We have lots of fun together. What more can a man of twenty-four want from life? From what I gather, fame and fortune haven't done you much good."

"You can say that again. So you're happy, Micky?"

"As a pig in shit. One of your expressions, Randall."

"Why does that young girl keep looking at me?"

"She knows who you are. Have you heard from Mary Wilson since she went to America? Wasn't the man she brought to the pub that night your agent?"

"She's chasing her dream, Micky. I'm no longer of any importance to her."

"There you go. Enjoy your whisky. The girls are calling to me."

"You're a lucky man."

"I know I am."

Alone, sad, with no idea what he was looking for in life, Randall sipped his whisky, trying to drink slowly. His mind went back to the tobacco farm in Rhodesia, in a place full of sunshine and smiling faces. He could see it all in his mind so clearly: the msasa trees in the bush beyond the tobacco lands, himself walking the family dogs, the birds singing to him from the trees, his whole mind and body brimming with happiness; down by the river, he took off his clothes and ran with the dogs into the clean, beautiful water, a duck quacking away in fright from the dogs; further downstream, the duck landed back in the water far enough away from the dogs to feel safe; through the trees, the sun bathed his shiny wet body with a soft warmth as he floated in the water on his back, the picture as clear in his mind as he sat up at the bar as it had been on the day.

"You are Randall Holiday?"

"Sorry. I was miles away. Do you know me?"

"Only by reputation. You're a famous author. Colleen and I were sitting down the bar watching you and the old man. Do you mind if we sit next to you? I'm Raleen. You don't have to buy us a drink if you don't want to."

"What would you like, Raleen?"

"A glass of wine would be nice. You see, I'm writing a children's book as I can't have my own children. Done all the tests. Nothing the doctors can do. So I'm going to have children in my imagination and live with them through my books. Do you live in your books, Randall?"

"Are you Randall Holiday the author?"

"I'm not sure who I am today."

"Colleen also likes wine. She's going to do the graphics. My friend is an artist. We met at school."

"Micky, give the girls a bottle of wine. They always say in life if you are going to do something do it properly."

"Can you help us find a publisher the way you helped Mary Wilson? Why are you smiling like that?"

"People, Raleen. Why don't you show me the book when you've both finished it, and then we will see."

"Will you really? That's so wonderful. Why are you here on your own? A famous man is usually surrounded by lots of people. You must have lots of fans. Now just look at that, Colleen. A whole bottle of wine. Thank you, Micky. Micky told us all about you, Randall. It must be so wonderful to be rich and famous."

"I rather think Micky only told you half the story. Oh, what the hell. Give me another whisky."

With Raleen on one side and Colleen on the other, there was no escape. Everyone in life wanted something. Life never changed. Mentally picking himself up off the ground, Randall tried to enjoy himself with the girls as the bar filled up on a Friday night at the end of a working week.

"We're not after you, Randall. Colleen and I are lovers. Have been since we met at school."

"The world grows stranger by the minute. Can't you get a doctor to fertilise you so you can have children? Isn't there something called artificial insemination?"

"As I said, I can't have children. And if Colleen had the baby it still wouldn't be right. Our child would only have one of our genes. Thank you for the wine."

"Did you read any of my books?"

"Not really."

Not sure if the children's book had anything to do with having babies, Randall watched them drink their wine. In Randall's experience, most things in life were about money. A kid's book of twenty-five pages of writing could be done in a month. And if it worked, sell at the same price as one of his novels.

"You've gone off again Randall."

"I have that habit."

"You will look at our book?"

"A man's word is his bond. Or so they say."

"How do we get hold of you when our book is finished?"

"Ask Micky. The barman knows everything."

Questioning whether drinking companions were better than drinking around the fire at home in solitude, Randall half-listened to the girls, Micky watching them all with a twisted smile on his face as he stood back waiting for the next order from his row of customers up at the bar. The music had been turned up, the people talking louder as the alcohol began to take effect. From what Randall gathered, Raleen had a job in an insurance company in what she called the claims department, Coleen working as a cashier in a grocery store, both of the girls twenty-four years old. By the way both of them looked at the men in the bar, the girls' sexuality was not one-sided. Or was the lesbian crap just another story? In life, he told himself, you never knew what people were really up to, which brought his mind back to Jane. Had she found a new, exciting life for herself? Would she be asking him for the twins once she settled back in her America? As he said to himself so many times, only time would tell.

"Have you ever had a threesome?"

"Not that I remember."

"You keep drifting away from us. Do you know what a threesome is?"

"If I did, I wouldn't talk about it to two girls half my age who I have only just met... Oh, you want another bottle of wine?"

"That would be nice. We'll have the book finished by the end of next month. How good is your American agent?"

"He and I are going through a problem at the moment as I won't do the publisher's publicity stunts. I refused to go on the Jay Leno show."

"You refused? But that's crazy."

"Not if you want the wolves back howling in your head. I'd better go. I need to phone Mrs Fortescue. Enjoy your bottle of wine. You haven't yet finished the first one."

"Aren't we pretty enough?"

"Girls. Really. I'm just an old goat."

"But you are famous. A celebrity. Celebrities can have anything they want."

Walking away from the bar without looking back, having paid and tipped Micky, Randall used the pub's payphone to call Mrs Fortescue. For ten minutes, Randall sat alone in the corner ignoring the crowd.

"We could take you home, Randall Holiday."

"Mrs Fortescue will be here in a minute. Sorry, I'm not in the best of moods today. Good luck with your writing and good luck with your lives. Tonight, as on most nights, I'm going to get well and truly drunk on my own."

"What a shame. It would have been fun."

"I don't think so, Raleen... There she is. She's the lady who looks after the twins... Thank you for being so prompt, Mrs Fortescue."

"It's my job. Your supper is waiting for you. Come along. I'm double parked... You left your phone in the car. It rang twice."

"Where did you put it?"

"On the coffee table in the sitting room next to the fire. The fire is burning nicely... Who were those girls?"

"I have no idea."

Imagining what two bisexuals would have got up to in a threesome, Randall let Mrs Fortescue drive him home, the complexity of the human condition blowing his mind. What were they all up to? Now, he'd seen it all.

Back at the house, he let himself out of the car, going to the back door and gingerly lifting the twins out before walking into his home while Mrs Fortescue parked the car in the garage. In the sitting room, he picked up the phone and went to voicemail, both messages from Jane asking him to pick up his phone. For the rest of his lonely, drunken evening around the fire he tried unsuccessfully to get Jane to pick up her phone, the music playing, the fire burning in the grate, the whisky bottle going down. With the guard in front of the fire, the whisky bottle almost empty, no sign of Mrs Fortescue or the twins, Randall went up to the bedroom in the hope of getting some sleep, another day in his life thrown on the garbage heap, the wolves back howling in his head. In the dark of the night, Randall woke up screaming from a nightmare in a world that was on fire, everyone running away from the final devastation, the world exploding around them into oblivion at the end of life, the human game finally over in a screaming mass of self-destruction. Unable to stop his shivering, his whole body shaking, Randall pressed his arms down across his chest, willing his fear to go away. In the dark bedroom, there wasn't a sound. Outside, the night was quiet. After a while, the shivering stopped. He was alone forever, no hope or purpose in anything. All night, soaked in alcohol from the day's drinking, Randall tossed and turned, everything in his life a hopeless nothing. All he wanted was a gun to shoot himself. When the morning light came up, spreading through the curtains, his misery reached its zenith. It was Saturday, the day James Oliver played his first football match, a son with a dead mother and a selfish, rotten father who wanted to kill himself instead of looking after his boy. Thinking of James Oliver instead of himself, Randall finally fell asleep away from his dreams. In his sleep, at last, he was as good as dead.

3

*W*hen Mrs Fortescue brought him his morning cup of tea his mind was a blissful blank, not a thought in his head.

"Enjoy your tea, Mr Holiday. Are you all right? It's raining cats and dogs. Don't think your boy will be playing football today. They say we have the worst climate in the world."

"Did you hear any noise last night?"

"Slept like a log. So did the twins. Breakfast in half an hour. Are you writing today?"

"I don't think so."

"Oh well. It's your life. Mrs Grainger will be joining us this afternoon. It'll take her a month to clean up this house. Her first job will be sorting out the attic and making herself a bedroom. Anyway, she's happy to get herself a job. What we all need, Mr Holiday. A job to do... Are you sure you are all right? My advice is to stop drinking alcohol. It destroys people. An expensive waste of time, drinking, But that's my opinion. And nobody ever takes any notice of my opinion. Never did and never will."

Not sure if Mrs Fortescue had not heard him screaming and was avoiding the issue, Randall tried to take control of himself. Though it seemed like a lifetime, Jane had only been gone three days, his phone preventing him from thinking clearly: too much booze had always clouded his mind. Jane was more likely wishing she had stayed in England with her children than chasing around promoting her book.

Instead of convincing himself she was coming back, Randall picked up his phone and tried again, his frustration exploding when it went to voicemail. For Randall, there was nothing worse in life than not knowing what was going on.

By the time he went down for his breakfast, he was seeing a more hopeful picture of Jane in his head: the poor girl was exhausted and had left her phone so no one could get hold of her, her publishers chasing her from one meeting with readers to the next in a world of manic publicity. Not only was she having to be nice and smiley to her readers, she had newspaper reporters and television crews asking her multiple questions, all of them driving her mad. He had been through it himself many times, none of it worthwhile. Jane was now finding out for herself why he had come to England to get away from the publicity and greed of business people in their constant push to hold their jobs or increase their wealth. Alone in the kitchen, eating his breakfast, the rain still bucketing down, the fear of Jane leaving him to bring up the twins alone began to fade. She would phone him when she was ready and not surrounded by people, people all around her being the reason she did not want to pick up the phone when he called.

After breakfast, he found Mrs Fortescue in the sitting room with the twins. He picked them up one after the other and held them in his arms, telling them both that before they could blink they would be back in the arms of their mother.

"Five months is a bit longer than a blink, Mr Holiday."

"Randall, please."

"It's going to be a long journey, Randall."

"Life's a long journey. And you are right. I must stop drinking too much whisky."

"Are you going to the pub today?"

"Not today. Not tomorrow. By Monday I'll be able to get back in my book, the story of the new South Africa... They really are cute. They say the only real reason for life is having children. Poor James Oliver. By the look of it, no football. The pitch will be flooded. Tomorrow I'll go to his school and take him to a restaurant for lunch."

"Not the Jolly Farmer?"

"No, not the Jolly Farmer. That place is dangerous."

"What do you mean by dangerous?"

"If I told you you'd think me crazy. But the world is crazy, Mrs

Fortescue. Never mind... I'm going to have fun watching these two grow up. Are you happy, Mrs Fortescue?"

"What a ridiculous question. Why do you write, Randall?"

"To keep myself company. Does Mrs Grainger like cats and dogs? I hope so. Just look at them. They all look so content. I rather think I'd prefer to have been a pussycat. Oh, how I hate hangovers. And I've no one else to blame but myself."

LATE IN THE AFTERNOON, to take account of the different time zone, Randall called Jane in New York, the phone ringing and ringing.

"How are my babies?"

"You answered the phone! I don't believe it. Where are you?"

"I'm in Barnes and Noble's bookshop sitting at a table signing my books. And here comes another girl with my book in her hand wanting me to sign it. I'll call you later. Agatha Stone has been so helpful. Manfred Leon should be really proud of her. It's all go, Randall."

"The twins are fine. I miss you, Jane."

"I miss you too. What time is it in England?"

"Five o'clock in the afternoon."

"Got to go... What's your name?"

"What on earth do you mean?"

"I'm talking to my new reader. I want her name and mine together on the inside cover. Don't you remember?... Gwendolen. What a lovely name... There you go, Gwendolen. Enjoy my book... I was speaking to my lover far away in old England... Yes, Agatha. I'm doing my best... And what's your name? Bye, Randall. Love to the twins. Call you later. Why didn't you answer my calls?"

"I left the phone in the car when Mrs Fortescue drove me to the pub."

"Have one for me. Can't drink on the job... There we go, Spike."

"Can't we talk?"

"You got a hangover? You sound agitated. Please. I'll call you later. I've never run around so much in my whole life."

"Are you enjoying yourself?"

"Of course I am. We're selling mountains of books. Before the day's out we're going to have to restack this table and we don't have enough books... What's your name, lady?"

"Bye, Jane."

"Bye, my love."

Randall got up from his armchair in front of the fire and walked across to the window. Outside it was still raining, the light almost gone. Feeling lost and lonely, all he wanted was a drink. At least she was having fun. Mrs Fortescue had been right: five months was going to be a whole lot longer than a wink. But that was how it worked... Going across to the television set on its trolley, Randall turned on the classical music channel.

"Mozart. My luck is in... And don't you even think of having a drink."

Back comfortably in his chair, the fire warm and welcoming, Randall tried to make up his mind whether to write about modern South Africa with all its politics or write a second book about Lawrence Templeton-Smythe in that old Africa at the start of the British Empire and take his character book by book through all the years of the twentieth century making himself and the reader happy: for Randall, there was nothing better than living in a fictional world, a world he created where people were happy with themselves and not trying to drown their sorrows in alcohol. Was she coming back to him? Who the hell ever knows what people were up to in the turmoil of modern life? Frustrated and sad, he got up and, walking across to the drinks cabinet, took out a full bottle of whisky.

"You've got as much self-control as a dead rat. Put it back, you silly old goat. She has a life too."

Back in his chair, Randall stared into the fire and listened to Mozart. It would take him three days to get the alcohol out of his system and have himself any kind of a life.

"A cup of tea. Let's go make ourselves a nice cup of tea. And no, Misty and Bob. We can't go for a walk. It's dark and raining. Do you dogs miss James Oliver? Of course, you do. We all miss our friends when we don't have them around. Come into the kitchen and I'll put out your food. You dogs look hungry."

By WEDNESDAY, the alcohol had finally drained out of his body leaving Randall feeling normal and able to think so he could go to his desk and write his book. The Sunday lunch with James Oliver in The Wagon Wheel had been fun for both of them, his son's days in boarding school with new friends taking away some of the pain from losing his mother. Even Mrs Grainger cleaning the house had made Randall smile, the old woman mostly keeping to herself in the attic when she had finished the day's work. Having food and a roof over one's head was more of a problem for old people than Randall had imagined; without a job, stretching government benefits to cover rent and day-to-day expenses was difficult. In the writing room with the fire burning in the grate, Randall sat up at his desk and stared at the blank sheet of white paper before picking up his ballpoint pen. His mind drifted far away from the present to an old Africa before colonialism, where the bush was largely inhabited by wild animals. The few indigenous people of that time scared of the lions and elephant, unable without guns to defend themselves. And into this world of sun, long grass and trees, Randall went with Lawrence Templeton-Smythe, having brought the Englishman back to the wilds from the estate in England he had bought himself from the proceeds of selling the ivory he had shipped back to England at the end of the first book. After two hours of describing Lawrence's surroundings, Randall put down his pen and smiled as the writing room and the warm fire in the grate came back to him. What Lawrence was going to do with himself in the African wilds by himself, Randall would only find out as the story unfolded. For the first time since Jane flew off to America, Randall found himself relaxed and happy without the need to drown his sorrows in alcohol, destroying his body and mind.

Going to the kitchen, Randall put the Collies on a leash and let himself out of the backdoors into a cold day with frost still on the ground, the dogs barking with pleasure as the three of them made their way into the woods and its leafless trees, the brisk walk doing all of them good. When Randall let the dogs off the leash they ran away barking.

"Come back, Misty and Bob! Nothing like a bit of exercise to make us feel good. Would you dogs like to live in Africa with the lions and the elephants? I didn't think so. Those elephants have big feet to trample you, and the lions love eating dogs. Come on. Let's run."

By the time they got back to the house, Randall was physically tired but his mind was electric as he thought through the next part of the story he was going to write.

"Lunch, Randall?"

"Thank you. A walk makes a man hungry. I'm back in a book, Mrs Fortescue."

"Is that good or bad?"

"Pays yours and Mrs Grainger's wages."

"Yes, I suppose it does. Tea or coffee?"

"Why not a cup of coffee?"

"You look happy today."

"I'm always happy when I've been writing. If I went to America next month for a week, would you be able to look after everything? The twins are as happy as crickets with you, Mrs Fortescue. You are very good to them."

"I love children. It was always my passion. I miss my own children and my grandchildren. But they have their own lives, and this, fortunately, for a few months, is mine."

"Maybe Jane will ask you to stay when she comes back."

"That would be nice. I'll take very good care of your home and family while you are away. One cup of coffee coming up. Mrs Grainger, maybe you too would like a cup of coffee? Why don't we all have a cup of coffee and sit together at the kitchen table? Then I'll make Randall his lunch.

4

_____

*R*andall arrived in New York at the end of February, no sign of
Jane at the airport which wasn't so surprising considering the
number of bookshops that required her presence. He took a cab to his
thirty-first-floor Manhattan apartment and let himself in, bringing a
broad smile to his face: the whole place smelled of Jane. In the bedroom
were some of Jane's clothes on the chair next to the bed, the bed still
unmade.

"You must have been late and had to run for it."

Smiling to himself, Randall made the double bed and went to see if
there was any fresh food in the kitchen, pulling out his phone as he went.
The phone rang as Randall waited.

"Manfred Leon. Can I help you?"

"Maybe I can help you, Manfred. I'm in my apartment on the thirty-
first floor, here for the week. I can do what you wanted and go on the Jay
Leno show."

"You must be joking. You turned him down. He won't ask you again.
He has more famous people than he can count wanting to be on his
show. How are you, Randall?"

"I'm sorry."

"You should be. Never ever again miss an opportunity like that one.
Godfrey Merchant nearly had a fit. Is Jane with you? Thought she was
with Agatha Stone signing books. They say for every book an author

signs for a reader it generates ten more sales, and so the word of mouth goes on. Successful book publishing is all in the marketing I'm afraid. You've taken yourself out of the public eye and your book sales are dropping, unlike Jane's which are climbing nicely and will do for as long as she keeps at it. You can't hide away, Randall, if you want to stay a successful author. You must move back to America. Your brother and Martha live in the same building, for goodness sake. And so does your girlfriend. Tracey. She works hard to promote her books for me. You're a naughty boy, Randall Holiday. Don't you miss your friends?"

"Have you heard of a stage actress named Penny Long?"

"I was her agent once. Trying to get her into films. She preferred the West End stage in London. Why do you ask?"

"Is she still alive?"

"I have no idea. I could find out for you."

"I met an old man in a pub who knew Penny when they were children living next door to each other. He still pines for her. It's a long story. I said I would try and find her for Jake Crawley who says Penny was the only true love of his life."

"When are we having lunch together?"

"What's wrong with today? Please don't give me a clip around the ear. Oh, and I'm not drinking."

"That's interesting."

"All that publicity business drove me to drink."

"Does the same for most of us. Just part of life. One o'clock here at the office. Lunch is on me."

"How is *Shakespeare's Ghost* coming along?"

"Depends on you, Randall."

"Is it typed?"

"Not yet."

"Have you given the hand script to anyone?"

"Not yet. Godfrey Merchant has gone off you."

"Can I repair the damage?"

"You can try. See you for lunch. Good to talk to you."

"I can hear you smiling."

"Of course I am. I'm your agent."

"Did you read *Shakespeare's Ghost*?"

"I did."

"What did you think of it?"

"As good a book as I ever read."

"Then why didn't you get it typed?"

"You've got to be a big part of the marketing or it won't work. Do you understand, Randall? We have to help each other or it doesn't work. We're a team. If you don't promote your books by helping us market them you'll have nothing to do, despite all your money. Jane's having fun with Agatha. The worst thing in life is boredom, you've said that yourself."

"Penny Long must have been quite old when you became her agent. She'd be in her eighties if she's alive."

"She was a great character actor in the latter part of her life. Many good films have characters in their sixties. They often make the film. It's not all about sex appeal and youth. I'll make some phone calls. Who is Jake Crawley, not that it matters? You can tell me the whole story over lunch. What are you writing at the moment?"

"A second book involving Lawrence Templeton-Smythe."

"I haven't even seen the first one."

"I haven't decided finally on a title. I'll tell you about it over lunch."

"Are you going to help us promote your book?"

"We'll see. Probably. My life's a mess."

WHEN RANDALL REACHED Manfred's office they went straight out to lunch, sitting at a table in an expensive restaurant surrounded by rich people. The whole place reeked of money. Manfred ordered himself a cocktail, giving Randall a smile.

"Are you sure, Randall?"

"Quite certain. I'm a drunk. When I drink, the after-effects make me miserable. Enjoy your Manhattan. Why did they call it after a place we live in?"

"I have no idea. You see that man over there with a pretty girl half his age? He's a film actor. There he goes. Now he's waving at me. Without my help, he would never have made it. So, how are your new babies?"

"They eat and sleep. Mrs Fortescue is looking after them. When does Jane start her world tour? A month and she's not out of New York."

"You have to do a job properly, Randall. It may take longer than five months. We'll see. Agatha is doing a splendid job. A real organiser is Agatha. One of the keys to a successful business is having dedicated and competent employees. I pay them well which helps. When the sales of

Love in the Spring of Life reach five million copies, Agatha will receive a fifty-thousand-dollar bonus."

"Have you sold the film rights?"

"I've had offers from four studios but as the sales go up, so does my price. You must remember that from *Love Song*. The more people who read the book, the more people that want to see it in the cinema. It's all a game of numbers."

"Where is Jane at the moment?"

"I don't have my notes with me to tell you which shop. When the shops close she'll go home to your apartment. Have you seen your brother Phillip or Tracey? Tracey loves her baby. Allegra. Such a lovely name. Now, what are you going to eat?"

"Is Jane going to write her own film script? She did a good job with Tracey's *Lust*."

"We'll wait and see. That part of it is up to the film producer. I'll recommend Jane, of course. More money for her and her agent."

"A rare rump steak, thank you, waiter. With lots of fresh vegetables. So all I have to do is go home and wait for Jane?"

"Something like that. I'll have the fish. And please don't cook it too much. Now, where were we?"

"You haven't mentioned Jay Leno."

"Why didn't you come over?"

"I'd found peace in the English countryside, away from the rush of people. Not as pleasant as Africa but the place I bought is quiet and away from noise. In my writing room, I live in Africa. Back in the bush. When I disappear into my mind I'm there, right there in the bush with the wild animals and a small tent to sleep in with a blazing campfire to keep off the animals at night. You should go to Africa, Manfred. You'd love it."

"I'm quite happy in New York. There's my list. You can read it now at the table or when you get home. It's a list of things you have to do to get your book sales rising again. You'd better put it in your pocket. Good to see you again, Randall. How was your Christmas?"

"My father and stepmother joined us. They miss Africa as much as I do. How long will it take me to do the jobs on your list?"

"Three or four months every year. Then you can go back to working for me. You see, in the end, despite all the publicity, it has to be a good book like *Shakespeare's Ghost*. Do I detect an element of you in the friend who wanted to stay anonymous?"

"I too want to live my own life in peace."

"When you've read my list and agreed to do what I ask, we'll get the book typed and edited and I'll send it to your publisher with an advance price that will blow their minds. Who knows? Jay Leno may even ask you again to go on his show. Food. Looks good. I'm hungry. You mind if I stop talking while I eat? The only way to enjoy good food. This fish tastes good."

"You said you weren't going to talk."

"You know how it is. I really enjoy your company."

"And I enjoy yours."

"There we are. Tuck in, Randall. That steak doesn't look too bad either. I love New York. It's always exciting. Something is always happening. Why I've never once been bored in my whole life."

"I'm never bored when I'm writing."

"But that's my point. You won't want to write if it isn't going to be published."

"I'll pay to publish my own book."

"That won't help. How's it going to hit the shelves?"

"If Godfrey won't take my book because I refused to go on the Jay Leno show, can't you find me another publisher?"

"And upset all the publishers? You must be joking. Part of an agent's job, a big part I might add, is getting his writers to promote their books. I can't be seen to be going against the system, it would ruin my business. There aren't that many publishers with clout. Maybe ten or twenty. I have to do what they tell me in the same way you must do what's on that list in your pocket. It was so sweet of Jane to ask me to be a godfather to one of her children. What were their names again?"

"Kimber and Raphael."

"Anyway, I can't and let's not start talking about religion. Your religion is what you were born to. And I was happily born Jewish."

Eating his steak, Randall watched Manfred finish his fish.

"You want dessert, Randall?"

"Why not?"

"Are we back on the same wavelength, old friend?"

"I think so."

"Penny Long. She was fun. Great sense of humour. Haven't heard her name in years. She never married. There was a story that she was a lesbian. In those days they kept it quiet. Now they come out and use it as part of their publicity. Gay rights. It's all about publicity. Getting the media's attention. Keeping your name in the news. They go into a bookshop and see a familiar name and pick up the book."

"You're not going to let me get away with it?"

"I hope not, Randall."

"You see, I look at money from a different angle. When you've got enough, why make more if you're not going to spend it? I have well invested what's left of my capital after my wives took their divorce settlements. The investment funds are watched by professionals. The income alone is more than enough to live on. You see, it's not just the money I made from my books but my inheritance from my grandfather. Ben Crossley left both myself and Phillip a fortune. I can't see the point in chasing more money."

"To keep you writing and let you have fun. How does that sound? Give me some ice cream and chocolate sauce. They make the best chocolate sauce in New York. You should try it."

"Thank you, waiter. I'll have the ice cream. What's your name? Does my friend tip you well?"

"Always. Two ice creams and chocolate sauce coming up."

"And coffee."

PART 6

FEBRUARY TO JUNE 1998 – ONLY TIME WOULD TELL

1

---

*J*ane Slater sat in the back of the cab on her way home after a gruelling day's work wondering what was going to happen next. Was Randall at home in the apartment? Was he going to demand she give up the tour and go back to the babies he will say she has abandoned? Were the twins being looked after properly by a stranger without even one of their parents? Was he ever going to marry her and would even that give her security for the rest of her and the twins' lives? Forty per cent of all marriages ended in divorce, most of them unpleasant, and he'd had two of them already. For the first time in Jane's life, she was going to be financially secure if she kept up the sales and maximised the film rights. With all that money she would never again have to depend on other people. Did he love her? Did she love him? They had fun when they were drinking together but drinking had its pitfalls. Since she arrived on the book tour, Jane had not taken a single drink. Last week she had turned forty. She felt old, an old woman in many people's eyes.

Having paid the cabbie and given him a good tip, Jane went up to the thirty-first floor and put her key in the door, pausing for a moment. Inside there was silence, no music playing. Jane quietly opened the door.

"Hello, my love. Are you there? Ah, Randall. The sight of you makes me so happy. What time is it?"

"Half past seven."

"Another long day. Do I get a hug?"

"You're going to get a lot more than a hug. You're crying."

"So are you. I so miss my babies. I abandoned them, Randall. Ran away to make money. Am I crazy?"

"I had lunch with Manfred. Gave me a to-do list. Maybe I'll have to compromise. Live four months of the year here and do what Manfred tells me, and the rest of the time writing in England away from people. A compromise. Oh, and I made the bed."

"I was in too much of a hurry this morning. Every morning. It never stops."

"Manfred says your sales are rising nicely. Make sure you invest your money wisely. Do you hate me for leaving the twins with Mrs Fortescue? I'll be back in a week. I just couldn't wait to see you. Phones are not enough. Are you mad at me?"

"Worried, but I've been worried since I left the twins in England. Are we going to have a drink?"

"I've stopped drinking."

"Thank goodness. So have I. So, how've you been, Randall?"

"Never felt more miserable in my entire life. But now with you, I'm beginning to feel better. How've you been, Jane?"

"Exhausted. It never stops. People. A constant flow of people. Having to be nice to people.. But it's been fun. Agatha's been a great support. It's life, Randall. You don't get something without working for it. Have you eaten?"

"Not tonight. You want to go out to dinner?"

"The last thing I want to do at the moment is go out to dinner."

"You're smiling."

"I'm so happy to see you. Come on. We'll make supper together and go to bed."

"Now you're talking."

"So tell me what's been going on at the Woodlands."

"Mrs Fortescue made me employ a full-time cleaner. She's moved into the attic."

"What's her name? How old is she?"

"Oh, you don't have to worry. She's an old lady in need of a job. Like Mrs Fortescue. You're smiling to yourself, Jane."

"A cleaner. I can't believe it. So, Spaghetti. We've got beef mince to use as the base for a sauce. I'm so tired all I want to do is go to sleep which isn't right."

"What else have you been up to other than signing books?"

"At the weekends I've been looking to buy an apartment. Part of my financial plan to spread the risk. Manfred introduced me to an investment consultant who looks after his financial affairs. Mason says the most secure investment of all is property."

"But I thought you were going to buy half of the Woodlands?"

"That's the property portion of your investment portfolio. This way we both spread our risks. Don't forget you also own this place and Rabbit Farm. You've invested heavily in property."

"Are you going to leave me?"

"No, of course not. We have the twins... Tracey loves her baby. She still hasn't tried to find out who the father is. We should go up and see her over the weekend. You remember the three musketeers?"

"Does she want to do a blood test?"

"I don't know... Tomatoes. That's what I need. Lucky I went shopping on Saturday... It's a bit weird you and I not drinking. By now we'd have begun to get pickled. Can you chop up the onions for me? Are you worried about Tracey taking a blood test? There's a chance you could be the father. That would be fun."

"Does she have a lover?"

"Tracey always seems to have a man. Only trouble is they are rarely the same person. She loves spending her money on good-looking men. Says you only have one life and youth fades quickly. I turned forty last week. Are my looks fading, Randall?"

"It's not all about age. I'm sorry I missed your birthday."

"Isn't it? We can celebrate over the weekend. But I often wonder. I was just so lucky getting myself pregnant. Tracey and I agree that without children, life becomes worthless. How's James Oliver?"

"He's perking up just a little."

"Let's eat in the kitchen. You can put out the spoons and forks."

By the time the meal was cooked and they sat down at the table to eat, Jane wasn't sure if it was good them not having a drink: in the past, alcohol had bound them together.

"What are you going to do during the day when I'm signing books?"

"I'm coming with you."

"Are you going to sign books?"

"If they want me to. The food's good. You're a much better cook than Mrs Fortescue."

"Will they be all right? I worry about them every waking moment.

I've had bad dreams. Nothing in the dream quite goes wrong but I wake on the brink of disaster. In my dream, I'm out shopping with the twins in the pram and turning around and the pram's gone... Are you writing?"

"Trying to."

"Haven't written a word since I went on the tour. Oh, well. Can't have everything, as they say. At least we have money. Without money, you end up on the bones of your arse like Mrs Fortescue and this Mrs Grainger."

"Have you seen your father, Jane?"

"Once. He and Sophie live quiet lives."

"Are they happy?"

"Who's ever really happy? All we can do is try to be happy. We're no different to any other species of animals on this planet even though we try and say we are different. Life's quite simple really. All the rules and regulations we like to call civilisation don't make the slightest difference to how we feel. But we all need money. Oh yes, we all need money."

"Do we? Our dogs and cats don't have money."

"But they have us to look after them. I don't think I really know what I'm talking about."

"Your eyes are almost closing."

"I'm just so tired, Randall. It'll be better during the weekend."

"And then I fly back to England."

"How it goes. You mind if I go to bed? It's up early again tomorrow morning."

"Where are you signing tomorrow? You haven't finished your food."

"Agatha wrote it down for me. The cab driver will know the way. Are we going to make love?"

"Depends if you fall asleep."

"Do you hate me? You look all tensed up."

"Even the mention of booze gets me wound up. Let's finish eating and get into bed and let you sleep sweet dreams."

"Let's both sleep sweet dreams."

Leaving the dishes in the sink, they walked into the bedroom, took off their clothes and got into bed. The moment Jane's head touched the pillow she fell into a dreamless sleep.

In the morning, in the taxi being driven to the bookshop that was next on Agatha's list, Jane's worry turned to becoming a lonely old woman once the twins grew up and flew the nest. Instead of coming with her, Randall had stayed in the apartment to read and digest Manfred's to-do list. A kiss goodbye was as near as they came to having sex.

"What's life all about, Jane Slater?"

"Did you say something?"

"Sorry, driver. Talking to myself. Do you have children?"

"We all have children... Here we are. Look at that. Your photograph is in the window of the bookshop. Are you really that famous writer? Are all those books piled up in the window yours? Big red sign: author signing books on Thursday, 26th of February. That's today."

"Why I'm here."

"Can I have one of your books?"

"If you come in and buy. All those books belong to the bookshop. There you go. I read your meter and added a tip. Have a nice day."

"You too. A famous author. Who'd have thought!"

"You've never heard of me, have you?"

"Haven't read a book since I left school. I'm a TV man."

In the shop, Jane introduced herself to the shop owner and looked around the shop. Her book was number one on the ten-bestseller shelf.

"Oh, you'll be number one today, Jane Slater. Your people put that photograph in my front window a week ago and made that pyramid of your books. The big red sign catches the public eye as they pass down the main street. Everyone likes to meet someone they are told is famous. Today I'm going to make lots of money out of your books. A lady from *People* magazine is sitting at the table we have prepared for your signing. Says she has an eight o'clock appointment. There'll be a trickle coming in for you to sign the book in the early morning, so it won't affect your interview with the magazine. By lunchtime, it'll be different. I'll bring both of you a cup of coffee. I'm so pleased you chose my shop for the signing. Once they know where I am, they'll come in again for other books. You're great publicity for my shop. I read your book and have no hesitation in recommending it. There's nothing better in life than reading a good book. What was the name of the lady again who set up the window last week?"

"Agatha Stone. She works for my agent... Hello, I'm Jane Slater. You must be from *People* magazine. There'll be a few interruptions but we'll still have plenty of time to talk. What would you like to know for your article?"

"I'm Emma Sanders. Nice to meet you. Do you live with Randall Holiday?"

"We have two children. Now, about my book."

"But you're not married."

"Does it matter?"

"My readers will lap it up. Makes a good story. Help you sell your books. What it's all about really. For both of us. How long have you known Randall?"

"As lovers? A bit over a year."

"And you have two children! That isn't possible."

"It is if you have twins."

"And you both live in England?"

"For the moment. We have two homes. Three, actually. We were friends. Good friends. And one night we became lovers and luck and joy came my way. At the end of my thirties, I became pregnant."

"Was it your first time?"

"Amazingly. My first love is all in the book."

"Did you deliberately not use a contraceptive?"

"That's a personal question."

"Are you going to marry?"

"Why don't we talk about *Love in the Spring of Life*?... Hello. What's your name? There you go. All nicely signed, Mavis. Enjoy my book. I loved writing it."

"Thank you so much. A book signed with my name by such a famous author. I'll treasure this book for years. Thank you again, Jane Slater."

"My pleasure... Now, where were we before Mavis interrupted us?"

"Can you take me right back in your life? We want your story. We don't want to retell the story of your book. People like to know about the person who wrote the book they're reading. Enables them to communicate with the author... Thank you. Just what I need. A cup of coffee. I drank too much wine at a launch party last night. New author. Haven't yet read his book. Took me out to dinner. He's so good-looking."

"Did you?"

"I'm not going to answer that question. Do you drink, Jane?"

"Tried to stop. Maybe tonight we'll have ourselves a drink. Randall is here in New York for a short visit."

"Is he coming to the shop?"

"He knows where I am."

"Can I wait for him?"

"You can do what you like."

"I've always wanted to meet Randall Holiday. He's good-looking too."

"How old are you, Emma?"

"Twenty-seven. Men. I love men."

"Are you married?"

"Whatever for? I'm ready with pen and paper. Let's have your story."

Trying to concentrate on her press interview, Jane's mind kept going back to Randall: would it matter if she bought them a bottle of whisky and an expensive bottle of wine? All she had to do the next day was sign books. There were no interviews scheduled. She wouldn't have to think. And if she left the moment the place closed instead of talking to Agatha when she came to the shop after window-dressing another shop for the following week, would it matter? Maybe Agatha would understand.

"What are you smiling about, Jane?"

"A bottle of whisky. Are we finished?"

"Where's Randall?"

"Leave him alone, Emma. He's mine. For the moment anyway."

"Thank you for your time."

"Write a well-written article."

"Are you going to read what I say?"

"Probably... There we are, young man. Signed. Enjoy your read."

"What's the matter, Jane? You didn't ask his name."

"This tour is destroying my life."

"Can I write that?"

"Please don't. I've enough problems. My babies are without their mother... I miss my babies terribly."

"You're crying."

"I don't care."

2

————

*B*y the time Jane reached the apartment with a bottle of whisky and a bottle of French wine it was seven o'clock in the evening. As she put the key in the door she could hear Randall's love for classical music.

"I'm home. The central heating makes this place so nice and warm. How was your day? Did you work out what you're going to do with Manfred? Had an interview with *People* magazine. They want you as well as me in the article."

"Supper's prepared."

"We need ice and two glasses. I bought us a bottle of whisky. Sometimes it's good to break the rules. Let's get pickled together and have a giggle."

"How many books did you sign?"

"Lost count. The shop owner was happy. I'm tired and exhausted but whisky and wine will perk me up."

"You bought wine as well!"

"You know what they say: if you're going to do a job, do it properly. Did you phone Mrs Fortescue?"

"Everything is under control. I'll get the ice out of the fridge."

"The music is lovely."

"Music is always lovely. Helped me so many times in my life."

"Let's have a drink. Tonight, I want to be happy... What's for supper?"

"Stew. Good old beef stew. We can eat any time we like. I know I shouldn't drink but I can't take my eyes off that bottle of whisky. Is it red or white?"

"The whisky?"

"The wine. If it's red, I'll open it now to let it breathe. Take it out of the bag. Red. French. Wow. That stuff's expensive."

"What money's for. If you got it, spend it. Not all, of course. Why are you giggling, Randall?"

"I always thought it was good whisky that made my mouth water. My mouth's dribbling at the thought of the drink."

"So, what's the plan?"

"I've done a lot of thinking, Jane, sitting here all day on my own. Manfred is right. If I can't publish I'll have to stop writing. If I stop writing there will be nothing to do. We have to promote our books whether we like it or not. And the twins need their parents to bond with. Only that way will we have a family. I'm going to fly back to England on Tuesday and bring back the twins."

"And Mrs Fortescue?"

"She and Mrs Grainger can look after the Woodlands and be there when we get back in the summer. We're going to live two lives."

"Oh, Randall. I thought I was going to die. Let's crack the whisky. Whisky and wine. Beautiful music. Stew on the hob as you call the top of the stove. And you and me, Randall. And my babies are coming back to me. What more can a girl ever want?"

"There you go. Lots of ice and lots of whisky. Cheers, Jane."

"Cheers, my love. To many lives full of happiness."

"I'll drink to that."

"What about James Oliver?"

"I've thought through that one. He's at a good boarding school that is giving him lots of friends, so seeing him every weekend isn't so important. If we are here during his holidays he can fly out and join us. He'll love America. This tastes so good. To keep our drinking under control we'll have a few breaks."

"Are you sure about the breaks?"

"Who knows? Out pops the cork. There's something about the sound of a cork coming out of a bottle. A joyful sound. *People* magazine. Never heard of them."

"Next week it's *Vanity Fair*."

"I did them once. Or rather they did me. It's so wonderful to be back with you, Jane. For a moment back alone in England, I thought I was going to shoot myself."

"Please don't do that. It's so messy."

"Peace, hope and happiness with my best friend and lover."

"Do you mean that, Randall?"

"Why would I say anything I don't mean? Scotch whisky is definitely the best. Must be fun up there in the Highlands perfecting the blend of a vat of whisky. We never think of the people who make our lives so pleasant because we don't know their names. Mozart, I thank for his music because I know his name. That he was the composer of the piano concerto I have enjoyed so many times. Music. Love. Happiness. Financial security. And a bottle of the best Scotch whisky."

"What's going to happen when the tour takes me out of New York? I still won't be close to my babies. Maybe leaving them in England with Mrs Fortescue when you come for a visit is right after all. It's all such a muddle. Whatever we do, it doesn't work. A woman should be a full-time housewife and bring up her children helping them grow. Show them how to avoid the snags. Give them that comfort and feeling of security. Let the man be the breadwinner and the wife look after the family home. How it worked before we women got ourselves in that maniacal pursuit of more money. Today, most families need both parents working for wages or they can't make ends meet. The women often make more money than the men, which never happened before women's liberation came along with all those activists shouting. Just another game of politics in pursuit of votes. What a world we've got into, they call democracy."

"Maybe I stay with the twins in England and fly out with them once a month to wherever you are?"

"I don't like the idea of my babies being carried onto aeroplanes. We talked about this before. They'd be constantly under stress, not knowing where they are or where they are going. And again, what are you going to do about Manfred's to-do list? Whichever way we jump there's a problem. Why isn't life simple? If anyone is going to fly around every month it should be me. Take a week's break from the tour."

"Your tour would never be over."

"What do we do, Randall?"

"I have no idea. Except tonight, just the two of us are going to get nicely pickled... There is a final alternative. We could both give up writing books and live off the interest from our capital."

"And be bored out of our minds."

"You got it. There'd be no challenge. Nothing new to think about. Just a daily routine with drinking too much booze at the end of the day... So there we have it. Maybe just play it one day at a time. Nothing works perfectly. Never did. It's called life. The same for all of us, Jane... You want me to top up your whisky?"

"And then we grow old."

"We never grow any younger. Now it's the forty decade. Then it will be the fifty if we stay healthy and live. I've never been sure what life was all about. What the purpose was. Why we were born. But we were and here we are... Is that better? Now I've drowned the ice. Cheers again. Tonight's giggle night. And making love night. Good, you're smiling. The twins are fine where they are. Secure and well looked after. Mrs Fortescue is an elderly woman who takes her job seriously. And she loves children."

"So are you going to do anything for Manfred?"

"Let's forget our agent. Forget about everything except ourselves. Tomorrow we'll get back to worrying."

"I love you, Randall."

"I love you too."

"But do we mean what we say?"

"Who really knows? The trick is to do and say what is right for the moment. What takes us through another day. Live today, Jane, and let tomorrow take care of itself. Now the music has changed and I didn't notice it change. Haydn instead of Mozart. Let's raise our glasses in thanks to both of them for creating such beautiful music that will last for all eternity. They've lasted hundreds of years. And will last hundreds more. Let's hope that happens to our books but I doubt it. Today, books and music are just about making money. What a world. But that's how it is. And by the time the twins grow up, it will have changed all over again, for better or for worse."

"Shakespeare will live forever."

"And so will *Shakespeare's Ghost*. Except he preferred to stay anonymous and enjoy his life without having to promote their plays. He just sat back up in his box and enjoyed the acting. Here's to William Shakespeare and his friend, whoever he might have been. It's the play that is more important. The creation of a great piece of art. You don't look so tired tonight, Jane."

"I'm more relaxed with you beside me. The stress has gone. You're right. Let's just enjoy today and let all those Shakespearian tomorrows you talk about take care of themselves 'to the last syllable of recorded time'. Now, were those words Shakespeare or his friend?"

"We'll never know."

After the stew, half a bottle of whisky and most of the red wine, they went smiling to bed, both of them happy by the look Jane saw on Randall's face. In bed, naked, they slowly, gently made love, the feeling more in Jane's mind than her body. With Randall holding her from behind Jane went to sleep. She woke once in the dark of the night, the sound of the New York traffic a faraway rumble, a pleasant, familiar sound. The dream came when she fell back into sleep where she found her babies. When she woke remembering a brief flash from her dream, Randall had rolled over, the sound of traffic almost gone. When Jane woke from her sleep for the last time, Randall was holding a cup of tea for her, standing by the side of the bed.

"Another day. Friday. I'm going to sit with you while you sign books, despite your work, the two of us together. Did you sleep well?"

"I dreamed I was with the twins. Everything was lovely. No panic this time when I woke. We're lucky, Randall. I shouldn't complain. I have everything a girl could ever want. Thanks for the tea."

"My pleasure."

"It's just a shame I'll be signing books instead of both of us writing by the fire in our lovely writing room, far from all the turmoil of people. Do you think mankind will live for all eternity? I doubt it. It's just a period of time for us at the moment. A brief flash in the onward process of evolution which will one day come to an end, this planet forgotten, a distant dead object going round and round in that strange place we call the universe. We must enjoy every moment we can when we have it. That lovely period in life called now. Let's soak together in a nice hot bath and then go out and visit the people, those fellow humans who like ourselves have no idea what it is all about. Today is making money day. How it works. This tea is perfectly delicious. I've always said there is only one way to start a day, with a nice hot cup of tea made for me by my lover. It's so wonderful to be with you again. Just the two of us. What's for breakfast?"

"Lots of toast and marmalade."

"And a bowl of cornflakes."

"And a bowl of cornflakes. The wolves have gone, Jane. No more howling wolves in my head. Lawrence Templeton-Smythe is talking to me in my head, the next story of his life coming alive. My fictional world, Jane. That's all I want. You, my children, and the world I create in my mind."

"But today it's the day of making money so we can live in comfort and follow the dreams of our characters. That's what we must understand. That we need both. Our dreams and the money to give us physical comfort to pursue our dreams and bring up our children."

"How is Margaret Neville?"

"Far, far away. But she'll come back to me when I start writing. When I go home to our place in the woods. She's always around, Margaret Neville. She's never left me since the day I created her. You must know what I'm talking about?"

"It's all as clear as crystal. I just can't wait for us to be alone again in the peace of our writing room. I'll go and make the toast while you think of Margaret Neville and bring her closer."

"We're nuts, Randall."

"Who cares? Nothing wrong with being a little mad. Makes living pleasant. Takes away the pain."

When Randall flew back to England on the Tuesday, Jane's feeling of insecurity came flooding back again. When she told Manfred on the phone during her book signing that she wanted a week-long break every month he laughed at her.

"And what's Agatha going to do? You can't chop and change. One job at a time. She plans ahead for you and keeps up the momentum. When you're in Australia and fly to England does Agatha come back here to the office or sit on her bum doing nothing? I thought Randall was going to stay in New York and now he's run away again. Running my business is a nightmare. I know what has to be done but no one listens to me. Is the bookshop full of people buying your book? Good. Keep at it. Keep your eye on the ball. Have a nice day, Jane Slater. Check your bank balance. Your publisher's made a big transfer into your account today. And tell Randall to behave himself. What's the matter with you two? I've made both of you rich and famous and where are my thanks? Mason will tell you how much tax you have to pay. You see, we're all organised."

"I miss my children."

"Then bring them to America."

"England's our home."

"What nonsense. I just don't understand people. You've enough money, the pair of you, to employ an army of nannies. One of Randall's rooms where he writes in his apartment is soundproofed. No problem, writing free of noise."

"Are you doing anything with *Shakespeare's Ghost?*"

"Not a thing. Let me get back to work. You should see my desk. There's a pile of files and the other phone is now ringing. It never stops."

"Sorry."

"I hope so. Keep up the good work, Jane. Your sales are soaring in every shop you visited. People are talking to each other about your book. Word of mouth. The best way for publishers to make a profit without spending half their money on advertising."

Staring at the dead phone in her hand, Jane looked up from the table and smiled at the next customer.

"What's your name? I like to write inside that this book of mine is for you and write your name before I sign."

"Conny."

"My sister's name is Conny... There you are, Conny. Love from Jane Slater. Enjoy my book. Now, who's next?"

Trying not to think back to her phone call with Manfred, Jane let the day go on, another day, another signing. By the time Agatha came in from her day of setting up another bookshop for a future signing, Jane was exhausted.

"Can we go for a drink?"

"I thought you weren't drinking? Lovely. There's a bar down the main road. I'd love to go for a drink. I'm going to get that fifty-thousand-dollar bonus, Jane. Five million copies sold. That's all we have to do to make me rich. I'm going to buy more clothes than you can imagine. Make the men come running. My aim in life is to find myself a rich husband. Your book tells us all the beauty of young, innocent love where two people fall head over heels with each other without any idea of anything else. People love it. Love the idea of love being all you need to find. But it isn't. Your young love, your Harvey, we found out later when he shouted his mouth off to the press, married not you but a girl from a rich family so he could get into the girl's family business. The story went viral helping your book's sales go into the millions. Innocent, perfect love of two people is one thing but it's all in the mind. A bit in the body of course. We can walk down to the bar. Didn't you tell me the truth about your own life when you broke up with Harvey instead of the perfect marriage you wrote in the book? That you ended up poverty-stricken working in a laundry. I wish I could write books like you and make that fortune. That's what we really want, Jane. Not love in the springtime of life. We want a fortune. We're lucky it isn't raining. When's Randall coming back? I'm to help him with his to-do list."

"I don't know."

"Why are you crying?"

"One minute you remind me of Harvey. Then you remind me of Randall. All I want is my babies."

"And a nice, stiff drink. Here we go. The door opens easily. Always do into a bar. Cheer up. Life always works out fine."

"So they say. You're right. I must stop feeling sorry for myself. What are you having? The drinks are on me. And thank you, Agatha, for your help. Every shop has been set up perfectly. I'm going to start with a double whisky."

"This place looks nice, Jane. We can eat at one of those tables. In two weeks' time, we fly together to Australia. Melbourne and then Sydney with a few towns in between. Got to keep up the momentum. Did you ever hear what's happened to Harvey?"

"He made a bit of his own money telling our story by writing articles for the odd newspaper. Good luck to him. Can't have been nice getting fired by his father-in-law and told by his lovely wife to get out of the house. He's even talking about writing his own book: the truth about love is the spring. It's all a game, Agatha."

"Can he write?"

"We'll have to find out... Why isn't Manfred going ahead with *Shakespeare's Ghost*?"

"He's trying to force Randall to behave himself."

"And if that doesn't work? He'll lose a good book. Doesn't make sense."

"There are plenty of good books."

"Are there? I wonder."

"Then we'll just have to see which one breaks first, Randall or Manfred. I'll have a glass of red wine. Didn't Manfred give Harvey a bit of your money? Told me once he paid two thousand dollars out of royalty every month into Harvey's bank account. Very generous of you for a man who dumped you and sent you financially down the proverbial plughole."

"I felt a bit guilty that all my money from the book wouldn't have come without that young love affair with Harvey."

"Did you want to bring him back? Money attracts men as well as women. We don't realise, but often we are being bought."

"My new life is with Randall and my babies. Looking back, it was all I ever wanted."

"But you're not married. Sorry, I'm saying things that I shouldn't. Manfred is having a lot of fun arguing about your film rights. He's got four producers running. All good movies come from a good story, mainly from novels."

"Have you ever been in love, Agatha?"

"I don't think so. Do we really know the meaning of love? Most relationships are a game of mutual convenience. It must be weird you sitting here and your children are on the other side of the pond."

"You can say that again. You want kids, Agatha?"

"Sure. We all want kids. Children, we hope, give us a future. I'm going to watch the saga of Manfred and Randall with interest. Maybe he should leave both of you alone and let you live in peace and just write your books. How much is Randall worth?"

"Millions. He always says, 'When you have enough what's the point of chasing after more?'."

"They all do it. They say making more and more money becomes an addiction. It's not so easy as people think to hold on to a fortune. The markets are so volatile. Many rich men have invested their money badly and gone bust. The only certainty with money is being able to create your own income. Why you and I are on this lovely book tour. I can't wait to go off and see the world. We're going to have fun. You'll feel just fine, Jane, after a couple more drinks. This is life in the fast lane. Just how I like it."

Listening to Agatha prattle on about her life, Jane thought back to Randall. She had tried to laugh off his comment about shooting himself, but was he serious?

"He said he wanted to shoot himself."

"Who?"

"Randall. He said with me away and Manfred not doing anything with *Shakespeare's Ghost* he had no life."

"But he's rich."

"Doesn't make any difference. I'm worried stiff, so far away. I'm being selfish; building up my own fortune; only thinking about myself."

"Stop worrying, Jane. Worrying never helped anyone. How's your drink going down? My wine tastes delicious and it's beginning to make me float. A drink after work is the best way to relax ourselves. With a few glasses of wine inside me I sleep right through the night."

"What if he's bought himself a gun? Hemingway shot himself and left behind his sons."

"Drink, Jane. Down the hatch. Let's both of us get a little drunk and have some fun. There's a man over there giving me the eye. I like it. It's so nice being young."

"I've just turned forty!"

"I haven't reached my thirties."

"Enjoy it while you have it."

"Have what, Jane?"

"What Randall calls the pull. Fifty thousand dollars doesn't sound enough of a bonus for getting me to five million sales. I'm going to ask Manfred to ask my publisher, Godfrey Merchant, to put in another fifty thousand dollars for you. Does Manfred pay you a good salary?"

"The best. Why I work so hard. Would you really do that for me, Jane? One hundred thousand dollars. Wow."

"It doesn't make sense."

"What doesn't make sense? A hundred thousand dollars?"

"No, silly. Me sitting here and my babies are all alone."

"Don't they have a nanny? And Randall?"

"They need their mother... Now I'm crying again."

"Let's change the subject. What do you know about Australia?"

"Absolutely nothing."

"Don't you want to go?"

"I want to go back to my babies and my lover. Why has Manfred been so difficult? People never leave us alone to our own devices."

"How life works. It's one long chase. Come off it, Jane. We're about to go around the world, all expenses paid by our publisher. What's wrong with that? We'll see things and meet lots of interesting people. Who knows, I might just find myself a rich husband."

"Is it really just about money?"

"Of course it is. Without money, life sucks. Don't you remember your days in the laundry?"

"Why I'm here building up my own money."

"Then stop moaning. You think he's going to come over? You're the luckiest girl in the world. You're rich and famous and have two lovely children."

"You're right. Thank you, Agatha. The drink is making me feel a little better. Shall I ask him to come and join us?"

"Don't be silly. He'll think I'm a whore. Let's change barstools and then he can't look at me. Drink and be merry. What my father told everybody."

"Where's your father?"

"He's dead. Died of cancer when I was ten. My poor mother. No husband and no money."

"I'm sorry."

"So am I. I never got over it."

"Who looks after your mother?"

"Financially? I do. With the help of my two brothers. You see, even if you were to lose all your royalty money, you'd still have children to look after you in your old age."

"He's coming over, Agatha."

"Oh, what fun."

Quietly, looking at their drinks, they waited.

"Hello. Aren't you the famous author, Jane Slater? I loved your book. Just finished it, in fact. May I join you for a drink? And what's your name?"

"Agatha Stone. I work for Jane's agent promoting her book."

"Can I buy you both a drink?"

"Why ever not? We're just getting started. And what's your name?"

"David. My friends call me Davy. What are you doing in my part of the world?"

"Jane's signing books. Did you buy her book from the shop up the road?"

"Last week. There was a big photograph of the author in the window. Why I recognised you, Jane, from the other side of the bar. Your book brought back wonderful memories for me. What are you two drinking?"

"The barman knows."

"Good. We'll have the same again, Simon. Known Simon for years. This is my favourite bar. How extraordinary to meet the author of a book I just read. *Love in the Spring of Life.* How it was with me. I'll never forget her. We never forget that first love. That time in our lives when everything is perfect. A book like yours appeals to everyone, the young and the old."

By the time Jane had finished her double whisky, it was time to go back to the hotel and sleep.

"I'm off to bed, Agatha. You don't have to come with me. You two enjoy yourselves. Simon can order me a taxi. Glad you enjoyed my book, Davy."

"One more drink for the road while Simon's getting you a cab."

"Why not? It's always one more for the road."

THE DAYS and weeks went on from shop to shop, country to country, bar to bar, all of it the same, all of it just making money. When Jane flew back to England, she hadn't seen Randall for three months, only spoken to him on the phone.

As Jane stepped off the plane at Heathrow Airport she was not certain if it had all been worth it despite the sales topping the five million mark and the film rights selling for two million dollars. With the feeling of excitement almost making her trip over her own feet, Jane ran out of the terminal straight into Randall's arms.

"Where are my children?" she demanded.

"At home. Safe. Come, the car's outside. Our lives are back. Even the sun is shining. June is bursting out all over. You remember that old song, Jane? We can be happy again. The shit's in the past. Never again, is what I told Manfred. I love you, Jane Slater. You have no idea how much I love you. The last three months have been the loneliest months of my life."

On the way out of London and into Surrey with Randall driving, Jane hoped that for once in her life it wasn't all about the money. She was going home with her lover to her babies and the peace of the English countryside, far, far away from people and all their madness. Would it work, she asked herself for the umpteenth time. Only time would tell. Gently, she put her hand on Randall's knee as they drove on through the Surrey countryside. When they reached the Woodlands it was four o'clock in the afternoon and the sun was still shining. Turning into the driveway, Randall began hooting the horn of the car. When they reached the house, Mrs Fortescue and Mrs Grainger were waiting outside the front door, with James Oliver and the twins. Everyone was smiling.

"Home, sweet home, Jane. From now on, this is where we stay. Are you happy?"

"Never been happier in my life... Hello, everyone. We're home."

PART 7

LATE JUNE TO JULY 1998 – A DEATH IN LIFE

1

_____

*T*he phone rang from inside the house, breaking Randall's concentration. Jane and Mrs Fortescue had gone into the village to do the weekly shopping, leaving Mrs Grainger to watch the twins. Lawrence Templeton-Smythe was walking through the African bush, rifle in hand followed by Tonga his servant, both of them looking for elephants as they chatted to each other in Shona. With his pen suspended over the page he was writing, Randall waited for the phone to stop ringing. When the ringing stopped, he went back down the rabbit hole into the mind of Lawrence and the hunt continued. Again the phone rang, breaking his concentration, the story again frozen. Patiently, Randall waited. The phone stopped and he went back into the book. Minutes later, the phone rang for the third time making Randall slam his pen down on the table he had put out under the walnut tree.

"Damn, the bloody phone. Who the hell can it be?"

Running into the house Randall picked up the phone that stood on the small table just inside the entrance hall.

"Why can't people leave us alone... Hello. Who's there?"

"Manfred."

"Manfred, what the hell do you want? I was a hundred years back hunting elephant when the phone started to ring."

"We're going to publish *Shakespeare's Ghost*."

"Whatever for? You've been saying for months you won't publish unless I go on a book tour. Jane's back and she's never going on a bloody book tour again. So, you want me to start running around the world to make you all money? Well, it's not going to happen. You're both wasting your time. You can tell that to Godfrey from me. I'm a writer, not a bloody publicist. Now, can I go?"

"We don't need your help."

"You mean I won?"

"I'm afraid so. If I asked very nicely would you come to the launch in New York?"

"There you go again. We're not going anywhere. I'm sorry to be rude and I do appreciate what you did for me in the past. Do what you like with the book. Throw it in the wastepaper basket for all I care."

"So you've started the second book of your historical African saga. Can we have the first book?"

"Are you kidding me?"

"*Shakespeare's Ghost* is nicely typed and read through by three editors. The odd error but basically nothing has changed from your handwritten manuscript. You don't have to come over for the launch if you don't want to. Your name is well enough known as it is. Go back to your book and enjoy yourself. How's Jane?"

"Wonderful. We're as happy as a couple of pigs in shit. That old saying that fully describes perfect happiness."

"Give her my love. Her book is still selling nicely. Enjoy writing the new book. I look forward to reading it."

"You mean I really won?"

"Game, set and match as they say on the tennis court. How's James Oliver and the twins?"

"I took him back to boarding school this morning. Spent the weekend with us."

"After the book's launched, I'll come over and pay you both a very quiet visit. Please go back to your book, it's what you do best... Are you there? You've gone silent."

"I'm gobsmacked."

"Have a nice day, my favourite author. What's the weather like in England?"

"The sun is shining. I'm sitting out on the lawn under the walnut tree with the dogs fast asleep next to my writing table."

"Give my regards to Lawrence Templeton-Smythe."

"Don't be silly, he's fictional."

"That doesn't make any difference. In your mind, he's a living person. Will be for millions of readers."

"So I really won?"

"Hands down. Total victory. I want your books, Randall. Have a nice writing day."

Knowing he would not be able to get back into the book with Manfred's words echoing through his head, Randall walked back into the garden and called the dogs. He could smell the cut grass from the early morning's lawn mowing, a job he had happily enjoyed. Walking the dogs in the woods would hopefully eliminate the telephone conversation and bring Lawrence Templeton-Smythe back into his head. The two Border Collies jumped up with excitement and followed him out of the garden and through the small wooden gate into the woods. Suddenly he was hungry but the food could wait, the fruit on the trees still not ripe enough to eat. A dove called to him from the branch of a big oak tree making Randall smile as the dogs ran away down the winding path between the trees. There was birdsong and the sound of bees. With the Collies, Randall walked down to the small stream and sat on the fallen branch of a tree, looking down on the water gently moving over the clean stones making a gentle trickling sound. The dogs ran off barking as they chased a rabbit. For that moment of peace, New York was as far away as the moon. All he could hope was that people would enjoy reading *Shakespeare's Ghost* as much as he had enjoyed writing it. After half an hour his mind had cleared of the clutter and he was back in the African bush. Getting up from his comfortable seat on the fallen branch, Randall walked back down the path between the trees, the birds still calling, the bees still humming, the Collies running around him. When he reached the small table he called his outside writing table, he sat down in his canvas chair and picked up his pen. For the rest of the morning, Randall was oblivious to his surroundings as Lawrence and Tonga continued their hunt, neither of them really caring if they found an elephant, their pleasure coming from each other's company and their walk through the warmth of the African bush. When Jane returned, he had finished the day's writing and was leaning back in his canvas chair, happy with what he had written.

"You want some lunch, Randall? Are you hungry? How did it go today?"

"I'm starving. Manfred phoned. He's publishing *Shakespeare's Ghost*."

"Oh, shit. You have to go back to America."

"We don't have to do a damn thing. I won."

"Oh, my goodness. Let's open the bar. Mrs Fortescue can bring us some lunch. We'll sit under the tree and celebrate. Oh, it's so wonderful to be home and free of all those people. Where are Raphael and Kimber?"

"With Mrs Grainger. Haven't heard a peep all morning. Give me a hug. I'm so relieved about Manfred you have absolutely no idea. And I told him you're not doing another book tour either. We can live our lives in peace and write our books."

"How's Lawrence and Africa?"

"How's Margaret Neville? I'll get the ice and the whisky. No, maybe not. The bar had better open at six o'clock. We both agree we have to control our drinking. Let's have some lunch out in the garden and tell each other our stories. My friend and lover is back again. Life is worth living. Poor old Manfred. Anyway, the problem's now over once and for all. We're free of them all. It's now just our family and writing our books."

"Can I read what you've written?"

"Not until I've finished the book."

"Why did people in those days want to kill elephants? It's so horrible to shoot such a beautiful animal for its ivory tusks."

"Money, Jane. In the book, though Lawrence doesn't know it, he and Tonga are about to run for their lives chased by a pride of lions. In the real world, all animals want to kill each other. You should have seen Misty and Bob chasing a poor rabbit when I went for a walk in the woods to clear my head of Manfred's conversation. We'll eat chicken tonight or whatever meat you and Mrs Fortescue are going to cook. Think of the poor chicken. Trouble is, we don't. We love roast chicken."

"I see you've cut the lawn."

"Did it to let my mind drift into the world of my book. Exercise always does that for me."

"Mrs Fortescue says we should employ a gardener. You've grown used to having Mrs Fortescue and Mrs Grainger around. Why not a gardener? You can tell him not to make any noise while you're writing. He can grow us lots of lovely fresh vegetables which are so good for us. Are you sure we can't have a drink? It's my first full day at home. The shopping's done. You've finished writing. The day is ours. How about a glass of wine so that we can raise our glasses to Manfred doing what you wanted? To a new book to live in the world and give other people pleasure... Where are Luna and Jasper?"

"Out hunting mice. Like that big cat in my book hunting men for its supper. You have that pleading look on your face, Jane. That 'please may I have a drink look'. Okay. You win. A bottle of wine under the walnut tree. Where do we find a gardener?"

"I'll ask Mrs Fortescue. I'll get the glasses. You pop the cork. Let's celebrate. I'm home, my love. And unless you kick me out, I'm not going anywhere. Not ever. When we've had a nice bottle of wine and eaten our lunch we'll have a nap. How does all that sound? Is the lion going to kill one of them?"

"I don't know. You can't shoot a lion when you're running away. Big cats run faster than men. We'll see tomorrow when I get back into the book. I do so love being back in Africa. Even if it's only in my mind."

THE DAYS for Randall passed in peace and happiness as he sat under the big tree in the garden writing his book and living in the mind of Lawrence Templeton-Smythe: for those hours he was Lawrence. Further away sat Jane at a second small table writing the story of nineteen-year-old Margaret Neville. Only when it was raining did they write inside. At the end of June, instead of opening the bar in the house, they walked hand-in-hand down the road to the Jolly Farmer where they sat up at the bar. To Randall's surprise Jake Crawley, the old man who had asked him to trace the girl who had changed his life when he was a young boy, was sitting at the other end of the bar with an old woman, both of them engrossed in themselves.

"It can't be."

"What can't be, Randall?"

"Penny Long. Manfred traced her and I put them in touch. Hadn't set eyes on each other for seventy or more years. That old woman has got to be the actress Penny Long. After they were caught doing naughty things behind the bushes by Penny's father, Jake was banned from ever seeing Penny again. They were ten years old and next-door neighbours. The best of friends. Jake said neither of them thought they were doing anything wrong looking at each other's private parts. It destroyed both of them. Penny became a lesbian and went into the theatre. When she became a film actress in her later years and went to Hollywood, Manfred became her agent. Now just look at them. Two eighty-year-olds behaving like love-struck children. Well, at least I did something good for once in my life. Let's go over and talk to them."

"Shouldn't we leave them alone? Let's have a drink. If he makes eye contact you can introduce me to them. Penny Long. I remember the name. She was a character actor."

"Micky, can we have a drink? Do you know who that old woman is with Jake?"

"Penny Long. In her heyday, she was a famous West End actress. So nice to see old people enjoying themselves together. Double whisky for you. What are you drinking today, Jane? So nice to have you back in England. A perfect summer. Can you believe it?"

"I'll still have the same as Randall."

"Coming up."

As they waited for Micky the barman to bring them their drinks, Randall stared across at Jake.

"He's seen me, Jane. They're both waving. Life isn't so bad after all. There we go, Micky. Cheers, Jane. What a lovely surprise. Jake and Penny back together after all those years. Makes you think. If the father hadn't lost his temper with Jake and kicked him off the property, they'd have married and had kids. Grandchildren. Even great-grandchildren. Instead, neither of them married and had children. What a waste of what would have been perfect lives. We'd better take our drinks and join them."

"I'm so lucky to have Kimber and Raphael. It's a waste of a life if you don't have children. You can carry my drink."

"At your service, madam."

"Why do you English have such strange accents?"

"I'm a Rhodesian. Born and bred."

"Both your parents were English. You're as English as they come."

Randall walked across with Jane to the other side of the bar carrying their glasses of whisky, stopping in front of the old woman.

"Hello. I'm Randall Crookshank. This is my partner, Jane. Are you Penny Long, by any chance? Hello, Jake. Do you mind if we join you?"

"Are you the kind man who put us in touch? We can't thank you enough. Yes, I'm Penny Long. Isn't your real name Randall Holiday, the famous author?"

"Jane here, my life partner, also writes books. Well, I'll be blowed. What luck my meeting Jake in this very bar. Isn't it strange how a casual meeting can have such huge consequences? We were both drinking alone. Always better to have a drinking companion. You and I, Penny, both have the same agent."

"I don't act anymore. Just a trifle too old at eighty-three. For days, Jake and I have been having so much fun filling in the gaps of our lives. We both love telling each other our stories. I've moved into Jake's small flat. Didn't seem to be any point living separately. Thank you so much, Randall. I've phoned Manfred twice to thank him. Happiness at last in the winter of our lives. When we were kids we were inseparable. Now we are again... Are you two married, Jane?"

"No. We live together. I gave birth to our twins."

"You should marry. Don't make my mistakes. I so envy you your children. The end of my life was so empty until now. Are you going to have dinner with us? One of the best parts of being a successful actress was my ability to save lots of money for my retirement. If you don't have money you can't afford to eat out. Many people in other parts of the world can't even afford to eat. They starve. At least that part of my life worked out. I've never gone hungry. I was just telling Jake about my father. He ended his life on his own. After what he did to me and Jake, I hated my father. He never understood. A self-righteous man who always thought he was right. My mother understood my problems. She and I kept in touch though I never went to visit them. I don't think either of them saw me on the stage. By the time I went into film and met Manfred, both of them were dead. That terrible day left both myself and Jake in a lifelong void. You see, I became a lesbian and hated men so there wasn't any point in my contacting Jake when I grew up and left home. Lesbians, however much they think they love each other, can't have each other's children. Let's go and sit over there round that table. How is it writing books? I've often thought of writing my memories. Now, maybe I shall, thanks to you, Randall Holiday."

"Write down your story, Penny. All of it. Tell the world the consequences of what your father did to both of you. It will get it out of your system. Make you both feel better. If you don't want to tell the world you hated your own father, you can say your story is fictional."

"Could either of you help me with the writing?"

"We'll read back what you do. That'll help. It's the story that counts. Not the perfect grammar. We'd love to have dinner with you. But be careful. If you don't write the story, one of us will pinch the idea. All my novels are based on actual events that have crossed my life. Even when I'm telling a story from the past. The past and present are all the same.

People's lives never changed. The turmoil of history has been repeating itself for millions of years ever since man evolved out of the oceans or wherever we came from. It was so wonderful to watch you both from across the bar being so absorbed in each other. Let's drink to your new happiness."

"Do you novelists really steal other people's stories? I wonder if, at my old age, I'm capable of putting down the story. I don't type very well."

"You could talk the story onto a computer but it isn't easy. I write with a pen. Always have done. Don't want a typewriter to get between me and my characters. All that clatter in the old days when I started writing. Manual typewriters. Can you believe the very idea in this day and age?"

"Maybe one of you could write the story for me. Are you both writing at the moment? Thank you for pulling out my chair, Randall."

"We're both absorbed in our latest books."

"Then my story will have to wait. Or I could write with a pen. Doesn't handwriting take a long time?"

"When you write slowly with a pen you are more inclined to get the words right the first time. The story flows forward episode to episode. Stops all that rewriting. I like to get my plot and sentences right the first time. Have a go, Penny. There's nothing better in life than having lots to do. Now, what are we going to eat, Jane? Supper is on us, Jake. May you both live to be a hundred."

"How old are your twins, Jane?"

"They will be a year old in September. Good luck writing your book. Apart from having babies, writing is the most satisfying thing in the world. A menu. I'm hungry. And I won't have to cook supper."

"Tell me about writing a book, Randall. How do you start?"

"At the beginning. 'We were ten years old when my father caught us behind the bushes, changing our lives forever.' From then on let the story roll. Read back the previous day's writing and pick up on the story. Your subconscious will have played your story forward. Once you get the next sentence you're off again. You have become the character. Much the same as acting on the stage."

"I always preferred the stage to film. Making a film is bits and pieces. Stops and starts. Takes ages to make a film. A play runs for maybe two hours without interruption. You are right. You become your character and communicate directly with your audience. Far more personal."

"Same as writing a book. You are telling your story to one person, the person who is reading your book. You can't see them or hear them boo or applaud. But it's the same feeling."

"Mostly I was so absorbed in my part I was unaware of anything other than myself and the other actors on the stage."

"Join the club. You're going to enjoy writing. So, tell us what it was like to be on the London West End Stage."

By the time Micky brought them a bottle of wine they had eaten the soup and were tucking into the steak, all of them talking ten to the dozen, a pleasant evening for all of them. After they ate dessert they began the walk back to their homes, Randall conscious of very old people not staying out late.

"Don't forget to get married, Randall. We'd love to come to the wedding. James Oliver can give away the bride unless you want to bring Jane's father over from America. There's a Norman church close to here. Jake showed it to me. Twelfth century."

"But I've had previous marriages. Can a divorcee marry in a church?"

"Ask them. We'll be in touch. Especially when I've finished my first chapter. And thank you, Randall, again. Before I made contact with Jake, all I wanted to do was die. There was nothing left for me to do in my life. Now I have my best friend back and a book to write. All thanks to you."

"Why don't you two get married in the Norman Church? Be a perfect ending to a perfect ending."

"Have you ever heard of two eighty-three-year-olds getting married?"

"If you love each other what's wrong with a solemn vow in an ancient building that has seen so many weddings over the centuries? Ask her to marry you, Jake. You're both smiling. Let the idea grow. Enjoy the rest of your evening together. What a lovely summer's evening. Jane and I are going home to drink a bottle of wine under the walnut tree and watch the stars come out. Not too many warm evenings like this in England."

"Will you come to our wedding?"

"Of course we will. Jane will be your maid of honour. I can give away the bride... Can an eleven-year-old boy give away the bride?"

"Ask him... Laughter. There's nothing more pleasant than the sound of laughter. Enjoy your wine under the tree. Jake and I are going to bed."

"To sleep, perchance to dream."

"You like Will Shakespeare, Randall?"

"Oh, yes. And his friend. Goodnight, dear friends, goodnight. I think I'm just a little tipsy."

As they walked away from the old couple, Randall looked back and smiled, seeing Penny and Jake's new happiness, Jake's hand round Penny's shoulder as they walked off towards his flat.

"You think they'd be as happy together if they'd been married sixty years?"

"You're being cynical, Jane Slater."

"Most couples end up arguing."

"We're not going to argue."

"Of course not. A Norman church. Didn't know buildings lasted that long. Let's leave it alone, my love. Only if people love each other should they stay together, not bound by a marriage certificate or the church. Half of marriages end in divorce anyway."

"I can see the beauty of a church wedding. The perfect setting."

"How could we use a church we have never attended just for a wedding? It wouldn't be right. We've never discussed religion and I don't want to start now. You and I have never been to church together. Isn't that saying enough? I don't want to put on a long white dress and pretend I don't have what they like to call illegitimate children. Our twins are as legitimate as children can be because we love them and always will love them. What's the point in trying to make it all seem better? We'll only be as happy as we want to be and that's all we can have from our lives. It's wonderful those two are together again. Would they have had a successful marriage if her father had not lost his temper with Jake? They will never know."

"A church ceremony would crown our love for each other. We'd have God's blessing."

"Do you believe in God?"

"I hope so."

"So do I. We all hope there's more than hell on this earth. But none of us really know who we are, where we came from or where we're going, other than being buried under the earth or burned to ashes. We only know what we have at this lovely moment, walking hand in hand back to the walnut tree and a bottle of wine followed by a gentle and beautiful sleep."

"I hear the call of an owl."

"It's so beautiful. The call of a night owl."

"I think I've made them happy."

"That you did, my love... You think they'll make a film of *Shakespeare's Ghost*?"

"You never know. I love you, Jane. Come on. Another few hundred yards and I'll pop the cork and we can sip our wine and stare at the stars."

By the time they made themselves comfortable under the walnut tree, one of the cats was stalking a thrush out on the lawn, Jane gently rocking the bouncy chair with her right foot, the twins lying quietly next to each other under a light blanket, Randall happy as a cricket.

"There's nothing better than holding a girl's hand with a glass of wine in the other. As the stars come out I'll have to stand out on the lawn to look up at them. That poor thrush. Good. The bird's flown. I love the call of a thrush. The perfect songbird. It's so nice to have helped those old people. Helping other people makes you feel good in yourself. Next week when you go shopping with Mrs Fortescue, I'm going to take myself on a walk and find that church. I know which direction it is. Every Sunday I hear the church bells ringing. A lovely sound. All those years and the bells were ringing, calling the faithful to church. I've never been inside the ancient church. Maybe I'll bump into the rector and ask him if he can marry us. We could give some of our money to charity and help the less fortunate. I wouldn't mind getting involved in a management of a charity to make sure my money is being used properly. Charity is like a business and has to be run properly. Just listen to all the birds singing. A summer evening in the English countryside. Cheers, Jane. Let our future live on and on just like today."

"What church did your parents come from?"

"The Church of England. There were many of their churches in Rhodesia. Spreading the faith of Christianity was all part of colonialism. Some even said the main reason for us going to Africa. You know, we haven't christened the twins."

"Is James Oliver christened?"

"Yes. By his mother. So is Douglas."

"We could both walk to the church on Sunday when the bells are ringing."

"The sun's gone down. Let's walk out and look up at the universe."

"You think God lives up in the stars?"

"I've never understood that part: if there is a God, where does he live? I asked my headmaster once. My headmaster was a priest. The school was run by the Church of England. He said he didn't know. When I asked him if I'd see my mother again in heaven, he said he wasn't sure. From then on I lost interest in religion. At least my headmaster was being honest. We don't know where we came from or where we're going.

Religion is a beautiful story. I've always regretted asking him about my dead mother when I was just a boy. Bring your glass. We can raise our glass to the heavens. Maybe my mother will be looking down on me. Maybe. There's so much in life we don't know. I like that idea of using my money for charity. Make my money have some worth. Now just look at the stars. I can see them as the light pales."

"He'll marry us if you give him enough money."

"Now you're being cynical again."

"Or telling the truth."

"Does it matter, if the money helps the less fortunate?"

"What's your advance for *Shakespeare's Ghost*?"

"I didn't ask him."

"Do you still miss your mother?"

"You always wonder about the person who bore you even if you never knew her. I'm half my mother. Bergit was a wonderful stepmother but she wasn't my real mother. Look at that. Just a sliver of a moon they call a sickle moon. I love this place. May we all live here in peace for the rest of our lives. We're so lucky, Jane. You have no idea how lucky we are. And back there, those two old people are finally tucked up in bed, side by side and fast asleep, and living in their dreams."

"Who was it who said 'religion is the opium of the people'?"

"I have no idea."

2

----

*O*n the following Sunday morning, the church bells began to ring, the sun still shining, both of them content from a good night's sleep.

"Let's go and find that church. I wonder who rings the bells? Come on, Jane."

"Can I come with you?"

"Of course you can, James Oliver. It's your weekend break. Let's all go for a walk. Mrs Fortescue will watch the twins. Come on, Jane. The bells are calling."

"Are you going to church? You have to dress properly for church. We'd all better get changed. How long will it take us to walk?"

"We're about to find out."

Half an hour later, Randall saw the bell tower in the distance, the bells swinging as someone below inside the church pulled the ropes. When they reached the entrance to the old church they went inside through the tall open door, the top of the door arched like the inside of the church. Inside, most of the benches were full, many of the people kneeling forward on the mats praying to God. A priest was standing at the altar at the other end of the long church holding a Bible, the beautiful glass windows rising high behind him showing colourful pictures of the saints. Randall found a space on a bench enough for the three of them. Quietly, looking in awe at the beauty around them, they waited for the service to begin.

"Let's all kneel and pray."

After prayers, the priest read from the Bible before the organ began to play, the great sound of music echoing through the ancient building as it had done every Sunday for hundreds of years. When the hour-long service was over, they followed the churchgoers out of the church, the priest now waiting outside the big front door to greet his parishioners and touch their hands.

"Are you three new in the parish? I haven't seen you before. When they have all gone, why don't you come to the rectory for a cup of tea and meet my wife?... Have a lovely Sunday afternoon, Roger. So nice to see you in church again."

"We've been away."

"I'm sure you have... Have a lovely Sunday lunch. Will you be attending church next Sunday?"

"We hope so."

"So do I... Now tell me, what's your name?"

"Randall Crookshank. This is Jane. This is my son, James Oliver."

"Hello, vicar. Pleased to meet you. We do call you vicar?"

"Larry is fine, Jane. Why don't you stand under that fir tree over there until they've all gone?... Hello, Mabel. Lovely to see you."

Randall walked to the side of the tall tree, not quite sure what was going on.

"He thinks we're married, Randall. Thinks I'm James Oliver's mother. We're tying ourselves in knots."

"That organ is so beautiful."

"You can say that again. And loud. The birds don't stand a chance. Why didn't you tell him you're Randall Holiday?"

"Because I'm not."

"I give up."

"Please don't give up, Jane. It's so unnecessary. Now look at that. The bells are ringing again. This time in celebration."

"You think that old house over there is the rectory?"

"We're about to find out. Here he comes. It's so amazing that people have been coming here to church for over a thousand years."

"Come along with me and meet my wife. She's sick in bed, I'm afraid. Been sick for over a year. God is calling her. It will happen to all of us when our time comes. So, tell me about yourself, Randall. Are you joining my church? I hope so. Once more today the sun is shining. Are you American, Jane? I can hear it by your accent. Your accent I can't quite work out, Randall. But the boy has an English accent. We just take this path between the fir trees to the old rectory."

"Do you have children?"

"Three of them. Flew the nest years ago and went on their journey. Life is one big journey, Randall. Thank you for opening the gate. First, we'll go to my wife's bedroom and say hello and then we'll go to the kitchen and make a nice pot of tea. I'm the Reverend Jones. Larry Jones. So nice to meet new parishioners."

"Can you marry a man who's been married before?"

"Depends if he was married in a church."

"Registry office."

"No problem. I rather thought you two were not married. And, young boy, where is your mother?"

"She's dead."

"I'm so sorry."

"So am I. Can I go and play with those dogs near the graveyard?"

"If you wish to."

"I do. See you later, Dad."

"Don't do anything silly."

"Why should I? Are you two really getting married? About time."

"Don't be rude, son."

"I'm not. You're always talking about it. I don't want to end up living with yet another stepmother... Life sucks."

"Where do you go to school, young man?"

"Cranleigh prep school. Part of your parish. It's run by you people."

"Do you like school?"

"Every minute of it. Especially playing cricket. This year I'm in the first eleven... Do these dogs bite?"

"They are my dogs and they don't bite. Their names are Frank and Johnny."

"Weird names for dogs."

"Go and play with them."

"What does it mean 'flown the nest'?"

"Going away. One day you'll fly the nest."

"I can't fly."

"Go and talk to my dogs."

"Yes, sir. As you say, sir. Which one's Frank and which one's Johnny?"

"Call their names and find out."

For Randall, it was a day to remember, a day he would look back on for the rest of his life. Near to the church and the rectory was a children's charity financed by the church and managed by the Reverend Larry Jones. When Randall offered a hundred thousand pounds to add to the coffers of the charity, the rector tried to smile. They had just left his wife's sickbed and walked through the old rectory to the kitchen.

"She's nearly gone."

"I'm so sorry for you."

"Thank you for your offer of money. Money always helps a charity. The children we support are those who have disabilities that parents struggle to cope with and need help with. Will your son be all right playing with my dogs? You must be rich, Mr Crookshank. What do you do?"

"I'm in the book business."

"They always say publishers make lots of money. Tea and biscuits. Why did you really come here today? Was it charity or marriage?"

"Both. I have plenty of spare time. I can help you run the charity. Helping these children and their parents will make me feel my money has some meaning and worth."

"I have spent the latter part of my life trying to help people. Without the church, many people would live without a roof over their heads. We try to look after the poor."

"I thought a divorcee couldn't be married in church."

"You came to my church today, Randall. You can come again and obtain a marriage certificate if I, Larry Jones, marry you in front of two witnesses. Then you can have God's blessing. We all want to atone for our sins. And however perfect people say they are, we have all sinned in our lives. Man is not the most pleasant of species even if we say God created him. There are so many truths and untruths in this world."

"What's the matter with your wife? Or should I not ask?"

"She has cancer. A long, debilitating and hateful disease. I've loved her since we were children. When she goes I shall be the loneliest man on this earth. Let's take our tea outside and watch your son playing with my dogs. When can you come with me to the charity's offices?"

"Tomorrow morning, if that is convenient."

"The donation of a hundred thousand pounds is always convenient. Now the bells have stopped ringing. Peace and happiness to all mankind. I never know which I prefer most, the morning service or evensong."

"Could we not join your wife?"

"We shall do that when we have checked on your son."

"Is she in pain?"

"All the time. She keeps calling to God to let the cancer go into her bloodstream so it will kill her. She'll be so happy in heaven. And when I die, with God's blessing, I'll be able to join her, our souls together forever without pain or suffering."

"My first wife, James Oliver's mother, died from breast cancer. Why he came to live with me."

"God tries us all."

"You have a beautiful choir, Reverend Jones."

"They say singing in a church choir is one of the most satisfying ways to enjoy oneself. Makes them feel good. An organ and a choir joining in music together. Your boy looks all right with my dogs. Let's go back and sit with my wife for a few minutes and then I'm sure you will want to go home. Shall we say nine o'clock tomorrow at the rectory? Where are you from, Randall?"

"Africa. My family was one of the last colonials."

"Ah, the old empire. Whether we did more harm than good is a matter of conjecture. Such a small island to have spread our wings so far. You can tell me more when I see you tomorrow. Now, look. It seems she is asleep. Ah, no, now her eyes are opening. Darling, we've come to share a pot of tea with a good man who is donating a hundred thousand pounds to our children's charity. Are you feeling pain?"

"I'm always feeling pain. Come and sit next to me on the bed... The parents will be so grateful. I miss my own children. Do you two have children?"

"Twins. Jane and I are going to bring them to your husband for baptism."

"Such a nice tea tray. Would you be kind enough to ask your wife to pour the tea for me? I used to enjoy pouring the tea. Now all I can do is lie and wait."

Drinking his tea, the sadness surrounding him palpable, Randall listened to Jane trying to make conversation with a dying woman, the smiles, the words, all of them forced. When the priest's wife closed her eyes, bringing tears to the eyes of all of them, the Reverend Jones led them out of his wife's sickroom into the rectory garden, a beautiful garden full of colourful flowers. After collecting James Oliver and separating him from the dogs, they began the walk back to the Woodlands.

"At least you won't be able to sing in the church choir."

"Why not?"

"You can't sing in tune, Randall. Neither of us can sing."

"What a strange day. One minute hope, the next minute sadness."

As they walked home along the side of the road Randall made his mind wander, letting it leap back a hundred years into the mind of Lawrence Templeton-Smythe and Africa. They were sitting in front of the fire, roasting a leg of buck Lawrence had cut from the carcase hanging in a nearby tree, the meat suspended on a piece of wire below a wooden tripod he had made from sticks that stood over the coals of the cooking fire. Total peace in the minds of Lawrence and Tonga, not even the memory of being chased by a pride of lions worrying either of them. The cart stood next to them half-filled with ivory they had cut from the elephant they had hunted, the four horses away in the surrounding bush, the animals grazing. There was birdsong and the sound of a troop of monkeys calling to each other from the trees.

When Randall and Jane walked into the garden of the Woodlands, Randall went straight to his desk under the walnut tree and picked up his pen. For two hours the story flowed as Randall lived again in his Africa. At the end of the day, Randall drove his son back to boarding school, leaving him at the gate with his small bag to run off and join his friends, the pain from losing his mother no longer visible. When he got back to the house, Jane had put the glasses out on the garden table, the bottle of wine ready next to the corkscrew, the afternoon sun still warm and pleasant on the side of Randall's face.

"He's slowly forgetting the pain of losing his mother."

"I'm so glad... Quite a day, my love."

"You can say that again. Just the two of us again. What's for supper?"

"I haven't asked Mrs Fortescue."

"Where are they? Where are the dogs?"

"Does it matter? There's you and me, my love. That's all that matters."

"How was your day's writing?"

"I enjoyed it more than watching that poor dying woman. Don't die on me. I couldn't handle what that man is going through. Why don't some of their kids come home?"

"Children have their own lives to live. Their own problems to face. Especially when they are grown up and have their own families. I'm sure they phone their mother and father regularly... Out pops the cork. Cheers, Jane. Do you want to get married?"

"You know, I'm not sure. It works as it is. You know that other old saying: 'if it works, leave it alone'. But maybe we should for the sake of the twins. Just look at them sitting up in the pram watching us drink. They look so happy... Have you spoken to Douglas lately?"

"I tried. Spoke to Clint who was rude as usual. Said my son was playing in the garden with friends. He's a real charmer, that Clint. Gets what was to become his wife to screw me for alimony, lives off my money and won't even call my son to the phone. To hell with them all. Let's have a few glasses of wine and leave the world behind."

"At least we are happy together. I wonder how many people in the world are truly happy?"

"Hopefully, most of them. Happiness comes and goes. The trick is to hold on to it. Never let it go."

"And live in the present, not in the past, or worrying about the future. They won't let you manage your money at the charity. You're giving your money to the church, and the governors, they have no doubt. Not even Larry Jones will have any control of the money. Let's just hope they do right with it. That the kids get some benefit. You write books, my love. You don't run charities. It's a bit like our tax money. Once they've got it they do what they like with it... Here come the dogs... There's nothing nicer than purring cats on my lap, a drink in my hand and the other gently pushing my children's pram backwards and forwards. Ah, the miracle of children. Thank you, Randall, for my children."

"Thank you for not using a contraceptive."

"And thank you, too. That night we first made love in your Manhattan apartment, could we ever have imagined it would bring us to an English countryside garden on a perfect summer's evening? Now look at this. Snacks to go with the wine. What's for supper, Mrs Fortescue?"

"Cold roast chicken and salads. Mrs Grainger will bring it out to you when you are ready. Such a beautiful evening. Not many summer evenings are like this."

"Thank you so much for looking after us."

"It's our job. Jobs both of us enjoy. And long may it last. Not even a cloud in the sky."

Not talking to disturb the evening peace, Randall ate snacks while they sipped their wine.

"Why are you so quiet, my love?"

"I'm listening to the birds calling from the woods."

"Why don't we ask Penny Long and Jake Crawley to supper?"

"I don't know their phone number."

"Must be in the book. Said he owned his flat. I'm sure Larry Jones would love to marry them. Didn't he say he'd also known his wife since they were children? I'll look it up and give them a ring. How strange life is. Without you meeting him in the bar, they would never have met again. Or was that meeting ordained? You never know... Maybe it's better to leave them alone. Do eighty-year-olds want to dine with forty-year-olds? What do you think the twins are going to do with their lives? My little children. My whole life sitting under a walnut tree. We should have some more children, Randall."

"We can try. Not that either of us take precautions. Let the gods decide... Here comes supper. Thank you, Mrs Grainger. Those plates are so nice and large and full of chicken and salads. This really is the height of luxury. I'm going to ask him tomorrow."

"Who are you going to ask?"

"The Reverend Larry Jones."

"And what are you going to ask the Reverend Larry Jones, my love?"

"When he will marry us. Let's have the rest of the bottle of wine. Then I'll open another. Then we'll eat our dinner. Cheers to us and our books. The books that gave us the money to buy this perfect home."

"I love you, Randall."

"I love you, Jane. To long life and happiness."

"To the wonder and joy of life. Are we going to invite the relations?"

"They will only come because they think they have to. And if we invite all the relations, we'll send invitations to everybody else and the press will find out, turning our wedding into a circus. We'll marry on our own with the priest and a couple of witnesses."

"And where are we going to find the witnesses?"

"We'll cross that bridge when we get to it."

"You're right. It's a long way for my father to come just to go to a wedding. What are we going to do for a reception?"

"Just you and me. I love it when you smile. Why is birdsong so beautiful?"

"Because they can sing in tune."

"Here, close to the woods, you can barely hear the sound of man. Why is man always so noisy? Engines. Radios. Shouting at each other. You want another glass?"

"Keep pouring. Those two are happy. It's nice."

"Which two?"

"Mrs Fortescue and Mrs Grainger. They have exactly the same as us even though they don't own the property. They'll be sitting in the back garden outside the kitchen door, none of us hearing each other's voices.

"It was the same on the farm in Rhodesia. The labour force was given food every week: maize-meal, sugar, salt, eggs, meat; milk came from the cows and they grew their own vegetables in their compound. We gave them the material to build their houses. Once the hard day's work was over they were at peace with themselves. There was no worry about being fired. The tobacco crop paid for everything. Now they're all unemployed, roaming the streets of the capital, Harare, selling anything they can find to sell. Street vendors. They must remember those days back on the farm with nostalgia. Now all the curing barns and grading sheds are doing nothing, no tobacco being grown. Nothing. And they thought kicking us whites out of their country was progress. Progress for Mugabe and his cronies. The rest they couldn't give a stuff about. What a world. All that time and money invested in a farming industry gone to pot as the new owners don't know how to farm and the few who do don't have the money to finance the growing of a crop."

"You're going on again."

"Writing about Lawrence makes me nostalgic about my own days in Africa. You've got to have money and know what you are doing to make a business successful. All those poor kids I knew when I was growing up on the farm. I often wonder what happened to them. Anyway, they have their political freedom. Maybe that's what they want instead of being told what to do by some white man."

"It's easy to talk like that when you're rich."

"I suppose it is. I was lucky. I was born into a family that had always had money. And do you know, if it wasn't for a man called Harry Brigandshaw, my family may not have gone to Africa. Or something like that. It's become a bit of folklore in the Crookshank family."

"There's that Harry Brigandshaw again. I wonder what he was like? As a person. He must have been a good man because you talk about him from time to time... I wasn't so lucky though, was I? Life in the laundry wasn't much fun."

"And then with Tracey Chapelle's help you wrote a book. We never hear from Tracey anymore. We were once all so close and now here we are thousands of miles away... You want to eat the chicken?"

"Not yet. I'm enjoying my wine... Mrs Crookshank. It's such an ugly name. Where did your family get it from?"

"Somewhere back in history it must have had a meaning. Who knows?"

"I'd prefer to be Mrs Holiday."

"Not going to happen. I'm a Crookshank and always will be. We'll write to all the relations and tell them we're married once it happens. Not even a breath of wind. I wonder what that bird is? I'm going to buy a book of birds and find out who they are. I loved my 'Birds of Africa' book."

"You're getting soppy again. Have some more wine. Why don't you pull the cork on the second bottle?"

"How many more kids do you want?"

"As many as possible."

"Do you think I was rationalising about colonialism? Making excuses?"

"Probably, Randall. Anyway, without colonialism we wouldn't have America. The biggest economy in the world. The world's most powerful democratic nation. Never forget one man, one vote. Wasn't that the anti-apartheid slogan?"

"And when they get your tax money the politicians do what they like with it. Did man ever find the right way to govern himself? From kings and queens down the years to democracy, and if you're not careful it's followed by anarchy as the economy goes to ruins. All I want to do for the rest of my life is keep as far out of people's way as possible. Who was it who said 'hell is other people'? Never mind."

"I love the sound of a cork popping."

"Do you know how many times we say that?"

"Every night."

"We drink too much, Jane."

"Probably. But who cares if we are happy? Give me a kiss, my love."

"My pleasure."

"It's so weird being forty."

"We didn't do anything on your birthday."

"Who wants to celebrate turning forty?"

"Do you feel any different?"

"I do. Forty is over the hill. Why do you want to marry an old woman of forty?"

"Because I love her. Have fun with her. The best of companions. You have to like the same things to live happily together."

"We both like drinking, Randall."

"And writing books."

"And enjoying our twins. Now the snacks are finished. You must always eat when you drink or you get stupidly drunk. Just look at them. They love being gently pushed... What are you going to do with your Manhattan apartment? It can't stay empty forever. And the way we're going it doesn't look as if we are going back to America."

"I'll get Manfred to find me an agent and let the place. Keep it as an investment. They always say making the money is not the most difficult part. It's holding on to it for yourself and the generations to come. Same with Rabbit Farm on the Isle of Man. I'll just keep it as an investment and a place to visit for a holiday. The neighbour looks after it. What are you going to do with your film rights once you have paid the tax? You'd better ask Manfred."

"What would we do without Manfred?"

"Don't put it to him like that or he'll have us back chasing the sales of our books and running in circles. Making the money is all one big game of catching the eye of the public and competing with everyone else's books."

"And in the future?"

"We'll just have to see. Nothing ever stays the same except this beautiful home of ours in the country."

"Enjoy today."

"And let tomorrow take care of itself."

"Cheers again, Randall."

"Cheers again, Jane. To many more happy days... Look at that. Over there in the apple tree. It's a squirrel. They are so cute. I love their bushy tails. He's eating something. Didn't know squirrels ate fruit. Thought they were nut eaters. When the nuts in the walnut tree are ready those squirrels are going to have a field day. Now I'm hungry. That's better. The chicken is good. So are the salads. We're in paradise, Jane. You want me to pass you your plate? Life in the slow lane. There's nothing better."

"Do you want to make love tonight, my love?"

"I always want to make love tonight."

"Oh, good. We can make a baby."

"You know, if someone a thousand years ago had said 'not tonight, darling', I wouldn't be here."

"There you go again."

"It's true. It's the luck of life. The odds of being alive must be billions to one. And then we are gone."

"Have another glass of wine."

"As you say, Lady Jane, lady of the manor. Look! Another squirrel. Am I getting drunk?"

"Tipsy would be a more polite word. We're both tipsy."

"Nothing wrong with being tipsy. How's your food going down?"

"It's so nice not to have to do the cooking. I'm getting lazy now we have Mrs Fortescue and Mrs Grainger."

"Life at forty, Jane."

"Life at forty, Randall. What are we going to do when we are seventy?"

"Sit out on the lawn and watch the squirrels while we drink our wine."

"Where shall we go for our honeymoon?"

"Right here. It's going to be you and me. We don't need other people. We'll spend our lives going down our rabbit holes into our books without being upset by other people. Living in peace... She must have put something on the chicken, it tastes so good."

"We could take a cruise around Africa."

"We'd spend our days worrying about the twins and James Oliver. Can't leave them behind."

"You're right. We've got what we want right here. The sun is going down. You want your sweater?"

"Not just yet. I'm going to go inside and put on some music. A little Gustav Mahler to blend with an English summer evening. I'll get you your sweater. Does it get any better than this, Jane?"

"I don't think so."

"Good. Tomorrow I'll make a wedding date."

"Shouldn't we listen to the birds instead of Mahler? When winter comes we'll sit inside around the fire and listen to your lovely classical music."

THREE WEEKS later in the garden of the rectory the Reverend Larry Jones married Randall and Jane witnessed by two members of the staff from the charity, all of them standing out on the grass of the lawn. For a long while, Randall stood hugging his new wife, both of them smiling, blissful smiles that came with finally finding what they both wanted.

"How long will it take you to drive back to your house, Randall?"

"A couple of minutes. Why do you ask, Larry?"

"I have a surprise for you... My wife told me to give you both her love on your wedding day. She would have loved being out here under the trees watching me marry you. But she can't get out of bed. God's will. May your marriage be as happy as mine and Sarah's. Happy days. And thank you, Randall, for another generous addition to the church funds."

"There you are, Jane. We're married. Let's go home. Thank you so much, everybody."

To Randall's surprise, the church bells began to ring as they walked from the garage where he had parked the car. On the lawn they could see the wedding lunch that had been laid out by Mrs Fortescue and Mrs Grainger, the tablecloth dotted with flower petals the ladies had picked from the garden. On one side of the table stood the silver ice bucket with a bottle of French champagne.

"What are the bells for, Randall? It's not Sunday."

"The bells are ringing for us. Just listen to them. Three bells ringing in unison. Those bell ringers really know what they're doing. Thank you, Reverend Jones... How do you feel, Mrs Crookshank?"

"Never better. Can life be any happier?"

"I don't think so. I'll open the champagne."

"Pop the cork, my love."

"And the bells are ringing... Just listen to our wedding bells."

∽

PRINCIPAL CHARACTERS

~

The Crookshanks

Amanda Crookshank — Randall's ex-wife
James Oliver Crookshank — Randall and Amanda's young son
Jeremy and Bergit Crookshank — Phillip and Randall's parents
Martha Crookshank — Phillip's wife
Phillip Crookshank — Randall's brother, central character of *The Game of Life*
Randall Crookshank — Central character in *Lovers for Today*

Other Characters

Agatha Stone — Jane's assistant in America during Jane's book publicity tour
Clive Hall — The owner of Croswell Hall in Surrey
Colleen and Raleen — Two young girls in the Jolly Farmer pub, Surrey
Corinna and Dirk Steenkamp — Eugene's parents who own the campsite in the Kokerboom Forest, southern Namibia
Emma Sanders — A journalist who works for *People* magazine, America

Eugene Steenkamp — Runs a campsite in the Kokerboom Forest, southern Namibia

Fred Whitemore — Works in a bottle store in Keetmanshoop near the Kokerboom Forest, southern Namibia

Godfrey Merchant — Proprietor of Merchant Publishers, America

Jake Crawley — An elderly punter at the Jolly Farmer pub whom Randall befriends

Jane Slater — Randall's girlfriend and mother of Kimber and Raphael

Kimber — Randall and Jane's baby daughter

Koos van der Merwe — An Afrikaner who runs the first campsite that Randall and Jane travel to in South Africa

Manfred Leon — Randall and Jane's American literary agent

Mary Wilson — A budding writer who Randall meets in the Jolly Farmer pub, Surrey

Micky — Barman at the Jolly Farmer pub, Surrey

Mrs Fortescue — An elderly nurse employed to look after the twins, Kimber and Raphael

Mrs Garraway — An elderly lady who rents out rooms to young people in Surrey

Mrs Grainger — Randall's housekeeper at the Woodlands, Surrey

Petra van der Merwe — Koos's wife in South Africa

Raphael — Randall and Jane's baby son

Reggie and Luke — Two punters Randall meets in the Jolly Farmer pub, Surrey

Reverend Larry Jones — Rector at the old church in Randall and Jane's village in Surrey

Stanley and Yvonne — Owners of the yacht that Randall and Jane sail on from America to Cape Town

Tracey Chapelle — Randall and Jane's New York friend, part of the 'three musketeers'

DEAR READER

~

Reviews are the most powerful tools in our kitty when it comes to getting attention for Peter's books. This is where you can come in, as by providing an honest review you will help bring them to the attention of other readers.

If you enjoyed reading *Lovers for Today*, and have five minutes to spare, we would really appreciate a review (it can be as short as you like). Your help in spreading the word and keeping Peter's work alive is gratefully received. Please post your review on the retailer site where you purchased this book.

Thank you so much.
Heather Stretch (Peter's daughter)

ACKNOWLEDGEMENTS

~

Our grateful thanks go to our *VIP First Readers* for reading *Lovers for Today* prior to its official launch date. They have been fabulous in picking up errors and typos helping us to ensure that your own reading experience of *Lovers for Today* has been the best possible. Their time and commitment is particularly appreciated.

Agnes Mihalyfy (United Kingdom)
Daphne Rieck (Australia)
Hilary Jenkins (South Africa)
Mike Carter (United Kingdom)

Thank you.
Kamba Publishing

Printed in Great Britain
by Amazon

41486739R00162